Dark Elf

Jordan Falconer

Mindancer Press

Bedazzled Ink Publishing Company * Fairfield, California

978-1-939562-00-5 paperback
978-1-939562-01-2 ebook

Cover art
by
C.A. Casey

Mindancer Press
a division of
Bedazzled Ink Publishing Company
Fairfield, California
http://mindancerpress.bedazzledink.com

For my dad . . .
I'm truly sorry you never got the chance to read and enjoy—
I think you would have liked it . . .

For Tammy . . .
Who just won't ever let me give up . . .

ACKNOWLEDGMENTS

Thank you Casey and Claudia for all your help and feedback—deeply appreciated :-)

CHAPTER 1

"For God's sake, Nightshade. Just kill them." Galvin snarled. He was a tall, white-haired figure with cold, glowing yellow eyes. "We have to get out of here before the sun rises, you know that."

Nightshade stared at the six women and children in varying stages of terror kneeling before her on the muddy ground. They were in shock, and some were sobbing. Nightshade stood with stooped shoulders and hung her head. Her dripping sword, coated in the blood of the human men who had tried to defend their loved ones to no avail, dangled limply in her hand. She tried not to see the carnage and the dead that lay about the clearing. All around, wagons lay overturned, their precious cargo of personal possessions scattered and trampled carelessly in the mud. Hacked bodies lay limp, their blood pooling in the once clean water of the recent forest rain. The night sounds had long since stilled, silenced by the tortured screams of dying horses and men.

Nightshade inwardly sobbed, yet outwardly held firm. The bloodlust had long since fled her system, and now she attempted to dredge up some image that would allow her to continue to slaughter the surviving humans. She looked at the captives and was captured by the frozen stare of a young, brown-eyed girl, no more than three. The girl did not understand what was going to happen to them, what Nightshade was required to do. The action was a deathblow to her resolve to be a good Dark Elf, and she tried to think up some reason for her not to do it.

"Here, let me." Galvin sounded close behind her. He spun her around. "Can't do it, can you? Coward." His handsome face twisted in a sneer of impatience and revulsion.

He slammed a gauntleted fist into Nightshade's face. She fell backward to the ground semi-conscious, blood streaming from the corner of her mouth. She rolled over to her side, spitting saliva and blood, sword forgotten, mud covering her clothes. Galvin swung his wickedly curved sword and beheaded the first victim. Blood spurted out of the clean shear to the neck as one of the other women screamed. The other five members of the scouting party lunged forward, eager for the taste of more innocent blood.

The rich smell of copper deepened in the early morning air, as the whoosh of metal sounded out in the silence, punctuated by heavy thumps as bodies and heads, separated from each other, hit the ground.

Nightshade slowly got to her feet. Her face ached. She grabbed her sword and sheathed it. She looked down in shame and felt Galvin approach her again.

"When we get back to the city, I will see to it personally that you are executed," he said coldly. "You shame the name of Nightsbane."

Nightshade felt a surge of loathing and finally found her tongue. "I am not a coward, Galvin. Kill me if you wish, but I am your best tracker. The king would most surely object." It was true. She could see during the day and at night, unlike pure Drow. This skill was the main reason her services were sought in scouting parties, despite the almost universal loathing the Drow had for her.

Galvin stood nose to nose with her, contempt shining bright in his eyes. "You rely on the king too much. I'm sure he could be made to see reason," he said in a silky voice.

A shiver traveled up Nightshade's spine.

He shot her one last glare and gracefully went to his comrades. They were looting the remains of the wagons, carelessly stepping on bodies in their excitement.

Nightshade watched his muscular back, hating him with every fiber of her being. Sickened, she carefully went to one of the overturned wagons the others had not reached yet and made an effort not to attract more attention. She pretended to root through personal possessions. She broke open a trunk with the hilt of her sword and stilled. It had a rag doll inside, packed lovingly away on top of a load of clean, pressed clothes. As she picked it up and turned it over, more self-loathing coursed through her at her part in the destruction done to undeserving lives.

One of her compatriots came up behind her. "Will you look at the garbage that the humans carry?" the tall Drow said, shaking her head in disgust. "It's a miracle they manage to do anything at all."

"Yes," Nightshade said, shaking her head, pretending amazement. She eyed the sky above. "Time to go to ground. The sun's coming up."

She left the female Drow to her wanton destruction of another's property and went to find Galvin. She had to lead them to a safe place for the duration of the day.

Sunstar opened her eyes and stretched sleepily, blind to the opulence surrounding her. Time to get up and face yet another boring day. Lessons were out for the moment, as her father's royal advisor was in the forest leading a group of Elven children and teaching them the Elven way.

She got out of bed and padded across the cold marble floor, pulling on her clothes as she went. She faced the mirror and saw the same thing she had seen the day before: golden hair, shimmering green, almond-shaped eyes, and the pointed ears of a Forest Elf. She was the eldest daughter of the Elven king, Darkwood, and had yet to convince him that she was old enough to sit in on meetings about matters of state and judgment of her people's disputes. She was sick of school and thought she had learnt all there was to learn there. She was much more interested in what made a good queen, and how to rule over her subjects with kindness and compassion.

Her only escape was Windwalker, the captain of her father's guard, who encouraged her curiosity. She knew that at first he had been surprised by her requests to know why things were done the way they were, then intrigued by her keen mind and gentle insight, and she had somewhat encouraged his fascination by her good looks.

They had become firm friends, and now teetered on the brink of becoming more. Sunstar was not sure if she wanted something more and tried to keep their relationship the way it was. Her father did not want to see it. In his mind, they were already married. It pleased him a great deal to know that her future consort was someone he trusted implicitly, was rational, and firmly grounded. Sunstar sighed as a surge of familiar, formless irritation washed over her.

Having made herself presentable, she went in search of breakfast.

She slipped through her bedroom doorway, headed toward the castle kitchens. The guards her father insisted on assigning her trailed behind. She went past the busy audience hall, barely noticing all the petitioners standing outside and waiting to see her mother, Queen Morningstar. She briefly considered saying good morning to her mother, but abandoned the idea. If she went into the hall, she would no doubt be dragged into another all-morning mediation session, and it was too beautiful a day outside to be stuck indoors listening to Elves complain.

She noticed a group of cloaked Elves at the door, their hoods pulled down to cover their faces, just outside the chamber. The other petitioners carefully stepped around them, and Sunstar wondered who they were.

Someone in the crowd bustled into a bodyguard, causing a muffled curse, and for him to brush against her. She stepped heavily and frowned in irritation.

Nothing for it now. I can't ignore them anymore. She turned around. "Are you both hungry?"

Jarrod, the more senior of the two guards, smiled at her. "Yes, Your Highness."

"Sunstar, Jarrod, Sunstar," Sunstar replied with a grin. "There's time enough for bowing and scraping when I assume the throne."

"Yes, S-Sunstar," Jarrod said with a slight frown.

The younger guard gave her a good-natured grin.

"Good," she said. "I'm starved."

They went into the kitchen, and the cook, Rivercrest, the mother of Sunstar's best friend, handed them each a plate of the oats, fruits, and nuts that Sunstar loved. They sat down and tucked into the meal with great gusto.

A young elfmaid, just a year or two older than Sunstar, rushed in to join them as they were finishing the last of their meal. "Sunstar!"

"Meagan," Sunstar said with a bright smile, eyeing the brown-haired, tawny-eyed Elf. "How are you this fine morning?"

"I'm well," Meagan said. "In fact, I'm fabulous. I've got the day off. You want to do something?"

Sunstar grinned even wider. "Love to. You have anything in mind?"

"Care to go out for a ride? It's been ages since I had the chance to just . . . wander."

"Okay." Sunstar abandoned her empty plate. "I'll just grab some food, and we can go."

"No need, already done."

"Not bad," Sunstar said. "I suppose you got the horses and all already?"

Meagan smiled at her, looking a little guilty. "Done." She grabbed

Sunstar's slim wrist and dragged her, laughing, from the kitchen, guards trailing unobtrusively behind.

They ran to the stables, and Sunstar made a beeline for her horse. She mounted and nodded at Meagan. Meagan grinned in return, and they galloped out of the stable. Sunstar glanced back at the cursing guards struggling to mount their horses. She laughed at the deception. She and Meagan curved sharply away from each other.

They left the city from different sides, circled around, and joined each other with the ease of long practice. No guards were behind them. They galloped off, still laughing, into the forest.

They slowed to a trot after a while and rode alongside each other with the ease of long companionship.

"Any ideas where you want to go?" Sunstar asked, breaking the silence as she turned to Meagan.

"Don't know really. How about the waterfall? If we go anywhere else, your guard is going to find us." Meagan waved a hand in the air.

"Waterfall it is then." Sunstar led the way through the forest, her horse plodding along at a steady pace. The early morning sunlight filtered through the trees, lighting up the way with pure streamers of gold. After an hour or so of companionable silence, they reached the waterfall.

Sunstar dismounted, Meagan behind her, and went to stand on a rock looking out over the river. The rushing water roared over the edges of the rocks on the cliff above, spray pierced by the sunlight, creating a beautiful, bright rainbow in the mid-morning air. Sunstar breathed deeply, enjoying the simple beauty of nature and the presence of her best friend to enjoy it with her.

"You hungry?" Meagan asked from behind her.

"Always." Sunstar turned and smiled at Meagan. She leapt off the rock with a lithe movement and sat on the cloth Meagan had spread on the ground underneath their feast.

"This looks terrific." Sunstar eyed all the food, deciding what best to eat first.

"Take something, I don't have all day." Meagan glared at her with mock impatience.

Sunstar laughed and selected a pastry. She munched on it contentedly while lying back on the thick grass.

Meagan moved to lie next to her when they finished. They stretched out, looking up at the pure blanket of blue lying across the heavens.

"It's so beautiful here," Sunstar said softly.

"Yes, it is," Meagan replied, glancing at Sunstar.

"Tell me, Meagan." Sunstar leaned up on an elbow, so she could look into Meagan's clear eyes. "Do you ever think about leaving here?"

Meagan stared back at her in confusion. "Whatever do you mean? This is my home."

"Yes, I know, but wouldn't you like to see more of the outside world?"

"Why would I want to do that? This is my home, and everyone knows humans aren't the nicest of races."

"True," Sunstar said. "But what about knowing more of the world before we settle down? I am expected to be the next Elven queen, but I know nothing of the outside world, and my father won't let me take on any responsibilities."

Meagan eyed her with some humor. "Well, look at what we've just done. We made a game of running away from your royal guard. And you wonder why your father thinks you're irresponsible."

Sunstar grinned, feeling an odd emptiness and restless dissatisfaction deep inside. "Perhaps. I know I have to stay here, but I want to see the outside world before I take up my crown." She fervently hoped that would be a long time away.

Meagan remained silent for a long time, then finally said, "Don't you want to settle down and get married? Windwalker is smitten with you."

"No," Sunstar said. Meagan had touched a nerve. Sunstar liked Windwalker as a friend, but deep inside she felt empty, knowing that he cared much more for her than she did for him. She thought her destiny lay outside the Elven forest, but had been unable to voice those thoughts before now. The Elves surrounding her loved her, and she loved them, but her heart did not truly lie there.

Meagan looked disappointed and a little hurt.

"I'm sorry, I don't mean to bite," Sunstar said. "I just get sick of everyone assuming I swoon over him. I don't." She sat up. "Why don't we go exploring?" She dredged up a favorite activity of their childhood.

"Okay," Meagan said, mollified. "I'd love to go exploring." She smiled at Sunstar. She opened her mouth as though she wanted to say something else, but sighed and shook her head. Sunstar shrugged. If it was important, Meagan would eventually tell her.

They quickly packed up the picnic. Sunstar led them into the forest, toward an area that they had never been to before, two hours' ride from where they were. It was now the middle of the day, and Sunstar knew they would have to leave soon, as they would be in trouble if they stayed out after dark.

They chased each other through the trees for hours, enjoying a simple game of Elven hide and seek all the rangers trained in to learn to move at one with the forest. It was Meagan's turn to find Sunstar, and she was having only limited success. The late afternoon sun shone through the trees—the wind rushed through the bushes and undergrowth. Sunstar grinned as she watched as Meagan bent and noisily searched the underbrush twenty feet from her.

"Sunstar?" Meagan stood and looked around, frowning. "Sunstar, where are you?"

Sunstar grinned and silently crept toward her, circling around her, within touching distance. A twig snapped.

Meagan whirled around, eyeing the greenery with some alarm. Sunstar pulled her legs out from under her. Meagan screamed and thrashed wildly as she hit the ground.

Sunstar threw herself on top of Meagan, her face a mere inch from Meagan's. She held her struggling limbs down. "Calm down. It's me." She laughed.

"Sunstar. You scared me half to death. I thought you'd gotten yourself into trouble," Meagan exclaimed and burst out crying.

"Ah, no." Sunstar eyed her with some alarm. "I'm sorry. I was just trying out a glamour my father taught me."

"Well, don't do it again. And your apology is *not* accepted."

Sunstar instantly felt sorry for the distress she had inflicted on Meagan. "Look. I really *am* sorry."

"I forgive you this time," Meagan said. "But don't do it again. I don't think I can take it." She gazed longingly at Sunstar.

"What ever do you mean, 'you can't take it'?" Sunstar gave her an alarmed look. She wondered how to stop what was coming.

Meagan leaned up and kissed Sunstar full on the lips. Sunstar enjoyed the sensation for a mere second, and then pulled back, breaking the kiss.

"Wait. Stop. Meagan," she said softly. "I love you as my closest friend. But that's as far as it goes for me."

Meagan blushed. Her eyes stuttering away from Sunstar's face.

Sunstar gently cupped her chin and pulled her back so they were looking at each other. Fresh tears wound their way down Meagan's face.

"Please," Sunstar said softly. "I don't want to lose you as a friend. We have been through so much together."

"Yes," Meagan said . "I can still be friends with you." She did not look or sound convinced.

Sunstar sighed inwardly. She felt guilty that she could not return Meagan's fervor and hoped that their friendship really was intact. She rolled off Meagan and gazed at the sky, noticing with dim alarm that it was late afternoon. She got to her feet, dragging Meagan with her. She pulled her over to their patiently waiting horses. They mounted.

"Look." Sunstar studied the fading light with concern. "We really have to get out of here."

Meagan stared at her, puffy eyed from crying. "What's the big rush?"

"We've wandered into the West Wood," Sunstar said.

Meagan's eyes widened in alarm. "But the Drow haven't been active here for ages."

"Actually, there was an attack last week. My father was keeping it quiet until we could confirm reports." Sunstar looked at the dense forest in concern. The light was rapidly failing. All around them, the forest was still, taking on a still more ominous tone in the expectant atmosphere.

"Well, I hope you know where we're going." Meagan looked anxiously around in the twilight. "I got lost quite a while ago."

Sunstar shook her head and bit her lip. If it had not been for the frantic dash right at the start of the day, they would not be out as far as they were. They had spent the entire day out a lot further than she would have liked. Now their options were extremely limited. Her father would be furious when they returned—*if* they returned.

She felt her blood run cold as she realized her bodyguards had never caught up with them. They should have been shadowing and audibly cursing her by now.

She wheeled her horse around. "We head that way," she said, pointing. "That should get us home."

"All right," Meagan said. "Good idea."

They rode a short way, toward thick cover. Sunstar surveyed the dense foliage, a dark blob in the gathering night. She glanced around and shivered.

Sunstar was extremely worried. Their only chance for survival was if the Drow were not in the region. She was not very worried about herself. Thanks to Windwalker she had learnt the basics of how to defend herself, but Meagan was another matter. She was a castle domestic, and had only been out for short day trips, apart from the usual overnight trips in the forest that all Elven children had while they were in school. Even then, Meagan had never really had the opportunity to attend much school, as she was kept busy in the kitchens.

Sunstar's horse suddenly screamed in pain and stumbled and fell. She barely had time to throw herself free as it thrashed and rolled. She was distantly aware that Meagan had also abandoned her horse and wondered why. Meagan was a second or so behind her and did not land well. She grimaced in pain as she got up and collapsed. Her left ankle would not hold her.

Sunstar's horse quieted, and she stroked his neck. She blinked and searched for any sign of why he could not get up.

"Oh, no," she moaned softly, looking at his rear leg. An ornate dagger lay buried in it up to the hilt. She checked Meagan's horse. Her mare was dead, a knife sticking out of her neck. Her blood soaked into the ground, and Sunstar felt sick.

There's no help for it now, she thought. *We have to try and hide. My poor horse.*

"What is it, Sunstar?" Meagan asked, alarmed.

"We're in trouble," Sunstar said.

She took Meagan's hand and led her into the bushes, trying not to make any sounds.

She parted the leaves of the tree and gasped in shock. A pair of gleeful red eyes gleamed back at her. She heard Meagan's whistling intake of breath as she prepared herself for a mighty scream. Sunstar's heart sank, and she stepped back.

CHAPTER 2

Sunstar was unable to make a sound as the forest came alive with Dark Elves. Meagan let fly an earsplitting scream, and Sunstar turned in a circle, eyeing the six Dark Elves that surrounded them. They were evenly spaced but Sunstar thought she saw a larger gap between two of them.

She lunged forward between them and thundered on through the thick forest, dragging Meagan behind her. She struggled not to panic and tried to lead them in roughly the right direction. The Dark Elves crashed through the greenery behind them.

Sunstar collapsed to the ground, pulling down Meagan with her. She rolled on top of Meagan and clamped a hand firmly over her mouth, willing her not to scream again. Meagan stared at her, bug eyed.

Sunstar tried to calm her panic as Windwalker had taught her. Her horse screamed behind them as the Dark Elves butchered him. She felt her heart sink.

"Spread out!" a voice commanded behind them. "They can't have gotten far."

The sounds diminished as the group of Dark Elves searched to their left, traveling away from them. They waited for long moments until after the sounds had ceased before Sunstar took a shaky hand off Meagan's mouth.

"Looks like we're in the clear for the moment," Sunstar whispered. "We have to head back now. I don't care if it takes all night."

Meagan nodded. She still looked terrified, but the raw edge of panic in her gaze had receded now that the sounds of pursuit finally faded to silence. Sunstar slowly and carefully disentangled their bodies. She soundlessly got to her feet, drawing Meagan up beside her.

The thud of a knife embedding itself into soft flesh froze Sunstar in her tracks. She whirled around to Meagan.

Meagan faltered and stopped.

"Sunstar." Meagan's eyes were wide with shock. She pitched forward into the startled Sunstar's arms.

"Meagan?" Sunstar stared at the ugly, ornate hilt sticking out of the center of her back. "No, Meagan, no. Stay with me."

Sunstar sank to her knees, clutching Meagan's body, tears trickling down her face.

"Well, well, well," a cold voice said close behind her. "Did she call you Sunstar?"

The voice sounded like it came from far away, and Sunstar answered before her mind could recover. "Yes. Yes, she did."

"Then you would be the Elven princess, would you not?" The voice was closer now, and warm breath tickled her ear.

"No, you have me confused with someone else," Sunstar said.

"I think not." The voice caressed her as a warm indigo hand caressed her silky hair.

Sunstar jerked her head away, jaw muscles tensing, feeling the warmth from a strong body too close to her for comfort.

"You are a most interesting prize. I have not had the pleasures of a princess for quite some time." The voice dissolved into an evil giggle.

Sunstar struggled to control her shudder. The warm body stood, dragging her up with it, wrenching Meagan from her arms. She was whirled around to face a tall Drow, all of about six-and-a-half feet, with long black robes covering his body. His white hair was long and silken, and his red eyes glowed balefully.

He touched her chin with a long, slim forefinger. She jerked away, and a ring of Dark Elves surrounded them. He seized her jaw with iron, uncaring fingers. "You are pretty," he continued in his soft voice. "I'm sure you will enjoy my gentle embrace."

Sunstar spat at him, and he laughed—a rich, full sound. He slapped her, knocking her to the ground.

"Tie her up," he ordered the assembled Drow. "We leave tonight."

Sunstar huddled on the ground, mind and spirit reeling with the turn of events. Iron hands hauled her to her feet and tied rough rope around her wrists. A stiff leather collar encircled her neck, and her captor pulled her forward into the night air. She did not move quickly enough to suit him, so he tugged sharply on the leash attached to the collar. She bent over and took an involuntary step forward, tripped over an unseen root, and fell to her knees. He grabbed her shirt front, tugged her to her feet, and tossed her forward with a soft snarl. She stumbled but regained her footing, and terror washed over her in a black wave.

Their capture and the sight of her oldest and best friend lying discarded on the forest floor haunted her, replaying over and over in her mind like a terrible nightmare. A deep, aching grief, mingled with numbing shock ran over her in waves, but she would not allow herself to mourn. There would be time enough for that later.

Now she was filled with trepidation at the prospect of the brutality she was sure they would visit on her. She felt sick with dread and emotional turmoil and stared sightlessly at the darkened forest.

The Drow, holding her leash, yanked it viciously, and she took a stumbling step forward. The Drow leader saw this and gave a brief snort of cruel laughter.

"Try not to damage her too much. She will be a good present for His Highness." He stepped toward the male Drow charged with the task of taking care of her. He leaned forward, glowing eyes cold and glittering. "If she is harmed by anyone other than me, I will kill you where you stand."

The Drow leading her nodded sharply, once. Sunstar glanced at the leader and felt her blood run cold at the absence of emotion in his eyes.

The male Drow pulled her forward again, this time a little more gently. Sunstar hurried to keep up with him, and it took all of her attention to scan the forest floor for the most obvious obstacles to her path. After stumbling over roots and rocks a few times—each time earning her a swift, almost hidden kick from the Drow in the line behind her—she learnt to shadow the movements of her captor. It helped her avoid the worst obstacles, but she still stumbled frequently, and the palms of her bound hands were soon raw from scraping against the ground as they cushioned her falls.

She was quickly exhausted from the punishing pace the Drow set, and her breath labored in and out of her lungs. Her exhaustion earned her sharp tugs on her collar—each one tearing more skin—until she felt the trickle of blood down her neck and a hard jab from the Drow behind her.

She glanced back at him, and he glared. He put his finger over his lips in a shushing gesture. She gritted her teeth.

They continued on through the forest, crossing creeks and traversing paths, until Sunstar was soaking wet and covered in filth from her numerous falls. Her hands and knees felt as though they were on fire, and she could feel blood dribbling down her neck. She had never felt so tired in her life, but the Drow would not let her rest. They pulled her forward with relentless intensity, looking for the slightest behavior to punish.

They continued on this way for an hour or so. Her captor slowed and sidestepped smoothly, allowing Sunstar's momentum to carry her past him. He shoved an iron hand into her back, and she fell to her knees with a sharp yelp.

He leaned over her. "Pay attention and move quickly," he snarled into her ear, giving her leash a vicious tug. Sunstar gagged and coughed. She tried to pull the collar away from her neck a little.

She was too winded to answer him, so she let her eyes show her anger and some measure of defiance. His own cold expression did not change, and he stared back into her eyes in a battle of wills that finally stopped when the leader motioned for them to continue.

When they finally halted in the early hours of the morning for a quick meal, she panted with exhaustion and leant forward, trying to catch her breath. Some of the initial shock had drained out of her system, chased away by the simple actions of survival. She felt almost dazed and seemed unable to focus on anything other than walking with the Drow.

Her Drow captor pushed her to the ground, and she stared up at him. He glared at her, wiping the hand that had touched her on the edge of his cloak. She frowned as an image of Meagan flashed through her mind. Meagan's blood coated his hands, and all he could think about was how disgusting it was to touch Sunstar? Did Meagan's murder mean nothing to him? Anger trickled into her, washing away some of the numbness.

The Drow leader dropped to his haunches by her side, smiling unpleasantly at her. "How are you doing, Princess?"

Sunstar glared at him, maintaining her silence. She was almost too tired to walk, and her wrists hurt beneath the ropes.

"Are you hungry?" He fingered a small trencher of food a stone-faced Drow female handed to him.

Sunstar remained silent, studying his handsome face. There was nothing to be gained by lying, and she had to keep up her strength if she had any chance of escape. She gave him a short, sharp nod.

"I thought so." He scooped up a small portion of food and held out his dripping fingers. "Here."

Outrage flowed over her. "You can't expect me to eat that way," she said before she could bite off the words.

He shrugged and put the food into his own mouth. "I couldn't care less, Princess." He tilted his head and studied her. "I really don't care whether you live or die. I was not sent to capture you, nor did I expect to find you. I could easily kill you, and no one would be any the wiser. I really should, since that would be much simpler for me. You are a needless extra mouth to feed." He eyed her, and Sunstar felt her blood run cold at his measured words. "But I did decide to bring you back to my king, and that is why I choose to keep you alive. If you turn out to be too much trouble for me, I will kill you. I don't need you and I don't want you." He smiled. "Now. Would you like something to eat?"

Sunstar's mind whirled, and she felt sick. His lack of compassion for her seemed to go beyond simple dislike. He seemed to see her as a thing no different to a rock or a tree. She realized in that split second that if she dared disobey him, he really would kill her. It was no idle threat. She *had* to obey him, or she would not live to see her parents and people again.

He watched her closely and nodded. "I see you understand me." He dipped his fingers into the trencher and held them out for her to suck. "Here. Eat."

She gently lipped his fingers, pulling the food off them, flushed with rage and shame. It was a rough stew of nuts and vegetables, along with a scarce portion of meat. It was strangely tasty. Her hunger turned into a wild animal inside her belly, and she wolfed down the portions he fed to her.

His soft laughter surrounded her, and a swift stab of hatred pierced her. She finally reached the end of the trencher, and he held out his dripping fingers. She stared at him.

"There's still more, Your Highness," he said, inclining his head.

She shook her head.

Suddenly she was lying on the ground, the side of her face stung, and her ears were ringing.

"You will take what I give you, or I will give you no more. Finish." He held out his fingers.

Sunstar gagged as she licked his fingers clean. Her hot eyes remained on his face.

He leant back and smiled at her. His smile did not touch his hot eyes. "Enjoying yourself, sweetling?" he asked in a mock sympathetic voice.

Sunstar glared at him with pure loathing. "When my father finds you—"

"It doesn't matter," he said with confidence. "He has no idea where you are. And he won't find out you are alive until it is far too late to save you, Princess."

Sunstar chose not to answer, instead she glared at him. She had not wanted to reply, but his actions had forced her. She held onto her anger. It kept her terror of the unknown at bay.

They traveled further after that, the pace set by the leader even more punishing than before. By the time dawn was upon them, they were many miles from where Sunstar had been captured, and the Dark Elves slowed and stumbled themselves as the light levels increased.

The leader finally pointed to a cave not far from the path they were on.

He blinked and flicked the moisture from his tearing eyes. "We will shelter in there for the day." He led the party into the welcoming darkness.

They milled in the cave, and Sunstar was the only one of the party able to stand upright under the low ceiling. The rest knelt on the floor and folded cloaks in preparation for the day's sleep. One by one they settled on the floor. They did not bother with starting a fire or preparing a final meal for the day.

Sunstar sighed and sank to her knees, thankful that walking was over for the time being. She could not remember ever being so exhausted. She was about to sink onto the cave floor when the leader knelt by her, smiling in a way she did not like. She watched him carefully.

His coldly handsome face was close to hers, and he caressed her. She jerked away as best she could with the thick collar around her neck.

"You will be with me during the day," he said, and Sunstar shuddered.

He untied her hands. She rubbed her sore wrists with numb hands, trying to restore her circulation. She waited a moment for him to remove the collar but he made no move to do so, and she sighed. She watched him warily and began to lie down.

"Oh, no, sweetling," he said, watching her closely. "When I said you will stay with me, I meant that you will *stay* with *me*."

With that, he drew her close with powerful arms. She struggled mightily. He lifted her from the ground, holding her close until her struggles ceased. He lay down with her and tied them together with the ropes from her wrists. She lay by his side, terrified, hoping he was finished with her, but it was not to be. He smiled and engulfed her in his brawny arms and pulled her on top of him. She waited but he did nothing else, and she released a whistling breath. His breathing evened out as he fell asleep.

Sunstar's mind roiled with disgust and loathing. Sleep was a long time in coming, despite her sheer physical exhaustion. She lay on top of him, listening to his strong, steady heartbeat, waves of dislike crashing over her. She felt soiled by the warmth that came off his body as he snored. She tried to push it aside, telling herself that she had to sleep to be ready for the next evening's march, but her mind kept bringing her back to the forest and memories of her capture.

She hoped that they had not traveled that far, and that her father would find her, but she knew her hopes were in vain. Her mind drifted back to the hapless Meagan, lying somewhere nameless in the forest, and the tears she had struggled to hold back during the night came to her full and unbidden. All the times they had shared together, and the future they would not have washed over her. The thought of her gentle mother's distress and her guilt for the unhappiness she had given to her family and friends ploughed through her. Tears poured from her eyes as she silently wept. She finally drifted into an uneasy slumber, husked out, disturbed by nightmares of Meagan dying, robbing her of precious rest.

Chapter 3

Darkwood, King of the Forest Elves, stood in his study, bending over a map of Elven lands and studying counters. He idly picked one up. The counters represented Drow movements through their land. Like most races, Drow traveled the fringes of Elven lands, going from one place to another. The Elves normally did not concern themselves with such minor matters as having public roads used by other races, but reports from the Elven rangers told them that there were more Drow, and they traveled further onto Elven lands than the ancient treaty between both peoples allowed.

"We had two more signs in the West Wood, didn't we?" a soft, feminine voice asked.

Darkwood looked up and into the eyes of his beloved Morningstar.

"Yes, we did," he said, smiling at her despite the grim subject. "What troubles me is that we don't really know why."

It was not the first time they had this discussion, and Morningstar nodded calmly, unsurprised. She opened her mouth to reply. The doors to the study flew open.

Darkwood turned to the open door with a frown. Windwalker, looking troubled, almost ran toward him. His eyes burned with an intensity that Darkwood did not often see.

"Yes, Captain?" Darkwood asked. "What is it?"

"Sire," he said, his eyes cutting to Morningstar.

Darkwood raised his eyebrows. Windwalker wanted Morningstar to leave, but why?

"Whatever you have to say you can say before both of us." Darkwood glanced at his wife. Windwalker often tried to shield her from bad news, but despite her delicate appearance, she was one of the strongest Elves Darkwood had ever met.

Windwalker bowed low. "Your will, Highness." He paused. "Patrols were dispatched to the West Wood this morning to search for more sign of Drow. Two guards did not return home last night, so I sent out a detachment to look for them. We found them—two bodies in the forest."

"Two bodies?" Darkwood frowned. "Do we know who they are?" His heart rate picked up, spurred by Windwalker's reluctance to meet his eyes, and his jaw tensed.

"Jarrod and Cerulean," Windwalker said. "We found Meagan—Princess Sunstar's friend—with a Drow dagger in her body. Two horses were butchered a little way away from her."

Morningstar gasped, and Darkwood, through the numbness and blood rushing in his ears, leaned forward and grasped the back of a chair in a white-knuckled grip.

"Sunstar. Has anyone seen Sunstar?" Darkwood was amazed that his voice was calm. His hands trembled.

Morningstar gave a low, strangled cry from behind him.

Windwalker grimaced and shook his head. "Her bed has not been slept in. We'll find her, I promise, Sire."

Darkwood's knees gave way, and he sank onto a couch beside the sobbing Morningstar. "Go and find her, Captain. Alert all the towns around our lands and let them know our daughter has been taken by the Drow. If they find her, please bring her back at once." He pulled Morningstar into his arms as Windwalker bowed and backed out of the study.

Darkwood's tears mingled with hers' as they sought comfort in each other.

"The Drow have her," Morningstar whispered.

"We'll get her back," Darkwood said. "Even if we have to go to war to do it."

"Let's just hope the guards find her before she is taken to Dragonar." Morningstar peered at him through red-rimmed eyes. "The Drow will kill her if she is taken there."

Darkwood nodded, his stomach twisted into terrible knots. He tried not to think about what would happen to his beloved daughter if they did not find her in the next few days. "She is strong. She will survive until we find her."

"I hope so."

Sunstar awoke with a start in the dusk of the next evening as she hit the ground with a hard thud. Her heart thumped in terror, and her breath came in short gasps as she fought to push away the remnants of sleep. She stared at the Drow scout leader, terrified and disorientated. He was looking down at himself in disgust, pulling his tear-stained shirt away from his chest. He snarled at her in wordless hatred. She shrank away from him, preparing to be slapped or kicked, but he merely glanced around the cavern at the waking Drow.

"Someone tie that up," he snarled, gesturing at her and grimacing in revulsion.

A blinking Drow rushed in to obey him.

The leader eyed her mercilessly and stood as best he was able and left the cavern.

Sunstar blinked. Her eyes burned and felt gritty with exhaustion. The Drow roughly tugged her to her knees and jerked the rope around her wrists. She groaned, and the Drow threw her down onto a rock.

Another Dark Elf approached her, holding a small trencher of dried fruit and vegetables. He quietly fed her, staring coldly at her as though she were a new and disgusting breed of insect. The ordeal was not as bad as when the leader had fed her, and without the odious, sensual pleasure the leader had taken with her.

She was dragged to her feet and led outside. She glanced at the Drow that had led her the previous evening, but he shook his head. She frowned as another took his place, and the night of walking commenced.

Her new captor was no better than the old one, and was in some ways worse. He never called her by her name. He called her something that her limited Drow vocabulary suggested had something to do with faeces. He never stopped for her and walked much quicker than her previous guide. She almost had to run to keep up with him, and when she stumbled she had to dodge his fists and feet.

The night's march was through a rugged, hilly section of forest, and he dragged her up and down slopes by the collar around her neck. After what felt like days of marching, the troop finally stopped for their midnight meal. Sunstar's captor yanked her to a halt.

She gagged and coughed, pulling the collar away from her neck. She glared at him. "That was unnecessary," she said when she was able to talk.

He gave her a measured look, then, like lightning, slapped her. Stunned, she sprawled flat on her back. Her head rang from the force of his blow.

He grabbed her by the collar, hauled her to her feet, and threw her against a tree. The air exploded from her lungs.

"I do not want to be near you," he snarled. "I wish you would die."

Sunstar frowned, revulsion twisting her features. She did not know how to respond. The leader looked at her and laughed.

"You cause us some trouble. I think it would be good if you were to relearn your place in life." He sat down on a convenient rock, watching her closely, and held out his hand to accept the trencher of food one of the Drow gave him.

"This is good," he said around a mouthful of food.

Sunstar's mouth watered, and she struggled not to give him the satisfaction of licking her lips and swallowing.

"You're not hungry, then?" he asked with what seemed honest curiosity, spoiled only by the loathing in his eyes.

Sunstar remained silent.

"More for me, then," he said airily and smiled. He scooped up more food and shoveled it into his mouth.

Sunstar felt an instant of disgust as her stomach grumbled loudly.

The leader smiled. He continued to feed himself. "Enjoying the rest, sweetling?"

Sunstar stared at him for a moment. His knuckles shone white as he gripped the trencher. She shrugged.

The leader snarled and opened his mouth, revealing half-chewed trail rations. He smiled. Sunstar frowned.

"If you want it, this is where you take it from," he said around a mouth full of half-chewed food.

Sunstar felt sick, and she sank back on her haunches, watching him carefully and trying to ignore the hunger snapping and snarling at her.

The leader remained silent, studying her closely.

They stayed that way, eyes on each other, weighing and measuring, until the meal break was over. A stone-faced Drow took his trencher from him. He pulled Sunstar to her feet and tossed the rope tied to the collar to the Drow in charge of her for the night.

"Take that back," he said coldly. "Make sure that when we go to ground it's not damaged."

The Drow nodded sharply, once.

The leader stopped and looked eye to eye with the Drow. "If she is injured, an equivalent portion of your hide will go missing."

The Drow nodded again.

The leader took his place at the front of the column, and the night's march continued.

By the end of the night she was bruised and bleeding and every muscle in her body ached miserably. The leader had not bothered to feed her during the night's march, and hunger snapped and snarled at her. In dawn's grey light she found herself tied to the leader once again, but this time slept peacefully, thanks to her terrible exhaustion.

This continued for another two nights, the leader taking every opportunity to taunt Sunstar and treat her as though she were an animal. All the loathing she felt for him continued to simmer. She felt the same toward the other Drow. She was universally treated as though she were an inanimate object, beaten and cursed at every opportunity—even when she was quiet her presence confused them. She thought it was simple curiosity on their part that kept her alive. She was sure that none of them had ever participated in a raid in which a prisoner had been taken and continued to live.

Halfway through the fourth evening, Sunstar knelt at the feet of the Drow leader. He liked it when she did that; it meant that he was less inclined to swing his fist into her face when they stopped for the evening. A shot of self loathing tore through her at the surge of hunger that accompanied the sight of the food on his fingers. She hated the degradation of eating that way and tried to tell herself that she did it simply to keep the peace with him.

He reached out a finger of food, and a figure stepped out into the small clearing in which they sat. The leader leapt to his feet, spilling the plate of food all over Sunstar. She quickly leapt back and sat heavily. Food fell away from her filthy shirt and she had to remind herself not to stuff it into her mouth. She watched them both with wide eyes.

"Galvin," the leader snarled. "Haven't I told you more than once *not* to do that?"

"Well met, Farouk," Galvin said, sarcastically. "What are you doing here? You should be patrolling near the Forest Elves."

"I know," Farouk said coldly. "Don't think to tell me my duties."

So he has a name, Sunstar thought, watching them warily. *Farouk.*

Galvin glanced back into the darkness and whistled softly.

Six new Drow entered the clearing. All were tall, the shortest being a good six feet in height, all bar one with the same silky white hair, indigo skin, and either softly glowing red or golden eyes. The final one was very different to her companions. She was well over six feet in height, pale, midnight haired, and had glowing eyes that were neither gold nor red. All the Dark Elves, save the female, eyed each other up and down. They seemed to be sizing each other up in anticipation of a skirmish.

The dark-haired Drow's gaze traveled over Farouk's party and stopped at Sunstar. She gave Sunstar the same frank appraisal that Sunstar gave her.

Galvin shot Farouk a final glare and followed the gaze of the dark-haired Drow.

He raised an eyebrow. "Well, well, well. And what do we have here? It's not like you to keep a prisoner, or are you going soft?" He approached Sunstar and gazed down at her, curiosity in his glowing eyes. Sunstar met his gaze unflinchingly.

"We have found for ourselves Princess Sunstar," Farouk said. "We—"

"You what?" Galvin interrupted smoothly, turning and staring at Farouk.

"We are taking her back as a gift for the king," Farouk said, not backing down from the stare. Galvin continued to stare coldly at him, and eventually Farouk broke and looked away.

"What is he going to do with an elfmaid, Farouk?" Galvin's eyes glittered, and he folded his arms. "Or were you lying and really planning on having fun with her before you got home?"

Farouk colored slightly, and Sunstar flinched. "She *is* a gift. I do *not* have to explain myself to you, Galvin."

Galvin smiled. His gaze bored into Farouk. "As it happens, we are headed home as well. We will travel together to make sure your little present arrives intact. With your kind permission of course, Farouk." His tone made it very clear it was not a request, it was an order.

"Very well," Farouk said. "I'm sure we have much to discuss."

Galvin leant forward to whisper something to the dark-haired Drow. "I'm sure you won't mind if Nightshade sees to her care. I don't trust leaving her to your tender mercies." He jerked his chin at Nightshade.

The dark-haired Drow nodded and slowly approached Sunstar. Her beautiful face remained expressionless, and Sunstar's knees shook in terror.

Nightshade stared at her. She stared back at Nightshade, a deer caught in hunters' sights. Nightshade shifted, and Sunstar forced herself to focus and break out of her haze. She stared back at

Nightshade with mostly fear, and not a little defiance. Nightshade met her gaze with expressionless eyes. Sunstar finally broke the stare.

Nightshade gently pulled Sunstar's face up so they were looking eye-to-eye. Sunstar stared back, tears brimming in her eyes. Nightshade's cold blue eyes gave nothing away. She gently released Sunstar's face and circled her. She took Sunstar's hands in a startlingly gently grasp and turned them, palms up. She eyed Sunstar's bleeding wrists. She looked at the leather collar and gently touched the drying blood on Sunstar's neck. She looked Sunstar up and down, and Sunstar became acutely aware of the tears in her breeches, dirt and thin smears of blood on her tattered clothes. Nightshade lifted the back of Sunstar's shirt.

"He didn't hurt you, did he?" Nightshade asked, very softly so that none of her compatriots could hear. She leaned in close, checking her neck.

"No, he hasn't touched me," Sunstar whispered. She suppressed her shock at the question from the Dark Elf. Why would Nightshade care one way or the other about what Farouk had done to her?

"Well, Nightshade?" Galvin demanded. "How does she look?"

"She's covered in bruises, and her wrists are bleeding," Nightshade said in her silky, deep voice. "Apart from that, I think she is unharmed." She paused. "We must attend to her cuts, or she won't live to meet His Highness."

Galvin gave her a cruel smile and turned to Farouk. "Isn't it lucky we came along when we did, Farouk?" he said with false good humor. "She might never have reached the city alive otherwise." He turned back to Nightshade. "Take her down to the river and clean her up. We'll move out when you get back." He tilted his head and regarded Nightshade. "You can handle a little elfmaid, can't you?"

Both scouting parties smirked and stifled their laughter.

Nightshade shifted next to Sunstar and nodded sharply, once.

Galvin snorted, satisfied. He turned back to Farouk. "To ensure that your luck remains good, Nightshade will take care of the princess until we are back in the city." He smiled, and his eyes shone with malice.

"As you will, Galvin," Farouk ground out. His eyes blazed.

"Nightshade. Take good care of her, or I'll kill you myself. *Slowly.*" Galvin jerked his head toward the darkness. "Move."

"Yes, Galvin," Nightshade said, with a hint of impatience. She took Sunstar's hand and gently pulled her forward.

Pure shock stopped Sunstar from tripping over her own feet and crashing into Nightshade's back. Nightshade pulled her close and walked forward slowly. Sunstar tried to follow her, but as soon as they were out of sight of the others, she yelped and tripped over a rock in the path.

Nightshade caught her by her shoulders and steadied her. "Are you all right?"

Sunstar nodded once, dimly amazed by the Nightshade's strength. She braced herself for a blow from Nightshade.

Nightshade turned and began walking. Sunstar took five more steps and tripped again and landed heavily against Nightshade. Nightshade patiently caught her and put her back on her feet again, and they continued walking. Sunstar could barely see anything and slowed down. Nightshade slowed with her. They finally reached the river, and Nightshade led her to the edge and pushed her down onto a rock.

Nightshade pulled off Sunstar's boots and shook her head at Sunstar's bruised feet. She gently guided them into the water, and Sunstar hissed at the cold and the almost instant relief from the aching bruises on her toes.

Nightshade very gently removed the collar from Sunstar's neck. "I don't think we'll be needing that anymore." She cast it to one side and gazed at Sunstar. "Are you going to give me any trouble?"

"I am going to try and escape. Surely you must know that, Drow," Sunstar said with an echo of her former spirit.

"You can't even see your way to walk along a forest path," Nightshade said. "By all means, try and escape. You won't be free for long."

Sunstar hung her head, wincing, savagely reminded that the Elf she was with was not a Forest Elf. No matter how dark her hair or blue her eyes, Nightshade was still a Drow.

Nightshade shifted beside her and put her pack on the smooth rocks. She pulled a spare shirt out of its depths and soaked it in the cold water of the river.

Sunstar moaned softly as Nightshade cleaned her neck and her wrists. Nightshade's touch was gentle and practiced, and she did her work with an economy of motion that fascinated Sunstar. After she finished, Nightshade ripped the sleeves off the shirt and wrapped them around the raw wounds on Sunstar's wrists.

"It would be more comfortable for you if you wore this shirt." Nightshade held out her torn shirt to Sunstar.

Sunstar looked down at the filth covering her tattered clothes. She nodded. Nightshade gave her the shirt and watched her as she changed. Sunstar hoped the darkness hid her bare body and refrained from looking into Nightshade's wary face.

When they were finished, Nightshade threaded Sunstar's arm through hers. Sunstar fidgeted as Nightshade began to walk back along the forest path. Sunstar felt uncomfortable being so close to a Drow, mingled with dim relief at the realization that clinging to Nightshade meant that she did not trip once.

They soon reached the Dark Elves sprawled in the clearing sharing a meal. Galvin looked up at them. He nodded at Nightshade.

Nightshade gently pushed Sunstar to a sitting position on a rock a little away from the others. She reached into her pouch and pulled out some trail rations. Sunstar waited to see what she would do. Nightshade's expressionless gaze never wavered as she handed Sunstar the food.

Sunstar stared at her, surprised. She wondered what Nightshade would do to her when she tried to eat.

Nightshade watched her carefully.

Sunstar looked down at the food in her hands, and her hunger roared to life. She fell onto the simple rations as though she had not eaten for months, gulping them down and licking her fingers.

"Have you not been fed?" Nightshade asked quietly.

Sunstar stopped and looked up at her. She could feel the color rising in her cheeks. "Yes, I have."

Nightshade looked as though she was waiting for Sunstar to add to this, but Sunstar remained silent and avoided her eyes. The moment passed, and she pulled Sunstar to her feet. They went and stood before Galvin.

Galvin eyed Nightshade, accepting her nod with an inclination of his head. "Let's move," he said to the others, and all the Dark Elves prepared to travel. He stood and went to Farouk.

Nightshade leaned toward Sunstar. "I can't leave the ropes around your wrists untied," she said softly, so the others would not hear, "because I know you will try to escape. I can make it easier for you, though." She retied the ropes looser around Sunstar's wrists and took her hand with firm but gentle fingers. Carefully guiding Sunstar forward, Nightshade took up her position close to the front of her squad, behind Farouk and Galvin.

CHAPTER 4

The entire troop moved out. Nightshade led the dazed Sunstar with considerably more care than the sadistic Farouk. Nightshade's strong hands took her around obstacles rather than through them, never losing their firm grip on her fingers.

Sunstar pondered this turn of events as they made their way through the forest. Her new captor *looked* vastly different to the other Drow with her silken black hair and startling blue eyes. She also *seemed* genuinely different. She was noticeably gentler than the others, and was universally treated with scorn by them. Sunstar had never heard of a half Drow before, and she burned with curiosity to know more about Nightshade.

"Nightshade?" she whispered. "Psst! Nightshade."

Nightshade gave no sign of having heard her.

She tried again, a little more loudly, but was rewarded with a jerk on her bonds and a quick glare. She lapsed back into silence.

They stopped for a quick rest an hour or so later, and Sunstar did not feel as exhausted as she had on the previous evenings. She had not stumbled too much, and although her feet hurt, they did not ache as abominably as they had. She sat down beside Nightshade, feeling more focused than she had before. Her wrists were still sore but the shirt covering her wounds was a benediction to her hot skin.

She glanced at Nightshade. "Thank you," she said so softly that Nightshade could not possibly have heard, but it did not matter. Nightshade could never accept her gratitude even if it had been welcome.

A few moments later their break was over, and Nightshade gently pulled her to her feet. She stepped closer to Nightshade, ready to continue walking. Nightshade gently pulled her into motion, and they continued through the forest until the Drow could not go any further.

The Dark Elves went to ground again in the cold, grey light of dawn. They found another cave with unerring accuracy to shelter from the light of the day. It was obviously known to the group.

Sunstar placidly submitted to Nightshade, defeated, knowing she would be tied to her during the day.

Nightshade leaned forward and loosened the rope surrounding Sunstar's wrist. She brought Sunstar's other wrist up and bound them both together, but they did not have to lie on one another. Sunstar realized that if she moved, Nightshade would immediately know.

Nightshade carefully pushed Sunstar to the ground. Sunstar's heart beat wildly in terror as Nightshade gently grabbed her ankles. She forcibly relaxed when Nightshade tied her legs together, covered her with a blanket, and gave her another to use as a pillow. She lay on the ground a short distance away, pulled her thick cloak around her, and fell into an instant slumber.

Adrenalin surged through Sunstar, and she was unable to sleep for a long time, despite her exhaustion and hunger. She did not understand why Nightshade displayed any level of consideration for her well being. Every Drow she had encountered displayed innate cruelty and a complete lack of empathy for her, yet Nightshade seemed different, but she was wary of drawing that conclusion. Was she mistaken simply because Nightshade looked more like an Elf than a common Drow? Was Nightshade really different? Or did she just hide her base nature better than the others did because of her obviously mixed blood? Perhaps she was as cold and cruel as the others and displayed compassion for Sunstar because it suited her—or Galvin—to do so.

After pondering this question for some time, she realized it did not matter. She was going to the Drow city and that was that. Nightshade's job was to ensure that she arrived in one piece and that was what she was doing. That was *all* she was doing. It would be insanely dangerous to assume any kind of common ground existed with Nightshade, or that the half Drow would be inclined to help her escape. Yet, despite Sunstar's resolved lack of trust, Nightshade's soothing actions and presence sent her into a deep, healing sleep.

The next evening she woke up to a gentle shake from Nightshade. She opened her eyes, blinking sleep out of them, as Nightshade untied her bonds and helped her to her feet. Nightshade walked her around, helping her to get some movement back into her stiff limbs. Sunstar stumbled more than once, but the ever-patient hand of Nightshade was there to steady her, emotionless blue eyes flickering once with something akin to sympathy.

Once Sunstar was able to move comfortably, Nightshade got her something to eat. Nightshade waited patiently while Sunstar wolfed down her breakfast, and then had some herself.

When they finished, Nightshade leaned forward and guided Sunstar to her feet. "We're going down to the river again. Your wrists need to be bathed and cleaned."

Sunstar nodded warily.

Nightshade led her down to the river, and the trip through the undergrowth was much easier than on the previous evening. Nightshade kept her close, gentle pressure on her arms letting her know if she had to turn left or right around obstacles. Once they were down at the river, Nightshade pushed her down onto the bank. She silently pulled Sunstar's boots off and helped her put her aching feet into the river. Sunstar watched her in fascination.

"Do you want to wash your face?" Nightshade asked, untying her wrists.

"I'm not pleasing enough to you, Drow? You don't like filthy Elves? You want me cleaner?" Sunstar asked coldly.

Nightshade did not respond and continued to untie her. She took the bindings off Sunstar's wrists and soaked them in cold water.

Sunstar hissed when Nightshade put the cold, dripping rags around her wrists. They became numb, soothing her pain. She relaxed slightly and shot Nightshade a wary glance. Nightshade's glowing blue eyes remained expressionless as she leaned forward and sank her hands into the cold river water.

She gasped and carefully splashed water onto her face, acutely aware of Nightshade's eyes on her.

Nightshade sat on the rock, watching her closely as she washed all traces of blood and tears from her face.

"We should head back to the others," Nightshade said when Sunstar was finished. "They will be wondering where we are."

"Aren't you afraid they're going to assume you're having sport with me? And beat you for it?"

Nightshade's eyes flashed with anger at the barb but she did not respond. Sunstar idly wondered why she was choosing to antagonize the one member of the scouting party that had done nothing but try and help her. She instantly upbraided herself. Help her? How was taking her away from her home to become sport for a sadistic monarch helping her?

They silently returned to the other Drow Elves.

Nightshade no sooner entered the clearing when Galvin strode forward with a snarl of rage. He backhanded her, hard, and she fell heavily against the ground, a thin trickle of blood running down her chin from the corner of her mouth. Sunstar collapsed beside her, dragged down by the rope connecting them. She shook with the sudden shot of adrenalin to her system.

"Where were you, coward?" Galvin planted his boot in the middle of Nightshade's chest, and he leaned his weight onto it.

"You told me to attend to the princess's care, and I am doing so," Nightshade ground out. "She will be sick by the time we reach the city if her cuts are not properly tended to."

Galvin spun and pinned Sunstar with an unforgiving stare. He grabbed her by the front of her shirt and hauled her to her feet. She shook with terror. He grasped her by her chin and roughly yanked her head upwards. She bit the inside of her lip to contain a cry of pain. He inspected her neck and threw her down. He turned back to Nightshade.

"You are lucky, human lover, that she really *is* damaged." He kicked her. "Get up. We march now."

Nightshade silently got to her feet and held out a hand for Sunstar. Sunstar stared at it in shock. She cautiously took it, and Nightshade pulled her to her feet. She looked into Nightshade's eyes and saw something akin to sympathy flickering in them. She looked away before a surge of tears threatened to overcome her.

The Dark Elves returned to the routine of the previous nights—Galvin and Farouk led the troop, Nightshade gently led Sunstar, this time tying them together with Sunstar's other wrist, and they journeyed on.

After a couple of hours of walking, they reached a rope bridge spanning a wide gully. Farouk quickly stepped onto the bridge, and Galvin stopped and put a large hand on Nightshade's chest, halting her forward progress.

"Not yet, human lover," he said coldly, nodding for the other members of the party to cross first.

Nightshade met his cold stare impassively, and Sunstar stayed close by her side. Sunstar glanced at the bridge, seemingly made solely of fraying rope and rotting boards that creaked ominously whenever anyone stepped on them.

"We go first," Galvin said as the last Drow stepped onto the bridge. "We will wait for you on the other side." He smiled, setting Sunstar's teeth on edge. He quickly followed the Drow onto the bridge and crossed.

Sunstar felt dim alarm and eyed the bridge with trepidation. She could not see much but saw enough to know Galvin was jumping from board to board. The bridge swung and groaned.

Sunstar shrank close to Nightshade.

Nightshade led her toward the bridge, seemingly calm. She stepped onto it, and it gave another screeching protestation. Sunstar took her hand, her own sweating as wave after wave of sheer terror crashed over her. The boards beneath her feet groaned and bent under her weight.

One of the boards snapped. She stumbled forward, crashed into Nightshade, and clung to her with desperate strength. Nightshade remained still and silent. She held firmly onto Sunstar.

"Look, it's starting to panic!" one of the Drow yelled from the other side of the gully, and the other Elves laughed.

"Let me cut the rope, Galvin," another Drow said. "We could get rid of two problems at once."

"There's a thought," Galvin said, glancing at Farouk.

Farouk glared at him.

"Oh, that's right." Galvin settled his weight back on his heels and crossed his arms. "That's your little present for the king. Nightshade, don't fall." He shook the rope hand rail. The bridge jostled ominously, and Sunstar squeaked.

The Drow laughed.

"See if you can make her squeak again," a tall, female Drow said.

Galvin jerked the railing again. Sunstar threw her arms around Nightshade and clung to her with desperate strength as the rope holding the foot boards snapped. The sudden shock to the other rope was too much, and it also snapped. A handrail followed close behind it.

Nightshade lunged for the remaining rope anchored to the other side. Sunstar clung to her with desperate strength. Her fingers dug into Nightshade's hard body. She yelped once in terror and then bit the insides of her cheeks to stop the shrieks of terror that threatened to erupt from her. Nightshade brought her knees up, and her feet took the worst of the shock as they slammed into the rock face.

Sunstar shut her eyes and buried her face into Nightshade's broad back, taking in the scent of wool, earth, and warm body.

"Don't drop me," Sunstar ground out as the Drow looked down at them and shook with laughter.

Nightshade shook her head in a barely perceptible motion.

"Come along, Nightshade," Farouk said. "Start climbing, or I'll cut the rope." He brandished a Drow dagger over the frayed rope.

Nightshade grunted with effort as she fought for footholds in the rock and inch by agonizing inch pulled them up the rock face.

"Look. She's all red," one of the Drow said.

"You need more exercise anyway, human lover!" another yelled.

"Move, Nightshade," Galvin snarled. "We haven't got all night."

Nightshade grimly pulled them both up and over the side of the cliff. Sunstar climbed the last few feet up and over onto solid ground. She lay flat, panting and breathing in dirt. Her fingers curled convulsively into the soil. She had never been so glad to be on solid ground.

"Very nice." Galvin crouched beside Nightshade. "Look at her knee." He pulled Sunstar over so she lay on her back.

Sunstar became aware of a stinging sensation in her knee and looked down. Blood oozed out of thick scrapes on one badly bruised knee. She stared at it, dazed. *I must have hit the cliff hard. I didn't even feel it.*

Galvin grabbed Nightshade's chin and yanked her head up so she was forced to meet his furious eyes. "I thought I told you I didn't want her damaged. Look at that. What's that?"

"She's damaged," Nightshade said.

"That's right. She's damaged," Galvin agreed, as though dealing with a difficult pupil. He raised a fist and punched her as hard as he could.

Nightshade crashed back to the ground. Blood streamed from her mouth.

Galvin shook his head and sighed in disgust. He grabbed her by the shirt and hauled her to her feet. Her head flopped forward, and he shook her. She moaned softly and straightened, looking dazed.

"Keep walking, human lover. And if she is damaged again I *will* kill you." He waited for a moment and stiffened at the lack of response from Nightshade. "What do we say to an order, Nightshade?"

The Drow Elves stopped what they were doing to watch the interaction. Farouk smirked.

"Yes, Galvin," Nightshade said softly.

He threw her to the ground and spat on her. The Drow laughed and turned back to Galvin and Farouk.

Sunstar crawled over to Nightshade and bent over her. She gently dabbed at the blood on Nightshade's face with a sliver of the rag bound around her wrist. Her fingers faltered at Nightshade's soft hiss of pain. "I know this doesn't mean anything to you. But thank you." She tried to smile.

Nightshade gazed at her. Her glowing blue eyes were still dazed but for a second they were filled with terrible sorrow and regret, which disappeared as swiftly as it came. Sunstar felt the sting of hopeless tears.

"Let's move out." Galvin shot Nightshade a quick glare.

Nightshade slowly and painfully climbed to her feet. She held out her hand to Sunstar. Sunstar took it and hauled herself to her feet.

They began walking, and Sunstar stayed close to Nightshade, who seemed unsteady on her feet.

CHAPTER 5

They stopped for a meal in the early hours of the morning, and Nightshade sat close by Sunstar as they ate together. Nightshade made sure Sunstar's plate was laden with the stew that the Dark Elves seemed so fond of, and Sunstar was full after the meal. She quietly submitted to Nightshade when it was over, and the march began again. When they stopped for the evening, Sunstar waited to see what Nightshade would do, but she did what she had done the previous evening—she tied them both together and gave Sunstar a cloak and blanket.

During the course of their travel over the next few nights, Sunstar slowly relaxed and came to trust that Nightshade would not punch or jab her when she stumbled or made too much noise. She noticed, with a bolt of self loathing, that she tried to be as quiet as possible so she did not draw the troop's attention, simply for Nightshade.

She tried to offer her appreciation to Nightshade in small ways. She gave her a smile here or there; she submitted to her murmured commands; she co-operated as best she was able. She found herself settling into a smooth rhythm with her captors and questioned why she was being so well behaved for them. It was her *duty* to try and escape from them.

Every night's march brought her closer and closer to the Drow city and diminished her chances of rescue by her father. The prolonged march in the outside world was also beginning to lull her into a false sense of peace. She *had* to make at least one attempt to escape them. She would have to wait for exactly the right time, but when would that be? Her only chance at freedom lay in the consideration that Nightshade gave her. She could try and run when Nightshade got her up during the day before the evening's march. Nightshade was half Drow and the chances of her being unable to see during the day were on Sunstar's side.

She bided her time quietly with this thought, and the perfect opportunity almost immediately presented itself. Nightshade woke her up, early as normal, and gently helped her to her feet. She untied the bonds connecting them and warily watched Sunstar as she moved around.

They were out in the open, and the other Drow were asleep in the undergrowth all around them. Sunstar cautiously stretched out her legs and surreptitiously watched Nightshade watch her. Something large walked through the undergrowth, and Nightshade tilted her head to listen to it. Sunstar watched Nightshade carefully, ignoring the forest sounds around them.

The undergrowth rustled again, and Nightshade turned her head to scan it.

It doesn't get better than this, Sunstar thought. She turned in the opposite direction and ran. She blundered through the undergrowth, glancing over her shoulder as she went. She could not see any signs of pursuit and smiled to herself.

She suddenly lay flat on her back, winded. She sat up, rested her weight on her elbows, and blinked at the corona surrounding Nightshade.

Nightshade held out her hand, and Sunstar took it. Nightshade hauled her to her feet.

They stood facing each other. Nightshade looked deep into her eyes, her own glowing blue unfathomable. Sunstar's breath came in gasps as she tried to get her wind back.

Nightshade took her hand, and they silently walked back toward the clearing the Drow slept in.

"I—" Sunstar began, her voice as loud as a bomb in the quiet forest. She wanted to make a disparaging remark, but sensed that was not what would come out.

"Shh." Nightshade glanced at Sunstar and shook her head, almost as though she were disappointed.

Sunstar felt an instant of guilt and then a surge of anger. *They* had kidnapped *her,* and she felt *guilty* for trying to escape? She glanced at Nightshade. It did not matter how gentle Nightshade was with her. Nightshade was her captor and therefore her enemy. She wanted to feel an answering surge of dislike and disgust, but nothing would come.

They went back to the clearing where Galvin and Farouk stood shoulder to shoulder waiting for them.

"What are you doing?" Galvin watched them both with glittering eyes.

"I heard something and had a look," Nightshade said. "Nothing."

Galvin took a step toward her so barely a whisper separated them. They stared deep into each other's eyes. Nightshade seemed relaxed, and Sunstar felt unwilling admiration she instantly suppressed.

"Really?" Galvin said.

"Is there something else you want to tell us?" Farouk asked. His gaze bored into Nightshade.

Nightshade shook her head. "No."

Galvin shoved her back a step. "See that it stays that way." His unspoken threat of violence lay over them like a pall of black smoke. His eyes promised murder. They continued to stare at each other in a battle of wills for another moment. He finally dropped his eyes, clapped his hands, and called for the scouting party to rise for the night's march.

Why, oh why am I doing this? Sunstar asked herself as she held out her hands for Nightshade to bind. She felt an instant of self loathing for the flash of guilt as she looked into Nightshade's glowing blue eyes. It became worse when she felt Nightshade's gentle grip as they took their place in line.

They began to walk.

Escape was not an option for her, Sunstar thought as she looked for another opportunity to try it. Every day she clung to hope and prayed that her father would suddenly appear with their army to rescue her.

Her fragile sense of peace and hope vanished like a puff of smoke on the evening of the twelfth night since her capture. They came up from their daylight resting place and breakfasted, as usual, but the Drow troop seemed different. They were more excited than they had been before and eagerly moved when Galvin call them together for the evening's march. Only Nightshade remained the same—expressionless and coldly calm. They walked for no more than an hour when Galvin and Farouk halted them. Sunstar looked around, blinking in the darkness. In the distance she could see black, jagged peaks outlined in the corona of the new moon, and she realized the darkness beside them was a monolith of a mountain.

"Nightshade, you'll have to carry her," Galvin said.

Farouk shot him an angry glance but remained silent.

Nightshade nodded. "Yes, Galvin." She glanced at Sunstar.

Sunstar stared at her, dread flickering through her green eyes.

Nightshade's eyes flickered in what looked like sympathy.

"Why?" Sunstar asked softly. "Please, Nightshade. Why?" She glanced up at the mountain and shivered.

"We're home," Nightshade said simply. "This is the mountain that covers our home city of Dragonar."

Sunstar felt panic welling in her heart, a wave of fear crashing over her. Her knees gave out, and she found herself in a puddle at the startled Nightshade's feet.

"I've got you." Nightshade gently guided Sunstar to her feet. Sunstar once again was witness to Nightshade's awesome strength as Nightshade lifted and carefully draped her over her broad shoulder.

Sunstar struggled to control her panic. It was one thing to be carried across a stream this way, quite another to be carried up a mountain. "Can't I walk?"

"No."

Sunstar took all her courage into her hands and threw it at the Dark Elf that had shown her so much kindness. She barely felt the inner criticism from the part of her psyche that was angry at her for meekly submitting to Nightshade.

Galvin and Farouk started up the rocky mountain path, Nightshade behind them.

The ground was flat for a few yards, and then began to slope upward. Sunstar closed her eyes and swallowed convulsively, trying to control the trickle of fear that was turning into a torrent inside her. She kept her eyes shut for a moment or so, but that was worse than trying to focus on Nightshade's broad back.

She bounced uncomfortably as they climbed a series of narrow stone steps. Sunstar glanced around and stiffened. There was a sheer drop beneath her, and they seemed far up. She was thankful she could not see enough to make out detail. Nightshade's strong arm held her in place, and she used the other hand to grab for handholds in the dark rock beside her. She resisted the urge to cling to her and sob. If her terror took hold of her, it would be a death sentence for them both.

They finally walked along a narrow path with the mountain on one side and a steep drop on the other. Sunstar felt Nightshade's gait become choppy, and she bounced uncomfortably. She realized with horror that Nightshade was jumping over breaks in the path, and she fainted for a few seconds from terror.

After what felt like hours of steady climbing, Galvin and Farouk led the way onto a ridge. It had a narrow opening, invisible from the ground below. The Dark Elves clustered around it and entered one by one, until only Galvin, Farouk, Nightshade, Sunstar and two other Drow remained on the rock shelf.

Nightshade, breathing hard, sank to her knees and lowered her cargo to the ground. Sunstar opened an eye and shuddered with alarm when she saw the blackness of the landscape below.

"Nervous, sweetling?" Farouk asked silkily, leaning over her with an unpleasant smile playing about his lips. "I will take you from here."

Fresh panic rose up in Sunstar's chest. "Why can't Nightshade take me?"

"You are quite taken with Nightshade, aren't you?" Farouk paused to glare at her, red eyes glowing, expression calculating. "It's because she can't see anything in the darkness below, can you, Nightshade?" He eyed them both pitilessly. "She's only half a Dark Elf, aren't you, Nightshade?" The other members of the party laughed in derision, Galvin included. Nightshade hung her head in shame.

Farouk grabbed Sunstar's hand and caressed it. Sunstar stared at him, expressionless. Only pride kept her from displaying any of the loathing she felt for him. He jerked her into the tunnel, Galvin and Nightshade following close behind, the other Drow bringing up the rear.

They traveled steadily down the dark tunnels. Sunstar's sight did not work in the blackness, and she blinked several times, fearing that she had gone blind. She felt another bolt of terror at being completely under the control of the sadistic Farouk. He set a pace that was too fast for her comfort, and she stumbled several times.

"Watch it, you clumsy fool." He dragged her forward until she regained her footing.

She could hear Nightshade behind her, and she seemed to be doing marginally better in the darkness than Sunstar. Nightshade occasionally stumbled, hissing when she was roughly hauled to her feet and thrust forward.

Sunstar's skin crawled where Farouk touched her. He idly ran his thumb over the back of her hand, and Sunstar's palms sweated with dread and fear. After a long period, they came to a stop.

A voice in front of them cried, "Halt! State your name."

"It is Galvin and Farouk, with both detachments," Galvin said.

The cruel voice turned jovial. "Ah, Galvin, it's good to see you back. We missed your presence at the Ring."

Sunstar did not understand this ominous comment and shivered. She was forcibly reminded that her journey was almost over. She peered into the dark, opening and shutting her eyes, but it still made no difference to her field of vision. Farouk shifted beside her and firmed his grip on her hand. She longed for the umpteenth time that it was the comforting, silent presence of Nightshade steering her through the blackness, not Farouk.

"I am back now, and we have a gift for His Highness," Galvin said, and Sunstar could hear the smile in his voice. "It is even better than the Ring."

"*Nothing* is better than the Ring," the voice said.

"How about a living Forest Elf?" Galvin said.

"You brought back a *prisoner*?"

"Not just any prisoner, but one the queen will also like."

"Well done, Galvin. We haven't had a good hunt in far too long."

"Oh, this one will be memorable," Galvin said softly.

Sunstar could feel rather than see his unpleasant smile. She took a step back at the sudden sight of his glowing eyes.

Farouk's cold laughter joined with Galvin's, and they pulled their respective charges forward again. As they walked past the guard post, warm hands reached out and roughly grabbed Sunstar's breasts and felt her with greedy fingers.

Sunstar stumbled.

"That's enough," Galvin commanded, jovial manner dissipating. "This one is for the king to decide." He shoved her assailant, and the hands left her body. The unseen Drow stumbled back, thumping against the wall with a grunt. She shuddered at the low moan that followed.

The party continued past the groaning figure and onward to the depths of the mountain. After what felt like hours, the uneven rocky surface of the path evened out to what Sunstar thought was a paved road, and she walked a little easier. The metallic taste of fear flooded her mouth, and foremost in her mind was the loathing she felt for Farouk, and a silent wish that they would allow Nightshade to lead her forward once more.

The gentle downward slope finally became a flat road, and Sunstar saw a very pale light. She blinked several times, afraid that her eyes no longer functioned properly. The uneasy visual sensation of the gentle blue glow caused her to lose her balance and stumble directly into Farouk.

She inadvertently tripped him, and he stumbled heavily. He tightened his grip on her and viciously swung her around.

"You stupid, clumsy moron." He dealt a brutal blow to the side of her face. She fell to the ground with a cry of pain. She held her face with a free hand, stunned. Farouk swung his foot back, in preparation for a savage kick in the ribs. Galvin shot forward and shoved him backward. At the same time Nightshade moved to Sunstar and checked her for injury. Sunstar felt Nightshade's gentle fingers touch her sensitive, burning cheek. She still flinched back from the contact despite Nightshade's soft touch, though instinctively she knew it was Nightshade. Nightshade's fingers faltered.

"Do not damage the king's property," Galvin hissed, Farouk's cloak bunched in his white-knuckled fist. He brutally shook Farouk to underscore his words. "Is she injured, Nightshade?" He tossed Farouk heavily to the ground and glared at the stunned Drow.

Sunstar felt Nightshade shift, felt the warmth of her body move away slightly.

"Yes, I think so," Nightshade said. "Nothing broken, but he has marked her."

From her point on the ground, Sunstar could feel Galvin's cruel smile, and Nightshade's inscrutable expression. Nightshade gently took Sunstar by the hand and pulled her to her feet, but did not let her go.

"It seems we cannot trust Farouk to bring her to the king unharmed. You will have to do it, Nightshade." Galvin laughed softly.

Sunstar felt a chill run up and down her spine at the sound.

"Bring her to the prison," Galvin continued almost conversationally, flinty gaze boring into the still stunned Farouk. "I'm sure the king will send for her when he is good and ready. We will go and inform him of Sunstar's capture, won't we, Farouk?"

"Yes, Galvin," Farouk ground out, while Nightshade nodded her acceptance of her orders.

Sunstar shrank into Nightshade's side, pushing her terror back by focusing on Nightshade. Prison? They were taking her to the prison? She felt distant relief. Taking her to prison meant delaying her death at Dark Elf hands. It meant time—time for her parents to find her and rescue her. It meant the Drow king would have plenty of time to forget about her. Her terror receded a little, and she moved willingly enough when Nightshade separated from the others and took her down road to the prison.

Nightshade gave a mental sigh of relief. She could feel Sunstar's trembling hand sweat. She longed to say something to Sunstar, but what could be said? Her fate was in the hands of her gods, her future not a bright one by any standards. She felt a real spark of rebellion ignite deep inside her. The Forest Elf that Farouk had captured was no more than sixteen Elf years of age, certainly untouched. From what Nightshade had seen of the elfmaid's remarkable green eyes, spirit and a good heart shone in her, sullied by intense terror, loathing, and hatred for her captors. *What would happen if we didn't reach the prison? Would they let us go or would they hunt us down and kill us?*

Nightshade led her down the twisting side streets, down further into the bowels of the earth, with a terrible, lingering feeling of wrongdoing. It was a strangely marked feeling. Of all the things she had done in her life, she knew this one was the one act she would regret the most.

Uncaring citizens jostled them, often stopping to stare and point. The air filled with their raucous laughter at the plight of the unfortunate Forest Elf.

"Look at the little Elf," one sang out. "Have you come to show us how well you fight?"

"Or have you come to show us how to fall in love with trees?" another added, laughing.

"Perhaps she came to us so we could show her how *real* Elves live," a third said, making an obscene gesture. Raucous laughter greeted this, and the crowd spat at her. Nightshade pulled her in close, protecting her as best she was able.

The taunts continued to follow them, and Nightshade hurried to take Sunstar to the prison, where she would be safe from prying eyes. She became aware of drops of water splashing onto the hand that held Sunstar's shaking fingers. She glanced at Sunstar and saw her tears. She hurried on with Sunstar, outwardly impassive, but inwardly forlorn. *Why?* a tiny voice inside her asked, shocked into speech by Sunstar's distress. *You hate this, it hurts you, so why are you doing it?*

Finally, barely suppressing a sigh of relief, they reached the prison—a large, neat structure. Nightshade entered, leading the quietly sobbing Sunstar. They ran into another tall Drow. This one was an older female with cold, glowing yellow eyes that glittered with ratty, intelligent curiosity.

"Goldeneyes," Nightshade said, inclining her head.

"Nightshade. And who do we have here?" Goldeneyes's gaze traveled all over the pretty, young elfmaid. Nightshade felt extremely uncomfortable at the intimacy of it.

"Princess Sunstar," Nightshade said. "Galvin asked she be held here until the king wishes to see her."

"*Princess Sunstar?*" Goldeneyes's eyes widened. "Ahh. Of course. We will take over from here." She gestured, and two guards came forth from the shadows as Nightshade loosened the rope tying her to Sunstar.

The guards roughly grabbed Sunstar as soon as her bonds were undone. They held her by her upper arms and dragged her back into the shadowy depths of the prison. It seemed to break through her paralysis, and Sunstar screamed and thrashed against them. They tightened their grip and controlled her writhing with ease.

"No, Nightshade," Sunstar screamed. "Don't leave me here. Help me."

Her cries were terrible to hear, and they gradually faded into the distance. Nightshade schooled her features into impassivity, struggling to control the shock running through her system at the force of Sunstar's pleas.

Goldeneyes chuckled. "It seems she's developed quite a liking to you," she said with hideous humor. She gazed at the passageway that Sunstar had gone down.

"Hmm." Nightshade shrugged and could not think of anything else to say, so she inclined her head in farewell to Goldeneyes, who was not paying any attention to her anymore. She turned and strode from the prison, back itching, struggling to control the uncomfortable urge to follow Sunstar.

CHAPTER 6

Sunstar struggled and screamed in the dim lighting as the guards pulled her backward down the passageway. She quickly lost sight of the motionless, dark figure of Nightshade. She willed the silent figure of Nightshade to come with her, desperate for her comforting presence in the foul prison. The guards took her past rows of moaning and howling inmates to the darkest cell in the prison. They opened the door and threw her onto the cell floor in a bone-jarring heap, and then strode back up the passageway, through cries and snarled insults.

Her heart hammered in terror, and tears cut slow tracks down her face.

She struggled to gain some measure of control over her fear. She focused on breathing and tried to relax her tense muscles. She allowed the adrenalin to flow through her system, leaving her weak and shaking in its wake. Some of the black cloud that had stolen her ability to think dissipated. She shifted so she was sitting cross-legged on the cold flagstones in the impenetrable blackness.

Fresh tears flowed down her face as a feeling of utter despair and hopelessness washed over her. She ached with homesickness for her forestlands, her parents, and friends. She tried not to think of what they would be doing, did not dare to entertain hope of rescue. Images of her trip with the Dark Elves to Dragonar trickled into her consciousness. She cursed herself for each time she had tried to be quiet, had tried not to struggle, or missed the opportunity to run. She thought of Nightshade's glowing blue eyes, Galvin's thin lips pursed into an expression of cruelty, Farouk's hungry gaze, and she shuddered.

Yet they were not the worst. Judging by the sly comments she had been subjected to throughout her entire trip, she knew the king and queen of the Drow were the worst of them all. *If I am lucky, they will kill me,* she thought, shivering. *If they do, will it be quick or slow? I hope it's quick, but I don't think it will be. I think it will be slow. They are too cruel and vicious for it to be otherwise.*

The only one who had shown her any redeeming features at all had been Nightshade, and now she was gone. She felt torn on the subject of Nightshade. Her original questions still remained: was Nightshade as psychopathic as her countrymen, her evil disguised by a thin veneer of good manners? What blood made up the half that was not Drow? Sunstar struggled not to ascribe any real redeeming features to Nightshade simply because she looked more like Sunstar than a full-blooded Drow. Yet despite her best efforts, comfort crept over her at the memory of glowing blue eyes and gentle hands.

Dread slowly regained its hold over Sunstar. She tried to think of ways to end her pain before it began.

A strong stab of self-recrimination suddenly hit her. *I can't end it. I just can't. I can't take any life, including my own. It's wrong. If my parents ever found out they would be doubly devastated.* All *life is sacred. Besides, what if the opportunity to escape is still before me? My death would be completely needless. I would have done it for nothing, and I've come so far already.* She took every scrap of courage in her hands, willing her fear to dissipate. *Speculation about the Drow is useless at this point. My path is set—I have been captured and I can't escape. They will do to me what they want, and I can't do anything about it. I will either live as a slave, or they will kill me.*

She tried to focus on her family and home to remain sane during the time she knew she would spend with the Drow—no matter how long or short that would be.

By nature she was insatiably curious and had a very positive outlook to life that had been subdued up to now, but had never left her. She drew on this and her reserve of courage to explore her cell, to see if she could find some means of escape. She cautiously knelt and carefully extended an arm in front of her and felt her way forward.

To one side of the cell, she felt a bunk, half-rotten covers moving uneasily as creatures crawled and slid under its rough surface. Her questing fingers repeatedly brushed against smooth, slimy things, rushing to evade her grasp. Aside from the bunk, a half-emptied slop jar, and fellow inhabitants, the cell was about ten feet square, empty of all other creature comforts. Shuddering, she returned to her original position in the middle of the cell.

Sunstar forced herself to remain calm. She sat cross-legged, hands clutching her knees, seething with terror of the unseen creatures lurking around the edges of her prison. She closed her eyes, delving into memories of happier times. In the midst of the ancient stench of bodily waste, scrabbling creatures, and cloying blackness, she returned to the forest surrounding her home, chasing her childhood friends in a game of never ending hide and seek.

"Did you hear—?"

"—Elven—"

"Captured, they said. I don't know—"

"—the Ring—"

Nightshade made her way home through the packed streets, seething with gossip of a captured Elven princess. She could not stop the feeling of disquiet deep in her soul. Memories of the wagonload of humans in the forest almost two weeks ago washed over her, filling her with a sense of regret. She could not stop another memory, hard on the heels of the first, of her first sight of Sunstar kneeling by Farouk's knee. Sunstar was covered in food, and Nightshade suspected Farouk was making her eat off his fingers. She felt haunted by a sense of failure, adding to her unease, and it grew stronger by the moment. She simply could not forget the look in Sunstar's eyes, so similar to the eyes of the child she had not been able to slaughter weeks ago.

She strode through the coldly ornate gates that marked the boundary to Nightsbane's Seat, past the contemptuous guards, into the large house. She was desperate to avoid her father, Nightsbane. She did not want to face the familiar loathing in his eyes when he saw his half-Drow daughter.

She strode into her austere chambers, finally away from prying eyes, and almost sagged with relief. She needed to think. She took off her cloak and armor and discarded them both on her bed. She went to her wardrobe, pulled out a meditation robe, and put it on with a sigh, trying to contain her roiling thoughts. Even here she had to be careful. Nightsbane was not above spying on her. She went into the inner door on the far side of her room into her meditation chamber. She sat cross-legged in the Circle of Meditation, drawn into the cold, stone floor.

She looked deep inside herself, feeling the disquiet, willing it to depart, but it would not go. The image of the little human's frightened brown eyes flitted through her mind, followed closely by equally innocent, almond-shaped green eyes. Shame washed over her in an immense wave.

What would Sunstar say if she knew Nightshade was part of a raid that had resulted in the deaths of a group of humans? Of women and children? Would those eyes still beg her for help? Her memory of Sunstar gave her all the whispered thanks, all the smiles, all the consideration that Sunstar had tried to show her during the trip to Dragonar. Each small event from their trip to the city came tumbling out after that, along with recriminations for not responding, followed by a terrible, all encompassing self loathing that made her shift uncomfortably in the Circle.

She felt Sunstar's ghostly touch after Galvin punched her for the terrible scrape to Sunstar's knee after the rope bridge snapped. She remembered walking through the Drow city to the prison and the sensation to go to Sunstar *immediately* became almost overpowering. She imagined doing it, and the resulting feeling of relief and pleasure rushed over her in a great tide.

Her mind suddenly shifted and ruthlessly fed her images of all the lives she had taken, all the riches, and she felt nothing but . . . revulsion.

Why? The little voice, not so little now, roared at her. *Why? Why are you doing things you hate? Why do you want to stay here with the Drow?*

The Drow had always hated her, and her father had taken every opportunity he could to beat her bloody. Every mistake had earned severe punishment. But her mother . . . she had been different. She had shown Nightshade the only love she had ever known in her early life, executed when her father had discovered she was trying to nurture gentleness and compassion in her only daughter. Nightshade had been promptly sent to the Drow guard, trained in all ways of murder and torture, taught to scout the forest and subjugate and destroy all she could not understand or control.

Nightshade was a good killer, of that there was no doubt. Her half-Elf heritage allowed her more latitude to see on the surface during the day, which made her an invaluable scout to her team members. Yet she had never enjoyed the brazen killing the Drow engaged in. She only did it because it was expected of her, and then when she had no other choice. She never engaged in cruelty, preferring to remain silent, uncomfortable with the atrocities she witnessed on a daily basis, carefully hiding her compassion and distaste behind a stoic façade.

The sense of wrong doing, which had always haunted her, that became stronger when the hunting party had encountered Farouk, now teased and tugged at her, forcing guilt to the surface.

The brown eyes of the child and Sunstar's eyes weighed and measured her, found her wanting.

These feelings were nothing new, but she could no longer stand aside and witness the slaughter and brutality the Drow enjoyed so much. She could not force herself to do it any more. Self loathing at her own weakness in not rebelling against the life she had been unwillingly thrust into washed over her. Galvin had been right—she was a coward, but not for the reasons he thought.

An idea of escape began to form in the back of her mind. The Drow would never miss her—they never accepted her in the first place. One lost scout was nothing to be concerned about—it was known to happen on occasion. She could easily slip away during the day on her next mission.

Yet she knew she would never wait that long. She would not leave by herself, not while a harmless Forest Elf rotted in the Drow prison.

She had seen the look in Sunstar's eyes, her gentle innocence and purity. She was capable of feeling the things Nightshade had never allowed herself to experience. Existence here would destroy the gentleness and compassion—the *life*—that burned so brightly in the Forest Elf. The Drow would steal Sunstar's soul and pervert her into something unrecognizable.

Nightshade would take Sunstar with her when she left. She would give everything she had for Sunstar's freedom and return to her people. She would do it simply because Sunstar had seemed to think, with her thanks and her smiles, that Nightshade was different to the other Drow.

I will free Sunstar, she thought. *I will do it because she doesn't belong here any more than I do. Even if this is the one and only right thing I will ever do in my life, it will be worth it. I will be free—we both will.*

For the very first time in her long and lonely life, Nightshade felt a tight band around her soul loosen as something slipped free, and she reeled inwardly at the unfamiliar emotion flooding through her—joy. In a sudden move that she could not remember doing since she was a very small Elf, she smiled. She laughed, a simple uncomplicated sound ringing out in the large chamber.

CHAPTER 7

Sunstar did not know how long she was locked in the cell. She was aware of a gnawing hunger, but that had been with her since the start of her capture and imprisonment. It seemed no worse or better than always. She pushed it to one side as best she could and stayed lost in the mists of her memory. She did not hear the cell door open, or the heavy-booted footsteps of the guards entering the cell.

They roughly hauled her to her feet, and she started in shock at the sudden, unexpected intrusion. The guards stood at attention, supporting her shaking body as Goldeneyes entered the cell. The jailer circled Sunstar, eyeing her with a half-lecherous, half-calculating stare. Sunstar struggled to stay upright despite the pins and needles in her legs and the pain in her knees.

"The king has asked that you be brought before him," Goldeneyes said after a moment's silence. "We can't have you looking like that for a royal audience."

Sunstar looked down at herself. She was filthy. She had not been given the opportunity to bathe while they had been on the road, so she was in desperate need of soap and water.

Goldeneyes roughly tore the shirt and breeches from her body. Sunstar stood there naked, too stunned to react. The old Drow moved close to her, greedily reaching for her smooth, young body. Sunstar flinched away.

Goldeneyes roared with laughter. "I like to see some spit in my elfmaids. Let's clean her up and bring her to the Ring."

The guards threw Sunstar to the floor. Goldeneyes's smile turned shark-like, and she took great, obscene pleasure in washing the struggling Sunstar all over, in intimate detail.

Goldeneyes finished, and Sunstar glared at her with fiery eyes, incensed beyond belief. "*Do not ever* touch me in such a manner again," she ground out through gritted teeth. "I am a royal princess, whether you like it or not, and a prisoner of war. You will treat me with a modicum of respect and by the rules of war."

Goldeneyes gave her a malicious smile. "You're a royal princess, now, are you?" she said in silken tones. "And you're to be treated according to the rules of war?" She tilted her head and regarded Sunstar with amusement. "Our peoples are *not* at war, in case you hadn't noticed. Even if they were, who, Your Highness, do you think is going to enforce these rules on us?" She gestured toward the smirking Drow guards. "There's no one here but us, and I can assure you not a word will be spoken about what happens here now. Never forget you are amongst the Drow, and we answer to no one but ourselves."

Sunstar and Goldeneyes locked heated stares in a battle of wills that lasted until one of the Drow guards shifted uncomfortably.

Goldeneyes flicked him a quick frown but kept the insulting, knowing grin on her face. She forced a rough prison garment over Sunstar's head. It was a little too large for her. The cloth hung loosely on her shoulders, and the hem of the tunic fell to somewhere just below her knees. The neckline was almost indecently low, and Sunstar had to struggle with the urge to pull it up further to satisfy her outraged sense of modesty.

The guards dragged her barefoot and stumbling from the cell. She pulled out of their grasp, determined to walk under her own power out of the dirty, stinking prison and out into the city streets.

It was not quite a parade through the city of the Dark Elves—the citizens did not exactly line the streets, but each and every one of them stopped what they were doing and turned to stare at her.

"There she is."

"Peel her flesh from her bones."

"I hope the king calls for her blood."

"Let her enjoy the Queen's Kiss."

The shouts from the crowd soon coalesced into a cacophony of screaming voices. Every now and again a comment, louder than the ones around it, bubbled up, drawing more laughter and catcalls from the crowd. They appeared to be ribald comments and for the most part Sunstar did not understand them.

She did quite clearly grasp what one young elfmaid yelled at her. "I hope the queen enjoys you as much as she enjoyed me." A horrible burn scar disfigured her once beautiful indigo features, a milky white eye staring at Sunstar with considerable malice and jealousy.

The guards pulled in close to her, shielding her from the worst of the refuse thrown at her, and from the indigo hands that reached for her, wanting to damage her.

The light was still almost too low for comfort, but Sunstar could see the royal palace off to her right. It was ornate and imposing, clearly intended to dwarf and subjugate the city around it.

An eerie blue glow lit the now neat city streets, and she could just make out ornate shop fronts lining the streets on both sides of her. The crowd here whispered and stared at her with an intensity that sent a shiver down her spine. Once she thought she saw a flash of black amidst the sea of white hair, but it was gone when she turned to focus on it.

They led her into a huge, solid structure dwarfing even the royal palace. Despite its size, it was still only a tiny speck inside the yawning chasm that harbored Dragonar. Several wide entrances were spaced at even intervals all along the circular perimeter. A steady stream of white hair and indigo skin trickled toward it, reluctantly parting to allow Sunstar and the guards to move through. The guards drew in close to her, shielding her from the jostling, punching, and shoving crowd.

Sunstar lifted her chin and squared her shoulders, resolving to firmly meet whatever came her way. The blood rushed in her ears and almost drowned out the sounds of the noisy crowd. They went through a wide entrance, and the guards dragged her down a hot, dark passage into a huge open area. She stumbled to a halt and looked around, blinking. She was in a huge, sandy ring in an arena, and she could barely see the walls enclosing it in the murkiness. She saw a flash of light out of the corner of her eye and turned to follow it. It came from an immense, shimmering blue globe, by far the brightest light source in the ring. Its surface shivered and shimmered uneasily, and it emitted random bursts of white light.

The guards pulled her into motion again, but stopped seconds later when she tripped and fell over. They hauled her to her feet, and she looked down to see what had caused her stumble. Iron rings stuck up neatly and out of the dirty sand. The guards fastened the heavy manacles attached to the rings to her ankles and wrists. The excited murmur from the crowd grew to a roar.

The stink surrounding her was almost indescribable. It was an uncomfortable conglomeration of excrement and old blood; sweating, unwashed bodies; incense to cover the stink; an uneasy undertone of sex. Sunstar concentrated hard on her breathing, trying to ignore the stench so she would not wretch. The jeers and catcalls continued, gaining in volume and strength.

"Silence!" a thunderous voice cut through the crowd noise like a knife, and the Dark Elves quieted in fits and starts.

Sunstar turned to face the source of the sound. She was able to make out three figures coming toward her.

The first was simply dressed in flowing, dark robes, with a hood pulled over its head. It carried a staff of plain design, with a simple crystal fastened to its tip. The crystal gave off its own pale radiance.

The other two, a male and a female, were more ornately dressed, and were holding hands. They walked across the sand as though it were crushed glass, carefully lifting their feet to avoid prolonged contact with the foul surface. Sunstar was able to make out their features as they came closer.

They were the most handsome Dark Elves Sunstar had ever seen. They were both much taller than Sunstar and had perfectly proportioned bodies. Each one's face was as striking and smooth as a carved sculpture. The blue light from the flickering sphere caused them to shimmer and shine with unearthly beauty. Each wore a simple circlet on their head and it was clear to Sunstar that they were the king and the queen.

"So this is our little prize." The king's voice rang out to reach each person seated in the stands above the Ring. "You are the Princess Sunstar are you not? Daughter of King Darkwood and Queen Morningstar?"

Sunstar heard the hooded figure chanting quietly beside them. She felt as though her body were encased in lead.

"I am," she answered anxiously, absurdly eager to tell the truth. She waited impatiently, desperate to be asked a question she could answer.

"I thought that fool Farouk was lying when he and Galvin came to see me. I was going to kill him for his stupidity. Then my queen," he gracefully inclined his head toward his mate, and she returned the gesture, "persuaded me otherwise."

"Pretty little thing, isn't she?" the queen said in admiring tones, as though speaking of livestock.

Sunstar felt her mouth form into a wide smile of pleasure at the queen's words. She made a titanic effort to clamp her mouth shut to keep herself from begging the royals to ask her any questions she could answer. She knew her eyes blazed with self loathing and fury.

"That she is, my dear." The king also spoke as though Sunstar could not hear them. He finally turned to address Sunstar directly. She hung onto his every word as though her life depended on it. "Quite frankly, I've no idea what to do with you, other than give you a slow and lingering death. You are lucky that my queen finds you quite comely. She has asked for you, and I agreed. My dear." He gestured at the queen as he gently released her hand.

The elegant, voluptuous queen lifted her chin and circled Sunstar, eyeing her appreciatively. "Yes." She stopped before Sunstar. "I think I can use her. Yes, my king, I will take her from your hands, trouble yourself no more."

Sunstar stood limply, swaying slightly, weeping inwardly with horror and disgust. She tried to ignore her immediate bolt of pleasure at the queen's words. The queen drew a long, elegant finger down the side of Sunstar's face, down her jaw, under her chin. She tilted Sunstar's face upward so she could properly see it. She leaned down and slowly and thoroughly kissed Sunstar. She pulled her in close so their bodies locked together, and ran her hands up Sunstar's body. She broke the sensual kiss, pulled back, and ran her hands across Sunstar's full breasts. Sunstar's breathing involuntarily hitched.

"Very young and delectable," the queen murmured as the lust-filled crowd strained to see Sunstar's shuddering reaction.

Sunstar's skin crawled with horror and disgust, despite her body's reaction. Loathing for the queen washed over her, and she felt sick with dread at what would come next. A single tear leaked from a hazy eye as the impotent fury washed over her.

"Take her to the queen's antechamber," the queen said as she turned away from Sunstar. "Hemlock, I will require your services." The hooded figure nodded and moved to follow the queen. She accepted the king's proffered hand, and they walked at a saunter from the Ring.

Hemlock stopped chanting, and the spell abruptly fell away from Sunstar. She felt dazed and weak, but grateful that the terrible urge to do the bidding of either royal had left her. She collapsed into her waiting escort's arms as they unchained her and half dragged, half carried her from the Ring.

Nightshade hid in a dark alcove in the main tunnel to the Ring. She shook with disgust and revulsion over the queen's plans for Sunstar. Her gut twisted, and she cursed the fact that she had been too late to simply walk Sunstar from the prison. She allowed the full force of loathing run through her and vowed inwardly that she would never let Sunstar come to any harm at the hands of the licentious queen.

What to do now? she thought. *There are too many spectators—witnesses—coming and going from the Ring, so I can't quietly kill the guards. I no other choice, though—I have to try and get her before they take her to the Queen's antechamber. We're going to have to hope no one sees, and then run and hide.*

The guards half dragged the semi-conscious Sunstar out of the Ring and up the shadowed passageway as the citizens roared their approval in the stands above. Nightshade tensed, lunged at the first guard supporting Sunstar, and pierced his warm heart with her cold dagger. His eyes widened in shock, and he sank slowly to the ground in death. Sunstar half collapsed beside him. The other guard drew his sword and took a swing at Nightshade. She ducked back, feeling the tip of the sword slice through her cloak. She glanced at the rip, and then lunged for him. She slipped inside his defenses and plunged her second long bladed dagger up through his chin and into his brain. Blood washed all over her hands as he gurgled and choked for a brief second or so. He collapsed into her arms, and she lowered him to the ground.

She quickly dragged both bodies into the alcove that she had used as a hiding place. Sunstar lay on the ground, moving her head from side to side. Nightshade quickly ran to her, knelt down beside her, and glanced around to make sure they were still alone.

Sunstar blinked at her. "Nightshade?"

Nightshade nodded. "Can you stand?" she asked urgently.

"Not without your help," Sunstar said.

Nightshade nodded. She slung Sunstar's arm over her shoulder and pulled her to her feet. Their height difference had to be almost seven inches, and it was not easy for Nightshade to stoop to help her walk.

"I'm going to have to carry you," Nightshade said as she scooped the Sunstar up into her arms. She caught an intelligible whisper and realized Sunstar was trying to say something. She leaned down to listen as she watched the passageway, alert for signs of more guards.

"Please don't hurt me," Sunstar murmured.

Nightshade felt herself crack a little on the inside. "I won't hurt you, and I won't let them hurt you either," she whispered, and smiled slightly, gazing into Sunstar's eyes, willing her to believe.

Sunstar's eyes fluttered shut.

Nightshade scanned the passageway for signs of trouble. She could see citizens in the distance, passing by the Ring, going about their day-to-day business. She could hear a murmur from the crowd still in the stands above the Ring. The passage remained mercifully deserted, but it would not be long before the queen missed her newest treasure. Nightshade made her way up the passage, Sunstar hanging limply in her arms. She stayed in the shadows as much as she could.

She reached the end of the passage and looked out into the street. It was almost deserted, since most of the population was still in the stands above the Ring. She shrugged her voluminous cloak over both of them and stepped out into the street.

Her legs felt as though they were encased in cement. Horrified, she felt her knees buckle. Her arms trembled, and she had no strength to stand or hold onto Sunstar. She sank to the ground, releasing the dismayed Sunstar as gently as she was able. Sunstar slowly tumbled onto the city street. Nightshade, on her knees, struggled to stay upright. She supported herself with a hand, blinking at the five dim figures walking toward her.

Her heart sank, and she steeled herself to meet her fate. Her soul cried out with horror and despair for poor Sunstar.

CHAPTER 8

"Well, well, well," came the king's mocking voice from above and beside Nightshade. "When Galvin told me of our young guest's attachment to you, I thought it best to keep an eye on you."

Galvin and Farouk laughed coldly, enjoying the spectacle of her fall from grace.

"I can see now that they are right. You *are* a coward and a weakling. You must be punished," he said in a conversational tone. Nightshade heard the whisper of cloth as he shifted. "Have you any good ideas, my queen?"

"Yes, I do." The silky voice of the queen drifted down to her.

Nightshade struggled to get her eyes into focus.

"Put her in the Ring and let the guards play with her," the queen continued. "After that, I think I will taste the fruits of my new toy. In the Ring for all to see, and little Nightshade can watch up close."

The king gestured, and a troop of soldiers ran toward them and surrounded them.

Nightshade felt dismayed at this latest horror in store for them. She was not concerned for herself—she knew she had earned death many times over for the terrible things she had done in her life. She glanced at Sunstar. They could not have Sunstar. Nightshade would fight to the last breath in her body to take Sunstar from Dragonar and back to the outside world.

The king waved his personal guard forward. They hauled Sunstar to her feet and dragged Nightshade along the ground.

"Remember what I told you, Sunstar. I *will not* let them harm you," Nightshade ground out through gritted teeth.

Sunstar's eyes flashed. "I know. I trust you."

All five Dark Elves laughed at this pathetic display of kindliness.

Nightshade's mouth curved into a smile. "Thank you," she whispered.

They were dragged back up the passageway, toward separate antechambers near to the mouth leading into the Ring. Hemlock followed them closely, waving a hand and muttering while the king and queen trailed behind them. Galvin and Farouk continued past them to go and take their seats in the box reserved for Drow nobles.

Hemlock followed Nightshade into the left antechamber, while the king and queen strolled out into the Ring to announce the new afternoon's entertainment to the assembled crowd.

The guards carelessly dropped Nightshade onto the low stone table in the center of the room. She shook her head, trying to clear her fuzzy senses. They roughly stripped her down to her underwear under Hemlock's cold gaze. She looked down at herself. She was not surprised to see that her body was on prize display for all eyes. Hemlock uttered a single word, and the enchantment lifted. She shook her head, fleetingly grateful that her senses began clearing.

Hemlock pulled his cloak back from his face, revealing a very handsome Drow, with perfect, clean and even, noble features. He could be mistaken for an athletic scholar from a distance. The illusion was quickly dispelled on closer inspection. His eyes were a shining gold, penetrating and intelligent. They were also extraordinarily cold when they betrayed any emotion at all.

Altogether, Nightshade mused, Hemlock would have been an utterly unremarkable though incredibly handsome magician, if not for one thing—he was known to be absolutely incapable of feeling any empathy at all toward his fellow creatures. His rise through the academy had been meteoric, and his ground-breaking magical experiments on living subjects were the talk of the scholarly world. He engaged in the most atrocious outrages against liberty and life for the pursuit of knowledge, and delivered his findings in a calm, considered tone of voice, more concerned with the outcome of his experiments than with the subjects involved in them. Even his superiors sometimes paled and expressed reservations about his most bloodthirsty studies. He always seemed surprised by this and brushed aside any objections as deliberate obstruction to his quest for knowledge. Nightshade hated him with a passion.

"When I am done with this, I am coming for you," she promised him in even tones.

"I think not," he said. "You will not survive what I have planned for you."

"Oh? And what is that?"

"You will find out soon enough." He shot a glance at one of the guards. "See to it that she is armored and brought out as soon as possible."

The guards flinched and bowed low, clearly afraid of the mighty magician.

Hemlock walked out of the room, leaving a deep well of peace in his wake.

Nightshade struggled, and one of the guards landed a heavy punch to her stomach, winding her. They dragged her from the room. As they passed the alcove Sunstar had been led into, she heard a soft voice sobbing, "Please, no."

Nightshade went berserk, struggling with the guards, determined to make good on her promise to protect Sunstar. The guards caught her easily, shoved her to the ground, and kicked her into submission. She curled up into a ball, heart aching at the heartrending sound of Sunstar's pain.

The guards pulled Nightshade to her feet, grunting in satisfaction that she was not going to give them any further problems, and dragged her as she struggled against them into the Ring. They took her to the center of the dirty sand and threw her down. The roiling, noisy crowd roared as she gamely got to her bare feet. She looked up at them. They were catcalling, screaming insults, jeering—a sea of hate-filled faces, howling for her blood, for her demise.

Hemlock quietly entered the Ring. He took up his position next to the king and queen. They were seated on their ornate thrones on the dais to one side of the Ring at ground level. As the ruling couple, they had the right to judge all contestants in the Ring and to witness first blood up close. Hemlock's lips moved, and the air in front of them shimmered as his magical shield, designed to protect them from stray blows, sprang to life. He examined it for signs of weakness and nodded once in silent satisfaction at its apparent perfection. He closed his eyes and chanted softly. He held up his staff, and a bolt of blue lightning shot from the tip, drawn into the sphere of blue light. The sphere pulsed and shone a brilliant azure, flooding the arena with light, causing everyone but Nightshade to hiss with discomfort.

Nightshade stared intently into the sphere. She could see dim figures form in the center of the glow. She shielded her eyes. They gradually became larger, and she saw it was a lightly-armored man on a horse, a heavily-armored man, carrying a barbed whip, walked easily beside him.

Nightshade and the assembled crowd gasped—the summoned warriors were Ginza. She thought quickly about what she knew of the Ginza. The Ginza was a warrior race arranged into a strict level system. There were ten levels, and numbers in each level were strictly regulated. Ginza warriors were trained to fight in pairs and a pairs' level was determined by the number of kills they had made of those in higher levels. The markings on the armor this pair wore told Nightshade they were at sixth level—almost the seventh. She felt her chances of survival plummet.

She kept them firmly in sight as they warily studied the circle in front of them. They spied her, and their unsettling white eyes lit up with apparent anticipation. They sized her up with cold, appraising eyes. She crouched in the sand and felt behind her for the sword she knew all contestants were entitled to. She closed her hands around the cold hilt and hefted the sword, testing its balance. It was of poor quality, as she had expected. She steeled herself. It did not matter. Nothing did. The end result was the same—she had to keep alive at all costs, during her match with the Ginza.

The image of innocent green eyes came to her, giving her the strength for battle. She straightened her shoulders. She took a deep breath, finding her centre and pushing emotion out of her mind, leaving raw instinct in its place. The scent of the Ring caressed her senses, heightening them and triggering her half-Drow blood. The old battle lust flowed into her, at once eerily familiar and completely different. Normally it was directed at any being standing and drawing air in front of her, but her desire to help Sunstar gave her the control needed to channel it to a fine scalpel aimed at the Ginza warriors.

She circled in time with them, her eyes flashing. She could feel her muscles tensing up, and she forcibly relaxed them. The image of emerald green eyes burned into her mind. The warriors finally appeared to be satisfied with the circumstances, and the swordsman spurred his horse into a gallop and swung his sword at her. She brought her sword up, and it shattered under the impact of his heavy blow. The crowd roared with approval as she staggered back holding the jagged remains. She saw a flash of movement out of the corner of her eye, and the whip cracked. She twisted to one side, rolled in the sand, and hissed as the barbs tore into the flesh of her back. The movement brought her directly into the path of the horseman. She rolled out of the way as his sword whooshed through the air to land square on the ground where her head had been seconds before. She lost no time leaping to her feet as the mounted man pulled around his rearing and snorting horse. She lunged straight at the man wielding the whip.

The whip cracked again, tearing more flesh from her bones, coating her in a sticky stream of her own blood. She tasted it, and it pushed her over the edge into a full Drow battle frenzy. Time stood still for her as she lunged at the man holding the whip. He seemed to freeze, and she pulled the whip out of his hands. He snarled and hammered blows into her unprotected body with his spiked gauntlets.

Nightshade, ignoring the pain of her many wounds, sidestepped him, flipped the whip easily around his neck, and pulled it tight as hard she could. The fight went out of him, and he clawed at his neck, gasping for air. She screamed and tightened the whip, and a brisk snapping sound escaped as his neck broke. The crowd roared, cursing her as she unwound the whip from his neck and took his knife. She let go of his limp body, and he fell heavily into the filthy sand, blood spilling out of his many wounds.

The mounted man snarled with rage and spurred his horse into motion. Nightshade reluctantly cracked the whip, and the horse screamed in pain as its legs became entangled, flaying flesh from bone. It tripped, throwing its rider into the dirt, and thrashed in the sand, screaming. The warrior rolled away, then darted forward and plunged his serrated sword deep into its throat. The horse's cries turned to wet gurgles as its struggles slowly ceased. Nightshade dropped the whip and threw herself at the warrior, snarling like an animal, and gave vent to great cries of rage. The crowd sighed in contentment as blood flowed and Nightshade's and her opponent's screaming escalated.

Nightshade caught glimpses of the king and queen, who stood to see more of the battle and strained to see flailing limbs and blood-soaked ground.

The Ginza warrior abandoned his serrated sword in favor of a long, wickedly sharp knife. Nightshade wielded the knife she had taken from the whip man. The warrior knelt on her, trying to pin her to the ground. He had one hand closed firmly around her throat.

Nightshade saw black flowers before her vision as he squeezed her airway closed. She collapsed on the ground, gasping for air, and the Ginza warrior plunged his knife deep into the side of her abdomen. She twitched once and lay still. The Ginza warrior slowly, almost casually, climbed to his feet. He stared upward at the crowd with wild, white eyes. They roared and stamped their feet in approval.

He saluted the crowd. Nightshade, behind him, grabbed her knife and lunged forward. His eyes widened in shock as she brought the knife up between his legs, instantly emasculating him. She pulled the blade from his body somewhere in his lower belly. He screamed, clutching himself. He sank to the ground, a torrent of blood spilling out onto the ground beneath him. Nightshade crawled forward, sucking in great breaths of air, clutching her burning side. She firmed her grip on the knife and then drew it quickly and efficiently across the warrior's throat. The blood jetted from his severed arteries, and his cries faded to watery gurgles, drowned out by the screaming crowd.

Nightshade collapsed, breathing heavily and moaning softly in pain. The remnants of the adrenalin in her system receded. It left her feeling hollowed out and saddened at the memory of the ugly spectacle of the battle. She was filled with self-loathing for her animalistic reaction to the spilt blood and prepared for death to take her slowly. She relaxed, feeling her limbs getting heavier and heavier.

She blinked her eyes open and saw the king and queen looking down at her. They nodded at each other and apparent approval hung about them in a noxious cloud. The hems of their garments were splattered in strayed blood.

"Now it is time for the second part of your punishment," the king said in a clear voice, but softly so only Nightshade could hear him. He glanced at his magician. "Hemlock, keep her alive."

Hemlock nodded and glided easily above the sand to Nightshade. He did not possess healing magic so he could not heal her. He could only hold her up so she could watch the second part of the show. He cast a spell over her so her agony increased, and she became alert and aware. She moaned in anguish as waves of pain crashed over her.

Sunstar, she knew, was next in the Ring.

CHAPTER 9

Sunstar, naked and shivering, was tied to the low, stone slab that served as a preparation table in the second antechamber.

"Please, no," she moaned as a clearly female voice cried out in agony and in the Ring. Waves of terror crashed over her. She struggled against her bonds. Any vestiges of hope that Nightshade might still be alive leeched out of her and left her in shreds. She wanted to scream and cry, but knew that it would not help her. Nothing would. It was the end.

The crowd roared. As though it were a signal to act, the attendants standing silently against the walls of the chamber stepped to her and pulled her off the table. Sunstar stood, unresisting, and tried to marshal the last shreds of her courage. She managed to regain a modicum of dignity when they took her by the arms and led her from the antechamber.

Sunstar's wildest nightmares had never prepared her for the sights that awaited her as she was taken into the Ring. Two unrecognizable, blood-soaked forms lay discarded in a wide puddle of gore, and she was terrified for a moment that one of them was Nightshade. She saw a flash of movement out of the corner of her eye and followed it. She saw Nightshade, half naked and heavily bleeding, supported by a robed figure that she guessed was the magician, Hemlock. Nightshade's beautiful face was a stoic mask, and her eyes tracked Sunstar closely.

The hateful crowd roared in appreciation of Sunstar's bare, young body on display for all to see.

The sight of the fallen Nightshade ripped another strip off Sunstar's tenuous grip on sanity. Dread caused her to whip around in an attempt to struggle free. The attendants tightened their grip, and she quieted, cursing herself for her momentary loss of control. She tried to push her roiling emotions to one side and focus on Nightshade, the only spark of compassion in the entire Drow city.

An altar materialized in the Ring in front of the blue sphere. The attendants held Sunstar tight and dragged her toward it. She tried to resist them as they threw her down and strapped her to it. She looked at Nightshade, and their gazes locked. Nightshade's mask slipped for an instant. Her pain and horror showed clearly on her face.

The queen left the nobles box and made her way to the altar, the crowd roaring approval at each of her slow, measured footsteps.

Sunstar stared wide eyed at the approaching queen. She shivered in terror and strained against her bonds. They were loose. The queen drew steadily nearer, and then paused and stared down at Sunstar.

Sunstar systematically tested her bonds.

The queen stood beside the altar and licked her lips in anticipation as she gracefully doffed her robe. She was naked, oozing sensuality that had the crowd moaning in appreciation of her virility. She bent over Sunstar, gazing at her in anticipation. Her eyes were dark with passion and lust, and she paused as if to savor Sunstar's beauty.

"No need to struggle, little one. This will only hurt if you make it." The queen's silken voice caressed her, washing intimately over her. Sunstar felt herself falling victim to the queen's otherworldly beauty, despite her loathing. She gradually stopped struggling as the queen slowly and sensually ran her tongue up the side of her body, pausing to taste a full breast, taking the nipple into her mouth, nipping it with her white teeth.

In the periphery of her vision, Sunstar saw Hemlock wave a hand at her.

"No," Sunstar said in a soft, drawn-out moan. The last vestiges of tension and hesitation fled her system, thanks to Hemlock's spell. "Please don't do this to me."

Hemlock amplified every sound uttered by the queen and Sunstar to torture Nightshade. The second the queen started talking, Nightshade allowed the adrenalin to flood her system. She braced herself. When the queen laid a hand on Sunstar, Nightshade launched herself off the ground and set off in a staggering run. Hemlock froze and stared at her, startled. Nightshade clutched her bleeding side and headed toward the altar.

Nightshade caught out of the corner of her eye the king leaping to his feet and heading for the queen and Sunstar.

Nightshade reached the altar, and Sunstar's eyes widened in surprise and hope. Nightshade grabbed the queen by the scruff of her neck and flung her as far away as possible. She began to untie Sunstar's hands.

The queen regained her footing, grace and sensuality abandoned, and lunged at Nightshade. Her hands dug into the open wounds on Nightshade's back. She curled her fingers, digging in deeper and pulling at Nightshade's flesh. Spongy bits of meat stuck under her long nails, and Nightshade screamed in agony.

Sunstar pulled back a freed fist, blindly swung, and connected with the queen's face. The queen flew back, unprepared for the blow. Nightshade straddled the queen and pummeled her for all she was worth, while Sunstar fumbled with the other restraints holding her down.

Hemlock looked on, his expression calm and calculating, he alternately tensed and relaxed, bolts of energy crackling between his fingertips, as if waiting for an opening to cast a spell on the captives. None was forthcoming as Nightshade and the queen rolled in the sand, fighting furiously.

"Nightshade," Sunstar said. "Help me. I can't stand by myself."

Nightshade heard her pleas and was distracted for an instant. The queen landed a solid blow to her knife wound, causing Nightshade to falter and clutch her side and howl in agony. The queen struggled to disentangle herself from Nightshade as the king rushed in to join her. She leapt back to escape Nightshade, giving Hemlock a clear shot at the two prisoners.

Precious time slipped away as Nightshade struggled to get her abused body working enough to collect Sunstar and escape. Hemlock chanted behind her as she stumbled forward, and she prayed to whatever gods would listen to her that they had enough time to escape.

She slipped and stumbled over to the kneeling, naked Sunstar, and slung a strong arm around her. She dragged Sunstar toward the flashing blue sphere. A leaden feeling slowly seeped into her legs and they began to give way. She strained forward one more time.

Sunstar's eyes were closed, her head pressed firmly to Nightshade's bloody chest. Nightshade's eyes watered, and she forced her semi-paralyzed legs to move. She dragged Sunstar with her, and they collapsed into the blue sphere. Sunstar lost the contents of her stomach as a sudden sensation of weightlessness gripped them both. Her body went limp as she passed out.

Nightshade was not so lucky. She remained conscious, and kept a tight grip on Sunstar. She found herself sailing through the air into a room. The wooden floor rushed up to meet her. She twisted just before they landed, and her body took most of the impact. An agonizing bolt of pain shot through her bleeding wound and pushed her over the edge into oblivion. She lost her grip on consciousness, and blessed blackness flooded over her.

CHAPTER 10

Hemlock sat back on his haunches, drained, the spell cast, but it was too late. He watched as the two Elves fell through the portal as the spell overcame them.

The king and queen both screamed in rage, and the crowd roared its disapproval at the unexpected action.

"Silence!" the king shrieked, and the crowd quieted in fits and starts. He bent over the kneeling and coughing queen.

"Hemlock, come with me," he continued, red eyes blazing as he scooped up the queen. He strode from the Ring past his silent, furious subjects, the queen in his arms and Hemlock on his heels. Hemlock followed him into the nearest passageway, and they stopped at the first antechamber—the one that had recently held Sunstar. The king put his almost senseless wife on the table. The attendants hovered around uncertainly. At his gesture they finally rushed in to cover her. She shook her head and tried to cast off the effects of the spell.

The king, after a brief look at the queen, turned to glare at the magician. "Hemlock. What happened?"

They escaped you half wit, Hemlock thought coldly. He stared at the king impassively, silent and inscrutable, waiting for him to finish his temper tantrum.

The king snorted and balled an elegant fist. "Find them, Hemlock. Find them, and when you have done that, let me know. I want to kill Nightshade personally, very slowly. My queen can have Sunstar to do with as she pleases."

The queen moaned softly behind them. Both Hemlock and the king turned and looked at her. Her elegant brow creased, and her anger came to the fore as the effects of the spell dissipated. She gave a low growl.

"As you wish, my Lord," Hemlock said, bowing. "I will require the services of some of your scouts. Galvin and Farouk, if I may." His kept his tone cool and respectful.

"Of course," the king said dismissively. His pupils dilated, and

Hemlock suspected he was planning what he would do to Nightshade once she had been found and caught.

Hemlock bowed, backing away from the fuming king and prostrate queen. He continued backing through the doorway, out into the dimly lit corridor.

He pondered the problem, during the short walk back to the palace. He barely noticed the citizens hissing in fear and shrinking away from him.

Nightshade had jumped through the portal to an unknown location somewhere in the world. He knew it was now because he had fixed the Portal to the present when he had called the Ginza to fight her in the Ring. That was good. It made finding her relatively uncomplicated. He simply needed to use the Eye. All it required was one of Nightshade's personal possessions.

He blindly walked through the palace, lost in thought. The guards averted their eyes at his passing. He calculated what he would need for the spell to invoke the Eye. The spell involved a blood sacrifice and a personal garment worn by the person being sought. He called in a servant when he had reached his dark, plain chambers. A scarred Drow soundlessly slipped into the room and bowed low before his master.

"Go to Nightsbane. Tell him my Eye needs a personal possession of Nightshade," Hemlock ordered without preamble.

The Drow bowed lower and slipped out of the room.

Hemlock leaned back in his comfortable chair, thinking deeply about the situation. He was not angry; he did not possess sufficient emotional capacity for that. Nightshade interested him. He had never encountered an individual who was quite so resistant to his magic. He considered asking the king to have her once he was done, as he carefully planned out a systematic study of half Drow endurance.

He looked up at a polite cough. "Yes?"

"Master, the possession is here," the servant said softly. He ushered in a frightened-looking Dark Elf clutching a leather jerkin.

"Come closer," Hemlock ordered.

The servant nudged the Drow closer. In a flash, Hemlock was on him. The magician plunged a dagger deep into the Drow's gut and pulled it savagely across. Blood fountained from the wound and splashed down the front of Hemlock's midnight robes. He coldly watched the Dark Elf gasp in pain and drop the jerkin so he could catch the intestines that were spilling out of him. Hemlock took a step back and grabbed a cup he had sitting on the edge of his neat desk. He took a healthy measure of the blood flowing from the Drow. He scooped up the wet clothing with the other hand.

"Drain the rest and clean up the mess," he ordered his servant with a dismissive wave of his hand.

He eyed the rich, crimson liquid as he went into his scrupulously clean spell-casting room. A pentagram was carved into the stones of the chamber. He lit the braziers at each point of the star. He bowed to all points, stripped naked, and entered the magic circle at the center of the pentagram. He pulled the filthy jerkin over his head and placed the cup on the floor in front of him.

He bowed low, closed his eyes, and chanted, becoming lost in the magic and coppery smell of fresh blood. His concentration centered fully on the bubbling stream of magic flowing through every limb. He could feel himself extending in all directions. He took the cup off the floor and drained it. The cooling blood dribbled down his chin, and euphoria seeped into his dark soul.

He felt streams of magic spill out of every pore, flowing off into the space surrounding him. His inner eye separated from his body, and he felt it as an almost sexual experience. He was unaware of the wild grin on his face as his spirit left his body. He screamed wordlessly with uncontrollable joy and floated out of the city and into the outside world. It was mercifully dark, and he searched the landscape with his keen ethereal senses, willing all animals to assist him. A snake returned a negative result, and a second later he wiped her mind clean. Crows dropped from the sky, stone cold dead—the path of magic tore their souls from them. Ravens gibbered, totally at his command. He gathered them close, planning to use them for more tracking when he got closer to his targets.

He did this repeatedly until the sun came up. In the burning, early morning pre-dawn, he saw a column of pure fire stretching to the heavens in the distance. He knew he had found them. He returned to his body, already planning a course of action.

CHAPTER 11

Nightshade's eyes fluttered open as she came to. She felt the weight of Sunstar's body on her, felt her move.

She covered Sunstar's eyes with her hand, and Sunstar began thrashing, moaning in terror. She sank her elbow into Nightshade's hard middle. Nightshade gasped, unable to cry out at the exquisite pain. She pulled her hand away from Sunstar's face.

"Please, Sunstar," she murmured when she was able to speak again. "It will be easier for you if you cover your eyes. It will help you adjust to the light. You have been in darkness for quite some time."

Sunstar relaxed as she heard Nightshade's voice. "What happened? I feel awful."

"We were in the Ring, and I took us through the Portal," Nightshade said softly.

"The what?"

"The blue sphere in the Ring."

Sunstar gasped. "I remember. All of it. Are you all right?" she asked, dread coloring her tone. Her eyes remained tightly closed.

Nightshade was reluctant to answer, but Sunstar's gentle tone spoke to her, as her words could never do. "I am injured."

"How bad?" Sunstar asked. "We have to get out of here."

"We have a little time," Nightshade said softly. "They have to find us first."

"Whatever do you mean? Surely they know where we are, if we went through that Portal thing."

"No." Nightshade shook her head. "It doesn't work that way. The Portal is aimed everywhere and at all times. When we jumped through, we landed somewhere, and at some time. They won't know where or when. They have to try and find us."

"Oh." Sunstar fell silent for a moment. "So *you also* have no idea when or where we are either?"

"Correct."

Sunstar's head fell forward, and she gave vent to a deep sigh.

A single tear escaped from her eye, trickled down, and landed on Nightshade's bloody chest.

"Sunstar?" Nightshade said in a soft, worried voice. "What troubles you? You are free to go." She was resigned to her fate. She knew she was slowly dying. She welcomed it. She had tried and succeeded—she was away from the Drow and she had helped Sunstar. Sunstar could leave and return home, a free and undamaged Elf. She would not even be forced to travel by herself. Any humans she found on the way would undoubtedly view her favorably and help her, as Elves were regarded with a special mysticism by other races.

A feeling of contentment crept over Nightshade, the first since she had made her decision to leave Dragonar. Another band loosened around her soul. She was free from her psychopathic countrymen, and it did not matter that it was only for a short time. What really mattered was that for once she had used her skills for good, rather than evil.

"I'm lost, Nightshade." Sunstar broke through her reverie.

"I can't help you anymore." Nightshade opened her eyes and saw tears run down Sunstar's face. "The battle took its toll. I won't survive for much longer. You are a strong Elf—you'll find your way home."

Sunstar was silent for a moment. "What if you didn't die, would you help me then?"

"I'm going to die," Nightshade said softly, with finality.

Sunstar leaned up blindly and grasped the tattered remains of Nightshade's shift. "But what if you didn't?" she said urgently. "What then?"

Nightshade, no longer able to move, stared at Sunstar's beautiful face. The innocent green eyes that had touched something deep within her dark soul and had been the catalyst to bring her into the light, were tightly closed. Sunstar's cheeks were tearstained.

Nightshade's strength was failing, and she slowly moved her arm up and clumsily brushed away Sunstar's tears. "Of course I would."

Sunstar leant into her touch but pulled away after a moment. "Lay still." She touched Nightshade and worked her gentle fingers down Nightshade's full breasts to her flat, muscular stomach. She found the sticky cloth covering the deep cut, which still oozed black blood.

Though Sunstar's touch was gentle, Nightshade moaned when Sunstar's fingers came in contact with her cut.

Sunstar flinched and jerked her fingers away.

Nightshade caught her wrist in a weak grip. "It's all right." She gently guided Sunstar's fingers back down to the weeping wound, her heart torn by the pity and sympathy wringing Sunstar's face.

Sunstar relaxed her fingers slowly and gained more confidence in her touch. She leant up the rest of the way and put the palm of her hand flat against the cut. Nightshade bit her lip, tasting blood and holding in her screams of pain.

Head bowed, eyes tightly closed, Sunstar sang. The song was wordless—notes of joy sounding softly in the still, dusty air of the warehouse they were in. The melody wound sounds of deep sadness, nestled in sea of shaky hope. Nightshade gazed at Sunstar's face in wonder, the gentle song winding through her and touching her deep inside her soul. She thought she would never again see anything as beautiful as Sunstar was now.

Deep shame tore through her. She knew she was not worthy of Sunstar's attention, thanks to the blood soaking deep and crimson into her past.

The blood seepage slowly stopped, and her side tingled, then became a deep-seated itch inside the tear, and slowly organs and flesh became whole and undamaged once more.

Sunstar's song trailed off, and her fingers touched Nightshade's side. Nightshade looked down. The skin was soft, clean, and unbroken. She slumped and collapsed on the floor next to Nightshade.

"It's done," Sunstar said. "You're healed. Will you still help me?"

Nightshade heard Sunstar stop breathing. Her eyes closed as a healing darkness began to claim her. "Yes. I'll not let them harm you," she whispered as she lost consciousness.

Sunstar awoke and cautiously tried to open her eyes. She blinked. The increase in light level was only mildly painful. She saw for the first time where they were. They were both lying on a rough wooden floor, surrounded by piles of cloth. At some point during the night, Nightshade had thrown a blanket over her to keep her warm, but she still shivered in the coolness of the night air. She looked down anxiously at Nightshade. Nightshade lay on her back, still, but was breathing much more easily and was soundly asleep.

She hesitantly laid a soft hand on Nightshade's cool forehead.

"I was wondering when you'd wake up," Nightshade said, and Sunstar flinched back.

"You're awake," Sunstar said.

"Yes." Nightshade paused. "We have to get moving, out of the city. Are you all right?"

Sunstar stared at her in surprise. She sounded genuinely concerned. Nightshade opened her eyes, and Sunstar stared into a sea of pale blue shining with blessed life in the dimness.

"I'm fine," Sunstar responded, just as softly. "What about you? Are you fit to travel?"

"We don't have a choice. It's night, and Hemlock will better be able to track us then. We have to get moving before he finds us."

"If we could be anywhere and anywhen, aren't we going to be safe for a while?"

Nightshade shook her head. "I think the portal was looking at another place at our normal time when Hemlock opened it."

"How do you know?"

Nightshade flinched. "I . . . they came from our time . . . in the Ring . . ." She bit her lip. She glanced back at Sunstar, glowing blue eyes haunted. "It doesn't matter how I know. Besides, it's safer if we assume that we landed in our own time." She sighed. "All that really matters is that Hemlock will be looking for us, and he will find us quickly."

Sunstar felt a sliver of dread slip into her heart. "What are the extents of his powers?"

"Dark Elves work best in darkness. His powers are greatly diminished during the day. He is at the mercy of the sun." Nightshade seemed reluctant to tell her any more than that for the moment. "I know we are in a warehouse. Why don't you take a look around to see if you can find us something to wear?"

Sunstar nodded and clutched the makeshift blanket around her body. She padded off to look among the stacks of cloth for something they could use as clothes.

Nightshade lay on the rough wood and cautiously stretched. She felt much better, but weak as a kitten. They were free of the Dark Elves for the moment, and she was grateful for the respite. She knew it would not last. A sense of hopelessness inched its way into her consciousness.

If they could escape from the Dark Elves—and that was a big if—she would deliver the princess back to her lands. What then? She was outcast from the Dark Elves, to be killed on sight if they ever found her. More than one Dark Elf would come looking for her. The Forest Elves would never accept her as kin, despite her Elven blood. None of the other races inhabiting the planet would accept her either. All they would see was a Drow, a bloodthirsty killer. Her only saving grace was that she did not completely look like a Drow, save for her eyes, which gently glowed in the darkness. They would give her away eventually, no matter where she went. In truth, she did not consider herself fit for companionship, knowing all the atrocities she had been a part of in the past, and what she would have to do to bring Sunstar home and free them both from Drow vengeance. Even the wild, alive feeling of freedom that was in her was not enough to overcome her guilt-laden, black thoughts.

A practical person, Nightshade tried to put those bleak thoughts aside. She concentrated on the next task at hand—Sunstar's freedom and return to the Forest Elves. She focused on testing her body and trying to get to her feet. She slowly got to her knees. Dizziness washed over her. She stayed there for a minute or so, allowing her body to recover its equilibrium. Then she tried the next step—getting to her feet. She slowly stood. She trembled, and her balance felt a little uncertain. Her stomach rumbled from neglect. The spots filled her vision again, and she waited for it to pass. She took deep breaths, head bowed.

A soft hand touched her arm, and she opened her eyes, only to stare into Sunstar's concerned, gentle, sea green gaze. She gave a brief smile at the unspoken question in those eyes, and that seemed to settle the fears she saw in them. She cautiously stretched, trying to will her body into health.

Sunstar gave her a hesitant smile. "Here." She thrust a bundle into Nightshade's hands. "I think these should fit you."

Nightshade studied the clothes that Sunstar had selected—breeches, a shirt, and a new pair of boots. A long dark cloak lay discarded on the floor close to them. "Perfect. Time to change."

She carefully pulled at the hem of her shift. Her skin tingled uncomfortably as the dried blood pulled away from her skin. She wrinkled her nose and tossed the ruined garment onto the russet-stained puddle on the floor. She looked back at Sunstar. Sunstar remained motionless, staring at her, and Nightshade raised an eyebrow. Sunstar blushed and pulled on the clothes—identical to Nightshade's—that she had selected for herself.

When they were dressed, long black cloaks concealing them, Nightshade turned to Sunstar. "Ready?"

"Yes," Sunstar said. "What are we going to do?"

"Our first order of business is finding out where and when we are," Nightshade said. "After that, we leave town and find something to eat. Unless you have any coin on you?" She smiled slightly at her weak attempt at humor.

"Not the last time I looked." Sunstar dug deep into her empty pockets and dredged up a return smile for Nightshade.

Nightshade looked around for a way out of the warehouse and led the way with unerring accuracy to the closest window. She wrapped a rag around her fist and broke the glass. She climbed through with Sunstar looking on anxiously.

Nightshade dropped lightly to the cobblestones and glanced in each direction for any signs of life. They were alone on what looked like a darkened city street, the scent of water suggesting they were by a river. She looked up at the window.

"Now you," she said softly. "I'll catch you."

Sunstar climbed through the window, and Nightshade grabbed her and held her steady.

"All right?" Nightshade asked.

Sunstar nodded.

Nightshade again looked up and down the darkened street. Any direction looked as promising as any other. "That way." She pointed.

She led Sunstar down the fragrant dockside street, through the mud, and stopped outside a scruffy tavern. A faded sign hung outside it, proclaiming it The Four Winds.

"Stay close by me," Nightshade said.

Sunstar nodded again.

Nightshade squared her shoulders and pulled the hood of her cloak over her head to hide her face. She gestured for Sunstar to do the same. Dizziness overtook her, and she paused a moment, waiting until the sensation passed. She strode up the rough steps with Sunstar close behind and opened the door to the tavern. The common room was smoky and hot, filled with laughing men. A troubadour sat close to the huge fireplace, entertaining some of the patrons with songs of the sea.

One or two men looked up in suspicion when they entered the tavern, but on the whole they were ignored. Nightshade went to the bar, Sunstar in tow. The barkeep gave them a questioning look. He was a fat, grizzled man with an oily, grey fringe of hair. He wiped his hands on his dirty apron as he approached them.

"What'll it be?" he asked.

"Information," Nightshade said.

The publican gasped and peered at her, she kept her features hidden in the shadow of her cloak. His eyes widened.

"You Elves are a long way from home, aren't you?" he asked in a loud voice, and several of the men at the bar blearily looked up from their drinks.

"That is not your concern," Nightshade said in a low and cold voice. "What town is this?"

"You traveled here and you don't know where you are?" His ratty, muddy eyes lit up with suspicion.

Nightshade snaked out an arm and grabbed him by his collar. "Where are we?" she asked in an icy tone.

The barkeep gulped and sweat broke out on his forehead. A couple of the patrons abandoned their tables and took a few steps toward the bar. "You're in the Twin Cities at the mouth of the Barook River."

"When is it?" she asked.

"Now," he replied, confused.

"What year is it?" she said, giving him a quick shake.

"The king is in the tenth year of his reign."

"Which king?"

"King Alistair the Fifth," cried the barkeep.

"Thank you." Nightshade dropped him back behind the bar. She turned around and glanced behind herself to make sure that Sunstar was still there. She took a step forward, and one of the men from the tables put himself in front of her.

"Who are you?" he asked with a smug air.

He was tall for a human man, a few inches shorter than Nightshade, and he stood too close to her. He was dressed in the baggy pants and shirt of a sailor. He had a thick thatch of oily brown hair, pockmarked skin, and a fuzzy growth of beard. He stared coldly at Nightshade, his slate grey eyes flickering with suspicion.

Nightshade sighed inwardly. She was acutely aware of Sunstar shifting nervously behind her. She did not want trouble and doubted that her shaky knees were up to it anyway. She put on her best menacing tone of voice, hoping it would deter him.

"That's none of your business," she said.

The man reached around Nightshade and roughly grabbed Sunstar. Sunstar gasped in shock.

"Who's your friend, then?" He grabbed the hood of her cloak and pulled it back, despite her struggles, to reveal her shining, unearthly beauty. "Well, well, well. What do we have here?"

"Get your hands off her." Nightshade lunged for them, her pulse racing. She took Sunstar's arm and pulled her out of his way. She had not wanted a fight, but if he insisted . . .

He snaked out his other arm just as she moved and dragged back the hood of her cloak. She grunted, and her mouth tightened in annoyance. His gaze slid over her skin. He paused and widened his eyes with shock when he looked—and really saw—her glowing blue eyes.

"I know you," he said. The inn fell silent as the other patrons climbed out of their seats and surrounded them. "You're that weird Drow. You're the one that killed my brother and his entire family."

Nightshade's instant reaction to his words was to deny it. She could not remember killing an entire family of humans, but was sure she would have tried to avoid it if she had been able. She clamped her mouth shut and felt her heart sink. It did not matter. Sunstar mattered, that was all. The sailors were going to kill them, or worse. If she was in perfect health, none of the men would still be standing, but she was not, and she still had Sunstar to protect.

The men murmured angrily as they moved in for the kill.

"What do you want to do with them, Farrow?" the barkeep asked, mopping the sweat from his brow with his dirty apron.

The man, Farrow, tilted his head. A couple of men grabbed Nightshade and Sunstar.

"You're sick, aren't you?" he asked softly, looking closely into Nightshade's tired and gritty eyes.

Nightshade remained silent.

He nodded, as though she had answered him. "That makes you so much easier to kill. But I don't want to kill you here. I have no desire to run from the king's patrols. We'll take you outside the city."

Nightshade had to suppress a smile. She could not believe their good luck. The sailors were going to quietly get them outside the city, disposing of one problem, and let them loose in the woods, disposing of another. Slipping quietly away from them would not be any trouble for either Elf, thanks to Nightshade's experience as a scout and Sunstar's natural affinity for nature.

Sunstar shifted beside her and shot her a concerned glance.

Nightshade glanced at Sunstar, as if on cue. "Remember my promise," she whispered.

Sunstar nodded. She grasped Nightshade's arm and squeezed. They gave each other an almost undetectable nod and relaxed. The drunken crowd roughly grabbed them. Nightshade saw Sunstar stiffen at the unaccustomed touch of the human men. One of them, a bald man with bad teeth, leered and licked his lips, and she shuddered.

They were tied up tightly, blindfolded, and carried stealthily through the malodorous city streets. The journey seemed endless. Nightshade tried to take advantage of the rest and plan. Concern for Sunstar nagged at her. Memories of confinement with the Dark Elves would be too new, too raw, for her to remain relaxed for long.

Their journey came to a halt an hour later. They were dropped carelessly onto the ground. The clean smell of night forest air surrounded them. The smells of sewage, humans, and city were long behind them. Nightshade felt her bonds loosened, and sweating hands lifted the blindfold from her eyes. She blinked, adjusting to the light levels, noting with relief that Sunstar was apparently unharmed, but terrible fear lurked in her sea green eyes. She was pale and sweating freely.

Nightshade got to her feet and moved in close to Sunstar.

"I've changed my mind," Farrow said, inebriated and staggering. "Get them."

Nightshade stared in surprise as the fifteen or so humans lunged at them. She realized, with a sinking heart, that rape in a quiet place was what they had in mind all along. She eyed their opponents, all senses on full alert. She knew that in her weakened condition she could never take them all on and win.

She took Sunstar's hand and lunged forward. She grabbed Farrow with her free hand and hurled him into four of his companions. She surged through the opening, dragging the ashen-faced Sunstar behind her. They hared off into the undergrowth, and she heard a snarl of rage from behind them. Footsteps crashed through the underbrush.

Nightshade ran, chest heaving, Sunstar straight behind her. She scanned the forest and spotted a thick layer of bushes. Sunstar saw where they were headed and eyed them fearfully. She skittered to a halt and tugged on Nightshade's arm. Nightshade stopped and gazed at her. Sunstar shook her head in frantic denial.

"No," Sunstar said, sounding raw.

"Yes," Nightshade said emphatically. "Please, I can't go any further. I'm exhausted. Please trust me."

Sunstar gazed at her and forcibly tried to relax. She gave Nightshade a small nod.

Nightshade nodded in return and gently squeezed her hand. Nightshade folded Sunstar into a tight embrace and led her into the bushes. They sank to the cold earth, and Sunstar lay against Nightshade. Nightshade held her close and rested her chin on Sunstar's head, covering them both in her black cloak. Sunstar clung to her, and Nightshade snuck a quick look at her. Sunstar kept her eyes tightly closed, and her ear on Nightshade's chest.

The men's footsteps sounded loudly in the still forest, the fresh scent of the night air surrounded them and caressed them. A group of booted feet thumped close by to them. One slowed and came to a stop close by their heads. Sunstar's grip on Nightshade tightened. Nightshade held her close, trying to give comfort with the feel of her body. Her muscles ached, and she was weary. The humans had only a slim chance of detecting them, but Sunstar did not seem to realize that.

Nightshade heard a thin, trickling sound and a stream of urine landed close to the top of her head. Under other circumstances, she might have found it amusing, but now she just sighed with disgust.

The man wandered off. The men sounded a fair distance away from them and lost in the dense forest. Nightshade waited until the sounds were very faint before she moved her head so her lips were close to Sunstar's ear.

"Can you move?" she whispered.

She felt Sunstar nod.

"Good," she whispered. "We have to get away from here before they double back. Can you move quietly?"

She felt Sunstar nod again. She had faith in Sunstar. She had learnt as a young Drow to move so the animals of the forest barely knew she was there. Sunstar, although she was only a teenager, would have the same abilities by virtue of her nature as a Forest Elf.

Nightshade forced her aching body to move. She assisted Sunstar to her feet and took her hand. They quietly slipped out of the bushes and into the forest, surrounded by the peace of early morning.

Nightshade nudged Sunstar into motion, and they jogged in the opposite direction to the men.

They ran for quite a distance, until the black spots in front of Nightshade's eyes forced her to stop. She labored to breathe and leaned heavily against a tree along the bank of a swiftly flowing river.

Sunstar touched Nightshade's shoulder. Nightshade gave her a questioning look. Sunstar, green eyes kind and concerned, bent over next to her.

"We have to rest. You're as pale as a ghost," Sunstar said. "I haven't heard the humans for a while. I think we're safe for the moment."

Nightshade nodded raggedly. "I . . ." Black spots consumed her vision. Her eyes rolled up in her head as her legs gave way. She fell forward into Sunstar's waiting arms as the darkness took her.

CHAPTER 12

Sunstar grunted and awkwardly sank to the ground under Nightshade's dead weight. Nightshade was much heavier than her willowy frame suggested, and Sunstar abandoned the idea of trying to move her further into the trees. She put her head against Nightshade's chest. She breathed a deep, heartfelt sigh of relief at Nightshade's strong, even heartbeat. She pulled Nightshade's cloak around her and smoothed her dark hair back off her forehead. A tangled mass of emotion surged over her. She felt the sting of tears in her eyes, and she bit her lip.

She's beautiful, Sunstar thought, studying her chiseled features. *She gave up everything and she's helping me.* The image of the warehouse came to the front of her memory, and the soft, gentle affirmation that Nightshade would stay with her until they returned to her people. *That makes it feel like she's my friend. Yes, I know we don't really know each other. I don't know what it is about her but I want her to stay with me. I want her to come home with me. I just don't think that's going to happen, though. Sooner or later she'll realize how beautiful the sunlit world is, and abandon me for it.* Home brought up another tide of emotion, and she bowed her head and sighed. *Not long*, she thought. It would not take long for Nightshade to bring her home.

She looked down at Nightshade in the still of the grey dawn, and then scanned the trees to one side and the river to the other. Her stomach rumbled, and she realized how hungry she was. She looked around. They were alone, and Nightshade would be safe while she went and found something for them both to eat. She made sure Nightshade was covered and as comfortable as she could be on the river bank, and then slipped into the forest, looking for a place to stay for the day.

Sunstar had an academic knowledge of survival in the wilderness, and it was the one set of lessons she had been fascinated by and scored high marks in. She had always felt the pull of the outside world, and realized with a rueful grin that she would now give anything to be back inside the Elven forest.

She reached a clearing in the thick trees with some shelter from the gentle breeze. There were scattered twigs and branches that would serve as firewood. She gathered them together, built a fire pit, and thought about the journey home. She felt a swift stab of fear at her poor knowledge of where she was and how to get home, and residual fear of Nightshade, that warred with her gratitude toward the half Elf. *What happens when the shock of our escape wears off?* she thought. *What will become of Nightshade? Will she stay as she is or will she turn into an animal? I don't know anything about her. I don't know why she is the way she is. I'm afraid.* She pushed the thoughts aside. All they seemed to do was spiral down into a dark place that stopped her from thinking clearly.

She gazed at her fire pit in satisfaction. She did not have a flint or a knife but it did not matter—she knew magic to create a small fireball and would use it. She turned and headed back toward the river, thinking to catch fish for them both. She realized with a small stab of sadness that the idea of the death of a living creature did not cause her as much difficulty as it once had.

She approached the edge of the water and felt deep within herself for her magic. Her hold on it was tenuous, thanks to her emotional turmoil, but she was able to focus enough to sing two large fish to the surface. They floated in a quiet pool of water, and she pulled them out, grimacing at the idea of killing them, now that the moment was upon her. She glanced back in the direction of the place she had left Nightshade and firmed her resolve.

Half an hour later, she sat before the fire pit, the fish wrapped in leaves beneath the coals, and watched flames dance before her. She stood, shoulders stooped with weariness, and went to check on Nightshade. Nightshade was still senseless beside the water, and did not look as though she had moved.

Sunstar stared at her and gently ran her knuckle down the side of Nightshade's face. "Sleep well, friend, and may your dreams be good ones," she murmured.

She painfully climbed to her feet and headed back toward the fire, so exhausted she could barely move. When she reached it, she wrapped herself up in her cloak and was asleep within seconds.

Nightshade slowly came to her senses. She felt dazed. She was distantly aware of lying on her back on the cold ground next to a river, judging by the roar of rushing water to one side. She sat up, blinking her watering eyes in the afternoon sunlight. She peered around. She could not remember how she got there. She took deep breaths of cleansing air and marveled at the feel of warm sunlight on her pale skin.

The barriers to memory abruptly collapsed, and everything that had happened came flooding back to her. She remembered the warehouse, the humans in the tavern, and Sunstar. She looked around frantically, but could not see any sign of Sunstar. She was alone.

Black despair gripped her. Sunstar had probably changed her mind and gone on without her. She knew where they were and that they were in their accustomed time. Why would she have stayed? For Nightshade? No—why stay for her? She represented one of the most evil races on the planet, and an ugly reminder of her imprisonment. An elfmaid as innocent and pure as Sunstar could not see past Nightshade's dark nature and had left.

Nightshade bleakly settled back to think about what to do next.

She had no doubt that the Dark Elves would continue to look for Sunstar. Sunstar had clearly hoped to reach her home before the Drow came for her. Nightshade briefly considered looking for her, but immediately ruled out the idea for two reasons. First, Sunstar had left without saying anything to her, so she obviously did not want her around anymore. It worked well for Sunstar to do that. Second, Sunstar did not realize that the Dark Elves would actually be tracking *Nightshade* to find her. If they separated, then Nightshade could buy the precious time needed for Sunstar to escape back to her own people.

Nightshade shifted uncomfortably. Her body was sticky with dried blood. She stood, stripped, and dove into the clear, river water.

She tried to ignore the sinking emptiness that was seeping into her soul. If they both escaped the Drow, what then? What of her? There was nothing she could do and nowhere that she could go where she would not be judged against the actions of her race. She was not sure whether she wanted to live or die. In fact, she wondered which would be better—life or death? It was a difficult question, so she pushed it aside for the moment. She still had work to do for Sunstar.

She tackled the next phase of her existence—face the consequences of her actions. She knew she had to fight them. She could not escape them, and they would not let her go. She had defied them. She gathered all her courage into her soul and prepared herself for when the Dark Elves came.

She dressed and sat in the sun and idly skipped stones across the steadily rushing water. After a little while, she felt a presence behind her.

"Nightshade?" a soft, hesitant voice asked. "It's good to see you're up."

Sunstar.

Nightshade could not keep the small sliver of joy that Sunstar had not abandoned her yet from entering her lonely heart. "I'm feeling much better." She turned to see Sunstar's lovely, shy smile. Her pleasure at seeing Sunstar slipped through her tight self control and she knew shone in her eyes for an instant before she could control it.

"Are you hungry?" Sunstar asked.

"Starved," Nightshade said, smiling slightly.

"Good," Sunstar said. "I did a little fishing and found something to eat in the forest." She hesitantly held out her hand, as though she expected to be refused.

Nightshade could not stop herself from looking at the hand in surprise, and then equally hesitantly took it.

Sunstar smiled broadly and helped her to her feet. She gave Nightshade's hand a gentle squeeze. She led the way to a hidden path between the trees, to the small clearing and the fire pit. Two leaves with fruits and berries lay close to the fire.

Nightshade stood back and waited as Sunstar cleared away the coals in the fire pit with a large stick and pulled two steaming bundles from beneath them. Sunstar carefully unwrapped one of the bundles of fish and served it to her. Nightshade accepted the proffered dish with a small grin, sat down, and dug in.

Soon they were sitting back, happily full.

"You're an excellent cook," Nightshade said.

"Thank you," Sunstar said. "My best friend's mother used to show me how it was done . . ." Her voice trailed off as her eyes overshadowed with pain.

Nightshade lapsed into an uncomfortable silence as guilt washed over her. She knew that Sunstar's companion had been killed in the attack by the Drow and guessed that was the person Sunstar was now talking about. She did not know how to start again, so the silence stretched out.

"May I ask you a question?" Sunstar sounded hesitant, almost as though expecting Nightshade to refuse.

Nightshade was surprised and cautiously said, "Yes, by all means."

"How come you can see during the day?" Sunstar asked.

"I am only half Drow." Nightshade's eyes misted in memory, and a thousand images of her time as a scout tumbled through her memory before she was able to shove them back.

"How *much* can you see during the day?" Sunstar asked, seemingly oblivious to Nightshade's tension.

Nightshade gracefully accepted the change and forced herself to relax. "I can see about as well as you can in the dark. My eyes hurt from all the light. I can hardly keep them open. About the same as it felt for you when we were in the warehouse."

"And you had to be led in the Drow city because you can't see in such complete darkness either?" Sunstar asked.

Nightshade shuddered. Her memories of being at the mercy of her mean-spirited companions were often painful and always humiliating. "Yes."

Sunstar looked surprised at Nightshade's clipped tone. She nodded, and the silence stretched out.

Nightshade stood. "We have to get moving. They will find us, and I want to be as close to your home as we can, when they do."

Sunstar nodded. "All right."

They quietly cleaned up the camp and walked in amiable silence.

Sunstar broke the silence. "Do you know where we are?"

"We are north of the Twin Cities, about a week from your home," Nightshade said. "You don't know? You know it's your accustomed time, don't you?"

"That close." Sunstar sounded excited. She glanced at Nightshade, light dancing in her eyes. "I know from remembering places on a map, and also have some idea of what humans are up to, so I know who their king is right now."

"I don't think you understand," Nightshade said. "Hemlock, the magician you saw with the king and the queen, will be tracking me—not you—with the Eye. It will take at most one or two nights to find us. After that . . ."

Sunstar shuddered. "What's the Eye?" Her brief elation disappeared, replaced by worry.

"All I know about it is that it's a spell he casts to allow him to travel the landscape without his body, and we will have some warning of it." She hoped Sunstar would not be able to tell she knew more.

"How will we know?"

Nightshade knew the Forest Elves revered life, and was unwilling tell her of the carnage that would be visited on the animal kingdom. "You will see it in the animals."

Sunstar looked as though she wanted to ask another question but it died on her lips. Nightshade stared at her expressionlessly.

"Can you hide us?" Sunstar asked after a moment.

Nightshade hung her head. "No. I am only a half breed, and did not inherit great powers of magic from either parent."

Sunstar abruptly stopped and faced Nightshade.

Nightshade looked down, avoiding her eyes, fearing the disgust she knew she would see in them.

Sunstar touched her muscular arm, but Nightshade's gaze remained firmly trained on the ground between them.

"Nightshade," she said softly, encouragingly.

Nightshade still would not look at her.

"Nightshade?" Sunstar's voice was gentle.

Nightshade finally gathered herself and looked at Sunstar, expecting the worst. She saw only a calm acceptance.

"Perhaps I can help," Sunstar continued. "I am a Forest Elf, and we use our magic to cloak our cities from outside eyes. I am not a magician either, but I can cloak myself, and with a little more concentration, I can cloak you, too."

Nightshade allowed herself to feel hope. "How old are you?" She knew Sunstar would be more in control of her magic if she were not too young. She only looked to be in her mid teens, but perhaps . . .

"I am eighteen," Sunstar said. "My father is a magician. My powers are quite strong, although they are not yet fully developed."

Nightshade smiled. The answer was much better than she expected to hear. "I think we have a chance," she said with a smile. It would be enough to keep them alive, though they would have to separate once they reached the Elven forest. She would be able to fulfill her promise to herself and bring Sunstar home.

They continued walking.

"Do you miss them?" Nightshade asked, thinking back to the riverbank and her mother.

"Yes, I do," Sunstar said, sounding surprised by the question about her family. "How about you?"

"I have left nothing of value behind in the Drow city," Nightshade said. "My father despises me and my mother is long dead." *She won't accept that. She will ask me more about my mother. She can see I'm half Elf.*

She felt Sunstar steal a glance at her, her slight frown as she caught Nightshade's brief flicker of pain at the mention of her mother. She quieted again. *Thank the gods,* Nightshade thought.

They walked on in comfortable silence through the lush greenery, each locked in their own thoughts. They stopped in the dying moments of the day in the midst of a clearing.

"I'm going to find us something to eat," Sunstar said, glancing at Nightshade. "Do you want to start a fire?" She stiffened slightly, seemingly bracing herself for a negative response from Nightshade.

Nightshade merely shook her head. "It's not a good idea—it's not safe. We don't have the time for it. We have to go to ground."

Sunstar looked up at the dying daylight. Fear flashed in her expressive green eyes.

Nightshade flinched at the obviously bad memories buffeting Sunstar. She wanted to reassure her, to touch her, but did not know how any gestures from her would be received. She stood awkward and still. "Sunstar, we are in danger during full night. It is still the cross over time. We have some moments to ourselves before we need to hide."

Sunstar's jaw tensed, and she nodded. "All right. I'll see what I can find to eat."

Nightshade watched her go. She turned to the way they came, hesitating for a second. She went a small way into the forest and picked berries off a bush, thinking Sunstar would probably enjoy them. Her heart warmed a little when she thought of Sunstar, but it was followed by a needle of guilt. Why had she taken Sunstar back to the city of Dragonar, when she had been planning to leave?

She filled her pockets with berries and headed back to the clearing to wait for Sunstar. Sunstar returned a few minutes later, as loaded down with food as Nightshade was.

"What's this?" she asked, staring at Nightshade's bounty.

"Something extra." Nightshade handed her the berries and gave her a half smile.

Sunstar grinned broadly in return. "Thank you. I love these."

They ate and sat back in the twilight. Nightshade looked up at the darkening sky.

Sunstar's good mood vanished. She nodded, although Nightshade had not said anything. "I know. We have to go to ground."

She moved closer to Nightshade and sat cross-legged directly in front of her.

"What is this glamour that you're going to cast?" Nightshade asked.

"Any creatures that happen by us in the night will only see a faint shimmering from the corners of their eyes. If they turn to look at us directly they will see the trees and undergrowth. They will only catch the scent of damp night air." She smiled. "Lie down close to me."

Nightshade raised an eyebrow at Sunstar, but obeyed, lying flat on the ground.

"Put your head in my lap," Sunstar said softly. "You have to be touching me. The land itself will hide us, but we have to remain completely still. I'll sing us to sleep and cast the glamour. This magic isn't being drawn *from* the land, it *is* the land."

Nightshade remembered how Sunstar stiffened when she had pulled her in close to hide them from the human men. She hesitantly moved back so her head was in Sunstar's lap.

Sunstar gazed down into Nightshade's eyes—eyes she knew were glowing blue. Nightshade felt completely defenseless for a second, and Sunstar smiled gently at her. Sunstar took a deep breath and closed her eyes. She sang a soft, soothing lullaby, which caressed Nightshade's senses, relaxing her and drawing her into a deep magical sleep. Her last conscious sight was of Sunstar bending over her, murmuring three words in ancient Elven.

CHAPTER 13

Hemlock tried again to find the missing Elves. Unlike the first night, where a pillar of pure white flame had shone to the heavens, nothing was revealed to his inner Eye. He was a patient Drow, his mental state almost timeless in its serenity, and he knew it was only a matter of time before they made a mistake, and he found them. He was thorough, highly intelligent, cunning, and resourceful. He never made any mistakes, merely out waited his opponents and capitalized on their blunders.

The door to his chambers crashed open, and the king strode through, the queen close behind him. Both monarchs looked more than a little angry.

"Hemlock." The king leaned forward, his eyes boring into Hemlock's. "When I call for you for a progress report, I expect you to deliver me one."

"Why bother if I have nothing to report?" Hemlock asked mildly.

The king growled and grabbed Hemlock by the throat and slammed him into the stone wall. Hemlock grunted as the air left his lungs, but remained silent.

"Your insolence is beginning to annoy me," the king said coldly, tightening his fingers.

Hemlock held his breath, meeting the king's eyes calmly.

The queen laid an admonishing hand on the king's arm. He shot a quick look at her, and she shook her head slightly. Some of the fury left the king's eyes, and he loosened his grip on Hemlock.

Hemlock slid down the wall and took a deep breath, staring at him without expression, hiding the anger that stung at him.

The king gave him another glare and turned to his queen. They strode toward the door of Hemlock's chambers, but stopped.

"Keep me informed of your progress," the king said coldly. "I don't care who you send, but I want daily reports."

Hemlock did not dignify him with an answer.

The monarchs strode from his chamber.

A frightened servant snuck into the chamber, shut the door behind him, and fell prostrate before the expressionless Hemlock. "Master," he gasped. "I'm sorry. His Highness threatened to cut me open if I didn't let him in."

Hemlock lifted his hand, muttering under his breath for a moment, feeling the magic pulse and flow around and through him.

The servant shot up into the air and slammed against the wall. He gasped and wheezed as invisible fingers tightened their hold on his throat.

"Never again," Hemlock said coldly. "Never again will you make this mistake."

He released his hold on the servant. The servant crashed to the floor, drawing great whooping gasps of air into his lungs. His chest heaved. "Yes, Master." He looked pathetically grateful at Hemlock's supposed forgiveness.

Hemlock gave him a cold smile, and the servant paled and stumbled from his chambers.

He continued smiling. The only reason the servant was still alive was because he did not have the time or inclination to train another.

He strode into his inner chamber, shedding his clothes, preparing to send forth his Eye. He imagined what it would look like if the king's flesh liquefied and fell away from his body. He felt his anger drain away from him, replaced by a deep well of calm.

He stripped, drank the rancid blood from the sacrifice, and cast his Eye into the air, wordlessly screaming in joy at the sensation of utter freedom. He hunted all night long, but could not find them. They had apparently vanished from the face of the earth.

He returned to his body, thinking that he should report his negative results to the king personally. He wanted to see the king grind his teeth in frustration. He left his meditation chamber and strode toward his bathing chamber. It would not do to present His Highness with a negative result while covered in dried, stinking blood. One had to maintain the illusion of obedient servant, after all.

For now, at least.

Nightshade awoke at dawn the next morning. She felt more alive and rested than she had over the past few days. She looked around, struck by the novelty of waking at dawn and sleeping at dusk. She forgot for a second or two about everything, and simply . . . was. It felt beautiful and full of promise.

Sunstar was still asleep. The urgency of their headlong flight through the forest cut through her haze and sank down on her like an almost physical weight.

Sunstar sat cross-legged, supporting Nighshade's head in her lap. Nightshade slowly sat up and turned to Sunstar. She laid a calloused hand lightly on Sunstar's shoulder and gently shook her. Sunstar started and lost her balance, and began to topple over backward. Nightshade lunged forward and caught her, then pulled her in close and saved her from the hard ground.

Sunstar's eyes opened, dazed and unfocused for a second. She seemed to come to, and her eyes widened at her sudden proximity to Nightshade. Nightshade struggled to suppress a flinch at the fleeting panic that went through her eyes. She could feel Sunstar's heart pounding, and she gently loosed her grip. The glamour dissipated so they became visible, and a startled deer grazing beside them bolted away into the forest.

"Good morning," Nightshade said. "If I had known that you were going to spend the night in that position, I would have asked you to lie down first."

Sunstar blushed. "Good morning. Yes, well, I suppose I should have mentioned it." She glanced down at her legs and grimaced.

Nightshade gently disentangled herself from Sunstar and stood, still feeling the tingle on her arms from Sunstar's body. She held out a hand.

"You're going to have to move a little to regain some feeling in your legs," she said.

Sunstar slowly and painfully got to her knees and took the proffered hand. Nightshade helped her to stand. She staggered and winced. She took Nightshade's arm, and Nightshade helped her walk around a little, until her legs were strong enough to take her weight. Nightshade watched her warily, and Sunstar smiled at her. Nightshade's trepidation vanished, and they continued on their journey.

They hardly exchanged a word for the first hour or so of their march.

Nightshade barely noticed. They had made it through the first night. Sunstar's glamour worked. There were no sign of the Drow.

She felt a glimmer of hope that Sunstar would see her beloved home again. She smiled ruefully. She wondered how Sunstar's parents would react if they ever saw her. What would they say to her? Would it be thanks or an order for her execution?

Nightshade's thoughts spiraled inwards. A small voice at the back of her mind yammered and snapped at her almost constantly. *Idiot. If you had run before you reached the city none of this would have happened. The king would never know, and you both would be free. Idiot!*

The morning progressed as they walked for several hours. The sunlight became brighter and brighter, robbing Nightshade of precious sight. She considered their situation. Stopping for hours during the day did not appeal to her, but she could not take them toward Elven lands while virtually blind during the day.

Nightshade was quietly grateful when they stopped for their morning meal. The sun stood a quarter of the way through the sky. She was having trouble seeing the path in front of them, and barely avoided tripping over several small obstacles. Sunstar went to her assistance and quietly took the lead. They ate in silence, and Nightshade listened carefully to the sounds of the forest around them.

When they were done, Nightshade hesitated, and Sunstar took the lead again. She walked through the forest, Nightshade close behind her. They finally reached a rough, pitted dirt road, and Sunstar stopped, glancing both ways up and down it. Nightshade, now completely blind, almost bumped into Sunstar's back.

"Which way?" Sunstar asked. "Right or left? Are you sure anyone uses this road? It doesn't really look like it."

"Left. I'm sure." Nightshade stepped forward and tripped over a large tree root. She stumbled into Sunstar. Sunstar fell, and Nightshade twisted at the last instant so she landed beneath Sunstar. She felt Sunstar shift on top of her.

"You can't see anything at all, can you?" Sunstar sounding worried.

"No," Nightshade said sadly. She kept her eyes tightly closed, and they were tearing badly. She gently disentangled herself and rose to her feet, bringing Sunstar with her.

"I'll lead you." Sunstar gently grasped Nightshade's hand.

Nightshade felt an instant of panic and pulled out of Sunstar's grasp. They could stop for a couple of hours until she could see something again and take the lead. She hated the feeling of helplessness, of not being in control. Trust did not come easily after living for more than forty years with the Drow.

"We could wait—" she began.

"No," Sunstar said firmly. "You told me we have to move quickly, and so we will. You will have to trust *me* to lead *you*, Nightshade." She sounded hurt.

Nightshade did not reply. She did not know what to say. She heard the pain and cursed herself for having caused it, after the kindness Sunstar had shown to her. Sunstar had never betrayed or hurt her and had never given her a reason *not* to trust her. Nightshade took a deep breath and held out her hand, eyes tightly closed against tears.

Sunstar took it with gentle fingers, squeezed it, and tucked it into the crook of her elbow. They walked down the uneven forest road.

"If you can't see anything, how did you know we had to go left?" Sunstar asked hesitantly.

Nightshade smiled. "There is nothing mysterious about it. We head north to your father's lands. I can feel the sun on my face, and it is still morning—so we are headed east. We must head north. So, left we must go."

Sunstar nodded. "It sounds so simple when you say it like that." She gently guided Nightshade along the smoothest path, trying to lead her the same way Nightshade had led her to the Drow city.

They walked down the road for several hours, stopping only for a brief, midday meal. Sunstar handed Nightshade her meal with a smile—she knew Nightshade could feel but not see.

They continued on into the afternoon. Nightshade pulled away from Sunstar again. She glanced around the road, blinking. Suddenly she stopped and tilted her head.

"Can you hear that?" she asked.

Sunstar listened closely and frowned. She could not hear anything, and was about to say so, when she heard the distant neighing of a horse. "What is it?"

"I can hear at least one horse. I think we have trouble ahead." Nightshade let go of the startled Sunstar's hand and ran forward, down the road. She tripped over obstacles but recovered her balance. Sunstar followed closely behind once she had recovered her wits. The sounds continued to get louder, and the road opened out into a human village.

Sunstar could see the village in roiling turmoil. Rough, dirty men on horses were milling around, destroying houses and wagons. Villagers ran, terrified and screaming, and the women clasped their children close and tried to hide. The bandits torched buildings, and one lone rider galloped behind a screaming woman, trying to grab the back of her dress.

"Sword!" Nightshade said to the deeply breathing Sunstar. She scented the air.

Sunstar eyed the ground frantically, searching for a weapon. She found one nearby, grabbed it, and threw it to Nightshade who caught it. Nightshade ran forward and joined into the fray, thrusting and swinging her borrowed sword with cold, calculated determination that made Sunstar wince.

Sunstar watched Nightshade's graceful form swiftly hacking and slashing at the opponents all around her, wounding and killing with unerring accuracy. She was so engrossed that she did not hear a human male come swiftly and silently up behind her, and clap a hand over her mouth. He dragged her backward off her feet. Sunstar grabbed at the dirty hand, trying to pull it away from her mouth. She tripped backward, managing in the process to kick him in the shins. She elbowed him solidly in the stomach as he staggered. He lost his grip on her mouth as he tried to grab the wounded area.

"Nightshade!" she screamed as the hand clapped over her mouth again, and she was surrounded by the stench of filthy human. The enraged human punched her in an attempt to make her more cooperative, and the air left her lungs in a rush.

Suddenly Nightshade was there. "Let her go," she said in her coldest voice.

"Why should I, Elf?" he asked. "I can do what I like. You can't fight me with your eyes closed."

Sunstar felt him stiffen at the sudden, inhuman, animalistic expression on Nightshade's face.

"Sunstar," she said.

Sunstar, wild-eyed and incoherent, struggled furiously. "Nightshade."

The sound of the struggle was enough for Nightshade. She lunged forward with her sword, and tore Sunstar downward out of his arms and stabbed him in the neck. Sunstar yelped as she felt the skin on her knees tear. Blood from the man's neck splattered the two of them, and

Sunstar struggled to control her bile. The man gurgled and clutched his throat. He collapsed to the ground, twitching.

Nightshade dropped the sword and knelt on the ground. Sunstar felt Nightshade's gentle hand on her shoulder and crept into her arms. Nightshade pulled her in close and rested her cheek on Sunstar's head. Sunstar felt helpless, and her tears washed some of the blood off Nightshade's neck.

Villagers slowly reappeared. They came from their hiding places to form a circle around the pair, eyeing the pointed ears and the blood.

"Thank you," a tall, strong young man said in an uncertain tone. Nightshade looked up to the source of the voice.

He gasped, started at the sight of her softly glowing blue eyes, and stared at her for a moment.

"By the Gods," he finally exclaimed. "You're that strange Drow that we've been hearing about. Why are you here? Come to finish the job the bandits started?"

Sunstar felt Nightshade stiffen.

The surviving villagers glared at them as their mood turned ugly. They moved in closer, searching the ground for any weapons.

"And so it begins," Nightshade whispered.

Sunstar's tears trickled down her face. She looked up from the safety of Nightshade's arms. "We have done you no harm," she said, voice cracking. "We saved you."

"So you could finish the job," another voice cried from the rear. Loud cries of agreement followed this.

"We don't need your help," the first man said. "Leave."

Someone at the back of the crowd threw a rock and it hit Nightshade on the cheek, drawing blood. She stood, drawing Sunstar in close. The crowd tried to surround them, but Nightshade saw a small gap in the wall of humans and slipped through it.

"We were trying to help you!" Sunstar yelled, as Nightshade took her hand and ran.

The villagers ran after them, pelting them with every object they could lay their hands on. Nightshade kept Sunstar ahead of her, shielding her from the worst of the rocks. They reached the border of the village and continued running. The villagers stopped there, calling insults and abuse as Nightshade and Sunstar continued to run.

Nightshade finally slowed to a walk, Sunstar breathing heavily beside her.

Sunstar turned and glared back the way they came. "Why didn't you say anything?" she asked, as Nightshade led them through the forest to the bank of the river.

Nightshade did not reply. She stripped off her clothes. "I want to get the blood off me," she said simply, stepping naked into the calm, clear water. "You should as well."

Sunstar looked down at her stained clothes, disgusted. She nodded, stripped off, and followed Nightshade into the water. They bathed in silence.

Sunstar got out of the water first and sat on a convenient, sun-warmed rock, watching Nightshade. She felt as though she were lightly coated in slime.

Sunstar was furious that the villagers had acted the way they had. They did not know Nightshade as she did, and they should not have judged her as they had. Had they not seen her fighting the raiders? Had she laid a hand on any of them? No. So why had they assumed she was there to do the same thing as the raiders?

Memories of the fight resurfaced. She had never seen such carnage at close hand, she reflected, as fear of Nightshade tugged guiltily at her. Her father's rule had always been peaceful. Sunstar still wanted an answer to the question she had asked. Why *hadn't* Nightshade defended herself against the villagers' harsh words?

She quietly watched Nightshade's statuesque body as she bathed, transfixed by her dark beauty. Grace, power, viciousness, courage, and compassion all combined into one magnificent package. Nightshade had promised not to hurt her and to keep her safe, and had always done so with such gentleness toward her. Windwalker had taken blood in defense of her home, but did she fear him? What made Nightshade any different from her father's soldiers? Could it be that she was wary now of Nightshade only because she was half a Drow and raised by Drow?

She thought back to her time in the Drow prison, her struggle not to ascribe any redeeming features to Nightshade simply because Nightshade did not look the same as the other Drow. She was dimly surprised that she did not feel that now. She had no doubt about Nightshade's gentler nature. She trusted Nightshade with her life and would continue to do so.

Could she accept the rest? Nightshade's ability to kill so easily? The fight had been bloody and lethal, that was true, but the humans were obviously barbaric in their interactions with one another. Did she blame them? What made *them* so different to the Drow? What was it really that separated the Drow from other races, if it was not the ability to kill?

Sunstar had been subjected to nothing but extreme violence and cruelty, and the only one who had shown her any sort of kindness was the one who was supposed to be her bitterest enemy, a symbol of the ugliest excesses she had ever witnessed—Nightshade. But Nightshade had never hurt her, and never would.

Sunstar kept her gaze firmly on Nightshade.

Nightshade finally got out of the water. She sat beside Sunstar on the rock. Her features were set in calm impassivity, as always, but her eyes told another story. The look in them was turbulent, as though dreading what Sunstar had to say to her, Sunstar realized with some shock. Why on earth would Nightshade think she was angry at her?

"Why didn't you say anything?" Sunstar repeated.

"They were right," Nightshade said simply. "I have no illusions about what I am. I have done unspeakable things."

"But you don't do them anymore?"

"No."

"Why?"

Nightshade did not answer. The silence stretched out, and Sunstar knew that Nightshade had reached her quota for the moment. She knew that, just as she knew in her heart she accepted Nightshade for who she was. Now it was just a matter of time to draw the tortured half Drow out of her shell.

"I won't give up on you," Sunstar said after a time. She stood and gathered her clothes. She snuck a look at the still face, hooded as always, and thought she saw a brief flicker of gentleness and longing there, gone so swiftly she thought she had imagined it.

They silently dressed and continued on their way through the forest. With the passage of the day, Nightshade's sight steadily returned, and she took the lead, staying close to Sunstar.

"I don't remember much about my mother," she began, haltingly.

Sunstar almost did not hear the soft words, and said nothing. She turned to regard Nightshade with an open look.

Nightshade's gaze turned inward, her expression pained, warring with a dim elation.

"I remember that she was the most beautiful Forest Elf anyone had ever seen. I remember that she loved me and tried to teach me the way of her people, but my father put an end to that. He trained me to kill, to be a good Drow. But I remember her and I have never forgotten."

"What happened to her?" Sunstar asked, after the silence had stretched out. She did not expect Nightshade to answer.

"My father killed her." Nightshade glanced at Sunstar. "He captured her, much like you were captured, took her back to the Drow city pregnant, and I was born. I was the only thing keeping her alive, and she loved me. I remember that—she loved me."

Sunstar hesitantly took Nightshade's hand and gave it a reassuring squeeze. "Her heart will be gladdened now that you have found your way."

A single tear flowed down Nightshade's face. "I have a long way to go." She wiped at the tear and released Sunstar's hand. Her shoulders sagged in relief, and a dim light entered her eye.

Something's changing inside her, Sunstar thought. *Is this the first time she's ever really spoken to anyone about her mother? About her love? How wonderful that must feel.* She thought of her own mother and felt a surge of love and longing. She nodded.

"Do you want to stay here for the night?" she asked, staying close to Nightshade.

Nightshade glanced up at the sky, and then at the long shadows cast by the trees. She nodded. "Why not? It's beautiful here."

Sunstar smiled. "Yes, it is." She clamped her mouth shut. There were so many things she wanted to say to Nightshade, so much she wanted to talk about but she knew Nightshade was overwhelmed, and it would have to wait.

She slipped into the forest and gathered food for their evening meal. When she returned to the banks of the river, Nightshade had a freshly caught fish on a fire she had built. They were silent before and during the simple meal, taking comfort in each other's company. When they were done and packed the remains of their food, Nightshade lay down as she had done the previous night. Sunstar sat cross-legged close to her head.

"Sunstar," Nightshade said. "You will never survive this trip if you stay like that. Lie beside me."

Sunstar did as Nightshade suggested. She gladly lay beside Nightshade. She needed to touch her, so she sidled up close so their arms touched.

Nightshade hesitated. She gently snaked an arm under Sunstar and drew her in close. Sunstar's heart beat wildly with memories of lying on Farouk's chest. She sucked in a deep, shaky breath. Nightshade released her.

"No, don't let go," Sunstar said. "I'm all right. It just takes a little getting used to." Nightshade's touch was *nothing* like Farouk's.

Nightshade nodded and firmed her grip around Sunstar.

Sunstar breathed deeply, calming her pounding heart. She moved in close to Nightshade again. She took in Nightshade's wild scent, rested her head on her broad shoulder, and slowly relaxed. She closed her eyes and softly sang. She felt Nightshade relax as she instantly fell asleep. The glamour shimmered around them, hiding them from prying eyes, and magical sleep overcame Sunstar.

CHAPTER 14

The next morning, they both awoke feeling completely refreshed. Nightshade felt her strength returning by the hour, and began to have a glimmer of hope that she would be able to help Sunstar escape when the Drow caught up with them.

Sunstar led once again during the middle of day, and they made good time. They joined a well-maintained and lightly-trafficked highway. They were heading into a human city, and it seemed to Nightshade as though Sunstar was not walking as quickly as she had before.

"Sunstar?" she asked. "Is there something wrong?"

Nightshade felt Sunstar shake her head.

"Not exactly," Sunstar said.

Nightshade turned toward her voice and lifted her chin in a silent question.

Sunstar sighed. "It's nothing, really. Just me being silly. I find humans to be barbaric, and I'm not looking forward to interacting with more of them."

Nightshade gave her a rueful grin. "We will be through the city quickly, and I will stay with you. I won't let them do anything to you."

She felt Sunstar nod and gently squeeze her hand. She smiled, and they lapsed back into silence.

The stream of traffic down the road grew slightly heavier.

"Do you know where we are?" Sunstar asked, breaking their comfortable well of silence.

"We are close to the Bordertown," Nightshade said, blindly scenting the air. She kept her eyes tightly closed. "We are taking a shortcut through it so we can get to your land a little quicker."

Sunstar lapsed into tense silence, and Nightshade let her be.

It was well into the afternoon by the time they reached the southern gate of the city.

Nightshade's sight gradually returned, and she took the lead, keeping Sunstar close to her. Sunstar seemed ill at ease in the throng of jostling humans.

"Do you think they will just let us through?" Sunstar held onto Nightshade's arm.

"They have no reason to stop us, and I haven't done anything wrong," Nightshade said with a wry grin.

Sunstar flinched. Nightshade knew the memory of the fight in the village was too new and raw for both of them.

"You have nothing to fear from the humans," Nightshade said. "They won't hurt you."

Sunstar nodded. "Just stay with me."

Nightshade gently squeezed her hand.

The town guard stopped them by the city gates. The guards clustered around the wagon belonging to the human family ahead of them.

"There." A young, stone-faced guard, pointed to the right. "Go there. Your wagon is to be searched."

"Why?" the human man asked.

"That does not concern you unless you are doing something you know you shouldn't." The guard peered intently at him. "Well?"

The man stared at him and snorted. He sharply clucked his tongue, and the tired cart horses pulled the wagon toward the right.

Nightshade and Sunstar stepped forward. The guard studied them with interest. He jerked his head to the left. "That way."

Sunstar nodded, and they joined the queue of thronging humans to the left. They finally reached the front of the queue after an interminable quarter hour.

An old man with grizzled hair, bright, shifty dark eyes, and bad teeth, eyed them up and down. Nightshade's defenses went up at the unwelcome attention, and she stiffened.

"What is your business here?" he asked by rote. His eyes were keen and alert, and he watched them carefully. A young soldier in a dirty uniform trotted up alongside him and whispered something in his ear. More guards emerged from the guard house by the gates and came up to stand close to him.

"We are passing through." Nightshade eyed the hands hovering close to carefully tended weaponry. She glanced around. They were surrounded.

"I don't think so," the watchman said.

Nightshade felt her heart sink. "And what do you think we are doing?" She raised an eyebrow at him, pinning him to place with her glowing blue eyes.

"I think you have kidnapped this young Elf, and that you're going to the town prison," he said, signaling the men. The milling, jostling farmers behind Nightshade and Sunstar drew back as the guards swarmed them. They tore Nightshade and Sunstar apart and threw Nightshade to the ground. She grunted as the air exploded from her lungs.

"Nightshade didn't kidnap me!" Sunstar exclaimed, but her protests were drowned by the sound of weapons being drawn. Sunstar looked on, anguished and helpless as they pinned Nightshade.

There were too many men for Nightshade to take on at once, so she allowed them to restrain her. She kept her eyes on Sunstar, singling her out, capturing her, willing her to know that she would be all right. They had nothing to fear. Nightshade would find some way to get them both out of this mess. She bowed her head.

A circle of six cautious guards carefully bound the unresisting Nightshade.

One of them bent over her. "Get up."

Nightshade nodded and slowly and carefully stood. Her wrists were manacled, and she was in leg irons. Both were a little tight—they had been designed for much smaller wrists and ankles. She looked down at the guards. The tallest one was several inches shorter than she.

"Move." The guard poked her with his pike.

Nightshade hissed as the sharp tip scraped against her behind. She glared at him. "I will go. Do not prod me. I am not a cow."

"No, you're a stinking Drow," he snarled and poked her again.

Her lips tightened. She took a step forward. "Take me to your prison, then."

He jerked the chains binding her wrists, and she took a step forward. The other soldiers formed ranks around her, and they walked through the gates and into the city streets.

The humans milling around stopped and stared at her.

"—look at the eyes—"

"—glowing—"

"—Drow—"

"—weird Drow—"

Nightshade tensed her jaw and tried not to hear the whispered words swirling all around her. The soldier leading her jerked to avoid a piece of fruit thrown at them, but it was only the first. Another followed after that, and then another. Soon they were pelted with foul-smelling fruit.

Nightshade tensed her muscles and bent slightly to avoid the missiles the humans threw at them. She kept grimly silent and concentrated on keeping her footing. Her leg irons were short, and she had to keep her stride very short to avoid falling on her face.

The crowd lining the streets openly jeered at her, and it felt like hours before they arrived at the human prison. Ornately dressed humans clustered around the entrance. Nightshade watched them as they eyed her curiously. A small child darted out from behind them and ran toward her.

"No!" The child's mother lunged for him. "No! Drow. They kill and eat small children."

The little boy screamed and cried hysterically.

Nightshade struggled to suppress a hot flush that she could feel rising under her collar. Her eyes shone with guilt, and an image of an overturned wagon tore through her mind.

"Stand back!" The guard leading her motioned for his comrades to widen the path into the prison.

Nightshade followed him into the darkness of the prison. She blinked and blew out a gusty sigh of relief that it was over. The guards led her to a desk. A soldier sat behind it, and the golden knots on his collar proclaimed him to be an officer.

He did not look up. "Take it to the end cell." He pointed with his quill, his eyes never leaving the parchment on the desk before him.

Nightshade frowned. *It?*

The guards threw her into the end cell, and she tripped and skidded on her knees. She looked up. She could not stand in the cell anyway. A guard entered the cell, flanked by two guards with crossbows trained on her. He cautiously removed her leg irons, and she stretched out with a sigh.

He darted from the cell, past the officer who had been sitting at the desk.

The officer entered the cell. She knelt and stared at him.

"Do you know where you are?" he asked, slowly and clearly.

"No," she said, blinking.

"You are in the Bordertown," he replied. "Why are you here?"

"I want to travel through your city with my friend. We are headed to Elven lands."

"The Drow are in the other direction. Or are you bringing her to a group of your countrymen?"

"No, I am bringing her back to her father's lands. I promised."

"I see I am confusing you," he said, slowly and carefully. "*Your* friends. Do you understand me? *Yours*. Not hers. *Yours*. You are bringing her to the Drow, are you not?"

"I am not a halfwit. I understand what you are saying to me. No, I am not bringing her to the Drow. I am bringing her back to the Forest Elves."

"Enough of your lies and deceit," he snarled. "Tell me where your forces are massing or it will be the worse for you."

"I am not lying. I do not know where the Drow are," she replied. *I wish I did, though*, her mind helpfully added.

He slapped her.

Her head rang from the blow. She narrowed her eyes. "Do *not* hit me."

"I will continue hitting you until you decide you are sick of the pain and start telling me the truth," he said. "How can you be so stupid? How can you think *we* are so stupid? What makes you think that we would ever believe that you travel by yourselves? Everyone knows Drow *always* hunt in packs. If you are here then there must be one close to us."

"I *am* telling you the truth." She gritted her teeth. "I do *not* know where the Drow are. And if I did it would be purely for the purpose of avoiding them."

"So you *do* know where they are."

"I just said no."

The officer turned to one of the guards. "Tell Lord Edgar that it freely admits to taking Her Highness. It claims it is traveling to Elven lands. It is obviously lying. Ask for his judgment."

The soldier saluted and ran from the cell block.

The officer turned back to Nightshade. "Tell the truth, and it will go much better for you."

"I *am* telling you the truth," she said. *And it is getting me nowhere. I understand why he thinks I am lying. Who would believe Sunstar would ever come willingly with one such as me?*

The officer's mouth set in a tight line, and he took a step toward her. She reached over his head and spun him around so the chains binding her wrists were pressed up against his throat. His breath whistled in and out of his lungs, and he clawed at her hands.

She held him close to her chest. "I asked you before and I ask you again now—please do *not* hit me." She took the chains away from his neck and threw him away, out of the cell.

He clutched at his throat, coughing and wheezing. He spat blood onto the flagstones.

The other guards rushed her and beat her. There were too many of them, and they overwhelmed her. They kicked and punched her as she lay on the floor. She curled up, trying to protect her chest and neck as best she was able.

After a while, the guards gave up, removed her manacles, and trooped out of the cell again. She lay dazed and covered in bruises. She felt a body close to her and opened her eyes.

The officer tangled his fingers in her hair and savagely pulled her head back. She blinked at him.

"Lord Edgar has ordered you to be hung at dawn tomorrow, Drow." He spat in her face and threw her head forward.

Nightshade waited until she heard the cell doors close and the snick as the key turned in the lock.

She sat up with a sigh. Let the humans think they could hang her in the morning. That did not matter to her so much. She would find a way to escape.

Her most pressing problem was that it had to be close to sunset. Hemlock would use his Eye to scour the landscape, looking for them. He would find them in an instant, if he happened to be looking in the right direction.

No. That was not quite right. He would find *her* in an instant if he was looking in the right direction. Sunstar's best protection was her separation from Nightshade. She was free. If they came, Nightshade would fight them and buy the extra time needed for the humans to protect her. The humans would *try* to protect her, and they had probably already sent for the Forest Elves. If Sunstar had to escape the city by herself, she could do it. She knew she could travel by day and cloak herself with a glamour by night. She would be safe until she crossed the border into Elven lands.

Nightshade smiled. She felt a little better than she had when the guards had first took her.

She settled herself down to wait.

"Look," a woman's voice said. "It's so still. Do you think it's still alive?"

Nightshade opened her eyes. Two ornately dressed and heavily perfumed women stood outside the cell, peering in at her. A human male stood close to them. They looked the same to Nightshade—the only difference was that the man wore tight breeches.

"Yes, of course it's still alive," the man said, amused. "Why would the guards put a dead Drow in a prison cell?"

"Do you think it understands us?" the second asked woman, leaning in close to the first.

They stared at Nightshade. She remained motionless and stared back at them.

"No," the man said finally. "I don't think it understands us. I don't think it's capable of thought the same way we are."

"Have you read the works of Erasmus?" the first woman asked.

The second woman shook her head but the man nodded. "I have." He smiled at her. "I suppose you're going to spout one of his wild theories? That they can be tamed and trained to imitate thinking, rational beings?" He snorted and shook his head. "It's highly unlikely. Theories that they have a functioning society have never been proven. They're cold, mindless killers, that's all."

"Well, isn't now a superb chance to study it? We have an actual Drow in captivity," the first woman said. "This is too marvelous a chance to pass up. We *must* study it."

"Haven't you heard?" the second woman asked. "Lord Edgar has ordered its execution tomorrow morning."

"Oh, that's a pity." The first woman peered at Nightshade, and then allowed her gaze to wander up and down Nightshade's body. "Good grief is this thing *female*?"

They all stared closely at her torso. Nightshade struggled to control a wild blush. She felt the tips of her ears burn.

"Yes," the man said slowly. "I think it is."

"This is exciting," the first woman exclaimed. "Erasmus postulated that the only purpose of a female was for breeding. It—*she*—certainly destroys *that* theory, doesn't it—*she*?"

"Oh, yes." The man clapped his hands together. "We must go and see old Erasmus and tell him that at least one part of his theory is wrong."

The three humans retreated, laughing and discussing her at the tops of their lungs. Nightshade rolled her eyes and shook her head, hoping she would not have any more visitors.

CHAPTER 15

Sunstar barely endured the spectacle of Nightshade bound and dragged away by the guardsmen like a common criminal. She shifted and came within a whisker of tearing her arm free of the watchman's grip.

Her heart ached for Nightshade. She had seen the glowing blue eyes as the guards had approached her; she saw the gentleness and the promise of safety in them. She swore to herself that she would free Nightshade. She would find some way to get her out of the town prison.

Sunstar turned to look at the watchman. She opened her mouth to speak but he cut her off.

"Princess Sunstar," he said respectfully. "Your father sent word to us that you were missing and asked us to keep an eye out for you. Lord Edgar asked that you be brought to him if you ever showed up here."

Sunstar felt a shot of happiness flow through her. Her father had not given up. Her people were looking for her.

She nodded. "Thank you."

The watchman signaled for a guard. A very young human male, barely old enough to shave, wearing a bright, clean, new uniform came jogging up to them.

"Please escort Her Highness to His Lordship," the watchman said.

Sunstar opened her mouth to speak, but the young man gestured before she could say anything else.

"This way if you please, Your Highness," he said, bowing elegantly.

Sunstar did not get the chance to say another word as he whisked her through bright city streets, filled with jostling, aggressive humans gesturing and arguing with one another. The smells of the market place gave way to the scents of the city, unwashed bodies, smoke, sewer, wet stone, and mud. He took her into an expensive part of the city where all the homes seemed to be elaborate and well kept. The roads were clean and well maintained. They went down a cul-de-sac, dwarfed by one manor, and the guardsman nodded at it.

"His Lordship's residence," he said formally.

Sunstar nodded. She wanted her audience with Lord Edgar to finish so she could find Nightshade.

He led the way up to the front gate to another perfectly groomed pair of guards. They bowed and opened the gate, letting Sunstar and her escort through. The young guard led her all the way to the huge front door. It opened as though of its own accord. They went inside.

Sunstar blinked as she took in the exaggerated opulence of the entrance hall. It was filled with finely carved marble sculptures, freshly cut flowers, floor to ceiling columns, expensive flagstones, stained glass windows, and afternoon sunlight. She felt amazed and slightly disgusted at the waste.

A liveried servant unobtrusively took charge, dismissing the young guard.

"Your Highness," he said, bowing as he backed away.

The liveried servant watched him distastefully and waited for him to depart.

Once he was gone, the servant lost no time in ushering the bemused Sunstar into the main hall. A handsome, vain-looking young man leant against the fireplace, watching her closely as she approached.

"Welcome, Your Highness," he said in a deep, rich voice. His perfume wafted toward her.

She smiled, instantly disliking the pale, effeminate human. "You must be Lord Edgar. Peace be with you and your house."

"Your father sent word of your absence from your home." He smiled, revealing his large, straight white teeth. His black eyes glittered. "We must send word that you have arrived safely. You must stay with us until he arrives. Enough of that, you undoubtedly require refreshment. Please, meet me after you have done so, and we will have some dinner." He looked away, dismissing her.

Sunstar sighed inwardly. Another liveried servant materialized, seemingly out of nowhere. He bowed to her and gestured for her to follow him. He led her through the richly-furnished manor to her room.

She stared at it, wide eyed. It was huge, almost as large as the Elven throne room at home. Large windows from floor to ceiling were opened on one side, allowing the afternoon light to filter in; golden dust motes speckled in the sunshine. An enormous, unlit fireplace dominated the wall next to it. A large, ornately-framed picture of a barbaric, somber human hunting scene hung on the wall above the fireplace. The other walls bore pictures of long gone scenery surrounding a castle. Light fixtures unobtrusively nestled between them. The back wall was dominated by a huge, soft, clean four-poster bed, velvet rope to call a servant within easy reach of any sleeper. The closet was made of the finest rare timbers and encrusted with gilt. The servant saw the direction of her gaze and opened it. It was full of long, flowing feminine wear of the type that Sunstar never wore unless forced to for state occasions. A bathtub stood in the center of the floor on a soft, deep rug. It was full of steaming water, courtesy of a servant that Sunstar had not seen enter the room.

She immediately stripped out of her filthy clothes and settled into it with a sigh, relishing the comfort. More servants appeared to assist her, but she waved them away, unused to being waited on hand and foot. She sank back in the warmth of the water, worry about Nightshade gnawing away at her.

She was pleased her father was coming for her, of that there was no doubt, but they still had to hide until he came. They were not safe from the Drow. She had to get to the town prison and to Nightshade.

Nightshade.

She would not leave her friend in the hands of the humans or the Drow. Nightshade did not deserve it. Sunstar wanted to help her, but how? She could not break into the prison to free her. She could not fight the humans, and even if she could there were too many of them. The only thing left to her was her magic, but that was only for defense, never to harm another life.

A plan began to form in her mind.

She dimly noticed the water had gone cold and got out of the tub. The stubborn human servants assisted her, and before she knew what had happened she was fully dressed again. They placed a mirror in front of her, and she eyed herself in disgust. She wore a long, stiff evening gown, down to the floor. It was the most impractical item of clothing she had ever seen, ornate, cumbersome, and it pinched in all the wrong places. She was amazed it fit at all—the tallest human woman she had seen so far stood a good six inches shorter than her.

Her eyes widened as she noticed the long shadows on the floor.

She glanced out the window. The sun had almost gone down, and she desperately tried to stem the rising flood of panic.

She turned to the servants.

"Please take me to Lord Edgar," she said, urgency coloring her tone.

"Yes, Your Highness." A maid dipped into a low courtesy. She gestured for Sunstar to follow her.

Sunstar picked up her skirts, inwardly rolling her eyes, and followed the maid. The maid halted before a closed set of doors, waiting only just long enough for them to open.

The second Sunstar set foot in what seemed to be the dining hall, a herald stepped out of the shadows.

"Princess Sunstar of the Forest Elves," he said.

Sunstar stared at him as he stepped back.

A dozen guests, laughing and sipping their wine, sat in the dining hall around a table groaning with food.

"Ah, here is our guest of honor." Lord Edgar rose, the men following him.

Sunstar approached the table. *I'll be damned if I courtesy for this strange-smelling human. Thank the gods these humans know nothing of Elven manners or etiquette.* She graciously inclined her head.

"Lord Edgar," Sunstar said formally.

"Please take a seat. Enjoy my hospitality."

Sunstar allowed herself to be seated, fighting the urge to flee.

"So you're Princess Sunstar," a coiffed and elaborately-dressed woman sitting opposite her said. Her strong perfume floated across the table in great tidal waves, buffeting Sunstar's finely tuned senses. "Is it true you were captured by the Dark Elves?"

Sunstar did not want to talk about it and hated being referred to as Princess. "Yes," she said, hoping that a minimum of words would cause the woman to close her mouth.

"Were they as nasty as we have been led to believe?" she asked, persistent.

Sunstar could not suppress a shudder. "Yes." She felt a shot of resentment that her capture by the Drow was treated as a colorful story to be told around a dining table.

"And is it true that one of those horrible Drow brought you into the city?"

Sunstar thought about how to answer this, schooling herself in patience. "Nightshade rescued me, and you put her in prison."

"Now, now, dear." The woman's male companion patted the woman's hand. "It's quite clear the princess is exhausted."

"You needn't worry about that awful beast." Lord Edgar patted Sunstar's hand in a patronizing manner. "It's been put in the prison and will trouble you no more, and will be executed in due course, as it well deserves."

"Have you decided yet? Are we to have a hunt?" one of the men asked.

"No, that would be totally barbaric. We will hang it at dawn."

"Oh, Edgar. You can't do that. This is the first Drow we've found alive. How are we to learn more about its hunting and camouflage techniques if you have it swinging at the end of a rope?"

"Yes," another of the men broke in. "It would be great sport to hunt a Drow. A marvelous test of skill, even if I say so myself."

Lord Edgar paused, eyes calculating. "It's an animal, so why not?"

"A Drow hunt." Another of the ladies clapped her hands. "How wonderful."

"Splendid," the second man said. "I'll—"

"She's not an animal," Sunstar cut in with considerable ferocity. "She saved my life over and over, and will continue to do so."

The table stuttered to silence as all the guests turned to stare at her with varying degrees of pity and surprise.

"Now, then, my dear." Lord Edgar leaned over her. "It's just an animal. That's all. Nothing more and nothing less. I'm sure it was able to mimic rationality and compassion, a little like a well-trained monkey, but you mustn't make the mistake of ascribing the nobler virtues to a thing that has none. It doesn't even have the potential to be a good person. You mustn't pity it."

Sunstar felt sick. "She. Not it. *She*."

Lord Edgar stared at her, perplexed. "What has *she* done to you?" Realization dawned in his eyes. "It's *brainwashed* you, hasn't it?"

"No. She has taken care of me. She is my friend." She pushed her chair away from the table and placed her napkin on the table next to her untouched soup. "If you will excuse me, I am a little tired."

She remained seated and closed her eyes. The guests silently eyed her in shock. She could not draw on the forest for power but she sang anyway, almost desperately. The guests looked on spellbound, entranced by the beauty of her song. One by one, their eyes grew heavy, and they fell asleep. They slumped all around the table, and the unfortunate woman who spoke first fell head first into her soup with a solid thud. Sunstar gracefully rose to her feet and made her way around the table, stepping carefully over the fallen servants. She gently took the woman's face from the bowl of soup with a murmured apology. She walked through the manor, singing, and everyone she encountered fell into a deep sleep.

Nightshade sat in her prison cell, head bowed. She could see a reflection of her glowing blue eyes in the polish of the stone. Everything around her was as clear to her as though in full sunlight.

Sunlight, she thought with a small snort. *It's probably dark by now.*

She hoped Sunstar was safe, and that the humans could keep her safe until the Forest Elves arrived. There was no question in her mind that the Drow would find her. Sunstar's only hope for survival rested on her. She had to try and escape the prison and leave the city. She hoped it would be enough to get Hemlock's attention. She could lead the magician away from Sunstar and fight him on neutral ground.

She hesitated, knowing that there was one thing left undone, and that was to apologize to Sunstar for taking her to the Drow city, for almost leading her to her ruination. Nightshade *deserved* to be sitting in a prison. She *deserved* to die for some of the things she had done.

She felt another moment of sadness and regret. She wanted more than anything to make her peace with Sunstar, but it could not be. She could not take the time to find her. If she did, it would probably be ruination for them both. *But, if I don't tell her, how will she know I'm sorry? How will she know what she meant to me? If I don't try to make restitution, isn't that going to mean I'm no different to any other Drow that ever lived?*

She heard soft footsteps approaching her cell and did not look up. She was sure it would only be another one of the parade of ornate humans who had gone past during the afternoon. They seemed to love gawking at the first known Drow in captivity.

"Nightshade?" a soft, hesitant voice said. "We have to get out of here."

Nightshade looked up.

It was Sunstar.

Joy at seeing Sunstar flooded her dark heart. Every doubt that she had about Sunstar's apparent regard for her gave way under her shy smile.

She gave Sunstar a broad return smile. "Sunstar. I'm very glad to see you."

Sunstar fumbled the door to the cell open. Nightshade could only wonder how she got the keys. She stumbled in and launched herself into Nightshade's welcoming arms Nightshade sighed and held her close, stroking her hair.

Sunstar pulled back and looked deep into Nightshade's eyes. "Did they hurt you?"

"No," Nightshade said, "I'm fine. You're right—we have to get out of here. It's full dark, isn't it?"

"Yes," Sunstar said, dread coloring her voice. "What are we going to do?"

"Can you cast your glamour here?" Nightshade asked.

Sunstar shook her head. "I'm not close enough to the forest. I can put the humans to sleep but that's all."

Nightshade nodded. "All right. We have to get out of the city. Now. Hopefully Hemlock hasn't started his search for us yet."

Sunstar nodded. Nightshade stood up and took her by the hand. She led Sunstar out of the cell and up the corridor to the guard's chamber. Sunstar took the lead, and they went past the sleeping prison guards and out into the city streets. The stars glittered overhead in the early night sky. Sunstar kicked off her uncomfortable shoes.

"Can you run barefoot?" Nightshade looked down at her bare feet.

Sunstar shook her head. "Not on these cobblestones and not in this horrendous thing." She tugged her skirts and looked down at herself in disgust.

Nightshade snorted. "I have seen worse."

"Where?" Sunstar asked.

"I'll tell you later," Nightshade said. "I could carry you?"

"Then let's go. We have to hide."

Nightshade nodded and bent her knees. Sunstar leapt onto her back and clung to her without cutting off her wind. Nightshade took off through the empty city streets at a dead run. After a nightmarishly long time, they broke through the gates on the other side of the city and ran out into the forest. Sunstar slipped off her back, and they dove into the undergrowth. Nightshade gathered Sunstar close to her. Sunstar sang, casting her glamour, and they both fell deeply asleep.

A single bird fell dead from the sky at their motionless feet.

CHAPTER 16

Hemlock's Eye scoured the landscape as it had done in the past, using the animals and birds of the forest to search for *them*. He had no luck so far, and was merely searching from rote tonight, enjoying the pure freedom of wheeling in the night sky. He caught a flash out of the corner of his left eye and whirled to focus on it. A pillar of pure white flame burned in the night sky. He raced toward it as fast as the old, congealed blood of the sacrifice allowed him. He was close to it when it abruptly went out.

He looked down at the dark earth below. Nothing could hide from his keen eyes. A human city lay nestled amid the thick trees of a forest close to the Forest Elf lands. It was ugly and painfully bright to him. He knew where *they* were headed, as he had done all along. The only question had ever been the direction from which they were traveling. Now they were closer to Elven lands and much easier to find, thanks to the much smaller area he had to search.

He brought himself back to his body in the Drow city of Dragonar, intent on studying maps of the region.

He opened his eyes and brought himself upright from his kneeling position. He padded to his study, still wearing the leather jerkin, black blood cold and dry on his smooth skin. A servant materialized with a robe, and he absently threw the blood-stained jerkin aside and pulled the robe on. He went to his bookshelf and opened one of his many well-kept books. He leafed through it, back and forth, until he found the map he was looking for. He tapped a spot on it and nodded.

"Prepare my bath," he said to his servant. "Inform the king that I am on my way to see him." The servant bowed low and hurried off to do his master's bidding.

Hemlock cleaned himself up and pulled on fresh robes. He called for his servant, and the one who had allowed the king entrance without his permission answered the call. He smiled and drew his dagger across the servant's throat before he had time to scream. His other servant materialized to collect the fresh blood.

He barely noticed this as he gracefully left his chambers and strode through the palace to the throne room. He knocked and paused, waiting for the king to grant him permission to enter. He pushed the doors open and strode in as soon as it was given.

The king and queen sat on their thrones, still as stone. Their hands were tangled together, and they watched him closely from the second he entered the room.

"Your Majesties," he said, inclining his head.

The king's mouth tightened. If he were anyone other than Hemlock, he would have been executed for his perceived lack of respect to the Drow monarchs.

"What news do you have for us?" the king asked, excitement coloring his tone.

"I have found them," Hemlock said simply. "They are near to the human city of Bordertown."

"We must dispatch a guard to go and bring them back."

"There is only one small issue," Hemlock interjected smoothly. "The princess is using a glamour to mask them. I don't know why she didn't use it earlier tonight. We will have to use some of your scouts to find their exact location."

"You fool—" the queen hissed, but the king put up a hand to silence her.

"You may have Galvin and Farouk. You might also consider including Nightsbane. I believe he would like to speak to his daughter." The king's melodious voice was quiet, though his tone was excited.

Hemlock allowed himself a cold smile. "Thank you. Will you be joining us?"

"Yes. I will send for the others," the king said. "When can we be ready to leave?"

"I require one hour," Hemlock said. "If you will join me in my chambers, I will take you to the city, and we will track them from there."

"You have my permission to do so." The king nodded, stroking the queen's hand.

Hemlock said nothing, but this time graced them with a bow. He turned on his heel and left.

Guards and servants shrank back against the walls as he swept by on his way back to his chambers. As soon as he entered, he went into his meditation chamber. He sat on the floor of his magic circle, visualizing the forest surrounding the human city of the Bordertown. Teleportation was an exact spell and required knowledge of the target location to an intimate degree. He had first-hand knowledge of the area due to the influence of the Eye, and he felt confident that he could get them to the right place. After an hour he emerged from his meditation chamber and met the king, Farouk, Galvin, a fuming Nightsbane, and a half-dozen Drows in his study.

"Is it true you've found them?" Nightsbane asked. He was a very tall, handsome Drow with shining white hair and fierce, glowing red eyes.

"Yes." Hemlock, pinned him with a cold stare.

Nightsbane began to sweat and looked as though he deeply regretted having spoken to Hemlock.

Once Hemlock was satisfied Nightsbane would not speak again, he turned to the king. "Are you prepared?"

"Lead the way." The king's eyes lit up with excitement.

Hemlock nodded and led the silent Drow hunting party into his magical chamber. They all gawked as he chanted softly, and the air shimmered in front of them.

Hemlock raised a hand and slashed it through the eye-watering air. A cut appeared, and he put his hands through it and widened the gap. They could see thick forest through it, and the smell of clean forest air trickled into Hemlock's chambers.

The king was the first to step through, followed by Galvin, Farouk, and Nightsbane. The Drow guard went after, followed closely by Hemlock. Hemlock stopped chanting when he had stepped through and he sealed the cut with a slender forefinger. The air stopped shimmering.

"Where are they?" The king glanced around, his eyes glowing eerily.

"They are here," Hemlock said. "But they are under a glamour, and we won't be able to find them."

"Then why did you drag us all the way out here?" Nightsbane demanded, apparently forgetting his earlier fear of Hemlock.

"We will have to use more arcane means to find them." The king looked around in the night in disgust. "We will track them by night." He stared at Nightsbane. "Your daughter will be bringing the princess back to her people. I am going to kill her for it."

Nightsbane's eyes lit up at the prospect of Nightshade's death, and he smiled.

"See if you can find them," the king said to Galvin and Farouk. They nodded and bowed low. They inspected the trees with the guards. The others waited quietly in their clearing for their return.

The king, Nightsbane, and Hemlock sat quietly for most of the night, waiting patiently for the others to return. The scouts returned close to sunrise, looking weary. The guards followed them, looking equally exhausted. Galvin and Farouk bowed low before their monarch. They exchanged a glance, and Galvin gestured for Farouk to speak.

"We found tracks, but could not find them," Farouk said, cowering.

The king nodded, gaze distant and calculating. He laid a restraining hand on the furious Nightsbane's forearm.

"We will go to ground for the day, and resume tonight," the king said.

They all nodded at their liege and found places to hide in the rapidly approaching dawn.

Nightshade's eyes fluttered open, and she rolled over, expecting to see Sunstar still fast asleep. Sunstar's clear, green eyes were open and watching her carefully. Nightshade smiled slightly and sat up, Sunstar rising with her. She stared at Sunstar.

"That really is an ugly dress," she said without preamble. "Is it as uncomfortable as it looks?"

Sunstar opened and closed her mouth several times. "Good morning to you, too. I'd love to argue but I can't. I think that says it all." She shook her head and sighed. "You have no idea." She straightened the skirts and looked down at it in disgust. "It's heavy, stiff, and very itchy."

"Well, it looks like I will be adding theft of clothing to my myriad of misdeeds." Nightshade bit her lip. "You can't walk through the forest, looking like that."

"I'm glad you said that, but you don't have to steal anything for me. I'll do it myself," Sunstar said. "Humans have the worst dress sense."

Nightshade smiled and stretched, working the kinks out of her body. She stopped when she saw the dead bird perched near to where their feet had been. Her blood ran cold.

"Oh no," she moaned.

"What is it?" Sunstar asked, concerned.

"They found us." She pointed to the dead bird.

Sunstar stared at it. "I don't understand. Is that the result of the Eye?"

"Yes, it is. You must have cast the glamour too late." Nightshade knelt and carefully touched the bird. "Cold. They are around here somewhere, but they must have gone to ground. We are safe for the moment, but we have to get moving. Can you walk in that thing?"

Sunstar looked disgustedly at herself, encased in the awkward gown. "Not that I really have a choice," she muttered. "Yes, I think so," she said in a louder tone of voice.

Nightshade nodded. She looked down at Sunstar's bare feet. "What about your feet?"

"They're fine."

Nightshade nodded again. She gently took Sunstar's hand. She led the way deeper into the forest, and Sunstar covered their tracks.

"Look at that." Nightshade pulled them to a halt after half an hour or so. She pointed into the trees.

Sunstar followed the direction of her finger and smiled broadly.

There was a small hut in the trees with a rough barn next to it. A desultory washing line sagged in front of it. Nightshade silently jogged up to it and pulled off a clean, patched shirt, jerkin, and rough breeches. A pair of boots lay on the ground below the line and Nightshade shook her head.

She jogged back to Sunstar and helped her out of the dress.

"How did they get you into this?" Nightshade fumbled with the buttons on the back.

"I don't know," Sunstar said. "All I know is that it took a long time, and I felt ridiculous and uncomfortable afterwards." She twisted and glanced at Nightshade. "Can't you cut me out of it or something?"

"I'm not carrying a knife." Nightshade grunted and finally managed to open the buttons at the back. Sunstar gratefully stepped free of the dress and pulled on the clothes Nightshade had gotten for her with a soft sigh of pleasure. They were almost a perfect fit for her size.

Nightshade nodded. "Much better."

Sunstar glanced down at herself, smoothing the jerkin. She glared at the discarded dress. "What do you want to do with that thing?"

Nightshade grabbed it and jogged back to the washing line. She draped the dress over it.

"What was *that* meant to achieve?" Sunstar asked when Nightshade rejoined her. "That wasn't exactly a fair trade, was it?"

"Maybe they will have some use for it." Nightshade pulled her into motion. "Maybe it's valuable? Who knows? Humans are an odd species."

Sunstar nodded. "I know."

They walked for some time and then stopped briefly for breakfast.

They passed a troubling, dark patch of undergrowth, and Nightshade's senses came to full alert. She pulled Sunstar to a halt, eyeing the greenery all around them, searching for something. She did not know what it was. She felt it as almost an itch deep inside herself.

"What is it?" Sunstar watched her in alarm.

Nightshade held up a hand, and Sunstar froze. Nightshade listened carefully and looked all around for signs of trouble. She heard birdsong, the rustling of small animals in the undergrowth, and the gentle chirp of insects.

"Nothing," she finally said, pulling Sunstar into motion again. She shook her head and tried to shrug off the feeling of being watched. They continued walking.

Sunstar looked haunted, and her black mood spread to Nightshade. It felt as though there was a clock silently ticking all around them, counting down to the end.

"Nightshade," Sunstar said at last, pulling Nightshade to a halt.

Nightshade eyed her carefully. She looked pale and miserable.

"Why did you help me in the Drow city?"

Nightshade pulled her into motion again. She thought about how to answer that and then settled on the truth, trusting Sunstar. "I wanted to."

"Why did you want to?"

Nightshade was silent for a long time, thinking, but unable to find a way to voice what was going on inside her. "I couldn't let them do it." She paused. "When we encountered Farouk in the forest, I saw a young Elf held captive by them, alive, having done nothing but walk in the forest close to her home. She did not deserve the fate that was in store for her, what they were going to do to her."

Sunstar watched the pain float across her features.

"Why are you still helping me?" Sunstar asked. "You could have just left me. I know my way home from here. We are close to the borders of my land."

Nightshade tried again. The remembered terrified gaze of a child bored into her tainted soul. "We killed a small girl," she said, lost in the memory of the blood of a small child, splashed crimson around her slaughtered family's wagon. The words burned their way out of her, unstoppable. "I am sick of killing and death. I wanted to leave and be free. I wanted to learn what more there is to learn of this world. I don't want to hurt anyone anymore." She drew in a deep, hitching breath. "I promised to keep you safe and take you home. I *want* to stay with you until you are home. The Drow can do with me what they please when you are safe with your family." She looked deep into Sunstar's eyes. "I am so sorry I took you back to Dragonar. I should have freed you long before then."

Nightshade felt her tears well up, and Sunstar pulled her to a halt. She looked deep into Nightshade's eyes. Nightshade's self control disintegrated, and the trickle of tears became a flood. She collapsed to her knees, hands to her eyes, and sobbed—great, terrible, heart rending sobs of pure misery. Sunstar knelt next to her. Nightshade felt herself drawn into Sunstar's embrace, the gentle touch of her hand as she stroked Nightshade's hair.

"Nightshade," Sunstar said, when Nightshade's grief finally eased a little. "I don't hold you responsible for what happened to me. You, indeed, were the only one who never hurt me. You promised not to let them hurt me. For that I owe you my gratitude. But you have never stopped helping me, and have stayed with me regardless of the risks, to take me home. You're doing it simply because I asked you to. No other reason. For that alone, you have shown you are my friend. No matter what you have done in the past, you are different now, and I will stand by you for as long as you will allow me to, as a good friend should."

Nightshade looked up into Sunstar's eyes, shimmering through her tears, and saw nothing but acceptance there. "You have been a friend to me as well. I want to see you safe home, back in the arms of your family. But when you are safe with them, you have to let me go—I have to face them, or you will never be free."

"I don't want to," Sunstar said evenly. "I can't do that. I like you too much." She smiled.

Nightshade smiled despite herself. "I like you too. I ask only one thing of you. If they do kill me, please don't let them take my body back with them."

Sunstar stared at her, a question in her eyes, mingled with joy at Nightshade's shared regard. "It's probably best if I don't know, isn't it?" she murmured. She looked deep into Nightshade's glowing, sky blue eyes. "My promise to you is that if you fall," she flinched as she said it, "I will personally make sure that you are brought back with us, and you will be kept safe."

"Thank you." Nightshade pulled Sunstar in close again.

She felt as though a mighty weight had been pulled off her shoulders. She felt a simple joy at actually hearing she did not disgust and revolt Sunstar. Another tight band released itself from around her soul as she regretfully let Sunstar go and stood.

"We need to get moving," Nightshade said. "We have to try and outrun them."

Sunstar nodded, and they continued to walk, their fingers comfortably tangled together.

"How was it for you in the town prison?" Sunstar asked hesitantly.

Nightshade was quiet a moment. "It was about as I expected."

Sunstar waited a moment but Nightshade remained silent. "And what had you expected?"

"Do you really want to know?" Nightshade asked, glancing at her.

"If I didn't want to know I wouldn't have asked," Sunstar replied.

"You won't like the answer." Nightshade sighed. "It seems most of them had not seen a Drow before. They came to the prison to see me." She smiled without mirth. "They talked about me, assuming that I was too stupid to understand them. They weren't particularly kind."

Sunstar took a deep breath. "That explains your fragrance."

Nightshade glanced down at her stained cloak. "No. That was from my walk through the city. The humans had an apparently inexhaustible supply of rotten fruit and vegetables, I think."

Sunstar flinched, and Nightshade remembered their walk through the Drow city to the prison.

"Some things are the same between all the races, aren't they?" Sunstar said.

Nightshade nodded. "Although I must admit it's easier than trying to dodge daggers and throwing knives."

Sunstar paled, and Nightshade nodded at a narrow path through the trees to their right. "The river is down that way."

She led Sunstar between the trees down to the rushing water. Sunstar sat on the bank as Nightshade took off her boots and walked into the river, fully clothed.

"You really like the water, don't you?" Sunstar said.

Nightshade's clothes were sopping wet. She stripped them off and draped them over a convenient boulder. "Yes. I love it."

"Isn't there any running water like this in the Drow city?"

"No," Nightshade said. "The water is volcanic, so it's always warm, and it often smells like bad eggs. The volcanic water is fine to bathe in. Fresh drinking water is hard to come by. It's boiled." She dived under the water and came up, wiping the excess water off her face. "Do you want to come in with me?"

Sunstar grinned. "I'd never turn down an invitation like that." She quickly stripped off her clothes and dived into the water with Nightshade. They bathed for a while and then climbed out of the water. Nightshade surreptitiously glanced at Sunstar. A tide of nameless emotion flooded over her, a strong undercurrent of pure pleasure beneath it that Sunstar felt something good for her. She watched Sunstar as she got into her half-dry clothes and held out her hand. Sunstar accepted it with a smile and squeezed it gently.

A couple of hours later, Sunstar led Nightshade through the thick undergrowth. Nightshade stayed close to her, tears leaking out of her tightly-closed eyes. Sunstar stopped and gently pushed Nightshade back. Nightshade sighed in pleasure as she found herself sitting on a thick log.

"Sit and rest," Sunstar said softly. "I'm going to find us something to eat."

Nightshade heard her move away and waited until she heard Sunstar return. She allowed herself to relax, her tense muscles protesting mightily.

Nightshade cocked her head in Sunstar's direction when she got close to her.

"Here," Sunstar said, "hold out your hands."

Nightshade obediently held out her hands, and Sunstar filled them with berries. Nightshade brought one to her mouth and bit into it experimentally. She gave Sunstar a broad grin.

"This is wonderful."

Sunstar nodded. "I know," she said around a mouth full of berries. "It seemed like the quickest thing to get on short notice."

Nightshade smiled. She felt Sunstar shift around the side of her, and then a gentle tug on her cloak.

"What?" she asked.

"Surprise," Sunstar said.

"Another one?"

Sunstar snorted a soft laugh.

There was the sound of ripping cloth, and Sunstar shifted again. Nightshade felt the sensation of soft cloth around her eyes. Sunstar tied the blindfold and moved back a step as Nightshade felt the soft cloth.

"Thank you. That helps a lot," she said, blindly facing the heat she could feel from Sunstar's body.

"You're welcome." Sunstar gave Nightshade's shoulder a gentle squeeze.

Nightshade smiled and was silent for a moment. It felt good to be able to acknowledge the small kindnesses Sunstar always seemed to show her.

They were companionably silent for a moment, and Nightshade felt the pressure of a berry against her lips. She grinned and nipped it out of Sunstar's fingers. Sunstar took one with a soft sigh of pleasure, and then gave another to Nightshade. They continued that way until the berries were all gone.

"We really should get going again, you know," Sunstar said after a little while, regret coloring her tone.

Nightshade winced and nodded. "Yes. We really should keep moving." The good mood that had infused them vanished like a puff of smoke.

Sunstar quickly cleaned up and took Nightshade's arm. "Come. We have to move and the ground is rocky."

"Yes." Nightshade stayed close to her. "I had noticed. This is the most difficult part of our journey, I think."

"To your left . . . why, where are we?" Sunstar asked. "Easy . . . tree root, a high one . . ."

"We are beginning the ascent of the mountains that border your lands to the south of your city. It will take us three more days until we are actually on Elven lands."

"This way . . . is all of the traveling like this?" Sunstar pulled Nightshade in close to avoid a dip in the path.

"Well, it could either be simple or difficult. Human bandits roam these mountains, as do renegade clans of Dwarves. Although the Dwarves do tend to stay underground." She nodded at Sunstar. "How do you not know this? These are the borders to your lands."

"I was not exactly encouraged to leave the palace. I am the crown princess. I am too valuable to be allowed out of the city." Sunstar sounded stiff and awkward.

"And yet here you are." Nightshade gave her a wry smile. "May I ask you a question?"

"I think I can guess what it is," Sunstar said, sounding defensive. "You want to know how I found myself in Farouk's clutches, if I'm not allowed out, don't you?"

Nightshade nodded. "But understand this, before you tell me—these are *your* lands. *Your* home. You have a right to walk your own land without fear of capture or death."

Sunstar was silent for long moments. "Put very simply I was out having a picnic with my best friend, and we wandered further than we should have." Her voice cracked, and her breath hitched. "My friend paid for it with her life."

"You blame yourself for your friend's death?"

Sunstar remained silent for another long moment, and then spoke so softly Nightshade had to strain to hear her. "*I* insisted we go out. It was *my* suggestion we go all the way to the waterfall. *I* wanted to play one last game of hide and seek. It was *my* decision to run east instead of south . . ." Her voice gained in volume, fueled by self condemnation and anger. "You know what the worst thing is? All I can see in my mind is Meagan's mother, bending over a pot in the kitchen and holding out a wooden spoon for us to taste whatever it was she was making. How am I to face her, look her in the eye, and tell her that Meagan was dead, and it's because of me?"

"Sunstar?" Nightshade asked softly.

"Yes," Sunstar said. "Yes. It's *all my* fault. *All* of it. And you, too. You nearly got killed for me."

Nightshade stopped and lifted up her blindfold, blinking in the bright light. She pulled Sunstar into her arms and gently stroked her back. They sank to the ground as Sunstar's tears raged against Nightshade's shirt, pouring out of her along with the terrible grief for Meagan that she had not been able to give voice to. She gradually quieted and wiped her nose.

"I must seem like such a child to you," Sunstar said, humiliated and snuggled into Nightshade's lap. She studied the laces on Nightshade's shirt.

Nightshade gently lifted her chin with a forefinger and gazed deep into her eyes. "No, you don't. Never. Your eyes say you are no child. And whatever has happened between the two of us has been of my own free will. I got hurt because of something *I* did." She smiled. "I understand why you are so upset." She paused, and Sunstar visibly relaxed. "You are young, and crown princess or not, you have an obligation to your people to understand the world before you take up your crown. How can you expect to deliver fair judgments to your people, to be a good monarch, unless you understand more about how the world works?" She gave Sunstar a crooked grin. "Although I must admit capture by the Drow is not a method I would have recommended as a lesson."

Sunstar snorted a laugh. She turned serious again. "How am I going to face my father after this? What am I going to say to him and to Mother?"

"Do what I would have done with my mother. Apologize to them. My mother always told me that she loved me. My blood never mattered to her, only that I told her the truth."

"Your mother was a remarkable Elf, wasn't she?"

"To have survived as long as she did amongst the Drow? Oh, yes." Nightshade looked down at Sunstar. "We should go to ground." She looked around and shook her head. "I had hoped to make better time."

"I'm sorry." Sunstar looked around them, at the lengthening shadows. "This is earlier than usual, isn't it?"

Nightshade nodded. "But now they are out of Dragonar, so they will be keeping scouts' hours. They will rise at sunset and go to ground at dawn. We best be hidden during both of these times so we can avoid them."

"I'm frightened," Sunstar said softly. "I don't want to get caught by them again."

"Don't be frightened," Nightshade said. "I *will not* let them hurt you. I swear it on my mother's grave. If . . . *if* they find us it will be when you are in your father's arms and the entire Elven army is at his back."

"What about you?"

"Don't worry about me." Nightshade looked up at the crown of the trees above them. "There." She pointed upward. "That is where we will spend the night." She glanced at Sunstar. "Yes?"

Sunstar gaped at her. "I suppose so."

"It's best," Nightshade said. "They won't think to look for us up there. Can you climb?"

"Not as well as you can. I fainted in terror as you took me to Dragonar, remember?"

"Well then." Nightshade stood up and gently deposited Sunstar on the ground next to her. "Hold on."

Sunstar leapt onto Nightshade's back and hung on for all she was worth. Nightshade nimbly climbed the tree and found a comfortable cluster of branches. They seemed to form a nest at the top of the tree.

As soon as they were at the top, Nightshade wedged herself comfortably into the vee formed by the branches. Sunstar lay on her, holding her close. She glanced up into Nightshade's gently glowing blue eyes.

"Ready?" she asked.

"I'm ready," Nightshade said.

Sunstar nodded and sang. They were both asleep within seconds, and the air around them shimmered and they faded out of sight.

CHAPTER 17

Nightshade slowly opened her eyes the next morning and blinked uncertainly in the dawn light. She became aware of the feel of a warm body in her arms. She looked down at Sunstar. Sunstar's eyes fluttered open and lit up with pleasure as her lips curved into a smile. Nightshade could not help but smile back.

"Good morning." Sunstar stretched as best she was able.

"Good morning." Nightshade glanced down. "Are you ready to go down?"

Sunstar nodded. "I'm ready."

Nightshade shifted, and Sunstar climbed onto her back. She looked back at Sunstar with a half grin. Sunstar nodded.

Nightshade stepped off the branch and leapt toward a neighboring tree. She caught a branch, using her momentum to flip around it, and let go when she reached the bottom of her swing. They flew down, and Nightshade grabbed another branch. They did this for most of the way down.

Sunstar clung to her and sucked in a whistling breath. Nightshade braced herself, half expecting Sunstar to shriek in her ear, but it never came. Sunstar remained mercifully quiet as she tightened her arms around Nightshade in a death grip.

Nightshade thought she would have to pry Sunstar off her, but once they were safely on the ground Sunstar let go and released a shaky breath.

Sunstar stared at her. "Where did you learn to do that?"

"I was a scout. It paid to move quickly," she said.

Sunstar nodded. "I'm sure it did." She shook her head, bemused.

They continued their journey and ate their morning meal as they traveled.

The trees gradually thinned out, and the forest became a plain, dotted with stands of trees.

There were no signs of any civilization for miles. They were completely alone in the wilderness.

Nightshade looked up at the sky, and Sunstar followed her gaze.

"What are you looking for?" she asked. "Dragons?"

Nightshade suppressed a grin and nodded gravely.

The smile fell away from Sunstar's face. "You're joking, right?"

Nightshade shook her head.

"No." Sunstar's gaze turned skyward. She turned back to Nightshade, a glint in her eye. "Are you sure? I never heard anything about dragons living anywhere close to our forest."

Nightshade grinned.

"Oh, come on." Sunstar pulled her to a halt. "Dragons?"

"Of course. Dragons." Nightshade pulled her into motion.

"I don't look that naïve, do I?" Sunstar said plaintively. "Everyone knows dragons are extinct."

Nightshade laughed softly.

"I will pay you back for that, you realize?" Sunstar said. "When you least expect it."

Nightshade smiled. "Yes, Your Highness."

Sunstar's face darkened at the use of her title, and Nightshade grinned.

"Be at ease, young elfmaid," she said. "If you won't believe in a dragon, how about looking up at the blue sky before I lose sight of it for the day?"

"Oh." Sunstar's expression became serious.

Nightshade saw her change in mood. "I didn't mean to upset you," she said, blinking. Her eyes were beginning to hurt from the bright light of the day.

"You didn't upset me," Sunstar said. "It's just that . . . sometimes I forget . . . you're my friend."

Nightshade was not sure what to do with the unexpected surge of emotion that flowed over her. *I care for her, and it hurts me to think of her in pain of any sort. I wonder if this is normal?*

"And you are mine." Nightshade looked into Sunstar's eyes, seeking something but not knowing what. Sunstar returned her gaze, shifting slightly. Her arms twitched by her sides. Her shoulders slumped, and she broke their shared gaze.

Nightshade quickly rubbed her eyes. The emotion buffeting her increased in strength, and she felt an instant of deep pain. She suppressed a sigh.

Sunstar smiled. "Well." She cleared her throat. "It *is* bright out here. Your eyes must hurt you."

Nightshade nodded, her eyes tightly closed.

She felt Sunstar reach around her and tie the blindfold behind her head.

"There." Sunstar took Nightshade's arm. "Let's keep going."

"Thank you," Nightshade said.

They walked on in silence for a few more moments.

This nothingness is enough to drive anyone mad, Sunstar thought. *How much further is this going to go on for? We've been walking for hours.*

The wind rushed through the high grass surrounding them, in an eerie, haunting monotone that made Sunstar feel ill at ease. She felt the gentle pressure of Nightshade's hand carefully holding her arm, and glanced up at her. Nightshade's beautiful face—what Sunstar could see of it—was relaxed.

"What is it, Sunstar?" Nightshade glanced down at her.

How do you do that? "Nothing," Sunstar said.

Nightshade smiled.

"All right." Sunstar threw up her free hand. "This plain . . . it's just so . . ."

"Like a flat stretch of land?"

Sunstar's lips twitched as she suppressed a grin. "Yes. Like a flat stretch of land." She laughed and squeezed Nightshade's hand. The wind moaned through the grass. Sunstar shivered and glanced around. The terrain was almost entirely featureless. The only landmark they had to navigate by were the mountains ahead of them.

"Are you all right?" Nightshade asked, breaking her reverie.

Sunstar shook her head and then remembered that Nightshade could not see her. "How can you stand it?" she asked at last.

"Stand what?" Nightshade asked. The wind rushed steadily around them, and Nightshade seemed to scent the air.

All Sunstar could smell was the long grass. "This place? It's like it's cursed." *I don't know how to explain the way it feels.*

"It's just flat ground. There's nothing here. Or is that the problem?"

Sunstar thought about it for a moment. "I think 'nothing here' comes closest to it. When I am in the forest I can feel it. Even when in a human city, and I can still feel something. A connection with the land. But here, there's nothing. It's like I'm walking through a painting."

"You mean you can't feel the magic in the land?"

"Yes. That's exactly it." She shuddered. "It's terrible. Do you know why it feels like this?"

"No," Nightshade said. "Not really. My education was limited."

"What *do* you know of this place?"

"It is called the Plain of Carnath. This and the lower half of the mountain before us was once a great city. Something happened to it—I don't really know what—but the city was destroyed, and the earth soured. The humans never knew the magic in the land had been warped until the Elves refused to walk across it."

"Elves *refused* to walk across it?"

"Yes. Elves didn't care for the sensation, although your people now travel this plain to the human cities. That being said, if you do, you tend to go through this place almost at a run."

Sunstar shivered. *I wonder what you would have to do to drain most of the life out of the very land itself?* "That's an interesting legend. And you say your education was limited? It seems quite extensive to me."

Nightshade smiled beneath the blindfold. "I've always listened and learned what I could from the other races we met."

Sunstar flinched. *Before the Drow you were with killed them, you mean?* She studied Nightshade. *How would that be? To be part of a group that killed everything they were with, and you couldn't stop them?*

She felt the weight of Nightshade's gaze and saw the rigid set to her jaw. She caressed Nightshade's hand and felt some of the tension drain away.

"What was said about the plain?"

"Before the humans settled here, this was once forest but there was a battle between dragons. Blood was shed when dragons were slain and it soaked into the ground, killing everything. It took years but eventually something grew, even it was just grass. It eventually became rich farmland. The land slowly healed itself."

Sunstar nodded and felt her cheeks warm when she realized Nightshade could not see her.

Nightshade stopped walking.

Sunstar frowned. "What—?"

Nightshade shook her head, moved a step away from Sunstar, and turned in a slow circle.

Sunstar felt her heart rate pick up but held her silence.

"I hear something," Nightshade said at last.

Sunstar grimaced and resisted the urge to shrink into Nightshade. "Like what?" she asked, distantly pleased that she had only sounded a little tense.

"Moaning. Soft."

Sunstar listened closely, frowning. All she could hear was the wind rushing through the grass.

"There." Nightshade turned to their left. "That way."

"All right." Sunstar took Nightshade's hand, and they walked toward the sound. After a moment or so Sunstar heard what Nightshade had been listening to. It was a long, weak, drawn out moan of pain. Sunstar tried to focus on it.

"This way." Nightshade quickly took the lead and stumbled over the deceptively flat ground. She stopped, and Sunstar's eyes widened.

"What happened here?" she breathed, clutching Nightshade's arm.

"Why? What does it look like? I can smell ash," Nightshade said.

"That doesn't cover the half of it," Sunstar said. "We're standing on the edge of a large circle of scorched ground. The dead are everywhere but someone is alive." Her voice cracked as she pushed back a wave of sickness. "I can't . . . I don't . . ." Tears spilt out from under her closed eyes. She felt a tide of raw, nameless pain break over her. Nightshade encircled her arms around her in a gentle hug, the soothing scent of linen and spice of Nightshade herself washed over her, giving her an anchor against the bitter scorching.

"Let's see if we can find the one who lives," Nightshade murmured. "You don't have to come with me. I can do it."

"I *want* to come with you." Sunstar fought the urge to wrap herself around Nightshade as tightly as she could.

"Let's go, then. If you can't, that's all right."

Sunstar nodded against her.

Nightshade took a step back, grasped Sunstar's hand, and led her into the desolation before them.

Sunstar stayed close to Nightshade so they were touching. She moved as silently as she could and scanned the burnt ground.

Oh Gods, she thought, faltering to a halt. *That's not burnt wood on the ground it's charred bodies.* She fought down her gorge.

"What is it, Sunstar?" Nightshade asked. "Do the fallen trouble you? Would you prefer to wait for me?"

"You *knew* there were bodies, and you didn't tell me?"

Nightshade nodded. "I knew."

"Why didn't you mention that to me?"

"I knew it would bother you. I didn't expect you to come with me."

Sunstar bit her lip. "Why wouldn't I go with you?"

"Into all this death? I thought it would bother you too much."

Sunstar shook her head. "No, Nightshade. Where you go, I go."

"The places I go to would not be good for you," Nightshade said.

"At least I know you'd come back to me if I went there with you." The words slipped out before Sunstar could stop them, and she cringed, expecting an unfavorable reaction.

Nightshade nodded, and a small smile played about her lips. She cupped Sunstar's face. "I will be where you are, Princess. I won't let anyone harm you if it's in my power to prevent it."

Sunstar almost sagged in relief.

The spell was broken as a low moan traveled around them on the wind, louder now that they were closer to it. Nightshade zeroed in on it and moved swiftly to a blackened figure lying under the charred ruins of a tree.

Sunstar hissed in shock and winced. Lying on the ground was a blackened little figure. Its face was a ruined landscape of boiled flesh; its fingers were gone and its blood slowly soaked into the ground.

Nightshade bent over it.

"Ah," the figure grunted in a cracked and boiled voice. "Who—?"

"My name is Sunstar," Sunstar said. "My friend is Nightshade. Can you speak?"

The figure moaned incoherently and tried to clutch at her. The scent of cooked flesh was sickening, and Sunstar struggled to keep her stomach contents.

Nightshade settled herself in the ash and reached for the small figure. It moaned in pain as she pulled it into her arms. Sunstar put a trembling hand on the dying figure's burnt forehead. Her vision blurred as her tears came.

"It won't be long," Nightshade said softly. "He is in his final moments." She turned her blindfolded eyes toward Sunstar and pushed up the covering and blinked in the sunlight.

Sunstar sniffed and nodded.

Nightshade held the little figure close, and he began to convulse. He finally gave a sharp cry of pain and stiffened, then slowly relaxed as death took him.

Nightshade put him gently onto the ground, leant over him, and whispered a few words in a language Sunstar did not recognize.

"What did you just say?" she asked, her voice wavering.

"I told him to go to his ancestors and be one with the land." She looked down at him. "He's a gnome."

Sunstar nodded. Waves of sadness washed over her. "Do you have any idea what might have happened here?"

Nightshade glanced at her and climbed to her feet. She held out a hand for Sunstar. Sunstar took it and found herself tangled in Nightshade's embrace.

"Do you know what happened here?" Sunstar asked.

"I can guess," Nightshade said. "I think they ran into a Drow scouting party."

Sunstar stiffened as burning shock flooded her system, followed by a wave of terror that robbed her of speech.

Nightshade's grip tightened. "Easy, Sunstar. They are long gone, and I'm not sure they know to look for us. We are too far from Dragonar for them to know we escaped, and it is by no means certain that anyone will have bothered to tell them."

Sunstar shivered and nodded, feeling a deep-seated unease that refused to die down.

"Let's leave here," Nightshade said. "We have to go."

"Shouldn't we take care of the dead?" Sunstar asked.

"Gnomes burn their dead in funeral pyres on occasion," Nightshade said. "That seems completely inappropriate considering the circumstances." She looked down at the small body. "The other option is to leave him here out in the open. That is also a gnomish custom."

Sunstar nodded. "We sing our dead into the land." She glanced at Nightshade. "How long do you think it will take us to reach the mountains?"

"Some time tomorrow," Nightshade said. "Why?"

"I can't feel the land," Sunstar said. "It means my magic won't work. I can't cast the glamour to hide us." A wave of terror broke over her, and she felt her hands tremble.

"It also means Hemlock's magic is impaired." Nightshade took her hands and caressed them. "No matter what, I won't let them hurt you. My promise to you—never forget it. I won't."

Sunstar tried to smile. "I always remember it but I worry about you facing down the Drow army."

"It hasn't come to that yet," Nightshade said. "And you don't know that it will."

Sunstar shivered and caved in to her urge to run. "Let's go. I can't stand this."

Nightshade nodded. She took Sunstar's hand and led her from the burnt ground. They walked toward the mountains.

"Is Hemlock going to find us out here?" Sunstar asked after a few moments.

"No. As you've noticed, there are no animals here. He can't use them so he must use more arcane means to find us. We will be safe if we go to ground."

"I don't know that I want to do that," Sunstar muttered.

"You have to rest," Nightshade said with gentle reproach.

The day was fast fading, and they cast long shadows. Sunstar glanced around them at the golden grass, caressed by the steady, moaning wind, almost a death rattle across the land. "I know. But I want to keep walking for a while."

Nightshade nodded. "All right. Are you hungry?"

Sunstar shook her head, and Nightshade nodded.

Sunstar's mind turned to the burnt gnome. She felt another oppressive wave flow over her.

"You're thinking of the gnomes," Nightshade said.

Sunstar nodded. "I can't help it. Do you know what happened to them?" *I really don't want to know but I can't let it go. What's the matter with me?*

"I think it was Drow cruelty," Nightshade said.

"Why would they do that?" Sunstar glanced at her.

Nightshade flinched. "Racism runs strong amongst the Drow. I'm sure they just did it for sport." She shuddered.

"Nightshade?" Sunstar shook her head. "Never mind."

Nightshade's jaw tensed. "You want to know how I know, don't you?"

Sunstar nodded unwillingly.

"I have seen it with my own eyes," Nightshade said.

"Oh," *What happened to them? What happened to Nightshade?* Sunstar drew in breath to speak again, and Nightshade pulled her to a halt.

Nightshade gently turned her so they were gazing into each other's eyes. "Why do you want to know?"

"It hurts," Sunstar said.

Nightshade stared at her for a moment. Fear lurked in her glowing, blue eyes. "I know it does." She regarded Sunstar steadily for a moment. "One night my scouting party was on this very plain, I don't know where. We came upon a campsite full of gnomes. I was ordered to kill the sentries but I made sure they heard me coming." She shook her head. "It didn't matter. The leader was behind me, and she killed them. She beat me senseless and left me unconscious. When I woke up, the party was ahead of me, and the campsite was in the middle of a fire. The gnomes were screaming and running . . . on fire . . . they were screaming . . ." Nightshade blinked away tears. "I couldn't help them. They were dead. All I could do was use my sword as they came out of the flames . . ."

Sunstar felt sick. She took a step toward Nightshade, and Nightshade flinched back, self loathing flickering in her eyes.

"Do you still think I'm your savior? I'm little more than an animal." Nightshade turned away from her.

Sunstar grabbed her shirt and pulled her in close. "You did what you had to do to survive, didn't you? You think I don't know that? You're wrong. The first time I laid eyes on you I could *see* you were different. Then you showed me with every word and touch that you *were* different to those you traveled with. What I could never understand was why you were with them." Her gaze bored into Nightshade and memories of their trip to Dragonar tumbled through her mind. "You're so different to *them*."

"You're different to *everyone*." Nightshade blinked away tears and terrible sadness. "You're the only one I've ever met who sees me, and is not revolted by me." She took a deep breath. "You really want to know why I stayed with the Drow?"

Sunstar nodded. "You don't belong with them."

"I don't belong with anyone, and that was why I did it. I was trained to be a Drow scout, and I was forced to do the things they did. They never accepted me, and thanks to what I did while with them, no one else can accept me either." She looked into Sunstar's eyes, her glowing blue eyes sadder than ever. “I was always afraid of being alone if I left. But now I know there are far worse things than being alone.”

“I am *not* here to judge you.” Sunstar pulled Nightshade into her arms and gave her comfort and strength as Nightshade had given to her so many times in the past. “You’re my *friend.*”

“And you are mine,” Nightshade whispered, sinking into her embrace.

Sunstar held her until the stars climbed into the sky. It felt good to hold her. Nightshade meant so much to her it terrified her to think of what would happen when they reached her father’s lands.

“We should really go,” Nightshade whispered.

Sunstar suddenly felt exhausted, the most tired she had ever felt in her life. “Can’t we just stay here?”

“If you want,” Nightshade said. “Hemlock can’t use his magic to find us.”

Sunstar sank to the ground, pulling Nightshade with her. “I don’t want to move,” she murmured.

In the final moment before sleep claimed her, she heard Nightshade’s soft reply. “Neither do I.”

Sunstar smiled and drifted off. Mercifully, there were no dreams.

CHAPTER 18

Nightshade was still asleep in Sunstar's arms when Sunstar woke up the next morning. She felt a surge of emotion that she was afraid to identify and gently pushed Nightshade's black hair back off her forehead.

Nightshade had told her a horrible thing the previous day, and she felt terrible sadness for Nightshade. *How did you survive with them for so long? I hope you want to come with me. I don't want you to be alone. I want you to stay with me and never leave. I care* for *you and* about *you.*

"Good morning." Nightshade opened her eyes, shifted, and stretched.

Every time you move away from me it hurts. "Good morning."

"Are you hungry?" Nightshade asked.

"Yes." Sunstar looked around. "Finding food doesn't look good, does it?"

"We're close to the river," Nightshade said. "I can catch some fish, and we can have a good breakfast. Assuming you really don't mind eating fish."

"My ideas about what I can and can't do have shifted over the past few days. I would love fish." Sunstar stared at her. "How do you know we're by a river?"

"I can smell it." Nightshade stood. She held out her hand and levered Sunstar up. "This way."

She led the way through the now waist-high grass. Suddenly they were by a river Sunstar was amazed she had missed.

She gathered together grasses and some desultory twigs she found into a rough fire. Nightshade waded out into the water, watching the slow moving current with studied concentration. She plunged into the water and pulled out a large fish.

Sunstar quickly turned her back and a moment or so later a dripping Nightshade squatted beside her and put the now dead fish onto the crude grill Sunstar had constructed.

Soon they were sitting on the bank of the river, feasting on fish.

"This is good," Nightshade said.

"Meagan's mother was a good cook. She made sure I knew something even if I never went near a kitchen my entire life."

"She taught you well. What was your favorite food?"

"She used to make a stew from vegetables." Sunstar smiled, caught in memory. Once again, she was a tiny elfmaid, running through the palace, giggling at the shouts from the guards as she ran by, Meagan calling from behind her to *wait, just wait, I can't run as fast as you, Sunstar.*

A wave of sadness swept over her.

A warm hand closed over hers, and she glanced up, blinking away tears. Nightshade drew her to her feet and pulled her in close. She led her around the embers of the fire, following the steps of a dance that was eerily known to Sunstar, with odd differences that took away some familiarity.

She looked deep into Nightshade's mesmerizing eyes. *I don't think I've ever seen her eyes this close before. They are the most beautiful sky blue I've ever seen. I only see strength and truth in them.*

"Every year there is a celebration in the city of Dragonar. It was the only one I ever went to, although for the past few years I haven't gone. It was a wonderful time for a child. Sweets, Elven stew, fine mead, and wine from the upper and lower worlds." She smiled. "I always loved to dance."

"And you are very good at it." Sunstar moved closer to Nightshade and slowed down the tempo a little. "We have feast days as well. I have a reason to love dancing."

"I imagine you do." A small smile played about Nightshade's lips. "It's time to build new memories, isn't it?"

"I already have," Sunstar said. "Some very good ones."

"So have I," Nightshade said, and the dance slowly ended. "Not all of my life has been bad."

"One day you and I are going to sit down together and talk. Really talk. You're going to tell me your life story." *I want to know everything about you.* I have *to know everything. I can't stop it. I don't want to.*

"I'm not sure how much of it you really want to know," Nightshade said.

"We'll decide as we walk." Sunstar regretfully released Nightshade and stepped back. She felt better now than she had moments before. *All it takes is one word from her, and everything gets better.*

Nightshade nodded, poured water on the hot ash, and buried the coals. Sunstar watched her for a moment, and then gathered together the remains of the fish for their midday meal.

"Are you ready?" she asked when she had finished. She looked at Nightshade to see her frozen and staring, wide eyed, at some point over her shoulder.

"Whatever's the matter?" Sunstar asked.

Nightshade took her arm, pulled her close, and turned her.

"Oh." Sunstar stared, shocked.

A small figure stood before the gently waving grass. It was transparent and watching them closely. It was of a species unfamiliar to Sunstar.

"It's a gnome," Nightshade said. "I think it's the gnome we were with yesterday."

A series of small figures slowly appeared to both sides of him, a group of spirits watching them carefully.

Spirits were not normally a source of concern, Sunstar reflected. They were as natural a part of living as death itself was. No, that was not it. It was actually the almost solid specter of a gigantic, onyx dragon with fierce, ruby red eyes, watching them closely that was causing them both some discomfort.

"Nightshade." Sunstar tugged at her sleeve. "It can't hurt us. It's a spirit."

Nightshade shook her head. "Not really. It's talking to me. They all are."

"What are they saying?" Sunstar asked.

The dragon's tail encircled the group, and the end flicked as it studied Nightshade with alien, unknowable eyes.

"No." Nightshade watched the dragon as closely as it watched her. "I am Nightshade. I am no Drow. I bring the Forest Elf back to her people."

The little figure of the gnome looked up at the dragon and spoke. His lips moved in eerie silence, and he gestured toward them.

Suddenly Sunstar yelped in pain as the sensation of a gigantic, powerful wave swept over her mind. It held her down, clawing through her memories almost as though it could not tell its own strength. She collapsed, and Nightshade caught her. She moaned at the terrible sensation of a staring eye in the center of her mind. It leafed through her memories like pages in a book. It finally withdrew after terrible seconds that felt like hours. She could not control her scream as it withdrew, the sensation like the slow withdrawal of a pole impaling her.

"Sunstar, are you all right?" Nightshade lowered her to the ground.

Sunstar felt wrung out, violated. She sat up with Nightshade's help.

"What did you do that for?" she asked when she could speak. "If you had asked I would happily have told you everything."

My apologies, little princess, the voice of the dragon boomed in her mind. *We are the guardians of this place. We are the dead. Our penance for our sins is to bring the spirits of the dead to their afterlife. We are permitted to extract retribution if lives are taken by force in this place.*

"We did nothing," Sunstar said.

You are innocent. I have seen into your heart, Sunstar, and yours, Nightshade. I will protect you as I protect all the others that enter my domain. I will watch over you until you reach the mountains, the dragon said. It nodded toward the gnomes, who bowed in return. *The Drow that did this will not live to see the other side of the plain. Farewell, Elves.*

With that, the dragon gave a mighty trumpet, causing both Sunstar and Nightshade to clutch their heads against the furious onslaught of the dragon's mental energy. It launched itself into the air, carrying the spirits of the gnomes. They wavered and disappeared after a few seconds.

"That's why Carnath has no magic," Sunstar said with a grimace.

"How?" Nightshade winced in pain.

"The dragons are using it all to keep watch over their land."

"What did it do to you?" Nightshade helped Sunstar to stand.

"It read my mind," she said. "It saw we had nothing to do with what happened and left us alone."

Nightshade nodded. "Thank the gods. I wouldn't even know how to run from a spirit dragon."

Sunstar nodded, and they continued across the plain. She stole a glance at Nightshade. *It read your heart, Nightshade. It was the first but it won't be the last. Not everyone thinks you're a bad thing.*

"You said we're what? About two days? From home, now?" Sunstar breathed deeply and looked at Nightshade.

They had been walking for an hour, eating the last of the fish as they moved. Nightshade, haunted by memories of the gnomes, wanted to be away from the Plain of Carnath. The terrain had finally become rocky, and they turned down toward the river, a solid line of trees to their left and the river to their right.

Nightshade stopped, sat on a rock, and patted it. Sunstar sat down beside her. "Yes. We should reach the top of the mountain the day after tomorrow. That's already your territory."

"Will you come all the way with me?" Sunstar held her breath. She looked as though she were bracing herself for something unpleasant.

"To your city?" Nightshade asked.

"All the way." Sunstar blushed. She looked into Nightshade's eyes. "What will you do after this?"

"I have no home," Nightshade said sadly. "And other races do not exactly think good things when they see me. I make my own way in the world now."

"You didn't answer my question," Sunstar said. "What will you do after this?"

Nightshade sighed and gazed at Sunstar. "I don't know. I don't know."

"You know," Sunstar said, "there's a place for you with me, if you want it. You're an Elf. You've done so much for me. Even a blind Elf could see you are good—"

"Enough, young princess." Nightshade put a gentle finger against Sunstar's lips. "I would love to come with you. I would like to know more about my mother's people."

Sunstar's smile lit up her face. "Wonderful!"

"Now there's just the small matter of the Drow to overcome," Nightshade said. "I must face them, or neither of us will be safe or free."

"I know," Sunstar said. "I know. I haven't forgotten about them. I can't."

Nightshade nodded. "One thing at a time. First we must cross into your father's lands."

"I know. We'd better keep walking." Sunstar got up and held out her hand for Nightshade.

Nightshade slipped into the lead ahead of Sunstar. She felt as though she was dreaming. She could barely believe the offer Sunstar had made to her, to go with her and live with the Elves. She felt hammered from all sides by a barrage of emotions she could barely process. The clearest of these was hope. There was something for her after Sunstar's return to her people.

For the first time since she had left the Drow, she felt as though she had a purpose beyond her current mission.

She knew that Sunstar's people would not accept her as easily as Sunstar had, but perhaps she could build a home in the Elven forest. A place she would not be hunted down as a criminal.

And then there was Sunstar. She would also have a friend to talk to on occasion.

Nightshade could not believe her good fortune.

She took them closer to the river, and the light gradually became blinding. She stopped and carefully felt for a rock to sit on.

She felt Sunstar approach and lean forward. A soft cloth covered her eyes, and a knot was tied at the back of her head. She reached up and touched the blindfold.

"What's this for?" she asked.

"I see smoke a way ahead through the trees," Sunstar said. "This is the best way to go through without any questions."

"What happens when the light dims enough for me to see?" A tiny alarm sounded in the back of Nightshade's mind, and she turned it down as much as she could. Her other senses were keen enough to make up for any shortcoming in her vision.

"We should be well away from them by the time that happens," Sunstar said. "Are you ready?"

Nightshade took her hand. "Yes, I am."

Sunstar took them up the rough path beside the winding river. The upward slope continued on for an hour or so, and then evened out into flatter land.

Nightshade heard the whoosh of foliage against their breeches and guessed they were walking through thigh-high grass.

"What can you see ahead?" Nightshade leaned forward. "Can you see ruins in the grass?"

"How did you know we were in grass?" Sunstar asked.

"I can hear it. Ruins?"

Sunstar was silent for a few seconds. "Yes," she said, sounding a little uncertain. "I think there are ruins ahead."

"Good," Nightshade said. "That's good."

"Only partly," Sunstar said.

"Why?" Nightshade frowned and scented the air as Sunstar pulled her in close.

"Sorry, rock," Sunstar murmured.

"I smell smoke. And cooking meat." Nightshade turned her head toward Sunstar. "We're coming up to a party of humans, aren't we?"

Sunstar sighed. "Yes, I'm afraid so."

Nightshade squeezed her hand. "The plan has not changed. We will go through them, and if they insist on us staying with them, we will do so."

"How are we going to explain the glamour?" Sunstar asked.

"If we are lucky we won't have to cast it," Nightshade said.

"Why?"

"If I'm right, these are the Palindor ruins. It's a place of powerful magic. Hemlock's Eye will not be able to penetrate it."

"Palindor? Why does that name seem familiar?" Sunstar asked.

Nightshade smiled. "It is a human legend. This was once the seat of the city of Palindor, and this was the castle of the king. He was wed to a beautiful human woman. An evil knight was a champion of the land and coveted the queen, thinking to make her his own. He wooed the queen, without the knowledge of the king. She spurned his advances, and he became steadily more insistent until she finally told her husband of the knight's betrayal of his oaths. There was a terrible battle and the evil knight was slain, but not before he killed the king. The queen, so distressed at losing her beloved husband, cast herself from the battlements, killing herself and their unborn child on the rocks below. Now their spirits are said to haunt this blood-soaked earth until time ceases."

"That's a highly unpleasant story," Sunstar said. "If this place is soaked in evil magic, wouldn't Hemlock's Eye have an affinity for it?"

"No, it's not *dark* magic, it's *death* magic. A curse soaked in the blood of a sacrifice. It's neutral. Animals tend to avoid this place because of that, so he won't see us. As for me . . . well, my essence will be hidden by the swirling magic in these ruins."

"All right." Sunstar sounded uncertain. "As long as you're sure."

Nightshade heard rustling in the grass on both sides of them and from behind them. She caught an animal scent in the mild breeze. The grass moved back and forth.

"I'm as sure as I can be," Nightshade said. "We are surrounded, by the way. There are humans to our right and left, and someone is coming up behind us."

Sunstar gasped, and Nightshade squeezed her hand. "Never forget my promise to you, Princess."

Sunstar drew in close to her. Nightshade felt her nod.

"Show yourself!" Nightshade pulled Sunstar to a halt.

She felt Sunstar draw in as close as she dared while still giving Nightshade room to move. She heard the tramp of boots through the grass and on the dirt path behind them.

"Well met," Sunstar said. "We mean you no harm."

"That's still to be seen," said a deep, gravelly, male human voice. "Who are you, and why are you sneaking up on us?"

"We are walking down a path," Sunstar said coolly. "That hardly counts as sneaking."

Nightshade heard the creak of leather as the one behind them shifted. It was followed by the soft hiss of a long-bladed dagger being drawn.

"We are headed back to Elven lands," Nightshade broke in. "We are just passing through. We mean you no harm." She held out her open hands.

"You are unarmed?" a younger male voice asked to their left.

Nightshade nodded. "We are Elves. We do not often arm ourselves, and then not without good reason."

"Can you not see the dark haired one is blind?" The first man snorted a laugh. "They are no threat to us." Nightshade heard him shift. "Come. Share a meal with us."

Sunstar drew in breath to speak, but Nightshade quickly cut her off. "Of course. But then we must leave. Our king is expecting us back."

"Of course," the older man said smoothly. "Follow me."

He turned and headed back to camp. Sunstar pulled in close to her, squeezing her hand convulsively. Nightshade wondered why she was so upset and cursed her lack of vision.

They went into the human camp, and Nightshade concentrated hard. She could detect five other men at the camp, besides the three that had tried to trap them. She smelt clean leather and oiled weapons.

The scent was mixed in with roasting meat and burning wood from the fire.

She frowned. She could hear what sounded like soft sobbing beneath it all. She sniffed the air carefully. No. It smelt too strongly of human and roasting boar. She would have to rely on her other senses.

She felt the sweat from Sunstar's palm and frowned. They moved away from the fire, and Nightshade suddenly lost her balance. She fell forward, discretely pushing up the edges of her blindfold as she did so.

The sun had passed its zenith and was going down again. Her vision was returning, and she blinked.

"Are you all right?" Sunstar helped her to sit down on the hard ground.

"I'm fine," Nightshade replied.

She and Sunstar leaned against a broken wall on weed-encrusted, cracked flagstones. Human men milled all around them, cleaning weapons and leather armor. It had all the markings of a bandit's camp. Horses were tethered nearby, and she could see two or three links of a chain on the wall beside them. They moved slightly, and Nightshade caught another whisper of a sob.

"I would offer you boar but I know you don't like animal meat," the middle-aged man said. "The best I can offer you is bread and cheese. Both are fresh."

Nightshade caught a glimpse of him. He was as tall as Sunstar and as thick as a tree trunk, all solid muscle.

"Thank you," Sunstar said. "That would be perfect."

Nightshade heard the rustle of figures moving around the camp, and the heat from a body as it knelt beside them. "Here," a man's voice said, gently handing her a plate. It had two thick slices of bread and an equally thick slice of creamy cheese.

"Thank you." Nightshade ate quickly, aware of Sunstar doing the same beside her.

Leather creaked. "So, friend," the first man said. "Why are two Elves wandering around in the wilderness?"

"We were visiting some human friends in Bordertown," Nightshade said smoothly. "How do a group of humans come to be so close to Elven lands?"

He was silent for a long time. All sound in the camp had ceased, and then she heard a brief, soft sound made by leather as the man shifted. "Visiting friends living close to Elven lands."

"It's a small world, isn't it?" Nightshade asked with a smile.

"Yes it is," the man replied.

"How is the traveling through the mountains?" Nightshade asked.

"Difficult," the man said. "There are many Goblin and Drow about."

"Goblin and Drow?"

"Oh, yes. The Elves have lost a princess, you see."

"Indeed."

"Captured by the Drow, so it is said."

"Ah." Nightshade nodded wisely.

"Who knows? They may have lost their captive."

"I see."

"And if they did, I'm sure the Drow simply want her back."

"Of course."

"But enough sour news for one evening. Let us celebrate new friendships."

Nightshade leaned back against the wall. Sunstar stayed with her, their shoulders gently touching. Nightshade could feel the tension almost thrumming through Sunstar's body.

"Come," the human man said. "Drink."

Nightshade felt a jug thrust into her hands. Her senses went on full alert.

"Why are we celebrating?" she asked as she pulled the stopper from the jug.

"We are out in the open and we are free," the human man said. "Who cares? Every night is a celebration. Drink."

"Indeed." Nightshade tilted the jug toward her open mouth. She poured the alcohol into her mouth and felt the fire in it. She allowed it to run out of her mouth and down the front of her shirt. She did not swallow any. She felt Sunstar shift beside her, and could imagine the strange look she was getting.

"Ah, ha!" the human roared. "That's the spirit."

He pulled the jug out of her hands and drank noisily.

Nightshade heard the soft rustle of chains and a sob. She focused on it and tried to determine what was making the strange noise.

"Do you hear that or are you too drunk?" Sunstar sounded a little sour.

"I'm not drunk at all," Nightshade said. "Yes, I heard."

"I think it's coming from behind the wall," Sunstar said.

"I thought so," Nightshade said. "It's dusk now, isn't it? I can't take this blindfold off or they will know I am no Elf."

"You *are* an Elf, Nightshade," Sunstar said. "A full-blooded one at that. We may not appreciate it, but Drow are Elves as are we. We are kin."

Nightshade hoped Sunstar's parents felt the same way. "Thank you."

"Come, blind Elf," the man ordered. "Drink. Drink."

The human handed her the jug, and she pretended to swallow deeply again. She handed it back to him, making a show of wiping her mouth.

The humans roared and whistled.

"Very impressive, Elf," one of the men said. "More."

The jug made its way around the circle again and the catcalls and cries of enjoyment grew steadily louder as the level in the jug dropped.

Nightshade was soaked in alcohol she had not drunk, and a little disgusted by the strong fumes. Sunstar sat rigidly beside her. The humans seemed to have left her out of their drinking game, and Nightshade wondered why.

"Are you sure you're not drinking their swill?" Sunstar whispered.

"I'm sure," Nightshade said. "They're all getting very drunk, aren't they?"

She felt Sunstar nod.

"Now it's time for the entertainment," the human slurred. "Go and get it."

Nightshade stiffened and longed to take the covering off her eyes. She heard the sound of bodies dragged up off the ground and stumbling over to the wall next to them. She heard a metallic, sliding scrape and a loud sob of terror. Sunstar gasped beside her.

"Nightshade," Sunstar said softly, before Nightshade could ask. "They have a little Goblin. He looks like a child."

Nightshade's mouth tightened as the sobs from the little Goblin became louder.

"No," he said in Drow. "No."

Nightshade turned so her blindfold was facing him.

"What did he say?" Sunstar asked.

"Who cares?" the human man cut in airily. "It's just an animal."

"No. Scared," the Goblin sobbed.

"Let's use him for target practice again," one of the other men exclaimed. "Same rules as before. If you miss him you take a drink. If you hit him you take two drinks."

"Sounds good," the first drunk man said. "Here, balance this on his head between his ears."

The Goblin began to cry, and Nightshade felt her gut twist.

"I want to go first," she said.

"Why not?" the human asked.

Nightshade felt for his hand and allowed him to lever her to her feet. He put his hands on her shoulders and pointed her forward. It took every ounce of her self control not to punch him as hard as she could. She felt him thrust a rock into her hand and made a show of swaying on her feet.

"Where is he?" she asked.

"No. Scared. No hurt," the Goblin wailed, sobbing piteously.

"Quiet. How am I supposed to aim with you blubbering like that?" Nightshade swayed back and forth.

Sunstar shifted on the ground by her. "By the Gods, Nightshade. No. Please. No. Don't do this. He's a child, not a straw target."

Nightshade shook her head. She wished she could take off her blindfold and look into Sunstar's eyes. Sunstar's tone indicated she really thought Nightshade would actually try to hit him. It saddened her.

Nightshade threw the rock and the human yelped in pain and thudded to the ground.

"Oh, no," she said. "I didn't hit the target, did I?"

"Sort of," one of the other humans said. "You hit Merton."

"Oh," Nightshade said. "Can I try again?"

"After you have a drink," the man said as the jug was thrust into her hands.

She pretended to drink again and burped uneasily. She swayed back and forth, accepting another stone from the humans.

"Hold onto him." Nightshade heard the man move, and the Goblin shrieked in terror.

Sunstar moaned beside her, and Nightshade was glad for the blindfold that hid most of her flinch. She threw the rock and it hit the human. He yelped in pain and slumped to the ground. His friends roared with laughter, and the Goblin cried.

"No," the Goblin screamed. "Scared. No. No hurt."

Nightshade threw another rock and another of the human men collapsed. They all roared with laughter.

"Give me another one," she said imperiously, swaying back and forth.

"No," one of the men exclaimed. "I want a go."

"If you take me to him I'll hold the target on his head," Nightshade said.

"You promise you won't help him?" the man asked.

"How? I can't see anything." She heard Sunstar's soft moan of pain and remained expressionless. Her heart twisted a little at Sunstar's distress.

"Come here, then," the man said.

Nightshade staggered toward his voice, tripping over her own feet. He laughed. She felt the man steer her to stand behind the Goblin.

She got down on her knees and enfolded a small, warm, leathery-skinned body close to hers. She could feel the Goblin shake with terror and his tears.

The man threw something at her, and she pretended to slip and covered the Goblin boy with her body. She felt cloth tear around her bicep and realized the human had thrown a knife. Her plan to allow the humans to drink themselves into a stupor evaporated, and she prepared herself to fight. She listened carefully to determine where the remaining humans were sitting around the campfire.

"No fair. You gave me rocks," she said.

"You're blind. No one wants a blind Elf to throw a sharp knife, do they?"

Nightshade laughed along with them, quickly feeling the Goblin's manacles. She had to free him first so he could hide. She thought she could undo them, but not by feel. She had to see them.

"Nightshade, no," Sunstar said. "Stop. Stop them."

Nightshade heard the sound of a hand striking flesh, and Sunstar's yelp of pain. Her temper snapped.

"What did you just do to her?" she asked coldly.

"She was whining, just like the brat," the man said.

"This has gone on long enough." Nightshade threw off her blindfold and strode across the ruins toward Sunstar before the humans had a chance to take in her glowing blue eyes.

She hit the human that had slapped Sunstar, knocking him

unconscious. The other men sobered and threw themselves at her. Nightshade gave into her instincts and let them take over. The human men were unconscious within minutes.

Sunstar quickly crossed to the Goblin boy and held onto him as Nightshade pulled all the human men into a neat pile to one side of the ruins. She rifled through their belongings. She found a coil of rope and used it to tie them up.

The Goblin boy gazed up at her, unblinking, tears leaking from the corners of his swollen eyes.

"No hurt?" he asked in Drow.

Sunstar glanced at Nightshade. "Do you have any idea what language he's speaking?"

"It's Drow. He said, 'No hurt,'" Nightshade said.

Sunstar looked down at him and shook her head. "No. No hurt." She met Nightshade's eyes as Nightshade tied the last of the bandits to his comrades. "Why didn't you put a stop to that earlier? Why did you let them throw things at him?"

"I was never going to hit him, I hope you know that." Nightshade's eyes stuttered away from Sunstar's face. "It's full dark. We can't leave these ruins until morning." Something large fell from the sky and crashed through the branches of a tree before hitting the ground with a soft thump.

"What was that?" Sunstar asked.

"That was a result of Hemlock's eye." She met Sunstar's eyes squarely. "We are trying to hide from Hemlock, and we cannot leave these ruins to cast a glamour. I think we both knew that when you saw the bandits here during the day. You and I both knew they were never going to let us go." She sighed. "I had hoped to drink them under the table and let them sleep it off. We could have been gone early in the morning with the boy."

"You want to take him home?" Sunstar asked.

Nightshade stared into the little Goblin's eyes and saw the same thing that she had seen in the human girl's eyes weeks earlier. There was fear there, but not of her glowing Drow eyes. It had slipped away from him to be replaced by something else—cautious hope.

"We can't leave him here, and we can't bring him with us. He's too young to be out by himself, so I'm guessing his home is in these mountains," Nightshade said.

Sunstar nodded. She was silent a moment. "I'm sorry."

"You really thought I was going to hurt him or that I would leave him here?" Nightshade asked quietly. "I suppose I would think the same if I were you." It stung, but she stoically met the pain.

Sunstar flinched. "No. I *know* you are not like that. That's not why I asked. I'm not apologizing for something I'm not guilty of. I'm apologizing because we're in this mess because of me. I chose to walk through a bandit camp. I chose to stay with them. I am the reason we're here now."

Nightshade shook her head. "This is not your fault. I am equally to blame. Do you really think you could have made me stay with these humans, if I hadn't wanted to? I'm glad we did this. Look." She nodded at the Goblin who was now staring adoringly at Sunstar. "If we *hadn't* stopped, we *wouldn't* have found him."

"You're right." Sunstar smiled. "We *have* to help him."

"I'm sorry too, Sunstar," Nightshade said.

"Why?"

"For thinking that you would judge me and think the worst of me. You've never done that. You've always been kind to me, despite everything."

"Never. I would *never* do that to you." Sunstar's eyes spoke volumes of the trust and fondness she had for Nightshade. She stood, unable to speak, and put her arms around her. She snuggled against Nightshade, face pressed against her chest.

Nightshade felt gentle pressure against her leg. She looked down and saw the little Goblin boy, wrapped around their legs, squeezing as hard as he could.

He glanced up at her and said something intelligible in Goblin, and Nightshade did not need a translator to tell her he had said, "Home."

CHAPTER 19

Hemlock's eyes fluttered open, and he gazed at the Drow king.

"Well, magician?" the king asked. "Where are they?"

Hemlock shook his head. "I cannot see them. We are close to Elven lands, and the magic in the land increases."

"So?" the king asked.

"It makes them more difficult to find, Highness. We will have to wait and continue to look for them by more arcane means." Hemlock glanced at Galvin and Farouk, who were watching him intently.

"Useless," Nightsbane muttered, and Hemlock pinned him with an unforgiving stare. He felt the urge to peel flesh from bone and idly wondered if he could use Nightsbane for the fresh blood he needed for the Eye.

"Go," the Drow king said to Galvin and Farouk. "Keep looking for a sign." He turned to Hemlock. "While you are looking, magician, we will also go toward Elven lands. That is where they are headed anyway."

Hemlock nodded, distracted. Killing Nightsbane would have to wait for a few days.

Sunstar watched as Nightshade bent over the Goblin and went to kneel by her side.

How could she think I would ever entertain the idea that she would be cruel to a child? Sunstar thought. *Because you once did,* her mind whispered. She flinched away from the thought. She thought she had gotten past the question of how different Nightshade was to any other soldier in her father's army. Every time she thought about Nightshade's Drow blood a small, treacherous part of her flinched. She had heard of Drow bloodlust, but had not actually seen it and wondered how to broach the subject with Nightshade.

She looked at Nightshade's broad shoulders, the silhouette of her hauntingly beautiful face, her dark hair and her blue eyes and felt a tide of nameless emotion wash over her. Nightshade meant so many things to her, and memory assailed her from all sides—the march to the Drow city and their flight from it, her softly spoken promise.

I won't hurt you and I won't let them hurt you either.

Nightshade sat against the wall again and patted the space beside her. The Goblin boy—freed by Nightshade—snuggled into Sunstar's lap when she took her place beside Nightshade.

He said a few words, and Nightshade replied. Sunstar looked at her.

"He asked when we were leaving. He's frightened. I told him we would go when the sun came up," Nightshade said.

Sunstar shot a glance at the unconscious humans. "I'm sorry we can't go any earlier."

Nightshade nodded. "So am I. I want to bring him home and return to Elven lands."

Sunstar nodded. They were companionably silent for a moment, listening to the crackle of flames in the campfire.

"Can I ask you a question?"

Nightshade nodded.

"What's your first memory of your mother?" Sunstar asked.

Nightshade gave her a brief smile, lost in the mists of memory. "Why?"

"I just want to know."

Nightshade was silent for a moment, and a small smile played about her lips. "I remember her arms holding me, her lips on my skin, and the warmth of her body."

Sunstar smiled. Her own mother felt the same way, as did her father. Her mouth tightened and a hard knot of sorrow formed in her gut.

Nightshade stared into the flames of the fire. "When I was little she sat me on her lap and let me play with cast off strips of leather." She smiled. "I didn't know it was cast offs from the armorer that she used to make knotted cords. I didn't realize until I was much older that they were to mark the days of her captivity with the Drow. I just thought of them as toys. She used to whisper in my ear about the wind in the trees and the river. She loved water, as do I." She fell silent for a long moment. "She always told me to obey my father. She said that he would be angry at me if I didn't. She said I half looked like him, and it was best for me if he never found out I wasn't like him in the places that eyes couldn't see." She looked deep into Sunstar's eyes. "What do you *really* want to know, young Elven princess?"

Sunstar studied her for a moment. Nightshade's eyes were gentle but shadowed from sorrow. "How did you manage to stay with the Drow for so long without them killing you? You are nothing like the other Drow that you were with. How did you survive amongst them for so long? How did you take other lives with little or no provocation?"

Nightshade winced at the directness of the question

Sunstar felt her cheeks warm. "I'm sorry. That was an awful question to ask you. It's really none of my business."

"It's all right," Nightshade said gently. "You won't be the only one who asks me that. Truth be told, I never killed anyone for sport. I was a soldier amongst the scouts, killing armed opponents in battle. My biggest sin was watching innocents slaughtered and not lifting a finger to help them." She sighed. "The worst was the little human girl." She looked into Sunstar's eyes. "Almost all Drow have a sickness of the mind. It is pleasure at the sight of spilt blood. Once a Drow starts fighting, the instinct for blood takes over, and a Drow will do anything to see it, to drink it in. Drow fighting tactics, society, philosophy, everything is designed around this sickness. I don't have it. I never did. My fighting ability comes from my Drow training. I am good at it, and I can see for longer than any full-blooded Drow when the sun comes up. That's why I'm still alive." She smiled. "You have nothing to fear from me. I won't hurt you."

"I know you won't," Sunstar said and nodded. "You said almost all Drow have this sickness. What happens to the others who don't have it?"

"They leave. They are outcasts and are shunned. If Drow meet them, they are killed on sight. I am guessing some live in your forest. It is easy to hide."

"Do you want to join them?"

Nightshade was silent for a moment and then shook her head. "I don't think so. I am only half Drow. I want to know more about my mother's people."

Sunstar relaxed a little. "Do you know your mother's name? Maybe I can help you."

"My mother's Elven name was Risingmist. I would like it if you helped me."

"I will see what I can find out." She looked into Nightshade's eyes. "You will come with me, won't you?"

"I will come with you." Nightshade's eyes showed a terrible uncertainty and naked hope.

"There is a place for you with us," Sunstar said. "You don't have to be by yourself."

"Your people will see the same thing that everyone else sees when they look at me. They will see my eyes and think I am a Drow."

"Perhaps so, but you will make them see otherwise," Sunstar said. "When I saw you, I felt kinship to you because you looked like me. But judging you based solely on that would have been very foolish. I have listened to you speak for yourself. You have become my friend, Nightshade, and I am sure you would not have been able to do that if you were even a little like a Drow."

Nightshade pulled Sunstar into her arms. "I don't think you will ever understand how sorry I am that I allowed the scouting party to take you back to the Drow city."

"It's all right," Sunstar said as Meagan's face flashed through her mind, along with a stab of sorrow and humiliation. "I take responsibility for my own actions. Put aside the question of whether or not I had a right to be in the forest, I disobeyed my father and went into the West Wood. We knew there were Drow scouting parties in the West Wood. It was my own stupidity that put me into this mess."

Nightshade nodded. "I understand."

They fell silent, gazing up at the blanket of stars overhead. The Goblin boy sighed and shifted in Sunstar's lap, making a soft sound of contentment. Sunstar lay against Nightshade, safe in the warmth and comfort of her arms. She thought about her mother and father and how hurt and upset they would have been, when told of her loss. She wanted nothing more than to see them and apologize to them.

She gradually drifted off to sleep in the safety of Nightshade's arms.

Sunstar opened her eyes and blinked against the early morning sunlight on her face. She glanced up at the still sleeping Nightshade and gently shook her. Nightshade opened her eyes and looked at Sunstar.

"Good morning," Sunstar said, struck by her beauty. She smiled.

"Good morning." Nightshade stretched, looked down, and

frowned. She quickly scanned the ruins around them. "Where's the little Goblin?" She scanned the ruins. "There."

Sunstar followed the direction of her gaze. The little Goblin watched the human men warily for any signs of movement. They remained still, snoring softly. He quickly darted forward and snagged one of the packs, and pulled it toward himself. One of the men snorted. The Goblin squeaked and froze. The man frowned in his sleep and settled down again. The Goblin released a gusty sigh.

He scurried to Nightshade and Sunstar, dragging the pack with him.

Nightshade said something softly to him.

He patted his chest. "Gargajin," he said, followed by more rapid speech.

Sunstar looked at Nightshade as she accepted the pack from him.

"He said his name is Gargajin. He also said he was hungry for meat," Nightshade said.

Sunstar pulled out the food—bread and cheese for them and a good portion of cold meat for Gargajin.

They ate well as they watched the humans closely for any signs of wakefulness. They remained out cold.

When they were finished, Nightshade quickly packed up the food and slung the pack over her shoulder. She said something to Gargajin, and he nodded enthusiastically.

"I asked him if he knew where home was, and could he show us the way," she said to Sunstar. "He said yes."

Gargajin slipped his hand into Nightshade's, and they began walking. The grasslands surrounding the ruins soon gave way to a rocky, upward path and stunted trees growing in the cracks between boulders. Gargajin stayed close to Nightshade. He looked around carefully, blinking in the full sunlight and occasionally rubbing his large eyes. He blinked and twitched his ears. There was no sign of any animals, and it put them all on edge.

"Nightshade?" Sunstar asked.

"Yes?"

"How is it that a little Goblin is able to speak Drow?"

Nightshade thought for a moment. "It's odd, I know. Drow and Goblins are not exactly allies. I am guessing that if the Drow go to ground in any of the caves in this region—and there are a few—the Goblins know about them and spy on them to make sure they don't move underground." She glanced at Sunstar. "These mountains are also home to a few holdout Dwarves."

Sunstar stared at her. "Dwarves? I thought they were all gone from here."

"These mountains are rumored to be filled with gold. I'm sure that more than one treasure seeker still enters them to find it."

"Gold?" Sunstar asked. "That's silly. These mountains were mined to extinction centuries ago by the Dwarves."

Nightshade nodded. "Perhaps so. Perhaps the current Dwarves are descendants of the original miners, who knows?"

"If there's nothing to mine, why stay?"

"It's home?" Nightshade shrugged.

Sunstar shook her head. "I'm sure that's not it."

Gargajin tugged on Nightshade's arm and said something. He pointed at a pile of rocks in the distance. Sunstar gazed at her and raised an eyebrow.

"He said, 'Rock. Home.' I am assuming that means the entrance to his home is somewhere in that vicinity."

Sunstar nodded and they walked toward the pile of rocks. Gargajin looked tense and scanned the stunted forest. Nightshade watched him and asked him a question. He said a single word back, and Nightshade frowned. She spoke slower and seemed to be repeating herself. Gargajin answered as slowly as she did. They both looked a little frustrated.

"What is it?" Sunstar asked.

"I asked him why he was so frightened. He's saying a word back to me that is not Drow. It has to be Goblin." She looked down at Gargajin, who was watching them both. "Unfortunately, I don't speak Goblin."

Sunstar held out her hand toward Gargajin, and he took it. He gave her a happy smile, overshadowed slightly by his large, sharply pointed teeth. He pulled her into motion again.

"I don't think it matters." Sunstar glanced back at Nightshade. "It doesn't matter what he's so frightened of. We're just going to have to deal with it. We said we were going to take him home."

Nightshade nodded. They walked over the open ground to the pile of boulders, and Gargajin tugged at her hand and jabbered in his unknown language.

She shot Sunstar a wry grin. "This must be his home."

Sunstar nodded. “Indeed.” She looked up at the sky. It was still early morning.

Nightshade followed the direction of her gaze, blinking in the bright light. “It will be fine, Sunstar. I am guessing we won’t be able to follow him all the way into the caves. He will find his way. It’s his home.”

They reached the pile of boulders after another hour of traveling across barren, rocky ground. They were breathing hard, and Gargajin ran ahead, yelling incoherently and waving his large hands around.

Sunstar jogged after him, followed closely by Nightshade. Nightshade was half blinded by the light and tripped into Sunstar several times. Sunstar grabbed her hand to lead her, and moments later they rounded the side of a large rock and stopped. Sunstar blinked in surprise. There was no sign of Gargajin.

“Where is he?” Nightshade asked from directly behind Sunstar.

Sunstar started.

“Sorry, I did not mean to startle you.” Nightshade scanned the rocks and stepped around Sunstar. “There.”

Sunstar followed the direction of her finger and saw a flash of leathery skin disappearing into a crease between two gigantic boulders.

“I thought you couldn’t see anything.” Sunstar made her way toward the crease with Nightshade close behind.

“It helps when I’m in shadow.” Nightshade frowned and stared over Sunstar’s shoulder. “Interesting.” They stood in front of the crack Gargajin had disappeared into.

Appearances were certainly deceptive. It was no crack. Two huge, round boulders stood twelve feet apart, bordering a twenty foot high door carved into a solid sheet of rock. Two massive columns framed the doors. Script was carved into the rock over the doors, but it was almost obliterated by time, and Sunstar could not read it. A crest was carved in the middle of it—a pick axe and half a hammer. The other half of the hammer had crumbled away.

“No, I can’t read that either,” Nightshade said in response to Sunstar’s questioning look.

“Well, it’s an abandoned Dwarven mine, anyway,” Sunstar said. “I don’t know which one.”

Nightshade nodded. “I don’t know either. I have not often traveled onto your father's lands this way, so I am not as familiar with this area as with others."

Gargajin, dwarfed by the immense doors, jumped up and down, gesturing them forward.

Nightshade and Sunstar exchanged a glance and walked toward the doors.

Sunstar put out her hand to the door. Gargajin grabbed it, shook his head, and mouthed something unintelligible.

"He says not to touch it," Nightshade said.

Sunstar smiled. "I gathered." She looked up at the doors, feeling uneasy. She could not say why; she wondered how much of it was because she now hated caves with a passion. She gritted her teeth and took Gargajin's hand.

He pulled them both toward a tiny door off to the left of the main doors. It was completely featureless and only three feet high. Sunstar felt an instant of panic and pushed it back.

"I will take him in." Nightshade glanced at her as they watched Gargajin. "You can wait for me out here."

He ran his fingers across the center of the door and stopped at a spot in the dead center of it. He pushed.

"No," Sunstar said. "I'm coming with you."

Nightshade gave her a small smile. "You're perfectly safe out here. And I won't be gone long."

"And let you have an adventure without me?" Sunstar asked with an attempt at lightheartedness. "No." Her feeling of unease increased, despite her bantering tone.

Nightshade gently squeezed her hand and snorted a soft laugh.

The door soundlessly opened inward, and Gargajin dove through the opening.

"After you," Nightshade said. "I'll be right behind you."

CHAPTER 20

Sunstar tensed her jaw. She nodded. She dropped to her knees and crawled through the opening. She found herself in a small, dark passageway, fresh air gently lifting the hair off her forehead. She fluttered her eyes closed and pushed back a cloying feeling of claustrophobia.

Gargajin hooted softly back at her, and she crawled after him. It felt as though they crawled forever through a narrowing tunnel, but it was only for a few seconds. She found herself in a chamber, barely large enough for the three of them.

Nightshade gestured toward the narrow opening on the other side of the tiny chamber. It opened out into a small tunnel, smaller still than the previous one. Sunstar winced. Gargajin nodded gravely.

"Go ahead," Nightshade said quietly. "I'll be right behind you." She bit her lip. "We have to find another way out. As soon as I went through that door, it closed. I couldn't see a way to open it from this side."

Sunstar fought back a feeling of raw panic. She felt Nightshade gently massage her back. Nightshade and Gargajin exchanged rapid phrases.

"He said the main hall is to our right," Nightshade said. "We can get out through the main doors."

"Why didn't we use them to get in?" Sunstar asked.

"I don't know. That's the part I can't understand," Nightshade said. "I think we will have to leave him soon. We're both simply too big to keep following him."

Sunstar nodded. "I quite agree."

Gargajin tugged on Sunstar's jerkin and pointed toward the small crawlspace.

Sunstar nodded and wiped her shaking hands against her jerkin. She tried to slow her hammering heart. She closed her eyes and dropped to her knees and then her stomach. She followed the waiting Gargajin through the small tunnel, dragging herself along by her forearms. Nightshade, directly behind her, seemed to be moving silently, and Sunstar felt an instant of envy.

After another interminable crawl through a nightmarishly narrow tunnel, they finally reached another opening. Sunstar groaned softly. The hole looked barely large enough for her shoulders to fit through.

"Nightshade?" she said, watching Gargajin scamper through it, thanks to his much smaller stature.

"Yes?" Nightshade said.

"I don't think I can fit through this hole."

She heard Nightshade shift behind her. "I can't see anything. How big is it?"

"I don't even know if my shoulders will fit through," Sunstar said.

Nightshade was silent for a moment. "You have to try. We can't go back. We *have* to go forward. Stretch your arms through the opening."

Rock bumped and scraped against Sunstar's back as she shifted. She put her hands through the hole, forcing down a surge of panic as rock scraped against her stomach and cheek.

"Gargajin!" Nightshade called.

Sunstar heard the scrape of the Goblin's feet as he jogged toward the hole. He grabbed Sunstar's wrists and tugged, grunting with exertion. He was much stronger than his small frame suggested, and Sunstar yelped as sharp rock carved a channel through the soft skin of her ribs and abdomen.

Gargajin's grip faltered at her soft sounds of distress, but it did not matter. More than half of her body was through the hole, and she pulled herself along with her hands, scraping the skin off them. She collapsed into a large alcove, breathing heavily. Gargajin hovered uncertainly by her, and she smiled encouragingly at him.

"Thank you," she said. "From the bottom of my heart."

Gargajin smiled and threw his arms around her in a clumsy hug, which she gladly returned.

She heard a soft grunt of exertion and turned to see Nightshade scamper from the same hole Gargajin had just pulled her through.

Sunstar stared at her, and Nightshade laughed softly at her expression of envy and awe.

"Living underground is good for something," Nightshade said. "And tight spaces are a standard part of Drow military training."

Sunstar nodded. "So it would seem." She leaned back against the rock wall, trying to regain her equilibrium and fighting her rising unease.

"Are you all right?" Nightshade knelt next to her.

"I'm a little scraped and bruised, but other than that I'm undamaged." Sunstar looked around.

The small opening they had come through was at the base of a rock wall that stretched up into the darkness. She leant against a side sheet of rock and looked up at a curtain of impenetrable blackness before her. She blinked. She thought she had seen a flash of light and frowned as she tried to find it again in the darkness.

She glanced at Nightshade. "What can you see?"

"I can't see the ceiling above us, so it's very high." She shifted. "We are against one wall of a gigantic hall. In the distance I can see a small fire. There are people around it."

Gargajin said something to Nightshade in a soft voice.

"Gargajin says he can't see," Nightshade said. "The entrance to the tunnel that leads to his home is across the other side of the great hall. He's blind in the darkness. We have to take him across to the other side. There's something living in the great hall that he considers an enemy, so we have to be careful."

"All that from three words?" Sunstar asked.

"They were, 'blind,' 'home,' and 'enemy.' It isn't hard to guess." Nightshade stood and held out a hand to Gargajin. She held out her other hand to Sunstar.

Sunstar took Nightshade's hand. "Did he happen to mention how we could get out of here again?"

"I can see the doors to the outside on our right," Nightshade said.

"You think we're going to just walk straight through them without any trouble?" Sunstar asked, a touch of sarcasm in her tone. Her nerves hummed with tension.

"I can even see the door handle," Nightshade said. "What's the matter?"

"Can't you feel it?" Sunstar asked. "It feels like we're covered in a shroud."

Nightshade nodded. "The sooner we help Gargajin, the sooner we can go back outside and into the forest. I trust your instincts, but there is very little I can do for the moment."

Sunstar nodded, pushing the feeling as far back as she could. She wanted to get out of the hall.

Gargajin gently tugged on Nightshade's hand, and Sunstar moved in as close to her as she could. Nightshade gave her hand a gentle squeeze and threaded it through her arm.

Gargajin and Sunstar clung to Nightshade, and she carefully steered them across the open space. She stopped about half way across, and her body went rigid.

Sunstar let out a soft, whistling sigh as she felt Nightshade's muscles tense. "What is it?"

"Drow. Three of them."

Sunstar's blood went cold, and her heart beat hard.

"They saw me," Nightshade said softly. "Don't move."

A raw surge of sheer terror tore through Sunstar, and she fell heavily to the flagstones beside Nightshade. Gargajin let out a strangled sob, and Sunstar groped for him. He shrank up against her, burying his face into her neck. She felt his tears on her skin and understood how he felt.

It was too dark for her to see Nightshade, but she could feel her shift her balance and brace herself for an attack.

She heard screams of rage in the distance and pounding footsteps as the Drow ran toward them.

Nightshade grunted and crashed to the ground as a figure collided with her at high speed. Sunstar heard the sound of fists striking flesh, grunts as the blows fell home, and the clatter of a sword or knife against the stones.

They heard the ring of steel on steel, and Sunstar gasped as she heard a grunt from Nightshade and a sudden yelp.

Gargajin yelped in terror. Sunstar whirled around and heard him grappling with a small figure.

The figure roared, echoed by Nightshade, and a heavy body crashed to the ground and lay still.

"Nightshade!" Sunstar yelled as another short figure joined into the fight. She suddenly found herself engulfed by a small, heavy male saturated with the scent of wild animal, dust, sweat, and leather. He roared in her ear and tried to wrap his hands around her neck. Her muscles bulged as she struggled to hold him off. She shoved upward, and he sailed over her head. He clung to her and they both rolled over backward. A small body hurled toward them, and the small male yelped. Gargajin growled. He bit down as hard as he could, and the Dwarf howled in pain.

A tall body flew toward them, and Sunstar heard a sickening thud. The Dwarf grunted, stiffened, and fell on top of her. A second later his weight left her body as a tall figure tossed him aside.

"Nightshade," she whispered.

Sunstar threw herself into Nightshade's arms. She trembled and squeezed as hard as she could. Tears of relief escaped from her eyes and soaked Nightshade's shirt. Nightshade tightened her arms around her.

"You're not hurt, are you?" Sunstar pulled back and peered at the shadow of Nightshade's face.

She felt Nightshade shake her head. "They won't trouble you anymore." Her arms tightened. "I suggest we leave here."

Sunstar felt Gargajin's arms encircle her leg, and she gave Nightshade one last squeeze and dropped to her knees. Gargajin put his arms around her neck and spoke two soft, unintelligible words.

Sunstar looked up at Nightshade. She felt Nightshade bend over.

"He said 'people' and 'home.'" Nightshade shifted. "I hear movement from the direction we were headed in."

Gargajin rustled through the pack he had taken from the human bandits. He thrust a package into the surprised Sunstar's hands and then ran from them, shouting a word at them.

"He said goodbye, didn't he?" she asked, pulling in close to Nightshade. She felt Nightshade nod.

Nightshade took her hand and pulled her in close. "We have to leave. The doors are straight ahead of us."

Sunstar nodded and could not control the shudder that went through her. The feeling of foreboding had gotten worse, and she felt as though eyes bored into the skin between her shoulder blades.

Nightshade stayed close to her, guiding her carefully across the uneven floor. They stood before the doors, and Nightshade pushed them open.

A small sliver of light shone through the crack between the doors, increasing in strength until the hall was flooded with light.

Nightshade yelped and turned her face away from the sun. The sun stood halfway across the sky. Sunstar blinked until her eyes adjusted to the increased light levels. She turned around and looked at the hall.

Three Drow Elves and two Dwarves lay discarded on the flagstones.

"Are they dead?" Sunstar asked.

"Yes," Nightshade said.

"Did they hurt you?"

"No."

"Thank the gods." Sunstar gave vent to a gusty sigh of relief. She had never been so glad to be out in the sun in all her life. She heard something rustle and looked down at her hand. It was the package Gargajin had given her. She opened it and looked inside.

"Hah," she said. "Gargajin left us with the bread and cheese. We won't have to live off the land tonight."

Nightshade smiled. "Good."

Sunstar took Nightshade's hand, and they continued their walk back to the trail that led over the mountains.

Hemlock blinked and opened his eyes. Something had woken him up. He quickly scanned the cavern but could not see what it was. The Drow around him remained immobile, snoring softly in the darkness.

He heard a soft buzzing sound and looked down at his pack. He understood at once what was causing it. He quickly rifled through the pack, dug to the bottom of it, and pulled out a small pouch. It was warm and shook gently as he held it. He opened it and looked carefully at the contents.

He tipped a polished, blood red stone out of the bag and into his palm. He felt it vibrate, and his lips curved into a smile. It was a scoutmaster's stone. It activated when a scout leader died. All scout leaders had them sewn into their robes. He closed his eyes and felt for the magic inside the stone. It was like flipping a switch, and an image formed in his mind.

He was on the ground in a vast cavern and could see an eerie, dim outline of objects and bodies strewn on the ground around him. One looked to be a Dwarf, and there was a partial outline of a pick ax on his helmet. There were more fallen Dwarves and two other Drow discarded on the ground. The stone itself was coated in blood so the images it transmitted were blurred. Then he heard the soft word that brought a rare, broad smile to his face: *Nightshade.*

He quickly repacked the stone and put it back into his pack.

"Sire." Hemlock shook the Drow king awake.

"What is it, magician?" the king asked in a husky voice. He leant up and rubbed his eyes.

"I have found them."

The Drow king, awake and aware, sat up. His cold gaze bored into Hemlock's. "Take us there. Now."

"No," Hemlock said.

The Drow King's mouth tightened, and he raised his hand to strike Hemlock for his disobedience.

"I cannot," Hemlock said calmly. "My magic is not strong enough to help us during the day, and it is but half way through the day. I have a suggestion if you are interested."

The King's lips tightened even further. He gave Hemlock a sharp nod.

"They must head back to Forest Elf lands. There is one road through the mountains. Let them take it. I will take us to a place that they will reach by the end of tomorrow. We will find them before they are able to go to ground."

"Why not tonight?" the king snarled.

"We cannot leave here until tonight, and by the time we do they will have hidden. We have to leave it until tomorrow night."

The king glared at him. "Very well, Hemlock. We will do things your way. But if they escape and the Elven army finds them, I will kill you myself."

Hemlock nodded. "We will find them, Sire. Of that there is no doubt."

"I have one further question, magician. How did you find them during the day if your magic does not work?"

Hemlock hid his contempt for the monarch's slow wits. "From a Drow scout leader. Nightshade just fought—and killed—three Drow in the area. It was more luck than skill, Sire."

"Well done, Hemlock." The king settled himself down to sleep again. "For that I will allow you to live another few days."

Hemlock barely managed to refrain from spitting on the king as the tall Drow drifted off to sleep again.

Allow him to live? The Drow king was lucky Hemlock allowed *him* to live.

Hemlock looked down at the sleeping figure of the king and wondered if he could use his blood the next time he cast the spell for the Eye.

CHAPTER 21

Nightshade and Sunstar walked down the forest trail. The brightest light of the day had passed, and Nightshade could see again. She glanced at the quiet Sunstar.

"A copper for your thoughts," she said.

"They're not worth that much." Sunstar gave her the ghost of a smile.

"It's the Drow in the Dwarven hall, isn't it?"

Sunstar glanced at her and nodded warily. She bit her lip, unsure of what to ask and feeling a terrible, ponderous uneasiness.

"I know there are always Drow scouts traveling outside the city. It is a simple fact of Drow life," Nightshade said. "I am sure that the king and queen have increased Drow patrols around the edges of your father's land. I expected it."

Sunstar went pale, and Nightshade pulled her to a halt.

"Sunstar," Nightshade said softly. "You know they are looking for us. You *know* that. But they will not even get a glimpse of you until you are back with your parents."

Sunstar could not think about it. The sight of Drow sent her stomach into a slow, forward roll of terror.

Nightshade pulled her into an embrace. "No fear. We have one more day of travel left, and we will be on your father's land."

And only one more day with you, Sunstar thought, breathing deeply and taking in Nightshade's gentle scent. *You make me feel so safe.*

They walked for another fifteen minutes before Nightshade pulled her to a halt again.

They stood by the side of a stream, surrounded by tall trees. A gentle breeze moved through the trees, and Sunstar shivered.

"We will rest here for the evening," Nightshade said. "You can tell me what's wrong."

Sunstar sank onto a smooth boulder, smiling despite herself. "Three days ago you would barely say hello to me." She shot Nightshade an amused glance. "Now you want to find out what's bothering me."

Nightshade returned her smile. "Three days ago, I couldn't feel anything besides self pity and guilt. Now I feel hope, and guilt is easier to cope with."

An image of Meagan's face swam to the surface of Sunstar's mind, and she pushed it back down. A terrible feeling of helplessness and humiliation welled up, and she let it roll over her in a slow wave. She shuddered at the deep-seated sense of panic mingling in with it.

She felt Nightshade's hand on her back as Nightshade knelt beside her.

"Sunstar?" Nightshade asked.

"How could I have ever been so stupid?" she asked. "I really shouldn't have run from my bodyguards. I should have waited for them. Meagan and I should never have been out in the forest so far." She looked beseechingly at Nightshade. "Look at what's happened to us. So many people have died or gotten injured for me. And for what. A prank that went wrong." She rested her head in her hands.

Nightshade stroked her back.

"I shouldn't really be saying anything to you about feeling guilty, should I?" Sunstar felt her cheeks warm as she looked at Nightshade.

Nightshade shook her head. "That's hardly fair. We have both lived very different lives. Is there any atonement for what I have done in my life? I don't know. I can't change what I have done. I can only try to start again from here." She bit her lip, fear of Sunstar's reaction lurking in her eyes. "I am an outcast from my society. Thanks to my Drow blood, no one will accept me, and they will always be suspicious and afraid of me. It is my lot in life to be alone." She tensed, naked humiliation and self recrimination in her eyes. "I'm not afraid of my death. I'm afraid of my loneliness. I'm afraid of my own cowardice. I knew from when I was too little to see above my mother's knee that it was wrong to hurt other living things. What did I do about it? I did what my father told me to do. What if I am always forced into roles others want me to play?"

"Then live, Nightshade. Find out." Sunstar bit her lip. *Please, Nightshade. Please say yes.*

Nightshade snuck her arms around Sunstar and pulled her in close. "I fully intend to. Do not fear for my safety against a swordsman, my princess. I am by far the best with a sword in Dragonar."

Sunstar squeezed her hard, fear swirling around her. "Can't you just come with me? Forget about them and don't fight them until the army is behind you?"

"Sunstar," Nightshade said gently. "We are almost in your lands. We could find your father's patrols tomorrow. We can both be safe. You don't know what's going to happen."

"No, I don't," Sunstar said. "But it doesn't feel good."

"Battle never does," Nightshade said. "Keep your faith in me. You will be sitting by the fire with your mother and father before the week is out."

Sunstar nodded. The shadows cast by the trees were long and drawn out. The feeling of foreboding got worse. By unspoken consent, Nightshade leaned back against a convenient tree, and Sunstar snuggled up against her. She cast her glamour, and they faded into obscurity.

"Galvin! Farouk!" the king roared.

"Yes, Your Highness?" Galvin asked, falling to his hands and knees and bowing before his king.

"Report, Galvin." The king scanned the darkness around them.

"There is no sign of them," he said. "Farouk is scouting the main trail. He is to report in an hour."

"We are over the borders and onto Elven lands, Highness," Nightsbane said quietly. "We could go to ground and wait for them. They will be in this area by the time we wake up. They should not be hard to find."

The king nodded. "All right." He turned to Galvin. "Go and get Farouk. We will wait here until evening." He glanced up at the sky. "Dawn is not far away. Move. Now."

Galvin jogged off to find Farouk, while the king turned and began talking quietly to Hemlock.

Nightshade looked down at Sunstar snuggled into her lap and felt forlorn. She understood Sunstar's feeling of foreboding; she felt it herself. They had so far been lucky enough not to see any Drow and to remain hidden from Hemlock's Eye, but it all had to end.

Nightshade felt grateful that Sunstar had shied away from direct questions about the Drow she had fought in the Dwarven mine. One of them had been a scout leader, and Nightshade knew that he had a tracking stone sewn into his cloak. If the king had a tracking stone on him he would easily be able to find them. She silently cursed. She had not wanted to kill the scout leader—she had not *intended* to kill him—but he had fallen heavily on his own sword, ending his life.

This would be their last day together. It would end today. Nightshade hoped that they would at least be close to the Elves before they did. She also said a silent prayer of thanks to the Elven gods that they had managed to get as far as they had before the Drow caught them. Sunstar had a real chance of reuniting with her family.

Sunstar.

She was so young and beautiful, and it felt like she knew Nightshade's heart better than Nightshade did. She thought about the shy smile Sunstar had given her after they escaped the humans in the Twin Cities. The wonderful feeling of exquisite pleasure when Sunstar had come to her in her cell in Bordertown. Sunstar had given herself to her without reservation, and had earned her trust. Nightshade had promised to keep Sunstar safe, and she wondered if Sunstar realized that with her actions she had made the same promise to Nightshade.

Nightshade felt much easier about the future than she had. She thought she would always be alone, but she knew that was wrong. Sunstar genuinely cared for her and *wanted* her to stay close. Nightshade felt something she had not felt since she was very little and sitting by her mother's knee—a sense of belonging, of family.

Sunstar's eyes fluttered open, and Nightshade sank into her gentle regard for a few moments.

"Good morning," Sunstar said softly and slowly disentangled herself from Nightshade.

"Good morning," Nightshade said. "Are you hungry? We didn't eat last night."

Sunstar nodded. "I would love some of Gargajin's bread and cheese."

Nightshade nodded. They shared a silent meal and then started their journey. Nightshade set a faster pace than they had traveled for the previous few days. Sunstar looked pale and grim, and her eyes darted around the trail.

"What is the first thing you're going to do when you get back home?" Nightshade asked, trying to distract her.

"Apologize to my parents," she said. "After that, I'm going to have a hot bath."

Nightshade laughed. "Yes, that *does* sound appealing."

"But you know what I'm going to do before all of those things?"

"What?"

"Wait for you," Sunstar said.

"Who said you would be waiting?" Nightshade asked. "I will probably be in your bath before you are."

Nightshade's attempt at humor had the desired effect, and Sunstar laughed softly. Her tension dissipated.

"I'll remember to keep it warm for you." Sunstar abruptly sobered. "I would love to introduce you to my parents."

"I will hold you to that," Nightshade said. "You will have to think up some creative way to introduce me. They'll probably clap me in irons as soon as they see my eyes."

"They won't," Sunstar said. "Despite all my other flaws, I am a good judge of character, and my mother and father both know that." She sighed. "The thing I am not looking forward to is facing Meagan's mother."

"What do you think will happen? What will she do?"

"She was never entirely comfortable with my relationship with Meagan because of our differences in rank. She was also uncomfortable because of Windwalker."

"Windwalker is your father's Captain of the Guard, yes?"

Sunstar shot Nightshade an odd look. "How do you know so much about us?"

"I was a scout," Nightshade said. "It was my business to know." She smiled. "Now, what of Windwalker?"

"My father considers him my betrothed." Sunstar bit her lip.

"Your father? What about you?" Nightshade asked. "What do you consider him to be?"

"One of my father's soldiers," Sunstar said. "And a good friend. No more than that. My father would never listen when I said I didn't want to marry him."

"Who do you want to marry?"

Sunstar shook her head. "I wanted to see more of the world before I thought about settling down." She glanced at Nightshade. "How is it that you're still a free Elf?"

Nightshade laughed. "I'm not considered worthy of Drow marriage. My father couldn't sell me or give me away. No self-respecting Drow would be caught dead with me."

"So there's no one?" Sunstar asked.

"Even if there were, they are behind me now. I left the Drow," Nightshade said.

"I'm sure we can find you a nice Elf to settle down with," Sunstar said.

Nightshade smiled despite herself. "Like you, I always wanted adventure before home and hearth. That hasn't changed a lot. I just need to be more careful when traveling."

"Do you want company?" Sunstar asked. "I know an Elven princess who would be happy to go out into the world with you."

"Do you? Perhaps I will ask her."

Sunstar took Nightshade's hand. She caressed it and gazed at Nightshade. Nightshade glanced down at her and gently squeezed her hand.

They kept walking.

Nightshade took them through the most direct route to the Forest Elven lands, knowing it was a race against time before they were caught. She hoped to encounter at least the Elven rangers out in the forest so they could bring Sunstar back to her father. So far, there was no sign of them, and she cursed silently. She was not sure they could go to ground for the evening and remain undetected.

"I think we should talk." Nightshade broke the comfortable silence that had sprung up between them.

"About what?" Sunstar asked.

"About what's going to happen to us. We are on the border of your father's lands."

"Isn't that good? Doesn't that mean we're safe?"

"Only if we find the Elven rangers quickly." Nightshade gestured to the trees and undergrowth surrounding them. "The Drow could be hiding anywhere in this, although if I were them, I would be hiding on Elven land. It means less searching for us."

Sunstar nodded, her jaw muscles tensing. She looked haunted.

"They will try to trap you. You have to run from them. You have to try and avoid the places they could have gone to ground." She pointed to a stand of ferns close to them. "There. That looks like a good place to go to ground. There's good cover. It's dark, and there's not much to crawl through and stay beneath cover. The other thing you should know is that Drow battle tactics are such that they will surround you and herd you toward the leader of the party. If you are ever caught by Drow again, don't run *from* them—run straight *toward* them. They won't expect it, and surprise will keep them disorganized for longer. The leader is almost always alone or only has one scout with them so it will be easier to escape."

Sunstar nodded. "Why are you telling me this? You should be with me when we run."

Oh, how I wish that were true. "I have to face them."

"And remember that you have to face *me* after all of this is done," Sunstar said. "Please."

"I haven't forgotten," Nightshade said with a smile, openly gazing at Sunstar. *You're very beautiful, even for one so young. Who holds your heart, young princess? I wish it was me because I love you, Sunstar, so very much so. I wish I could tell you, but I can't.*

Sunstar's eyes showed a terrible, deep-seated pain and fear.

"Rest easy, Princess," Nightshade said. "I will take care of you. You will be free."

"My freedom is best if you are in it," Sunstar said. "Remember that, Nightshade."

"I have never forgotten," Nightshade said as they continued to walk. "I also remember each and every kindness you showed to me when I led you to Dragonar. Why did you do it? Why didn't you fight me harder?"

Sunstar was silent a moment. "I didn't know I could escape anywhere without being caught. And you were so kind to me compared to all your companions. You never did the same things to me that they did. Even if I couldn't get away I could count on you not to hurt me."

"Not hurt you?" Nightshade said. "I will never forgive myself for taking you all the way back to Dragonar. We should have run before then."

"It's done," Sunstar said. "My entire life for the past few weeks has been full of, 'if only I hadn'ts' and 'I wish I'ds.' I can't go back and change *any* of it. I can only try to live with it." She paused. "As must you, Nightshade."

Nightshade nodded. "Even if nothing ever goes right for me again, I will make sure that you are free. No matter what, promise me—you run for your life. Run as you have never run before."

"Only if you are behind me."

"I will be behind you. You must trust me." She squeezed Sunstar's hand. "It will be today. I can feel it."

"How can you be so sure?" Sunstar asked. "Maybe we can make it all the way in."

"Now they will be getting desperate. Hemlock's Eye will not work properly in your forest because of your magic. They are here. They are waiting for us. I think they have had enough clues to where we landed and how we are traveling." She glanced at the whey-faced Sunstar and smiled. "Rest easy. You should escape. We are making enough noise to wake the dead, and the rangers patrol to the borders of your lands. We will be found."

"Come with me," Sunstar said softly. "Promise."

"I will try," Nightshade said. "It's all I can tell you."

Sunstar nodded, pale and unhappy, and remained silent. Nightshade let her be.

They walked through the thick forest that marked the border of Elven lands. The shadows lengthened into late afternoon, then into sunset. Nightshade led the way. She felt a deep-seated sense of unease, and she tried to pinpoint the reason for it. Something teased and tugged at her senses. She slowed, listening to the sounds of the forest. It was eerily silent. Alarm bells sounded in the back of her mind.

She pulled Sunstar to a halt. Her heart thumped wildly, and she looked all around them. She looked past Sunstar's startled face. She was unable to shake her unease, which was rapidly sliding toward a terrible feeling of dread. She homed in on a thick stand of trees. The undergrowth grew rampant in and around the ancient boughs.

"What is it?" Sunstar watched Nightshade with considerable alarm. She lifted her foot. They both looked down and saw a dead bird. It was covered in ants. "Oh no." She moaned.

Nightshade nodded, looking at the trees. "If I were going to ground for the day, that's where I'd be. We have to run."

"It's so close to dark," Sunstar said. "Can't we just hide? Won't the glamour hide us?"

"No, we're too close to them for that." Nightshade shook her head and willed her legs to move forward. "Hemlock's powers are strongest when it's dark. We can't hide from him if he's close, and he will be. We have to run. Now."

Nightshade grabbed Sunstar's hand, and they ran into the forest.

Nightshade hoped against hope that they would run into the Forest Elves. They loped through the gathering dusk, through the border onto Forest Elf land. Sunstar's face was pale and taut with terror.

Nightshade felt helpless—she knew they would be trapped.

Hemlock shook himself awake from the magical sleep that bound the Drow during the day. He looked around at his companions, snoring contentedly all around him, and felt a shot of irritation that he quickly stifled. He prepared himself to cast forth his Eye to scour the landscape for the two fleeing Elves.

He slipped carefully out into the clean forest air of the early evening. He cleared a space in the undergrowth, and sat cross-legged. He emptied his mind, and became still as a statue. He drank some of the fresh blood he had obtained by killing one of the Drow guards. He paused for a moment, allowing it to infuse him, and then took another deep swig. He felt the wild joy take hold of him. His spirit felt buoyant; he launched his Eye into the air.

He saw the flaming pillar of pure white fire almost immediately. It was close to them, and he studied its position carefully, memorizing the landscape so he could safely cast a teleportation spell. He gave a savage laugh and raced toward the white fire. He saw the two young Elves fleeing for their lives, heedless of the disturbance in the forest. He brought himself back to his body with a solid thud. He shook himself, leapt to his feet with his customary speed, and rushed to wake the king.

A flight of dead crows showered Nightshade and Sunstar, falling to the ground all around them.

"He's found us." Nightshade slowed down and pulled Sunstar to a halt. After a moment, they heard a tearing sound close by that she recognized with dread as the magician's teleportation spell.

"What was that?" Sunstar cocked her head. She looked pale and ill.

"Teleportation spell." Nightshade gripped Sunstar's shoulder with gentle fingers. She looked deep into Sunstar's terrified green eyes. "You have to go now."

Sunstar stiffened with terror as the reality of the situation sank into her. "Please don't leave me." Tears flowed down her pale face. "You promised you would stay with me."

"I promised not to let them hurt you, and I won't. You also asked me to escort you to your father's land, and I've done that too. Now it's time for me to go and face them."

"You can't, they're going to . . . I don't want to lose you." Sunstar took in a great sobbing breath. Pain and misery for Nightshade shone in her eyes.

"They won't get past me," Nightshade said, with a rueful smile. "They trained me too well. If they do come after you . . ." She did not want to upset Sunstar any more than she already was. "Go that way." She pointed ahead of them further into the forest. "And don't stop for anything. I'll be right along behind you." She gave Sunstar a small smile. She could see by the pain in her eyes, mirroring her own, that they both knew she was lying.

Sunstar sobbed and grabbed Nightshade in a fierce hug. Nightshade relished the contact and laid her cheek on Sunstar's head.

"You mean so much to me. And I will never forget you." Sunstar's voice cracked, and she breathed deeply.

"Goodbye, Sunstar," Nightshade said. "Take care of yourself. Now go."

She disentangled herself from Sunstar and watched her run off into the trees. Sunstar paused to take a brief look back before she disappeared.

CHAPTER 22

Sunstar continued her headlong rush through the trees. Her heart thumped with terror. She distantly heard the Drow king speak behind her.

Sunstar cursed herself for being a coward and grimly kept thoughts of Nightshade's courage at the forefront of her mind. She knew that the calm, glowing blue eyes would torment her to the end of her days. She ran, hoping against hope that she could reach safety before the Dark Elves found her again. This time there would be no Nightshade if they did.

Thumping footsteps followed Sunstar's headlong rush through the forest. She knew Nightshade was lost. Her lungs burned with fatigue, and her blood ran cold as the footsteps gained and came around at her from both sides. Laughing voices filled with malice encircled her. She instinctively knew one of them was Farouk.

She tripped over a root and fell headlong on her face. Footsteps came up behind her, followed by the whoosh of arrows from the trees overhead. A strong male hand gently helped her to her feet, and she found herself looking through her tears into the surprised, dark eyes of Windwalker.

"Sunstar?" he said softly in wonder.

"We have to help Nightshade," she said wildly. "Please, Windwalker, go and get her."

"Who is Nightshade?" He stared at her, calm and commanding.

"That way." She waved her arm behind her. "Go and get her. Please, Windwalker. Please find her. Don't let them take her."

He nodded slowly and signaled one of the guards surrounding them to take her.

"Guard her." He indicated three of the other guards around them. He nodded to the other guards that had slipped forth from the bushes to join him. "Come with me," he said, and they ran in the direction she had just come from.

Nightshade steeled her jaw and calmly moved in the direction of the Drow. She did not bother taking any precautions to hide herself. She strode out in the open, virtually daring them to stop her. She could see them up ahead, and her heart sank. Her father was at the forefront. She stopped directly before them.

The king, Hemlock, and Nightsbane silently stared at her, and the Drow guards formed a circle around her.

"Nightshade." The king sounded gruesomely jovial. "We've been looking for you." He smiled unpleasantly.

"I will not let you harm Sunstar," Nightshade said. The mantra soothed her soul. She knew both she and Sunstar were beyond their reach, that Sunstar had touched her in some indefinable way.

The king laughed at her. "Get her," he snarled to the Drow soldiers. They leapt in with loud cries, determined to kill her. Nightshade felt another band loosen inside her. She easily disarmed a soldier and liberated his sword. She was surrounded by carnage in very short order. Five soldiers lay dead or dying in pieces around her. She eyed Nightsbane, Hemlock, and the king with cold eyes.

Nightsbane looked on, respectful of her fighting abilities. His hate for her radiated from him in cold waves. He jumped in with an arrogant snarl, sword drawn, and tested her defenses. They attacked and parried, and he was hopelessly outmatched. She lunged and caught him unawares. He gasped and looked down in surprise. Her borrowed sword stuck out of his gut. He sank to his knees with a grimace, valiant tugging at the sword. His arms went slack and his eyes rolled up in his head as he pitched forward, dead.

Nightshade felt her knees go weak, and she looked up with dread to see Hemlock silently chanting. She fought with every ounce of her remaining strength, but still sank slowly to her knees. She inwardly wept for her failure of Sunstar. Her arm went limp, and she feebly grasped for Nightsbane's discarded sword as the magic held her firmly in its grasp.

The king left his place by Hemlock's side, where he had been standing with his arms crossed and a cold expression on his handsome features. He knelt in front of her and drew his dagger. He carefully ran it down the side of her beautiful face, cutting it deeply. Nightshade gasped in pain.

"That's only the start," he said, softly, lovingly. "I'll have all eternity to torture you."

Nightshade mustered every ounce of strength she had left and grabbed Nightsbane's sword. She lunged forward with it. A cry escaped her lips as it cut through the king's icy cold, black heart with contemptuous ease. He touched the fatal wound and a single, strangled intake of breath passed through his lips. He brought his bloody hand back up to his face and stared at it in wonder.

Nightshade stared at him uncertainly, sickened by the further bloodshed, yet she felt somehow vindicated by his loss of life. The king lunged forward, gathering every ounce of his dying strength, and plunged his dagger into Nightshade's side. It tore through the scar of the wound that had been recently healed by Sunstar.

Nightshade went rigid with agony and screamed as Hemlock muttered a spell of pain amplification at her. He strode across the clearing, absently kicking the corpse of the king aside. He clubbed her viciously over the head, and she grayed out.

No! her mind screamed at her. *I don't want it to end like this.*

She forced herself to full consciousness as he dragged her under a bush. She bled heavily from the dagger wound.

He looked down at the crimson stain and smiled. "You will make a fine test subject," he said with satisfaction. "You can give your life to a noble cause." He closed his eyes, and his lips moved.

She forced her abused body to rally one last time. She grabbed his neck in one hand and squeezed his windpipe, robbing him of the ability to chant. His eyes bulged, and his face went purple as he tried to breathe. She held on grimly as he thrashed, in too much agony to scream as his flailing hands hit her bleeding wound several times. He finally lay still but she kept her hands around his throat for several minutes. She let go and looked closely at him. His neck was black and his sightless eyes stared in horror. She felt sick for a minute and then awareness slowly sank in.

The entire scouting party that had come after she and Sunstar was dead.

Nightshade smiled.

Sunstar was safe. She was free. They *both* were.

There was no sign of the Forest Elves, and Nightshade realized that there probably would not be. Sunstar would reason Nightshade was behind her, and they would both head back to the Elven city.

Perhaps Sunstar would wait, perhaps she would not—it made no difference to Nightshade's fate.

Nightshade, despite her promise, could not follow.

I really did want to see the Elven city with my own eyes. I'm sorry I won't be able to do it. I'm also sorry I won't see Sunstar again. An image of Sunstar flashed through her mind, her haunting beauty when she had sung and healed Nightshade. A tide of raw emotion bubbled up from deep inside her. Most of it was a wild, primitive joy at a feeling of pure freedom and a deep love for Sunstar, but it was tainted by the terrible sadness at the knowledge that her love could never be. Sunstar's face stayed in the front of her mind, and she felt the sting of tears.

"Nightshade," a small voice said close to her, speaking Drow. "Hurt?"

Nightshade started and moaned softly as her heart rate picked up. She turned her head toward the sound and saw a little Goblin face peering at her. He looked dismayed and frightened.

"Gargajin?" she held up a clumsy hand. She tried to push the pain and weariness aside. "Yes. Hurt."

Gargajin cautiously crept forward and laid a cool hand on her forehead. "Safe. Heal."

"I can't heal myself, little one. I don't have the magic to do it."

Gargajin shook his head, looking frustrated. "No. *Heal.*" He sat beside her and put a device on her chest. It looked like a small brass circle with a ruby in the centre. He whistled softly and pressed it.

Nightshade felt the ground falling away from beneath her, and she gasped in pain as sudden weightlessness gripped her. She felt an odd, jarring sensation that made her yelp in pain. She felt herself wrenched downward and her knife cut tore. The pain was instantaneous, monstrous, and overwhelming. She lost consciousness.

Sunstar sank to her knees, breathing hard, trying to calm her nerves. Nightshade's cry of pain echoed in her heart and soul, threatening to shatter her into a million pieces.

She had promised to take Nightshade's body home with her if Nightshade fell. She immediately shied away from the thought. *Come to me, Nightshade. Please, please live.* She was only distantly aware of the Elven guards that remained close around her watching the forest for any signs of the Drow.

She waited anxiously for Windwalker to return. Every sound in the night forest made her tense. She replayed her final moments with Nightshade over and over in her mind, until she felt ragged and bloody on the inside. What if Nightshade really had fallen? What then?

She heard movement in the forest an hour or so after Windwalker had left her to find Nightshade. She sat up, watching carefully with the guards. Windwalker appeared in the clearing with only two of the guards he had left with.

"We have found Drow bodies in the forest, Highness," he said. "No one was alive when we got there."

"No," Sunstar said, and the denial gave way to a soft moan. It turned into a low, sobbing cry of pain, and Windwalker flinched. She closed her eyes, steeling herself and pushing back her misery. "Take me to them. Perhaps I can help you."

"It is not a place for a princess and an elfmaid," Windwalker said.

Sunstar glared at him, her anger tinged by terrible, burning resentment. "Where do you think I have been for the past month, Windwalker?" She clamped her jaws shut to stop any other words from coming out. *Something terrible happened to me, Windwalker. Whether you like it or not, you* will *acknowledge it and you* will *treat me like an adult because of it.*

"I'm sorry." Windwalker blushed. "Was it that bad?"

Sunstar stared at him, silent, and her resentment deepened. He made it sound like she had been made to go outside and play for her own good. Deep inside she heard the echo of a promise that made life bearable: *I won't hurt you and I won't let them harm you either.*

Windwalker got to his feet and gestured. "This way, Princess."

Sunstar nodded and walked beside him back to the clearing where she and Nightshade had parted company. She sobbed on the inside, her pain a high keening for Nightshade.

He did not stop. He led her further into the forest, toward six more Elven guards. They stood around a row of corpses, watching the forest warily.

Sunstar struggled to control her bile. She looked at the face of each corpse, steeling herself to see Nightshade's beautiful features, relaxed in death.

"That," she said, pointing to one of the bodies, "is the Drow king. That is a scout leader called Farouk. He is Galvin. I don't recognize any of the others." She looked up at Windwalker. "Did you find any more?"

Windwalker shook his head. "It took us all this time to find these." He nodded toward a path of torn foliage. "Down there, there is a lot of blood in the bushes and signs of a struggle, but no more than that."

Sunstar felt the tears well up. Hemlock and Nightshade were missing. She had failed the one promise she had made to Nightshade. "Show me."

"But, Sunstar—" began Windwalker.

"*Now*, Captain."

Windwalker bowed to her as was befitting her rank. He led her further into the forest, following a path of broken undergrowth to a dark space between two trees.

Sunstar knelt and leant into the undergrowth. The greenery was torn and flattened as Windwalker had said, but there was also a great deal of blood. She crawled into the crushed undergrowth and looked carefully around. She reached forward and felt in the leaves. Her fingers encountered something smooth and woven.

"Windwalker, there's something here."

Windwalker went into the bushes next to her and frowned when he felt the cloth. Sunstar backed out as he leaned in and pulled on the cloth.

"Help here," he said, and one of the guards jogged to him. They pulled a body out of the undergrowth. "How was this missed?" he asked the guard sharply.

"You aren't supposed to see a Drow Elf when they go to ground," Sunstar said, leaning over the body. It wore a black cloak. Her heart hammered in dread, and she braced herself for a terrible blow.

Her hands shook as she pushed the cloak away from its face. Her shoulders sagged, and she felt exhausted. *Hemlock. It's Hemlock. Not Nightshade.* She sank back onto her haunches, breathing a bone deep sigh of relief.

"This is Hemlock, the Drow king's magician," she said.

"That is all we found," Windwalker said.

Sunstar nodded. "Please search again." She closed her eyes. Where was Nightshade? "I want to go home. I need someone to come with me." She glanced at Windwalker. "What happened to Jarrod?"

"Both of your bodyguards were killed by the same Drow who took you. We think they were killed first," Windwalker said. "You will have to do with me for now." He smiled, and she could see the pain of loss lurking in his gaze.

Sunstar shook her head and sighed. “That’s terrible. I didn’t mean for them to get killed. It is nothing but a waste of life and for what? A stupid, elfling prank.”

“Sunstar—” Windwalker reached for her.

Windwalker’s concern felt stifling, and she pulled out of his grasp. She felt sick from the knowledge of her part in Jarrod’s death and pain over Nightshade gnawed away at her.

“Stay here,” she said shortly. “Look for Nightshade. I am going home.”

“Let me send some guards with you,” he said.

Sunstar nodded. “I expected no less.”

Windwalker turned and signaled to the guards. The six that were guarding the bodies in the clearing came forward. “Take Her Highness back to the city.”

The guards saluted and formed ranks around Sunstar.

“I’ll ask Father and Mother to send out more guards,” she said.

“I have the rangers to help me,” he said.

“You’ll still need more help,” Sunstar said. “More Drow will come.”

“But you’re safe here. You’re home,” Windwalker said.

“The Drow king is dead. You would be foolish to think the Drow will let his death go unpunished,” Sunstar said. The more he spoke the angrier she got at him. Why was his only concern ushering her back to the palace to be a useless ornament when the entire Drow nation was about to land on their heads? She turned to the guards. “How far to the city?”

One of the guards bowed. “If we start now and don’t stop, we will reach the city by early afternoon tomorrow.”

Sunstar nodded. She felt as though she were a tightly wound spring. “I’ll send out more troops when we get back to the city.”

“Yes, Sunstar.” Windwalker gave her one long, last, searching look.

Sunstar turned away from him, trying to rein in her bitterness and only partially succeeding. She gestured for the guards to lead the way.

Three hours previously she had been quietly thinking that she and Nightshade had gotten lucky and that they would be able to make it all the way to her home without interference by the Drow. Now she was walking toward home, feeling everything other than happy. She felt miserable. She had lost Nightshade, and she could not honor the one request Nightshade had made of her. She did not even have the comfort of knowing if Nightshade had died quickly or not.

It hurt so badly she was beyond tears, and was thankful that they were walking so she did not have to interact with anyone. She blindly followed the guard in front of her, watching him carefully since she could barely see the path. She imagined the gentle touch of Nightshade's hand, and her tears welled up and spilt over.

She felt empty. She did not feel safe as she had expected she would once she was back on her father's land again. She could almost hear Nightshade's gentle admonition, and her lips twisted into a wry grin.

They stopped in the middle of the night for a quick meal, and Sunstar found herself starting to walk off into the forest to forage. She stopped herself and sat down, horrified. The guards clustered around her, and the youngest one, holding a pack, passed out trail rations.

Sunstar watched the forest carefully, alert for any sounds she could not identify. She chewed carefully, straining her senses to hear. A small animal crashed through the undergrowth, and she quickly stood, tilting her head and straining to hear any other sounds.

"Highness," the Elf with rations said. "It is nothing but an animal."

"How can you be so sure? Drow are cunning enough to mimic anything. You could be sitting on an entire scouting party and you would not know it." A memory of how the undergrowth came alive with glowing eyes sprang to mind.

"We are deep in your father's territory," another guard said. He was staring at her as though she had gone half mad.

"It doesn't matter," Sunstar said sadly. "Fortunes can change very quickly."

She looked around, trying to penetrate the darkness. She blinked several times. Her nerves sang with tension. She abruptly realized that she did not feel safe. She felt safe traveling with Nightshade but not her father's guards. She sighed.

They quietly finished their meal and marched again. Sunstar felt a little easier when dawn's grey light pierced the early morning sky. Yet she still felt unsafe, despite their proximity to the city.

She imagined what it would have been like to walk into the city with Nightshade. Nightshade would have been unsure of herself but she would have done it for Sunstar. She would also have been happy that they were finally home.

They passed farms once they got closer to the city, and an

occasional Elf sat on a fence by the road, watching them walk past. She tried to smile for the Elves watching them, but often failed. She was too tired, and her heart ached too badly for her to be in good spirits.

They finally reached the city in the middle of the day, and Elves lined the streets, watching as they headed toward the palace. Sunstar felt her cheeks burn and kept her eyes firmly trained on the road. The ghosts of memory snapped at her, and she once again found herself walking down a Drow street, pelted with rotten food, yet still sheltered by Nightshade's cloak.

They reached the palace, and one of the guards moved more quickly to the castle.

"Stop!" Sunstar called.

He pulled to a halt and saluted.

"I will bring the news of my return to my parents myself," she said. "Go to the officer of the watch and ask for another detachment of guards to be sent out to Windwalker. On my authority."

"Yes, Your Highness," he said.

"Please dismiss the guard and return to the barracks. Get some sleep," she said.

He saluted and backed away slowly. He called the dismissal to the assembled guards, and they dispersed.

CHAPTER 23

Sunstar stared up at the castle with a deep sigh. Her mother and father would be furious with her. What would they say? What words could they possibly use on her that she had not already used herself? Would they try to lock her in her rooms until she turned old and gray? The last possibility was the most appealing of them all. Her distress was too overpowering to be around company for too long. All she wanted to do now was go to her rooms and let out her tears for Nightshade.

The guards at the palace doors looked shocked and gave her a belated bow. She walked past them with only the most cursory of glances. She had to force her legs to move. Every step felt like a millstone, every second an eternity of dread at her parents' reaction to her presence. Every moment was a step closer to facing Meagan's mother and begging for forgiveness.

She thought about Nightshade's promise and squared her shoulders. If Nightshade could stare down the entire Drow nation, then Sunstar could face two harmless Elves, even if they were angry parents.

She approached the doors to her father's study, and the guards came to attention. They stared at her, round eyed.

"Is Mother in there?" Sunstar asked.

"No, Highness. Your mother is in the audience hall," the younger of the guards said.

"Go and tell her I am back in the city," she said.

The guards saluted, and the younger of the two rushed off to do her bidding. She knocked on the door.

"Enter!" Darkwood, King of the Elves and Sunstar's father, called.

Sunstar went into her father's study and closed the doors behind her. Her father was bent over his strategy table. His long, thick, blonde hair, like her own, hung free and half hid his handsome face. He ran his fingers along the contours of a map, studying it carefully. She felt a surge of love for him.

"What is it?" he asked without looking up.

"Father," Sunstar said. "I'm back."

Darkwood looked up, and his eyes widened. "Sunstar."

She opened her mouth to speak but before she could utter a sound, her father had her in his arms, squeezing her for all he was worth. She squeezed back, unable to speak through a rushing tide of almost overwhelming love.

He held her at arm's length and studied her. "Daughter. You've returned. You must be tired. Do you need a healer? You must want a bath! Are you hungry? You must—"

"Sunstar?" a hesitant voice asked behind them.

Her father released her, and she turned around to see the tear-stained face of Morningstar, her mother.

"Mother?" Sunstar felt tears swim to the surface. She hated more than anything to see her mother upset with her.

"Sunstar." Morningstar ran to her and pulled her into a close embrace. Darkwood encircled them both with his long arms.

"Oh, my beloved Sunstar," Morningstar said. "You must be exhausted. You must—"

"Mother, Father, I'm fine. It's so good to see you. I'd thought I'd lost you forever." Sunstar squeezed Morningstar's tall frame as hard as she could. She reveled in the hauntingly familiar scent of her perfume, her warmth, and her love.

"Well, you haven't," Darkwood said, his voice thick with tears. "We're still very much here and very glad to see you."

"I'm sorry," she said. "I'm so sorry. I didn't mean for any of that to happen. I didn't mean to hurt you."

Morningstar pulled back a little. Her eyes seemed a little clearer. "You are forgiven, daughter. We will discuss it after you have refreshed yourself. But suffice it to say that what happened to you was punishment enough for a silly prank."

Sunstar silently nodded. She felt sick. *A silly prank? Oh, Mother, what I did was a million times worse than that.*

"Why don't you go and have a nice, hot bath, and come and eat with us," Morningstar said.

Sunstar flinched as an image of Meagan's mother shot through her mind.

"It's all right," Morningstar said softly, stroking her arm.

Sunstar nodded and sighed. She backed out of her father's study and headed toward her own rooms.

Sunstar sank into her bath half an hour later. She looked at the boots sitting by her bed. They were the ones Nightshade had taken from the farm for her. She would not go back to wearing her old boots. These were surprisingly comfortable, and a perfect fit.

She glanced around her room and saw that she was alone.

She took a deep breath and felt her shoulders relax. She stopped pushing down the memory of glowing blue eyes, and simply . . . let go. Memories of Nightshade tore through her, the strongest being the feel of her arms as she held Sunstar for the last time.

Go that way and don't stop for anything. I'll be right behind you.

You mean so much to me. I will never forget you. Sunstar squeezed her eyes shut. Never had truer words been spoken. *Nightshade,* her heart screamed. *Where are you? I love you. Come to me. You* promised.

Tears welled up out of her eyes and streamed down her face. She sighed and lay back in the bath water, feeling the heat soothe every bruise and scrape on her body. It hurt too much for her to simply sit still, so she restlessly bathed and lay back in the tub, simply soaking.

"Are you feeling any better?" a soft voice asked from beside her.

"Mother," she said, taking in her mother's beautiful face. "I think I'm as good as can be expected."

"Your father is waiting for us. We should talk." Morningstar ran her concerned gaze over Sunstar. "Can you talk?"

Glowing blue eyes stared at Sunstar from the mists of memory, and she fought back a rolling wave of pain. She nodded. "I think so. Some of it, anyway."

"Good enough." Morningstar held out her hand.

Sunstar got out of the tub, toweled herself dry, and dressed. She looked down at her boots. She slowly pulled them on, relishing the feel.

"Where is Windwalker?" Morningstar asked, from her seat at the table by the window.

There was a knock at the door. "Come," Sunstar called and turned her attention back to her mother. "He is still out in the forest. He is looking for survivors."

"Survivors?" Darkwood let himself in and sat at the table by her mother.

Sunstar squared her shoulders and stood. It was time to tell them everything. They would be angry, but they had to know for the good of their people.

"Yes, Father. Survivors." She sighed and bit back a surge of misery. It all seemed to have happened so long ago. She sat down at the third chair at her table and looked out of the window at a brilliant, cloudless blue sky. She drew courage from it.

Her parents exchanged uneasy glances.

"Mother, Father," she said. "I did something very stupid and got myself into trouble."

"I think we understand that part, daughter." Darkwood's blue eyes flashed with anger and then softened. "But we love you no matter what. Tell us. Tell us what happened."

Sunstar nodded. "Well, it all began about a month ago . . ."

Sunstar found that she could not stop talking once she started. She pulled out every detail for her parents' examination, almost begging them to be angry at her. She told them about traveling with the Drow, the queen in the Ring, Nightshade, and their flight from the city. Her parents remained completely silent during her soft speech, looking concerned, horrified, and pained in turn. By the time she spoke her last word, her shoulders shook with the force of her bitter sobs, and she covered her face with her hands.

She felt herself pulled into her father's arms, and he held her as the worst of her grief racked her. Morningstar stroked her hair, gently soothing her.

"This Nightshade," Darkwood said quietly. "What of her?"

"I don't know." Sunstar breathed deeply and tried to keep her voice steady. "Fallen, I think." Her reserve broke completely, and she sobbed again. Her father's arms tightened around her, and she felt more forlorn than ever. Saying the words out loud to her parents made Nightshade's probable demise real, and her pain became exquisite.

She finally quieted a little, and her father led her to a small divan on the other side of the window. She sat down into her mother's embrace.

"We're not angry," Morningstar said. "We're both more hurt and disappointed than angry."

Darkwood nodded. "And this is the last we'll say on the subject. I think what happened to you was punishment enough. I will tell you that I am disappointed in you. You know better than to behave like a foolish, irresponsible Elfling. Your best friend is dead, and your people are at the brink of war with the Drow because of this."

"Brink of war? How? How can *their* attempts to kill *us* bring *us* to the brink of war with *them*?" Sunstar pulled back and stared at him, blinking uncertainly. It felt like she was living in a bad dream. It was almost as though he was so concerned with avoiding an armed conflict that the matter of her kidnapping would go unanswered.

"The Drow king is dead, daughter," Morningstar said. "They will expect compensation for that."

Sunstar stared at her, feeling as though they were speaking different languages. *Compensation? They're worried about* money*?*

"You're serious?" Sunstar snorted a laugh and threw up her hands. "First, he died in pursuit of me, while trespassing onto Elven lands. He was in the process of trying to kidnap me again. *Again!* Second, an Elf did not kill him, Nightshade did—and she was a citizen of his country."

"No," Darkwood said. "Trespass is true. But Nightshade ceased to be a citizen of Dragonar when you invited her back here to live. She became a citizen of our nation. Or rather, had it restored. Her mother was a full Elf, Risingmist, yes?"

Sunstar nodded. Her sense of dislocation became worse.

"So technically they could say they were not on our lands—you did, after all, say this was at the border, and an Elven citizen killed their king," Darkwood said.

"Are you telling me that the Drow are saying they want us to pay for the murder of their king?" Sunstar kept opening her mouth and asking questions, but it felt as though she could not understand them any more than she could understand her parents' concerns.

"No, not yet." Morningstar exchanged a look with Darkwood. "But they will."

"How do you know they are going to want money?" Sunstar wished Nightshade was with her. "How do you know they're not going to ask for me to be returned? You can't turn them down, can you?"

"We can turn them down," Darkwood said. "You are an Elven citizen, and we do not give up our own so easily."

"And you are our daughter," Morningstar said. "We love you. We won't give you up for anything."

"That's true," Darkwood said. "We won't give you up for

anything." He leaned forward and stared into her eyes. His own shone with unalloyed sadness. "This is the outcome of your prank, daughter." He sighed. "They will hunt you for a long time, if they ever stop."

"I was on *Elven land* when they took me. My *prank* was running from my bodyguard, that's all. Everything that happened afterward was me escaping my unlawful captivity." She bit her lip. "I should have let them kill me." She looked up as her parents gasped and studied them in turn.

"Daughter," Darkwood said. "Don't say that. Your mother and I would have been devastated if anything had happened to you."

And I'll bet you wouldn't have gone to war over me. "So what am I to do now?"

"*We* will wait and see what the Drow do." Morningstar exchanged a grim glance with Darkwood. "And we will give you new bodyguards."

I don't want a bodyguard, I want my beloved Nightshade alive and by my side. "All right. But I reserve the right to choose my own bodyguard."

"What? You want someone old and slow so you can take advantage of them again?" Darkwood asked. "I don't know what's going on inside you, but please try not to compound one mistake with another."

Sunstar flinched and gaped at him. She felt the same resentment toward him as she had toward Windwalker. What was the matter with them both? Did they really both think she had learnt nothing? That she had not understood any of what happened to her?

"Get out," she said, softly and coldly.

"I beg your pardon?" Darkwood's green eyes, eerily similar to hers, flashed.

"You heard me. I said, get out. I meant it," Sunstar said. "How shallow and stupid do you think I am, Father? Do you really think I am going to shrug this off and go skipping into the forest pulling daisies?" She stood up and glared at him. "My *best friend* is dead, and *I* am the one who has to face her mother. Jarrod is dead, and I can't ever apologize to him for what happened. *Nightshade*, who understood me as no one else ever has, who only ever wanted peace, is dead. And for what? Me. I am *not worth* any of this." She took a step forward so barely a hair's breadth separated them. "When the Drow come calling, I will be there for them. I will deal with this, because this is *my* problem, not yours. I will take my bodyguard and leave you to your precious nation. You can dither over what to say to the Drow as much as you like."

Morningstar laid a restraining hand on both Darkwood and Sunstar. She exchanged a long look with Darkwood. He nodded and turned back to Sunstar.

"I see you *do* understand," he began. "You understand that you must face the consequences of your own actions. That is good. But you have forgotten something even more important. You are the crown princess of the Forest Elves, and we cannot simply hand you over to the Drow. We would not do that anyway. Despite what you seem to think, we love you. You are our daughter. On top of that, you are correct. You were on Forest Elf land when you were unlawfully taken by the Drow. That was an act of war, in and of itself. It would be an unmitigated act of gall to presume to demand any type of restitution for the death of their king considering that little fact."

Morningstar gently cupped Sunstar's face. "I can see the one question you are asking yourself. You don't think we would have come to get you, do you? You think we would have let you rot with the Drow. You are very wrong, daughter. We would have moved heaven and earth to reach you."

Sunstar snuck her arm around her mother, and she cried again, amazed that she still had tears left. "I'm sorry," she whispered. "I can't help it."

"I understand," Morningstar said.

"Why don't you try and get some sleep? It's very late," Darkwood said.

Sunstar glanced at the window. The sky was dark. It was full night, into early morning. She suddenly felt exhausted. She nodded. "Perhaps you're right. I *am* tired. Good night, Mother and Father."

"Good night." Darkwood pulled her into a gentle embrace. "Why don't you help your mother tomorrow morning in the audience hall?"

Sunstar forced a smile. She was not sure she could sit through hours of indignation over petty matters that made no difference to anyone but the petitioners. She had much larger concerns, and she wanted to be by herself. "Thank you, Father. That sounds like a fine idea."

Her parents kissed her good night and left.

Sunstar sank back onto her soft bed, bone weary and wide awake. She felt cold and lonely. She was accustomed to sleeping on the ground with Nightshade, and her bed felt almost too soft. She stretched out her arm, feeling the empty space in the bed next to her. She wished with all her might that Nightshade was next to her. She longed for the comfort of Nightshade's arms and the feeling of safety.

She closed her eyes and let the exhaustion take over.

CHAPTER 24

She ran through the forest, Nightshade straight behind her. No matter how hard she tried, she could not move faster than a slow trot.

"Run, Sunstar!" Nightshade pulled even with her and glanced back over her shoulder. "Can't you hear them? They're right behind us." As if on cue, the sound of footsteps crashing through the undergrowth drifted from behind them. The terrible ripping sound that signified Hemlock's teleportation spell started.

"I'm trying," Sunstar gasped. "I can hardly move."

Nightshade grabbed her by the upper arm, and the first arrow struck the ground by Sunstar's side. The air ahead of them shimmered and a crack, saturated in darkness, became visible in the shimmering.

Nightshade yelped.

Sunstar skidded to a halt and turned to look at Nightshade. She screamed when she saw the arrow shafts quivering from Nightshade's back.

She knelt over Nightshade, frantically searching for signs of life.

A large hand dropped on her shoulder . . .

" . . . Sunstar."

A hand was on her chest, holding her down onto the bed.

Sunstar thrashed and sat up, breathing hard. She looked around wildly, prepared to fight to the last of her strength. Where was Nightshade?

"Sunstar," a gentle voice said again. "You're safe."

The voice penetrated her numb mind, and she looked around. Morningstar sat beside her, looking alarmed and concerned.

"Mother," she said, sighing. She shook from the aftermath of her nightmare.

"You're safe, daughter," Morningstar said. "You had a nightmare."

Sunstar released a shaky breath and pushed her sweat-soaked hair out of her face.

Morningstar pulled her into an embrace. She gently stroked Sunstar's hair. "Just a nightmare."

"A bad one." Sunstar grimaced at the remembered sounds of arrows thudding into Nightshade's body.

"Do you want to talk about it?" Morningstar asked.

Sunstar shook her head. "My escape from the Drow. That's all." She frowned. "How did you know to come in here?"

"Oh. They told me." Morningstar smiled and nodded at two Drow standing in the doorway. Sunstar tried to dive out of bed and run, but Morningstar held her back. "Where are you going, daughter?"

Sunstar twisted out of her mother's embrace and leapt off the bed. She got her feet tangled in the bedclothes and fell heavily. A split second before she hit the floor . . .

. . . the room shifted, and she sat bolt upright in bed. She clutched the sheets and stared owlishly out of the window. Bright sunlight streamed into her rooms.

She released a deep sigh. She looked down at her bed. The sheets were twisted and sweat soaked, and she herself felt damp. *I'm not going to sleep again unless I'm too tired to dream.* Her eyes felt as though they had grains of sand in them, and her head pulsed and snarled with a deep-seated headache. She got out of bed and rang for a servant.

An hour later she was freshly bathed and clothed and headed toward the audience chamber. She had foregone breakfast. She was not hungry. She doubted she would ever feel hungry—or happy—ever again.

She made her way through the crowd of Elves milling around the audience chamber. There were farmers, merchants, travelers, and common Elves. She tensed, uncomfortable in the sea of life surrounding her. She longed to escape to the solitude of her rooms but forced herself to stay put. She had told her father she would be there.

She saw a familiar contingent of hooded Elves standing by themselves in a quiet corner. They were the same ones she had seen on the morning she had been captured. She wondered why they were still there. She could not see their faces. Her senses went on alert, and she approached them slowly.

"Who are you?" she asked, conscious of the crowd of Elves around them.

"We are subjects of King Darkwood," a male voice replied. He sounded muffled thanks to his cloak.

"Why do you wear a cloak inside?" she asked.

"I cannot see, Highness," the robed figure said. The others pulled in close to him.

"Why are you here?" she asked.

"We come to see our king," the cloaked Elf said.

Sunstar reached out a shaking hand. The cloaked Elf remained completely still, waiting for her touch. She gently pushed the cloak back and gave a hiss of horror when she saw his face.

"You are a Drow," she said, taking a step back. "No, not another dream." Her heart hammered in her chest, and she almost stumbled in her haste to back away from him.

"What?" he said, surprised. "No. This is not a dream. You are safe. I mean you no harm."

His eyes were tightly closed against the light. He fumbled around the top of his cloak until he found his hood and pulled it over his head so his face was once again hidden. He sighed with relief as the other cloaked figures moved in close to him.

None of the other Elves were paying any attention so Sunstar relaxed a little. If they were truly dangerous every Elf in the palace would be fleeing for their lives.

"What is your business here?" she asked, unable to refrain from taking a step away from him.

"I am a farmer with a border dispute with my neighbor," he said.

"What dispute is this?" Sunstar asked.

"My neighbor allows his cattle onto my land to graze. I do not want them there. They eat my produce," he said. "My neighbor claims I settled there illegally although I bought my land as he did."

"Where is your neighbor?" Sunstar's treacherous palms were sweating.

"Here," an Elf said from beside her. He was close to seven feet tall, extraordinarily handsome, with cold hazel eyes and a cruel sneer on his lips.

"Come with me." Sunstar beckoned them both forward. "Only you two," she said as the Drow's fellow cloaked Elves—and Sunstar suspected they were also Drow—took a step toward her.

"I can't see, Highness," the Drow Elf said.

"Take my arm. I will guide you." Sunstar pushed back the ghost of another hand on her arm.

"Your will, Your Highness," the Drow said with a bow.

"Your names?" Sunstar asked as the crowd parted to allow her and the two Elves through.

"I am called Snakeheart," the Drow Elf said.

"And my name is Shiningopal," the Forest Elf said.

Sunstar pushed her way through the doors into the audience chamber.

They paused for a moment as Morningstar looked at her scribe to see who was next.

"These two are next," Sunstar said.

Morningstar looked up. "Sunstar." She frowned as she saw Sunstar and her two companions.

"What have we here?" she asked.

"A border dispute." Sunstar held out her hand for the patents that both carried. She sat down next to her mother.

Sunstar opened one, and Morningstar the other. Sunstar studied the patent carefully. The sale was legal. She traced her finger against the borders of the land and looked over at the patent Morningstar held. They could see which borders were common. They were along the edge of a road that led down to a lake. The patent Morningstar held told another story. It showed the two farms bordered each other, and that Shininopal held the access to the lake. Sunstar studied the parchment carefully. She could see that the lines between the farms looked darker than the other marked borders. It was clever fake.

Sunstar looked up. "I see no true common borders. There is a road that neither of you owns that runs between your properties. What have you to say to this?"

"I do not understand," Snakeheart said slowly. "There is very clearly a fence between our properties. A gate separates the two. If I want my livestock to have water, I must go onto Shiningopal's land."

Sunstar was silent a moment, watching them both. Shiningopal shifted uneasily, looking anywhere but at her or Morningstar. He shot his neighbor a quick look of revulsion. Snakeheart stood still as a statue, looking carefully forward. He showed no tension at all.

"You annexed our highway didn't you, Shiningopal?" Sunstar said.

Guilt flickered in his hazel eyes, hidden quickly by a mask of righteous anger. "He's lying." He shot Snakeheart a vicious look. "He's a filthy, lying Drow. I am an honest farmer."

Sunstar gave him a wintry smile. "I think *you* are dishonest, Shiningopal." She leant back in her seat and studied him carefully. "I think that Snakeheart is not the only one using this land that you are clearly charging a toll for. I think you've been doing that to all of your neighbors, haven't you?"

"Highness, how dare you?" He pulled himself up to his full height and looked down his nose at her. "Who are you to presume to judge me? You are an irresponsible wretch with no regard for those around you."

Sunstar's heart twisted, and she flinched at his words, but remained carefully expressionless.

Morningstar leaned forward eyes sparking with anger. "May I remind you, my good sir, that you are addressing the crown princess and my daughter, not some common serving wench."

"Thank you for that instructive comment," Sunstar said to Shiningopal, before Morningstar could say anything else. "But what I have done, I alone must answer for. Not you. But that is beside the point. We are not discussing me, we are discussing *you*. You are here, apparently, because you are a liar and a thief."

"A liar and a thief, am I?" Shiningopal asked. "At least I'm not a murderer."

The Elves in the audience chamber gasped and then stilled, carefully watching the interaction between the two. Sunstar glanced around the room, quickly taking in the universally cold expressions from her fellow Elves.

"Sir, you speak out of turn," Morningstar said coldly.

"No, Mother," Sunstar said. "Let him speak. I'm sure he's not the only one here thinking these things." She gently stroked Morningstar's arm until she felt her relax. She turned back to Shiningopal. "What are you accusing me of? Actually killing my friend or being irresponsible and allowing my friend to get killed?"

Shiningopal folded his arms and stared down his nose at Sunstar. "It doesn't matter. The results are the same either way. Your friend is dead, your guards are dead, and we will face retribution from the Drow."

"We face retribution from the Drow no matter which way we

turn," Snakeheart said. "Or are you stupid enough to believe they will ever leave us alone?"

"Silence, Drow. Your friends send raids, we all know that. Now they want blood. We should give it to them." He turned to Sunstar. "You brought this upon us. You are the one they want so you should give yourself up to them."

Shiningopal took a step toward Sunstar, and Snakeheart stood in his path.

"If you want her you will have to come through me first," Snakeheart said. "You will not lay one single hand on this elfmaid while I still draw breath." He turned to the Elves in the audience chamber. "If you think the Drow will ever leave you alone you are sadly mistaken. They have seized on this opportunity because they can, not because it is warranted." He turned back to Shiningopal. "She is young, and she made a foolish mistake. I don't think it is one that she will ever make again."

"No." Shiningopal shot back. "We will hand her to the Drow ourselves when they come calling."

Some Elves nodded in agreement, some stared at the floor while still others shook their heads in disgust. Sunstar watched them all as though truly seeing them for the first time. She wondered if they had always been so unthinking and spiteful.

Sunstar got off the throne by her mother's side and went to stand beside Snakeheart. She was surrounded by Elves and she virtually dared them to take her. She looked up at Shiningopal. "What I find most interesting here, Shiningopal, is that you are less concerned with declaring my guilt than you are with distracting everyone from the true issue. You stole from the crown and extorted sums of money from your neighbors." She held up both patents. "Your patent is false. The real ones have a mark on the parchment." She turned and signaled for the guards. "Take this Elf into custody." She gazed at the darkness hiding Snakeheart's face. "You will get your access back to the lake. Shiningopal's property is to revert to the crown and will be sold. The proceeds will be reparations for the extortion his neighbors have suffered."

Snakeheart straightened. "Thank you, Princess." He gave her a deep bow.

Sunstar nodded. "You're welcome."

The sea of silent Elves parted to allow another Elf through. Sunstar flinched at the sight of Meghan's mother. Guilt overpowered her.

"Rivercrest—" she began.

The sound of Rivercrest's hand striking Sunstar's face was as loud as a whip crack in the silent hall. Sunstar fell to her knees, humiliated.

"Do not speak to me, you murderer." Rivercrest's voice rose to a scream. "My daughter trusted you. She was in love with you. And you killed her."

"I'm sorry," Sunstar whispered.

"Sorry won't bring her back, will it?" Rivercrest snarled. "I told her you were irresponsible. I told her you would bring her nothing but pain." Her chest heaved and spit flew as she ground out her words. "She harmed no one and nothing. She worked every day of her life. And you, you self-absorbed monster. All you've ever done is get her into trouble. You *knew* you weren't supposed to go into the West Wood. You *knew* to be back before nightfall. You *knew* to take your bodyguards, but did you do any of these things? No. Why? Because you are an irresponsible, selfish brat. Everyone else has always taken care of the problems you create." Her self control and anger snapped, and she fell to her knees, sobbing.

Morningstar quietly got off her throne and tried to comfort Rivercrest, but she pushed her away.

"I will leave this room and be gone forever," Rivercrest said. "I am done serving you."

Morningstar nodded. "I understand."

"No, you don't," Rivercrest said. She spat at Sunstar, turned on her heel, and left.

Sunstar flinched. She glanced around the hall but saw nothing but strangers. She backed away from them. They were right. She felt naked, stripped bare. All of her secrets were on display for her people. Would any one of them ever truly know or care how sorry she was?

Snakeheart reached for her and snagged her shoulder. His hand was gentle. "May we talk, Princess?"

"What more is there to say?" she whispered. "She was right. I *was* a selfish brat."

Snakeheart shook his head. "No, not really." He turned so the opening in his cloak faced the assembled Elves. "Have you all forgotten that she was on *our* land when she was taken?"

There were cries of "No!" from scattered Elves throughout the hall. The majority remained silent and stared at them. Snakeheart held out his hand for Sunstar.

"Please, Highness," he said. "Come."

Sunstar took his warm hand and allowed him to pull her to her feet. "We can go somewhere quiet. And my name is Sunstar."

He bowed. "Thank you, Sunstar."

She felt every unforgiving stare at her as a thousand pound weight. She awkwardly led him to the alcove at the rear of the audience hall. She drew the curtains and pushed him back down onto one of the seats.

Snakeheart pushed his hood back and cautiously opened his eyes, hissing in pain. Sunstar saw a flash of glowing green and gasped.

"You're not full Drow either, are you?"

"I am," he said. "My eyes are simply a different color to the norm. It happens to those of us who are not as other Drow."

Sunstar nodded. "You don't have the mind sickness that other Drow do?"

"No," he said. "How did you know about that?"

"Nightshade," Sunstar whispered and flinched, bowing her head. She wanted Nightshade's arms and strength.

Snakeheart nodded. "This Nightshade would have joined you?"

Sunstar nodded. "I hoped so. I still do. We have not found her yet." She paused. "What did you want to speak to me about?"

Snakeheart gave her a bitter smile. "When I was young, I was out in a scouting party. My brother was with me. We ambushed a group of humans in the forest near Yarnook—it is a town a day's walk from the Twin Cities. It was a party of six men and it was an easy kill for us. We did not realize that we had disturbed a larger party of fourteen men, and the remaining eight set upon us in the forest. Drow do not take their wounded, and my brother was wounded. I left him, as a good Drow does. We headed back to Dragonar, but after a night's march, I could bear it no more and went back for my brother. I found him. The humans had tortured him. It had not been an easy death. I hunted them down and when I found them, I saw that they were just a group of cowering human men, preying on the weak." He sighed. "I left them and the Drow and have not returned since."

"You regret having left your brother in the forest?" Sunstar asked.

"No," Snakeheart said. "He was an animal. I feared my father more than I hated and feared my brother. I saw that the only thing that separated humans and Drow was physical appearance. I came here. Now I see that all that separates humans and Elves is physical appearance."

"That's not true," Sunstar said, shocked.

"Really?" Snakeheart asked quietly. "If I put my hands over your eyes and said, 'I found a young female in the forest. She was kidnapped and tortured. She escaped. I'm bringing her home,' what would you assume? Would you think it was a Drow bringing her home? Would you always think it was a Drow that did the kidnapping? Very little separates the species, Sunstar."

"What is the point of all this?" Sunstar asked. "What are you trying to tell me? Not to feel any regret because no one is really any better than anyone else? Or just that the Drow are more predictable than I'm giving them credit for?"

"You assume that Elves are somehow more special than any other species, that they should be held to a different standard to anyone else. It is not true—from what I have seen of the Elves today, I would dare to say they are no different to any other species. Everyone seems so concerned with how to avoid the wrath of the Drow that they seem to have forgotten that the Drow committed a crime against a sovereign power during an unlawful trespass. You must remind them all of this, and you must remind the Drow that they do not have free run of another nation's lands."

"And how do you propose I do that?" Sunstar asked, half angry.

"You must face the Drow."

"I can't face them. The thought of it makes me sick."

"You *must* face them."

"And how do you propose to do that without bloodshed?"

"Return their dead to them and go from there."

CHAPTER 25

"That's your grand plan? Return their dead and hope for the best?" Sunstar said, outraged. "Are you aware that one of them is their king? What will they say when they see their king is gone?"

"No, you misunderstand," Snakeheart said. "Drow society is on the brink of implosion, thanks to what has happened here. The Drow monarchy is passed through the male of the line. The Drow queen will only be monarch until a male of the king's line comes forward, and that will only be after much bloodshed." He paused for a moment, and then continued in a firmer voice. "Drow are left where they are fallen—if they are considered to have fallen in battle—because the magicians reanimate them. It is the height of shame to be returned to life by a magician. The reanimated dead are used for slave labor."

Sunstar struggled to control her gorge. "So if the king was returned and reanimated, the living dead would rule the Drow?"

"Until the battle for succession is decided," Snakeheart said in a carefully neutral tone. "In any case, the Drow will be so busy fighting amongst themselves that they will leave you in peace for a while."

"So I get to cause civil war amongst the Drow by returning their dead?" Sunstar said. "That's no choice at all. So why not just tell the Drow he's dead and let them fight amongst themselves?"

"You could do that. But I can assure you the queen will come after you because she will no longer be queen." Snakeheart shook his head. "The new king will certainly kill her. Her life will be measured in minutes once the Drow find out His Majesty is dead."

"Oh, Sunstar," Morningstar said quietly.

Sunstar turned to her mother. "I didn't see you there."

Morningstar sank onto a seat by them.

Sunstar gave her a brief, humorless smile and turned back to Snakeheart. "So my choices are as follows. First, I can do nothing. We bury the dead and leave the Drow to their own devices. They won't know the king is dead but will soon guess because he never returns home. They will enter our lands to investigate, will find me alive, and the queen will attack us because her life is now to be measured in minutes. Second, I can return the Drow king to his people, he will be reanimated, and the queen will attack us because her life is now to be measured in minutes. Third, I can inform the queen that her husband is dead, and the queen will attack us because her life is now to be measured in minutes."

"Sunstar—" Morningstar began.

"I said, *is that it*, Snakeheart?" Sunstar asked.

"Those are your choices, and that is why you must face them," Snakeheart said. "But please do not overlook one important point. It is the *queen* that has issue with *you*. Not the Drow as a race. Not the Drow who becomes the new king. He will not trouble himself with you since you helped his ascension to the throne. It is the queen. *Your* people are not in danger. *You* are. By staying amongst your people *you* put us all in danger from the queen, because something as trifling as a city of Forest Elves will not be enough to stop her from reaching you."

"I have to leave again," Sunstar whispered. She felt numb. "I must choose between myself and our people, and that is no choice at all." Snakeheart's words echoed and ricocheted inside her mind.

"Sunstar," Morningstar said. "You can't leave here. You are the crown princess. You have an army to protect you."

"Mother, I can't." Sunstar held up her hand. "Listen to me. I made a terrible mistake when I ran out of the city with Meagan, and every decision I have made since then has made things worse." She paused for a moment. "I have done nothing but shiver and cower behind others. Everyone but me has paid the price for my indiscretions. Now it is time for me to stand by myself."

"Sunstar," Snakeheart said. "I will go with you."

"Didn't you hear what I just said? This is my problem, and I won't allow anyone else to pay for my mistakes."

"I heard you," Snakeheart said. "And as a loyal citizen of this nation I will not allow any member of the royal family to go and face an armed opponent without an honor guard."

"You want me to take you out there just so you can fight for me?" Sunstar asked.

Snakeheart shook his head. "I can and will teach you to fight, Princess. I will go with you."

"Why?" Sunstar asked. "Why would you do this for me? And don't tell me anything about Elven nobility."

"The Elven nation has always been confused about how to treat us former Drow, Your Highness, but at least you never hunted us as other races do. We can own land and live with other Elves, and we can make lives for ourselves."

"We are Elves. We do not choose to take lives," Morningstar said, and Sunstar winced at the self satisfaction in her words.

"Yes, we do," Sunstar said. "And we make sure to shun the ones that do it in our defense."

"Sunstar."

"It's true." Sunstar felt exhausted. Her head ached. "It's all very well to say all life is sacrosanct, but we live a lie. It's a hypocritical philosophy, and you know it."

"You don't know what you're talking about." Morningstar stared at her as though she had grown horns.

"I think she does, Your Highness," Snakeheart said.

"Silence." Morningstar glared at him.

"No, Snakeheart, speak," Sunstar said. "We must put aside philosophical conversations for the moment until we have more time. What do you propose we do about the queen? Where to meet with her?"

"Sunstar, enough of this," Morningstar said. "You *are not* going to face the Drow queen."

"Mother, let me alone." Sunstar controlled her temper with difficulty. "All this is my fault. If I stay here and hide behind you, more innocent Elves are going to get butchered, and for no good reason. I am not worth it. Nightshade was worth it. Snakeheart is worth it. But I am not."

"Why, Sunstar, why?" Morningstar asked.

"I have learnt a lot about the world, even though I have not spent much time in it," Sunstar said. "I have seen humans defending their homes from raiders. I have seen one Elf turn her back on her entire people and way of life simply to help me escape the Drow. Everything she did for me after that was because I asked her to. It did her no good to help me, and yet she did it, regardless of the cost to herself. If I am ever one tenth as good as she was, I will have lived my life well." She looked her mother in the eyes. "I did the wrong thing and I will deal with my own problem."

Morningstar sighed, and her mouth tightened in displeasure. "You will not reconsider this reckless choice of actions?"

Sunstar firmed her jaw and shook her head. Her mother simply did not understand that she had changed. She was not as thoughtless as she had been before. She understood what she was proposing and she knew what the consequences of her actions would be.

"I will try this one more time, daughter," Morningstar said. "Listen to me and listen well. Your first mistake was your silly prank that cost valuable lives. This will be your second—to endanger your own life by fighting the Drow by yourself. You are not a common Elf. You are a member of the royal house. You cannot place yourself in danger like that."

"Mother," Sunstar said with relentless gentleness. "That's as may be. But you forget one thing. I am not the only child you have. You forgot my brother and my sister. If I am killed, one of those two will wear the mantle of heir to the Elven crown. Even as a royal I'm not worth all that much."

Morningstar flinched. "Then perhaps the one argument I have left is the one that will persuade you. You are my daughter, and I love you. I don't want you to do this. I don't want you to get hurt."

"So we are closer to the truth." Sunstar felt as though Morningstar had twisted a knife in her heart, and she could feel herself bleed. "None of the other trappings really matter, do they? You don't want me to go because you are my mother and you don't want me to get hurt?"

Morningstar flushed. She nodded her head. "It is that simple, daughter."

Sunstar shook her head. "If I were any other Elf none of this would matter. But I am your daughter, and you are a queen." She sighed and flinched inwardly at the tears she could see building in her mother's eyes. "Remember this. I love you. So many nights I prayed for your arms. I prayed for yours and Father's love. I now try and repay some of the love you've given me, and to honor you by showing you I *have* learnt something. I want our people to be safe so I will go and take care of my problems with the Drow. I do, however, ask you for a small company of soldiers. I am not stupid enough to think that the queen will travel by herself."

Morningstar shook her head. "You have painted me into a corner, daughter." She got up and walked to the door, bowed as Sunstar had never seen her before. "Do as you wish. I will not help you nor will I stand in your way."

She left without looking back.

Sunstar felt sick. She turned back to Snakeheart. "What do you suggest?"

"I suggest we leave before your father finds out," Snakeheart said. "Even if you cannot get a group of soldiers to help you, you still have me and my friends."

Sunstar dredged up a smile for him, despite the misery in her heart. "Thank you, Snakeheart." She stood and paced, suddenly restless. "What do you propose we do?"

"Meet me by the northern gates at dawn tomorrow morning," Snakeheart said. "We will talk more then."

Sunstar nodded, and Snakeheart stood and began to leave. "Thank you, Snakeheart."

He inclined his head. "My pleasure, Your Highness." He pulled his cloak over his head and quickly left.

Sunstar took a last look around the alcove, seeing echoes of her mother. It hurt. She hoped that her mother would one day forgive her for doing what had to be done.

Sunstar sat on the windowsill in her room, looking out over the marketplace far down below. It was a hive of activity, the same bustle of Elves that had been in the marketplace for centuries. She hoped it would stay that way for centuries more.

I love Mother. I hope she forgives me. I would hate for this to be our final parting.

There was a knock at the door.

"Come," she called. The cool breeze lifted the hair off her forehead, and she smiled at the scent of flowers that it carried.

"Your mother told me what happened."

Sunstar turned and saw her father staring at her. He stood halfway into the room, his penetrating gaze weighing her, measuring her.

"May I sit?" he asked, gesturing toward one of chairs close to her.

Sunstar nodded, eyeing him warily.

"Don't look at me like that," he said as he sat down. "I see no point in exchanging pleasantries. Your mother told me about your little . . . discussion . . . this morning. She says that you are going regardless of what we have to say about it."

She gazed at him, his handsome features, vivid green eyes, and thick blonde hair, so like her own. She felt a surge of love for him.

"Please try to understand. I really don't want to hurt either one of you. Despite appearances to the contrary, I love you both very much. But something Snakeheart said has put all of this into perspective for me. He told me that the Drow are not after you or our people, they are after *me*. If I don't face them, they *will* be after our people, and I can't have that."

Darkwood held up his hand. "You are putting me in a very difficult position. I understand well both your mother's and your views, and I must choose between the two. When do you plan on moving forward?"

Sunstar gave him a suspicious stare.

"Please," he said, shaking his head. "I will not put either you or Snakeheart in the dungeon, nor will I lock you in your room. You are not a child, and you can make your own choices, good or bad."

"Tomorrow at dawn by the northern gates."

"Good," he said, standing. "I will let you know what I think by then."

Sunstar nodded. "Thank you, Father." She smiled. "I love you."

"I love you too, daughter." He cupped her face and smiled sadly at her. He gently kissed her forehead and then turned and left.

Sunstar looked out of the window. The day had lost some of its luster for her.

CHAPTER 26

Nightshade opened her eyes and found herself lying naked under a rough blanket that covered her bare breasts and reached down to mid thigh. She frowned in confusion and stretched cautiously. Her body felt absolutely fine.

She frowned and lifted the blanket. There was no sign of the knife wound. She had been healed.

She sat up, and was unable to suppress a soft groan.

"No, lie down," a small figure said in Drow, as he rushed toward her. "You have been badly injured and you must regain your strength."

"Who are you?" Nightshade asked in Drow. The small Goblin looked old and wore the robes of a wizard.

"I am Yargon, royal wizard of King Gilgrich," he replied. "You are Ragnath's friend."

"Ragnath?" Nightshade asked. "The little Goblin boy?"

"Yes. *Gargajin* Ragnath."

"Gargajin?"

"It means 'prince' in Goblin," Yargon said.

Nightshade's eyes widened. "I thought it was his name."

Yargon smiled and shook his head. "Yes, he has only begun to learn Drow and doesn't know many words yet. All in good time. King Gilgrich asked that he be told when you awoke." He quickly crossed to the other side of his cluttered room and pulled out Nightshade's clean and neatly folded clothes. "We don't have anything that would fit someone as large as yourself so we laundered your clothing."

"Thank you." Nightshade began to lift the blanket, and Yargon squeaked and turned his back.

"I have a bathing chamber behind that door," he said in a high and strangled voice as he pointed to a small door to one side of the room.

Nightshade smiled. "Thank you." She stood and reached over him to pluck her clothes out of his hands. She paused for a moment, allowing a sudden feeling of lightheadedness to pass.

She stepped through the door Yargon pointed to and found herself in a large, airy bathing chamber. It was lit by candles in a series of alcoves. Water flowed down a rock face into a basin carved into a slab of stone. She cautiously put her hand in the water and found it lukewarm.

Perfect, she thought. *Certainly better than freezing river water.*

She bathed and dressed and quickly made her way back into Yargon's chamber. She dropped to her knee, as was Elven custom, since she seemed to be in the presence of a monarch. King Gilgrich—dressed in richly-appointed clothing—sat at a table, talking quietly to Yargon.

"Ah, Nightshade, is it? You're awake," King Gilgrich said. He gave her a broad smile, revealing impossibly sharp and pointed teeth.

"I am awake. I assume I have you to thank for my healing?"

Gilgrich nodded.

"Thank you, Your Highness," Nightshade said.

"You're welcome. It was the least we could do to help one of the Elves that rescued our son from the human slave traders."

"It was my pleasure," Nightshade said with a smile. "He is a good little boy."

"And my only son," Gilgrich said. "You know he followed you when you went toward Elven lands? He saw the fight with the party of Drow." He leaned forward and eyed her closely. "He is why you're still alive. What happened, Nightshade? We heard some talk of a kidnapped Elven princess?"

Nightshade bowed her head. "It is a long and complicated story, Your Highness."

"Then tell me," Gilgrich said quietly. "We have all the time we need." He pulled a rope that hung on a nearby wall. "And we will eat while we talk."

Yargon nodded. "May I remain, Your Highness?"

Gilgrich waved a hand. "Of course." He patted the chair beside him. "Sit, Nightshade."

Nightshade sat, wondering where to begin. The Goblin King seemed kindly, and she felt at ease with him. She finally took a deep breath and began right at the beginning. It took her hours to tell, and when she finished the table was littered with plates and empty trays of food.

"Well," King Gilgrich said. "I assume that now you want to go back to the Elven forest? For your Sunstar?"

Nightshade bit her lip. Every second she spent away from Sunstar felt like an eternity. She felt pain deep within herself, and everywhere she looked she saw almond-shaped, green eyes. It made her want to cry.

"Yes, I would," she said. "But first I must offer my thanks. It is not enough for the kindness you have shown me, but it is all I have."

"There is no debt," Gilgrich said. "You saved my son's life. Not many would. We are Goblins, and we know what other races think of us."

She remembered the way villagers had thrown stones at them after she had interrupted a raid on their home. The humans could not see beyond her glowing eyes. She thought of Ragnath's sobs and his terror, the sounds of misery from a child. "I don't. I know better than that."

Gilgrich gave her a genuine smile. "I believe you do." He nodded. "There is one further favor I would like to ask of you. I would like an introduction to the Elven monarchs."

"May I ask why?" Nightshade asked. She needed one herself. She was uncertain of her reception with the Elves, less so of their response to a missive from the Goblin king. *But what does it matter? All I can do is try. I will ask Sunstar when I see her again. She will listen to me, and I can at least try and repay his kindness.*

"I would like a treaty with the Elves," he said. "I need some help policing this part of our lands. We are on the border with the Elves, and it would help if they sent more patrols."

Nightshade nodded. "I am more than happy to help you, Your Highness."

"Good," King Gilgrich said. "We had planned on starting out tomorrow. The slavers and Powrie Dwarves are massing in the forest by the abandoned Dwarven mine, and we need some help."

Nightshade grimaced at the mention of the Dwarves. "You plan on going to the surface from there?"

"Yes, to see their numbers and also to give the Elves plenty of time to see that we are coming." He leaned forward and patted her knee. "Rest, now. Tomorrow we will go forth to your Sunstar."

Nightshade gave vent to a bone-cracking yawn. She felt completely exhausted and husked out. Yargon jabbed her and pointed to the bed, his wrinkled lips pressed into a determined, straight line. Nightshade smiled at him and nodded.

"Thank you," she said. She dragged herself over to the pallet and collapsed on it, asleep before her head hit the pillow.

Sunstar walked toward the Northern gates of the city. It never occurred to her to saddle a horse. She blinked and shrugged in the early morning light. She had not had breakfast. She had been too tense to eat after a night of vivid, cruel nightmares where Nightshade died over and over again.

She nodded to the guard. He came to attention.

"Tell my Mother and Father you saw me come this way and at what time," she said.

"Yes, Your Highness," he called back.

It was not much but at least they would know that she had set out to do what she had promised.

Another guard silently saluted her, and she waved back and resolutely walked out of the city gate.

Snakeheart stood fifty meters from the city gates, waiting for her. He blinked and looked at her with his unnerving glowing green eyes.

"Well met, Snakeheart." Sunstar clasped forearms with him. "Are you alone, or did you bring your friends?"

"They came with me. Our farm is in the other direction," he said. "Your friend also joined us."

Sunstar frowned. She had not invited any friends. Snakeheart saw her frown and waved a hand. A cloaked figure came out of the shadows, stopped, and stared at them.

"Who are you?" Sunstar asked. "Take off your cloak."

"All right, Princess." A handsome, black-haired Elf pushed back his cloak. His eyes were so dark brown they were almost black.

"Thank you," Sunstar said. "Who are you?"

"I am Takhisis," he said. "I am Captain Windwalker's second in command. King Darkwood thought you could use my sword arm."

"How come I never heard of you?" she asked.

"I got promoted while you were away," he said.

Sunstar shot him another quick glance and sighed. His explanation did not help. She still did not recognize his name. She felt colder and lonelier than ever, and wished with all her might that Nightshade was with her. She shook herself. Wishing for Nightshade would not help her.

She nodded and turned back to Snakeheart. "All right, we're out in the open. What are your plans for now?"

"First, I will introduce you to my comrades. Follow me." Snakeheart turned and walked away without looking back.

Takhisis shot him a mistrustful look.

Sunstar gave him a reassuring smile. "Trust me, lieutenant. If he wanted us dead, we would be dead already."

"That makes no sense," Takhisis muttered. "If he tried to harm you, he would be dead before his sword left his scabbard."

"I hate to tell you this," Sunstar said, "but if he were of a mind to hurt either one of us, we would both already be dead, consequences be damned. Drow are outstanding fighters and do not suffer from the same philosophical objections to violence that we do."

"Or that you pretend to have." Snakeheart coolly eyed Takhisis.

Takhisis scowled at him.

"Play nicely," Sunstar said. "We will be companions for a while, and I have no desire to pull you apart all the time."

Takhisis and Snakeheart exchanged a glance that was saturated with dislike.

Snakeheart turned off the road and led them a way into the forest. They stopped under a heavily shadowed tree, and Sunstar blinked. She could barely see anything, despite the gathering dawn.

Snakeheart gave a low whistle, and five Drow materialized out of the undergrowth. Two were female, the remaining three male. Sunstar blinked at the difference in their eyes. There was no glowing red or gold amongst any of them. They were all greens, blues and browns.

"Those two," he pointed to the females, "are Obsidian and Onyx. They," he indicated the males, "are Ironheart, Flamestrike, and Firestorm." He turned to the Drow. "Sunstar and Takhisis."

The Drow inclined their heads and stared without expression at the two Elves.

"Sit." Snakeheart sank down onto a convenient rock, and the others followed his lead.

"Shouldn't we move?" Takhisis asked.

"I won't be able to see anything in a few moments," Snakeheart said. "We are in no hurry."

"Do you trust me to lead you?" Sunstar asked.

Snakeheart stared at her, his surprise evident in a minute furrow of his brow. "It would be nice, but I wasn't expecting you to do it."

"I don't mind, and if we have to move, it's the easiest way to do it."

Snakeheart exchanged a glance with the other Drow. Obsidian nodded slightly and the rest followed suit.

"All right. We agree." He straightened his long legs. "Now, you must tell us more. Who was found with the Drow king? What happened?"

Sunstar took a deep breath, almost embarrassed. She did not feel comfortable talking about Nightshade. It was still too raw and fresh. "We had finally made it back over the mountains onto Elven lands when . . ."

She told it quickly and well, and when she finished, Snakeheart shook his head and exchanged a grave glance with the other Drow.

"What?" Takhisis kept his gaze on Sunstar, as though carefully weighing and measuring her.

"All Drow scout leaders have a jewel sewn into their cloaks," Snakeheart said. "The jewels are all linked to a parent stone. The jewels are activated when the owner of the cloak's blood is spilt. It transmits the blood awareness to the parent stone. Normally it is only the leader of the Drow scouts that pays any attention to the activated jewels, but in this case, since Galvin and Farouk were both with His Highness, I'm sure the queen had watched the parent stone as well. There is a possibility that she already knows that the king is dead."

"So we walk into a trap?" Takhisis said.

"The queen is a powerful magician," Snakeheart said. "If she wanted to teleport into Sunstar's bathtub I'm sure she could do it. In fact, I'm sure she would have done it by now. No, she must not know, or the princess would already be dead."

"How could she not know? Isn't it just as likely that she's preparing herself for a meeting with me?" Sunstar marshaled her courage. She was dimly amazed she sounded as relaxed as she did.

"Perhaps we have some leeway," Snakeheart said. "She will not be able to return to Dragonar, and until a new heir comes forth to make a claim on the throne she is in charge. I think you are right. I am guessing she will take this time to prepare a nasty surprise for us." He fell silent for a moment. "She might also be interested in this friend of yours, Nightshade."

"Why?" Sunstar asked. "We never found Nightshade."

"Perhaps Nightshade is already back in Dragonar," Takhisis said.

"That would be the most logical explanation for why you haven't found her."

Sunstar flinched. "That doesn't matter for now. We must focus on the task at hand. We must find out about the queen." She sighed. "What also matters now is that I'm nowhere near the city when the queen comes looking for me." She glanced at Snakeheart. "I am thinking that we go back to where I was found. If I were the queen, that's the first place I'd start looking."

Takhisis unwillingly nodded. "I agree, Highness."

"As do I," Snakeheart said.

"Do you know if Windwalker and the others are still in the forest there?" Sunstar asked.

Takhisis shook his head. "I doubt it. Your father called them home."

"If the queen is going to go where the bodies are, what if they are on their way back here?" Sunstar asked.

"We will meet them on the way," Takhisis said. "It will be a caravan, and not easy to miss."

"All right," Sunstar said. "Then let's head back to the clearing."

They all stood. The Drow pulled their cloaks up to shield their faces from the sun. Sunstar took Snakeheart's hand and tucked it under her arm. The other Drow followed suit so a chain formed behind Snakeheart.

CHAPTER 27

Sunstar soon discovered that it was much more difficult to lead a group of blind Drow than one Drow. She finally called a halt after they had tripped and collided with one another for the fifth time. Sunstar and Takhisis each led two Drow, and the final one—Snakeheart—held onto Onyx, who in turn held onto Sunstar.

Sunstar walked behind Takhisis, paying careful attention to his broad back. She had asked her mother for a contingent of soldiers, but she had said she would not help. If Sunstar had ordered guards to go with her, they would not have refused her. Her father would never refuse a request for protection. So why did he send only one soldier? One she had never heard of? She knew that she did not know every soldier in her father's army, but she did know his officers. So why had she never heard of him? Even before she had been captured by the Drow?

"What unit were you with before you were promoted?" Sunstar asked.

Takhisis remained silent.

"Lieutenant?" she asked after a few minutes.

"I'm sorry, Your Highness," he said. "I'm trying to listen to the forest."

"Meaning?"

"I'm listening to make sure that we have fair warning if anyone comes near us. This area of the forest is never completely quiet."

"Why?" Sunstar asked. "These are our lands. Why aren't they free of bandits?"

Takhisis remained silent.

Sunstar heard Snakeheart sigh behind her and fought the urge to turn and roll her eyes at him. He would not be able to see her anyway.

The Drow were naturally silent, and Takhisis refused to talk, so it was a silent party that traveled through the forest for the next few hours until the midday break. They stopped and sat down in a clearing, and Snakeheart pulled out a small bundle of food from his pack. He handed it to Sunstar with an apologetic shrug.

Sunstar glanced at Takhisis. He leant against the trunk of a tree with his eyes closed. Sunstar felt a surge of dislike and smothered it. Her father had asked him to come along for a good reason despite his apparent lack of grace. She wondered why he would not tell her what unit he had been in until his promotion.

The package contained the same trail mix she had eaten with the Drow during their march to Dragonar, and Sunstar grimaced. She looked up sharply at the sound of a low chuckle. Takhisis remained beneath his trees, and the Drow silently waited for her.

She dealt out the food, and the Drow took it with silent bows of thanks. She walked to the tree and nudged Takhisis. He opened his eyes and stared at her. She held out the package.

"Hungry?" she asked.

He stared at her with distaste. She shrugged, backed away, and stifled another swift surge of dislike. She went and sat down next to Snakeheart.

"I don't like him," Snakeheart whispered.

Sunstar smiled ruefully. "I don't either. I don't care how good a swordsman he is, I don't want to end up with him as a bodyguard."

Snakeheart nodded. "If you want, we will teach you how to fight as a Drow."

Sunstar thought about Nightshade, her fearlessness and her incredible skill with a sword, and smiled. "Thank you. I would like that."

Snakeheart nodded, and she could feel his approval although she still could not see him.

"Finish up," Takhisis said abruptly. "We move out in five minutes."

Sunstar bit off a sharp retort. She rewrapped the package of food and gave it back to Snakeheart. He quickly put it back into his pack and took Sunstar's arm.

The march through the forest in the afternoon was as silent as it had been in the morning. The Drow stayed close to Sunstar, and she led them carefully around objects so her charges rarely stumbled.

The Drow led by Takhisis were not so lucky. He took no care with them at all and frequently cursed when they stumbled. Sunstar held her tongue for as long as she could, but her temper finally erupted after Ironheart fell to his knees going over a large root. Takhisis hauled him to his feet, then shoved back Flamestrike and Firestorm while muttering under his breath.

Sunstar struggled to hide the surge of dislike his actions provoked. She wondered if she had ever been like that. In a flash she thought of the question that Snakeheart had asked her. *If I put my hands over your eyes and said, "I found a young female in the forest. She was kidnapped and tortured. She escaped. I'm bringing her home," what would you assume?*

"Clumsy idiot," Takhisis muttered. "Watch where you're going."

Sunstar closed her eyes and listened again to the tirade. She could not hear any difference between him and the Drow that had taken her captive. The realization saddened her.

"Enough, Takhisis," she said. "That's quite enough."

"He hit me on purpose." Takhisis shoved Ironheart.

"He cannot see anything," she shot back. "Ironheart, are you all right?"

"Yes, Sunstar," Ironheart said as he dusted off his knees.

"Lead them *nicely,* Takhisis," Sunstar said coolly. "Or I will have you clapped in irons and dragged back to the city with the same care you are showing to our friends."

"*Our* friends? Oh, these are not *our* friends. They are *your* friends," Takhisis said coldly. "You really think you can do what you want to me? I think not. By whose authority do you think you can do this?"

"*My* authority," Sunstar ground out through gritted teeth. "I am the crown princess."

"And an irresponsible ass," Takhisis said equally coldly. "You want to send me away? Fine. Go right ahead. But I'm sure your parents will have something to say about your stupidity at staying with full-blooded Drow in the forest after dark."

Sunstar felt shocked to her core for a precious few seconds, and she hesitated. *I trust Snakeheart*, she told herself as she tried to crush the thread of doubt and fear worming into her heart. She felt a moment of disgust in herself. Out of both of them, Snakeheart had shown her ten times the kindness and civility of Takhisis. What right did Takhisis have to question Snakeheart's honor?

"See? You don't trust them either." Takhisis folded his arms and looked down his nose at her. "Why did you bring them?"

"Silence," Snakeheart ordered. He turned to Sunstar. "I understand that you have your doubts, and that is well. It is good. But make sure they remain *your* doubts." He turned to Takhisis. "You will remain silent and keep your opinions to yourself."

"Are you threatening me, Drow?" Takhisis stepped toward Snakeheart and shoved him.

Snakeheart quickly sidestepped the brunt of the impact, and Takhisis's momentum took him past. He grabbed Takhisis's arm and pulled it up against his back. Takhisis yelped in pain.

"If I wanted you dead, you would be dead, lieutenant," Snakeheart said. "As you so rightly point out, I am a full-blooded Drow, and I do not require sight to fight an opponent."

"Enough." Sunstar finally found her tongue and calmed her heartbeat. Snakeheart's words reminded her of Nightshade's abilities, and she felt a stab of pain. "Let go of him, Snakeheart. Let's try to get to Windwalker with no lives lost, shall we?"

Snakeheart let Takhisis go. Takhisis glared at Snakeheart as he took Ironheart's arm.

They walked through the afternoon. Sunstar was pleased that although Takhisis still led the Drow with an ill-concealed lack of grace, he no longer cursed at them when they stumbled.

Sunstar wondered how many other Elves felt as Takhisis did towards their Dark Elf population.

"No, Sunstar," Snakeheart said quietly.

"No, what?" Sunstar shook herself out of her reverie.

"No, not all Elves are like Takhisis," Snakeheart said. "Our neighbors treat us with courtesy and respect, with the exception of Shiningopal." He was silent a moment. "But even then, Shiningopal treated all of his neighbors as a nuisance."

Sunstar smiled. "One day all of you and I are going to have to sit down and talk. I would love to know how you come to be here, when you have an entire world to choose from."

"It is because you are kin," Obsidian said.

Sunstar almost started. She had not heard the female Drow speak before.

"I would like to think so," Sunstar said. "But I don't know if we all feel that way."

"It is enough, Princess," Obsidian said.

Sunstar nodded, wondering if she believed it or not.

Snakeheart pushed his hood back off his head and eyed Sunstar, his glowing green eyes lightening in the gloom.

"You say this is where you were found?" he asked.

Sunstar nodded and bit her lip. The clearing was empty. There was no sign of either Windwalker and his guards or the bodies they had found. The forest itself was quiet, and Sunstar closed her eyes. She listened carefully and scented the air. It was unusually silent. Takhisis had gone further into the forest toward the bushes where Hemlock had been found. Sunstar steeled herself. She wanted to follow him, but was afraid they had found Nightshade. She wanted to believe Nightshade was still alive.

"Where are they?" Snakeheart looked around and blinked.

"How much can you see?" Sunstar asked.

"It's still too bright for me," he said. "But at least it doesn't hurt quite so much anymore."

"Snakeheart," Firestorm called.

Snakeheart and Sunstar joined Firestorm, who was scenting the air. His hood was thrown back but he kept his eyes tightly closed against the too bright dusk.

"What is it?" Snakeheart asked.

Firestorm kept scenting the air, and Snakeheart shot him a quick glance and did the same. He frowned.

"What is it?" Sunstar asked.

"Blood," Snakeheart said shortly. "A lot of it."

"Are you sure?" Sunstar asked. She looked in the direction Takhisis had gone in.

"I'm sure," Snakeheart said. "Who can see?"

"I can see a little," Obsidian said.

"Good. See if you can see any of the bodies that were supposed to be here," Snakeheart said.

Obsidian nodded, and they spread out. Sunstar followed Takhisis and went further along the trail toward where they had found the Drow king. There were no signs of any bodies, and there was fresh blood splattered all over the path. Sunstar forced down bile, feeling a deep disquiet sinking into her soul. She struggled to control the feeling of dread washing over her in cold waves.

"Looks like they're gone," Takhisis said, suddenly from beside her.

She yelped and jumped.

He gave her a surprised look. "Pardon me, Princess." He smirked and bowed. "I didn't mean to startle you."

"That's quite all right." She was caught unawares by a surge of dislike so strong she struggled with the urge to slap him. “What have you got to report?”

“Well,” Takhisis said, frowning. “There are no bodies up the trail. None. No Drow, no Elf.”

“Where is Windwalker?” Sunstar turned and walked back to Snakeheart and the other Drow. She trusted them more than she trusted Takhisis.

“He could be well on his way back to the city,” Takhisis said. “We will stay here overnight and return in the morning.”

“Since when do you give the orders?” Snakeheart emerged from the gloom.

“I am in charge,” Takhisis said. “Not you. *I* see to the welfare of the princess, not you.”

Snakeheart drew in breath to argue.

“Enough,” Sunstar said. “Snakeheart, did you find anything?”

“I’m not sure,” he said. “There was fighting here a short time ago, that is all I can tell you.”

“Your recommendations?” she asked, pointedly ignoring Takhisis. She could almost hear him grind his teeth.

“We should stay here tonight and head back in the morning,” Snakeheart said. “We need to rest before we return. We’re all tired,” he continued as Sunstar looked set to argue.

“We should at least eat something,” Takhisis said.

Sunstar nodded. She was hungry and tired, despite feeling strung out. Her nerves were singing, and she did not completely understand why.

They rejoined the other Drow in the clearing, and Onyx and Flamestrike scattered to gather wood for a fire. Takhisis produced a package of trail rations when they returned and dealt out the food.

Snakeheart stared at it suspiciously and shot a glare at Takhisis. Takhisis color darkened, and his brow furrowed in anger.

Sunstar stepped between them. “Enough. Play nicely. If all you’re going to do is fight, say nothing at all.”

Takhisis and Snakeheart glared at each other.

They all sat down to eat. Takhisis sat on one side of the fire, the Drow clustered around the other. Sunstar sat in the middle, rolling mental eyes.

After they had finished, Sunstar sat with her back against a convenient rock and sighed. She felt exhausted. Takhisis watched them carefully, his eyes bright.

Sunstar felt as though her head weighed a thousand pounds, and her fingers and toes tingled.

She looked at Snakeheart. His eyes were closed, and he was leaning against Ironheart. Ironheart also looked as though he was asleep, and Sunstar felt an instant of alarm. She wanted to open her mouth to speak but found with horror that she could not speak. Her mouth would not move.

Her hands, feet, head, chest, all would not move.

Takhisis got up from his spot before the fire with a chuckle. "There was a little something in your dinner, Sunstar." He nudged her with his foot and snorted. "I have a buyer for you." He stood and whistled toward the trees.

Sunstar turned her eyes toward Snakeheart. His eyes were open and staring in horror.

Sunstar wanted to scream as a group of horribly familiar human men came out of the undergrowth. They approached the camp and quickly slit all the Drows' throats, save Snakeheart. Sunstar wanted to scream in agony as their lives bled out in a crimson flood in the dirt before the flames.

"You forgot one, Merton," Takhisis said coldly. He pulled his knife and strode toward Snakeheart.

"No," Merton said. "We didn't forget. He'll fetch a high price. He's a full-blooded Drow, and look at those pretty eyes of his."

"Equal share?" Takhisis asked.

"Of course." Merton tilted his head to one side. "Take off that ridiculous mask, would you?"

Takhisis chuckled and reached for a point beneath his ear. "Bothering you, is it?" He tugged, and it looked as though his face came off in his hands.

Sunstar stared. In place of handsome Elven features was a human male. His face was swarthy and a mass of scar tissue. One of his eyes was gone and the socket was filled with pus. Sunstar struggled to control her bile.

"That's better. Let's put them to sleep. We'll burn the other Drow bodies. We don't want them waking up on the march, do we?" Merton did not wait for a response. He quickly bashed the hilt of his sword across the back of Snakeheart's head. Snakeheart slumped, unconscious.

Sunstar drew in breath but a blinding pain erupted in the back of her head. Consciousness deserted her, and she knew no more.

CHAPTER 28

Sunstar opened her eyes. The air burned with predawn light. She was lying on the ground, close to Snakeheart. She cautiously tried to move, and her entire body protested. She glanced at Snakeheart but could not see his face.

The clearing they were in did not look familiar. They had been carried overnight. She wondered for a few moments what had happened to Ironheart and their other friends. Had the humans really burned them or left them to rot where they fell? Would the Drow be looking for them to reanimate them, or were they safe where they were? Either way, she and Snakeheart would go back after they had finished with the slavers and the Drow queen. They deserved at least that much.

A shadow fell over her.

"You're awake," Takhisis said. "Good."

Sunstar rolled over and saw the tall human staring at them with cold delight. She wished she was unbound so she could tackle and pummel him.

"Who *are* you?" she asked.

"You want to know who I am as opposed to where you are? Charming. That's an example of the type of thinking that got you into trouble to begin with."

"I have no interest whatsoever in discussing whatever trouble you think I was in," Sunstar said coldly. "My life and actions are *not* any concern of yours. Given that you appear to be a slave trader, I really don't think you're in any position to discuss morality with me."

He strode over to her and backhanded her, followed with a swift kick to the ribs. Fresh agony exploded in her body, and she moaned in pain.

He knelt over her and pulled her head back by her shaggy fringe. "You want to know who I am? I am the one who brings you back to Her Highness."

Sunstar felt her blood run cold. "You mean the Drow queen, don't you?" Her voice faltered, and she cursed her weakness.

Takhisis nodded. "I most certainly do. And if it makes you feel any better, she's paying premium rates for you."

"Idiot," she said coldly. "Of course I don't feel better. I'm trussed up like livestock and suffering the presence of a human who killed almost all of my traveling companions."

Takhisis smiled. "Strange world, isn't it?"

Sunstar glared at him. She felt a rolling wave of anger and tried to push it down. She would have to keep calm and her wits about her if she was to escape with Snakeheart.

"Where are the other Elves from the clearing? And how did you get so close to my father's city?"

Takhisis tilted his head and regarded her. "That's all for me to know and you to find out."

"Your answer, I assume, would be the same if I asked you where we were going," she said.

Takhisis gave her an insultingly superior grin. "Almost. I'd tell you that you were well on your way to meet Her Highness."

"When my father finds out about this—"

"Grow up," Takhisis snarled. "Why do we always expect Daddy to come rushing in on his charger? He's not coming, believe me. By the time he realizes there's a problem you'll be long dead."

Sunstar growled at him, unrestrained hatred rolling over her in cold waves. Snakeheart stirred beside her, groaning softly.

"Oh, look," Takhisis said. "It's awake."

"My head," Snakeheart muttered. He shifted. "Sunstar, is that you?"

"It's me, Snakeheart," Sunstar said.

"Are you harmed?" he asked.

"No," Sunstar said.

"No more talking," Takhisis said coldly. The bushes rustled around him, and he stood. "Merton." He greeted the human who approached him. "How's it look?"

"We're clear," Merton said. "Road looks good all the way to the mine."

Mine? Sunstar searched her memory for any mines that were on her father's land. The only one she could think was the one that she and Nightshade had been in with Gargajin before they had reached Elven lands.

"Good," Takhisis said. "I just want to get paid and get the hell out of here."

Merton regarded him for a moment. "Agreed. Let's move out." He glanced over his shoulder. "Boys. We're leaving."

The forest came alive as bandit slave traders filtered in through the undergrowth. Dawn's early light shone through the trees, falling on Sunstar's skin. Takhisis and Merton exchanged a quick glance.

"It's time for you to go to sleep again, Princess." Takhisis pulled a flask out of his jerkin and shook it.

"No," Sunstar said.

"*Yes*." Takhisis pulled her head back by the fringe and forced the bottle to her open lips. He poured, and a bitter taste flooded her mouth. She coughed as it coated her throat and windpipe. She unwillingly swallowed.

"There." Takhisis released her as she rolled sideways, gagging and coughing.

"Ah, no," Sunstar moaned as her arms and legs began to tingle. She was unconscious by the time her lips went numb.

❧

"Look, I think she's waking up."

"It's about time. We're nearly there, and I'm sick of dragging her around."

Sunstar opened her eyes, and she blinked to focus on her surroundings. She was lying out on the flat ground by the doors to the Dwarven hall, and the human bandits were clustered around her. Snakeheart, still out cold, lay on the ground beside her. They rested in the deep shadow of the doors, and the sunlight had a golden hue that told her it was either dusk or dawn again.

Takhisis bent over her and gave her a smile that did not touch his remaining eye.

"Good evening, Princess," he said with gross civility, and Sunstar suppressed a shudder.

Merton knelt beside him. "We have a buyer for you. She's very keen to see you again. She said you would remember her."

Sunstar stared at him, silent. She understood the Drow queen had paid for her. She allowed the silence to stretch out until Merton dropped his eyes and shook his head.

"Well?" she asked. "What are you waiting for?"

"We're waiting for the buyers we have for him." Takhisis nudged Snakeheart with the toe of his boot.

"Who are already here." A small male emerged from the bushes by the hall doors. He was no more than four-and-a-half feet in height, massive through the shoulders and arms, and had a long beard that reached down to his knees. He stank abominably, and wore a crimson cap.

"Who do we have here?" he asked with interest, leaning over Sunstar with his ham-like fists resting comfortably on his thick thighs. She suppressed a shudder at the stench of unwashed body coming off him in waves.

"Princess Sunstar, Crown Princess of the Forest Elves," Takhisis said.

"Oh, ho!" The Dwarf straightened and clapped his hands. "What a prize." He grinned evilly at Takhisis. "Does her father know she's out and about?"

"I have no idea," Takhisis said. "I was just trying to figure out how to get into their city for her when she came out to me."

"Very impressive." The Dwarf glared at Sunstar. "How easy you make it for him." He looked beyond her. Sunstar followed his gaze to Snakeheart, feeling a measure of cheer when she saw Snakeheart's unblinking, glowing green eyes. He had recovered from the vile brew they had been fed.

"He's alive," the Dwarf said in some amazement.

"As requested," Takhisis said in satisfied tones. "Have you got the money we asked for?"

"We will see," the Dwarf said, a strong measure of malice flashing in his eyes. "If he can see well in the dark we will pay for him."

"He's a Drow," Takhisis said. "Of course he can see well in the dark."

"His eyes are different to a normal Drow's eyes. You won't get paid unless he sees as well as a normal Drow does."

"And how do you propose we test that?" Takhisis asked.

"We will take him into the mine and test his sight. One hundred gold pieces if he is intact and fifty otherwise."

"Two hundred gold pieces and not a piece less."

The Dwarf straightened. "One hundred." He put his hands on his hips and eyed Takhisis without mercy.

"*Two* hundred."

The Dwarf pointed to his hat. "Do you know why I wear a red cap?"

Takhisis shook his head, and gave the Dwarf a wary look.

"I am a Powrie," the Dwarf said. "The blood of all the lives I have taken is on my cap. It needs another dunking, and I will use your blood if you try and cheat me. I may use it anyway." He stared at Takhisis, his cold eyes showing the truth of his words. "The final price is one hundred gold pieces if intact, your death if he is not. Take it or leave it. If you leave it, I will kill you where you stand, human."

Takhisis paled ,and Sunstar struggled to control a surge of bile. A Powrie Dwarf. They were on par with Drow.

"Agreed," Takhisis said, his black eye smoldering with hatred and anger. The other humans shuffled their feet, aware that he had made a loss with the bargain.

"Let's go in there, then," the Powrie Dwarf said.

He approached the large doors, and other Powrie came out of hiding by the entrance. The humans hissed in shock and grabbed for their swords.

He pulled a war hammer out of his belt and rapped it on the door three times. A great, hollow booming sounded behind it, followed by ear splitting squealing and a howl of protest as the door swung open by itself.

The Dwarves did not stop to wait for anyone. They strode into the hall.

Takhisis and Merton exchanged a glance and pulled Sunstar and Snakeheart to their feet.

Sunstar's heart beat hard from the adrenalin whipping through her system. It was time. The Drow queen had come for her. There was no escape.

She glanced back at Snakeheart, and he gave her a quick smile of encouragement. Sunstar could not understand why he looked so relaxed. It did not matter if either or both of them were free. They were facing down too many opponents, including a detachment of Powrie Dwarves.

Takhisis dragged her into the hall, and she glanced around at the immense, empty space. She blinked and stared at the spot where Nightshade had fought the Drow. They were gone. Sunstar wondered who had gotten rid of them.

"Who's this?" The Powrie turned to a couple of the human bandits who led a group of tattered Elves into the hall.

Sunstar stared in shock, as did Windwalker, as they took in each other's captivity.

"Windwalker," she said.

"Highness," he called back.

Their captors slapped them.

"We found them." The man tugged at Windwalker's ties and pulled him to the ground. "In the clearing."

Takhisis eyed them curiously. "Well done. Perhaps our buyer will want them as well."

Takhisis grabbed Sunstar and dragged her into a chalk figure drawn on the floor. He threw her down and knelt on her. She struggled but he was much stronger. He took out his dagger and sliced open her forearm, dripping blood into the exact center of a circle. It pooled in unnatural symmetry as though the chalk mark were a bowl to hold it.

The air became charged, and everyone took a step back. The chamber filled with the same low light that pervaded the Drow city. Sunstar heard a ripping sound and a tear formed in mid air reaching to the ground. She gaped as the Drow queen stepped through.

She snarled and waved a hand. The doors to the hall flew shut with a hollow boom loud enough for everyone to clap their hands over their ears. Sunstar, unable to cover her ears, shook her aching head, hoping the ringing in her ears was only temporary.

"Little Sunstar." The Drow queen approached Sunstar. "How good it is to see you again." She ran a finger along Sunstar's jaw, and Sunstar jerked her head back.

Sunstar marshaled all of her courage together to still her shaking. Of all the scenarios that had gone through her mind, bound as a slave before the Drow queen had not been amongst them.

"Don't touch me," she said coldly.

"Let go of her," Windwalker said.

A human punched him in the stomach and glared at him as if to dare him to say more.

The queen ignored him. "Where are the others?" she asked Takhisis.

Takhisis eyed her and nodded sharply. More humans appeared, carrying large sacks between them. They put them on the floor, and Takhisis used his dagger to cut the closest one open.

The stench of rotting flesh filled their nostrils, and Sunstar fell to her knees, gagging violently.

The queen glanced at her, amused, and knelt by the bag. She ran her hand down the rotting face of the Drow king. She bent over and kissed his lips gently. "Farewell, my king."

"Our pay?" Takhisis said. "We have fulfilled our end of the bargain and wish to be away."

The queen stared at him. "Yes, of course." She reached into her robes and pulled something out of it. Takhisis hissed and took a step back.

Swift as a striking snake, the queen lunged at him and blew a handful of sparkling dust into his face. Takhisis buckled, coughed, and gagged. His tortured breathing echoed in the chamber, followed by his soft whimpers of pain. His whimpers soon changed to cries of pain and then great, searing gusts of agony as his flesh liquefied and streamed off his body in fatty runners.

The terrible noises coming from him abruptly ceased. Sunstar blinked and saw a long arrow sticking out of his throat.

The Queen stared at the arrow. "I am betrayed!" she screamed, twisting and looking all around the great hall.

A rough voice screamed a command, and the humans and Drow queen were engulfed in armored Goblins wielding swords.

The Powrie, despite their declared love of bloodshed, grabbed the bound Elves and pulled them toward a side alcove.

"Quick!" The lead Powrie grabbed Sunstar and pulled her along. They sat the Elves against a wall in a side chamber with the armed, grim-faced Powrie watching the entrance closely.

A Goblin spotted them, raised his dripping sword, and called a command. A detachment of Goblin soldiers disengaged the humans and raced toward the side chamber. The Powrie cursed and fought back.

"Quick," Snakeheart said. "Untie me or they are dead."

"Who said the Goblins are on our side?" Windwalker asked as Sunstar and Snakeheart scrabbled around so they were back to back. Sunstar ran her fingers along the knots of his bonds. It was a simple knot, and she easily tugged it loose

"Thanks," Snakeheart gasped. He quickly flexed his hands and untied the ropes at his ankles.

The Powrie backed into the chamber, overcome by the force of sheer numbers. Goblins lay dead and dying all around them, but only one Powrie had fallen. The others nursed assorted injuries but all still fought as though possessed. Snakeheart grabbed a fallen Goblin sword off the floor and engaged the lead Powrie.

"Sunstar," Windwalker said. "My bonds."

Sunstar nodded and backed toward him. She felt the knots holding his hands together, and quickly freed him. Windwalker grunted thanks and hastily untied his ankles. He reached behind her and loosened her bonds, and she pulled the ropes from her wrists and ankles. The other Elven guards who had untied each other's bonds sprinted across the chamber in search of free weapons.

Snakeheart fought like a Drow possessed and inch by inch the Goblins and Snakeheart overcame the Powrie. Sunstar stayed back against the wall, cursing her lack of fighting skill. She watched dispassionately as blood splattered the alcove.

A sound from the passageway to her right caught her attention.

It was a dreadfully familiar tearing sound.

Sunstar looked in the gloom to her left, and saw the queen's red eyes staring balefully at her.

"Snakeheart. Help," she screamed as the queen lunged for her. She tried to pull out of the queen's grasp but she was a split second too late. The queen's fingers tightened around Sunstar's wrist, and she chanted.

Sunstar felt a surge of raw panic and fell backward into the queen. She spun around and put her open palm into the queen's throat. The queen coughed and doubled over, releasing her grip on Sunstar.

Sunstar blindly dove out of her reach and skidded along the passageway on her knees, crying out in pain. The queen snarled, dove at her, and grasped the back of her shirt.

"My life is over because of you, Elf." The queen pulled her backward. "I will have my revenge for this."

"No," Sunstar said. "You've already taken everything I ever loved." Her temper snapped.

"Let her go," a new voice said.

Sunstar looked up at the figure striding toward them. Her heart lurched painfully at the sight of glowing blue eyes.

"Nightshade," Sunstar whispered in heartfelt relief. Her shoulders sagged, and she released a breath.

A barest flicker of a smile flitted over Nightshade's beautiful features at the sight of Sunstar. Her eyes blazed with emotion that matched Sunstar's.

The queen's eyes widened and blazed red. "It is good you could join us, little Nightshade." She glanced at Sunstar and chanted softly.

Sunstar felt sick as she recognized Hemlock's paralysis chant. She tried to lunge at the queen, but her muscles felt as though they were made of lead. She sobbed inwardly as the queen gave her a smile that did not touch her eyes.

No, not Nightshade, she thought as she watched Nightshade run toward them, cloak billowing as she tried to draw her sword.

The queen held out her hand and whispered a few words in Drow. Nightshade stopped dead and fell to her knees, inches from the queen. Her eyes shone with rage.

"You will not touch her," Nightshade said through gritted teeth. "I will kill you before I let you hurt her."

The queen laughed softly. "You are hardly in a position to threaten *me*, Nightshade." She tilted her head and studied her. "I can do whatever I like, and you can't stop me."

She smiled and turned toward Sunstar, who was leaning against the wall. She stroked the side of Sunstar's face and gently cupped her cheek.

The queen turned to Nightshade. "This bothers you, doesn't it?" She ran a finger down Sunstar's neck to the smooth skin of her chest. "You . . . love . . . her, don't you?" She knelt before Sunstar and kissed her.

"No." The pain in Nightshade's voice was almost palatable.

Sunstar fought back her gorge, feeling the softness of the queen's lips with revulsion, the warmth from her skin, the brush of her silky hair against her skin. The queen broke the kiss and smiled as Nightshade fought against the enchantment.

"Nightshade," Sunstar said through gritted teeth. She felt deep inside herself for the strength to move. She focused all of her brute strength in one finger of her hand, and after a second or so it twitched. *I can free myself,* she thought with a wild surge of pure joy.

"I can see the desire in your eyes," the queen said to Nightshade. "You *love* her. This is priceless." She laughed.

Sunstar's heart ached for Nightshade and for herself. She groaned as she forced her wrist to move.

"Sunstar, I'm sorry," Nightshade said, and Sunstar looked at her.

Nightshade's eyes blazed with undisguised rage, mingled with deep pain and humiliation. Her mouth worked.

"Don't say you're sorry. *Never* be sorry for that." Sunstar forced her stiff legs to hold her as she stood. She stumbled forward.

The queen's eyes widened, and she gasped. Her face twisted, and she snarled as she lunged at Nightshade and groped for the dagger almost hidden in her belt. Sunstar crash tackled her. They collided with the still kneeling Nightshade, and all three went over in a heap.

Sunstar felt the queen's hand close around the cold hilt of her long, ornate dagger. Sunstar grunted, her hand weak against the iron strength of the queen's arms, and her grip faltered as the queen pulled the dagger free. The queen batted her back, and Sunstar crashed to the ground, half stunned. The queen moved forward, fast as a striking snake, and straddled Sunstar. She held the dagger above her head, screaming in rage.

Sunstar blinked as she saw hands grab the queen's wrists from behind and pull her backward with stunning savagery.

The queen yelped in pain and tumbled backward, legs bent at an awkward angle. She lay stunned for a moment, and Sunstar scrabbled away. Nightshade stood over the queen with her sword drawn, glowing blue eyes blazing with rage.

The queen screamed as Nightshade brought the sword down as hard as she could. It pierced her cold, black heart, and a ribbon of black blood spurted from her lips. She clutched at the sharp blade of the sword, her fingers cut to ribbons.

Her eyes dimmed as the life fled from her body.

Sunstar's paralysis broke. "Nightshade." She stumbled to Nightshade. "Don't leave me. *Please* don't leave me. Stay with me." She threw her arms around Nightshade and squeezed her as hard as she could, blinking away tears. She breathed deeply, taking in Nightshade's clean, spicy scent, and moaned softly in pleasure.

Nightshade's closed her arms around her. "Sunstar," she whispered. She sank to her knees, Sunstar firmly in her grip, and kissed the golden crown of her head.

Sunstar looked up into her glowing blue eyes. She drank in the sight of Nightshade's beautiful features. *I love her more than life itself.*

She claimed Nightshade's soft lips in a kiss of love and possession. She felt the feather-light contact as a tingling shock that went all the way down to her toes. Nightshade tightened her arms around her as the kiss deepened. Sunstar felt adrift, carried along by Nightshade's desire, her own roaring and crying out for her touch. Nightshade pulled Sunstar onto her lap. She held her close and gently stroked the skin over her ribs through her tattered shirt. Sunstar gently deepened the contact, tightening her hold on Nightshade and reveling in her warm, strong body. She wanted to crawl inside Nightshade. Her body responded, and her hands became restless.

Sunstar broke the kiss, her breathing uneven, feeling Nightshade's rapid heartbeat, and ran gentle, trembling fingers along the smooth skin of her jaw. She gazed deep into Nightshade's eyes, seeing the deep well of her love reflected back in them.

"I love you," she whispered.

"I love you too," Nightshade said. She smiled.

"I missed you. I wanted—needed—you with me."

"I came to you as soon as I could."

"I thought you'd fallen. You said you would be behind me, but you weren't." Sunstar's breathing hitched. "But here you are. You came back." She swallowed her tears of relief.

"I came. I promised you I would. Nothing can keep me from you," Nightshade said. "Hemlock couldn't use his teleportation spell with your people so close, so he dragged me off into the bushes to wait for them to leave. I was unconscious but recovered a lot faster than he thought I would. He will trouble us no more."

Sunstar nodded. "We found his body. It's here in this hall with us."

"We must burn it," Nightshade said. "All of them."

"I know. That will be the next order of business. We must also see to the fallen Drow that came with me."

Nightshade's eyebrows rose. "*With* you?"

Footsteps pounded up the passage toward them, and Snakeheart knelt beside them, blinking in surprise at Nightshade's glowing blue eyes. Windwalker looked over his shoulder, blinking at the sight of Sunstar snuggled in Nightshade's arms.

Nightshade stiffened, but Sunstar quickly stroked her arm. "It's all right, he's with me. This is Snakeheart."

Snakeheart grinned. "And this must be Nightshade." He held out a forearm, and Nightshade clasped it.

"Thank you," she said. "Thank you."

"You're welcome," Snakeheart said. More footsteps pounded toward them, and he stood. "We should show the others you are all right."

Nightshade nodded. "The Goblins will be distressed if I don't show myself soon."

Snakeheart quickly stood and left to give them precious few moments of privacy.

"They're with you?" Sunstar asked, allowing Nightshade to pull her to her feet.

"Yes, they are," Nightshade said. "You're not going to believe this."

"In a minute." Sunstar pulled her to a halt before they met the others. "Please, tell me you're not going to leave? You're going to stay with me?"

Nightshade nodded and gazed deep into her eyes. "I won't leave you, Sunstar. I will stay with you for as long as you will have me."

Sunstar gently cupped her face. "Thank you."

Nightshade smiled and leant into her touch.

They walked through the corridor of Goblins that began at the start of the passage and out into the main hall.

The air in the hall was cool, thanks to the main doors that someone had reopened. Soft light from the night sky bathed them in ghostly light.

Nightshade led Sunstar up to a crowned Goblin. He was dressed in ornate armor, and he watched her closely.

The Forest Elves in the hall close by the Goblin king gasped when they saw Nightshade. Sunstar spared a glance for the still shocked Windwalker.

Nightshade went to one knee before the king, and Sunstar quickly followed suit.

He looked at her and fired off a few words in Drow.

Sunstar shot a quick look at Nightshade.

"He said that his son spoke highly of us both and wanted his father to meet us."

"It is truly a joy and a privilege to meet you, Your Majesty." Sunstar formally bowed to the foreign regent.

Nightshade translated for her, and a cloaked Goblin standing by the king's side whispered a few words and gestured.

"It is also good to meet my son's rescuer," the king said.

Sunstar started as she realized she could understand him. "Your *son*? Gargajin is your son?"

The Goblin king smiled. "Gargajin means 'Prince' in our language. He is young, and his Drow is not good, so he did not know the word for it. His name is Ragnath." He gestured toward his soldiers. They parted, and a small figure hurtled through and threw his arms around Sunstar and squeezed tightly.

"Sunstar," he yelled. "You're alive."

"Thanks to you." She pulled back and gazed at Ragnath with a grin. "It is good to see you, young friend."

"It is good to see you as well, my Elven friend." He turned to his father. "Have you asked them about a trading treaty yet?"

"No, son." The king patted him on the head. "We have not yet finished with thanks and pleasantries."

"Trading treaty?" Sunstar asked. "Tell me more."

The king smiled. "All right."

CHAPTER 29

Close to dawn, Sunstar stood outside with Nightshade, watching the pyres with Drow bodies burn. The Elven guard stood behind them, watching closely for any unforeseen movement.

Nightshade felt at peace for the first time in days. Sunstar had made it. She had gone home. She glanced down at Sunstar, scarcely able to believe her good fortune.

"What's the smile for?" Sunstar squeezed her arm.

"It feels strange," Nightshade said.

"What does?"

"Not running," she said.

Sunstar nodded. "I know." She grinned. "But now we can get on with the business of living." The smile fell away from her face. "Although I think it will take a lot before my parents trust me again."

"Why?" Nightshade asked.

"They're going to think I made the same mistake twice," she replied, nibbling her lip.

"Tell me," Nightshade said gently.

Sunstar told her everything as the pyres burned hot and brilliant before them. Nightshade felt distantly grateful that there was no sign of movement from the dead. She listened carefully to Sunstar's story.

"You know what the worst of all these things is?" Sunstar asked when she finished.

"What?" Nightshade said.

"The sight of blood doesn't disturb me anymore, and I don't see life as an absolute. I see it in relative terms." She gestured at the pyres. "I'm not sorry I left the city, despite the loss of life. We almost lost a detachment of guards, and would have, had I not come."

"You sound like you're trying to justify your actions," Nightshade said.

"I am," Sunstar said. "I have been plagued endlessly over the past few days by Elves who are eager to point out my youth and stupidity. I had an enormous fight with my mother about coming out here at all."

"If you hadn't come out, you probably would have been kidnapped by the slavers," Nightshade said. "Windwalker and his detachment would be dead."

"And Snakeheart's friends would still be alive."

"Let go, Sunstar," Nightshade said, openly regarding her. A haunted look lurked in Sunstar's vibrant green eyes, and her forehead was newly furrowed with care lines. "If you could go back over the past few days is there anything you would change?"

Sunstar thought about it. "No. I made my choices when I got back to the city because I wanted to fix what I had done wrong."

"Then explain it to your parents the way you just did it to me. I will help you."

Sunstar smiled. "Thank you, Nightshade."

Nightshade put an arm around Sunstar and pulled her close.

They stayed until the fires burnt themselves out and then went back into the hall. Snakeheart was sitting down near the ancient, cracked Dwarven throne with the Goblin king, Ragnath, and their personal guard.

"Nightshade, Sunstar," he said, smiling and bowing as they approached.

"Snakeheart," Sunstar said. "I'm sorry. I'm sorry about all of this, and that you lost your friends."

Pain flitted across his handsome, indigo features. He nodded. "I'm sorry too."

Sunstar flinched.

"I don't blame you. It was their choice to come with me. I never asked them to." Snakeheart tensed his jaw. "But I will miss them. We were family."

"If you ever want to talk," Sunstar said. "You have shown me you are *my* friend."

"And mine for protecting Sunstar," Nightshade said quietly. "I would be pleased to count you as a friend, Snakeheart."

"I would like that," he said. "It can get quite lonely, even amongst the Elves."

"Then we must think of a way for you to be close to us," Sunstar said.

"How about we do it simply because we want to?" Nightshade caressed Sunstar's hand. "I don't want to hide anymore. Can't we be friends simply because?"

Sunstar smiled. "Yes, and I agree." She sighed and turned back to the silent king, Ragnath, and Snakeheart. "I would like to take my leave of you and retire for tonight."

The king nodded, and Ragnath gave them both a final hug for the evening.

"I think we will be taking our leave of you," Gilgrich said.

"But I thought you wanted to come and meet my parents," Sunstar said.

Gilgrich smiled. "I have the treaty as I wanted, and I must organize my people to live up to our end of the bargain."

"Are you sure, Your Highness?" Sunstar asked. "We would love to have you."

"I will come and visit one day." The king smiled and revealed his sharp teeth. "And in the meantime, I will consider us friends."

"I would consider it an honor, Your Highness," Sunstar said. "Safe traveling."

"You too, Princess," Gilgrich said with a bow.

Nightshade and Sunstar bowed low in respect to the Goblin king. They watched as he marshaled his troops and gathered their wounded. They filed away into the darkness, after one fond, farewell wave from Ragnath.

After he left, Sunstar, Nightshade, Snakeheart, Windwalker, and the two remaining Elven guards left the hall and headed toward the forest. Sunstar could feel Windwalker's eyes on her, and she glanced back at him. He watched her carefully, his eyes also taking in Nightshade's slim beauty.

"I just want to talk to Windwalker quickly." Sunstar touched Nightshade's arm. Nightshade looked down at her and smiled.

"Yes," she said. "I have felt his eyes on me for the past hour."

Sunstar grinned and dropped back so she was walking beside Windwalker.

"Windwalker," she began.

"So this is your choice?" He waved a hand at Nightshade and Snakeheart, who was walking with her.

"It is," Sunstar said. "I never meant to hurt you."

He looked down at her and gave her a genuine smile. "You haven't really. I think that was of more interest to your father than to either one of us. I'm still trying to take in the fact that she is real."

Sunstar laughed, and he joined her. In that brief moment, the two became friends. Sunstar squeezed his arm and trotted forward to Nightshade again.

Nightshade quickly took Sunstar's hand and gave it a gentle squeeze. "We're in the forest again." She glanced at Snakeheart. "I think it's time to go to ground for the night."

Sunstar was about to argue, but the second her mouth opened, her comment turned into a bone-cracking yawn.

Nightshade called a halt to the march. "Let's rest," she said to Windwalker, and he and the other two Elves nodded in agreement.

Windwalker looked at the guards. "We will take the watches during the night. Sleep well, Your Highness, Nightshade."

They nodded to Windwalker as he turned to the remaining Elves.

"Tomorrow we will go by the clearing for your friends," Sunstar said to Snakeheart.

"No need," he said sadly. "They were burned by the humans. I woke before we left the clearing. The humans were that civil at least."

Sunstar nodded. "I'm truly sorry."

He waved his hand. "It's all right. We all felt happy to help you. It was good to feel useful again. Good night." He turned and laid out his cloak beside the fire the Elves were making.

Sunstar watched him closely, her mind turning over his words. She liked him. He wanted a purpose in life outside farming? She could give him one. She turned back to Nightshade. "Come with me."

"What about your guard?" Nightshade glanced at Snakeheart and Windwalker.

"We're on my father's land, and I'm with you," Sunstar said. "I think I'm safe, don't you?"

Nightshade smiled and nodded.

Sunstar took her hand, and they headed toward the trees. She looked back at the visibly tense Snakeheart, and gave him a small grin. He relaxed and nodded slightly, then settled down before the fire with the Forest Elves.

They walked for a few minutes through the thick trees—Nightshade carefully leading Sunstar—and stopped in a small clearing.

"Here." Sunstar sang, and the air shimmered around them.

Nightshade raised an eyebrow at her. "Why didn't we do this while we were running?"

"It's not a glamour that could have hidden us from Hemlock. This is just privacy," Sunstar said. "Peace. That's what I want with you."

"We have our whole lives together."

"We won't often have our lives to ourselves. I'm the crown princess, and we will be married. We will be plagued by duty and obligation. One day we will look back on this night, and we will long for the time when it was still all ahead of us."

Nightshade spread out her thick cloak beneath them. She knelt before Sunstar and touched her face with trembling fingers. "Is that what you want? To be married to me and ruling over the Elven people?"

"I want to marry you more than anything." Sunstar knelt and leant into her touch. "I don't know. I always wanted to travel but now I'm not so sure."

"Would you trust me enough to travel with me?"

"I love you. I'd go anywhere with you," Sunstar said.

Nightshade claimed Sunstar's lips.

"I love you," Nightshade said when they broke. "I will never hurt you, and I will never let anyone hurt you either."

"I want to make the same promise to you, but I don't know how," Sunstar said.

"Didn't you know?" Nightshade cupped her face with gentle hands. "You've made that promise to me many times over, without ever having had to speak the words." She kissed Sunstar, pulled her in close, and teased her shirt from her breeches.

She slipped her hands under Sunstar's shirt, up the smooth skin of her ribs, and paused to cup her breasts and gently squeeze her nipples.

Sunstar shivered and swallowed convulsively at the sensation. Her hands shook, and she almost tore Nightshade's shirt from her body. She caressed the smooth, silken skin of Nightshade's chest and full breasts. She watched Nightshade with the eyes of a lover as she kissed and nibbled her soft skin. Nightshade shifted and pushed Sunstar down onto her back. She ran her fingertips along the soft skin of her belly, lower, to her breeches.

Sunstar moaned as Nightshade kissed her way up Sunstar's jaw line, nibbled her ear, and the soft skin of her neck. The feel of Nightshade's breasts pressed against hers drove away her reason. She felt Nightshade's touch as a trail of fire down the sides of her body and as she tugged her tight breeches down her smooth hips. Nightshade's kiss was not far behind, and Sunstar came almost as soon as Nightshade's lips closed on her. She stiffened and moaned, heart hammering, feeling boneless. She gazed into Nightshade's hot, glowing blue eyes and saw her love and desire.

"I love you."

She rolled Nightshade onto her back, kissing and tasting every available inch of skin that she could find. The days of torment from the sight of her smooth skin, her hard muscle, and her beautiful, glowing blue eyes tore at Sunstar as she lost any semblance of self control. She kissed and nipped Nightshade all over, driven by Nightshade's soft moans and cries of pleasure. Nightshade came too soon for Sunstar's liking, clutching her with painful strength and pulling her up so they lay tangled together.

Sunstar smiled in pleasure at the sensation of bare skin against bare skin along the entire lengths of their bodies. She kissed the skin of Nightshade's chest, tasting the salty flesh, feeling the heat from her.

"I love you, Nightshade," she said. "More than anyone in the world."

Nightshade tightened her arms around Sunstar. "I love you, too. With everything inside me." Sunstar felt Nightshade's lips against the crown of her head. "I don't want to go back to the others just yet."

"Neither do I." Sunstar glanced at their scattered clothing in the clearing.

"We really should get dressed." Nightshade followed the direction of Sunstar's glance.

Sunstar nodded. "I know that wasn't the best idea but . . ."

Nightshade nodded.

Sunstar released her with a sigh, and they dressed.

"I know there'll be more time when we're home," she said, staring at Nightshade's now fully-clothed body.

"Yes, there will be." Nightshade smiled. "As much as I hate to admit it, I'm exhausted."

Sunstar opened her mouth to argue but it turned into a bone-cracking yawn. The days of light, restless sleep, misery, and tension had taken their toll. She slowly and regretfully nodded. "All right. But when we get home . . ."

Nightshade nodded. "We're staying together." She pulled Sunstar to her.

Sunstar nodded. "This feels so familiar." She snuggled into Nightshade's warm body.

Nightshade smiled. "With one difference," she murmured, then gently kissed Sunstar.

"Oh, yes." Sunstar wrapped herself around Nightshade and kissed the skin visible beneath the vee of her shirt. "Good night, Nightshade."

"Sleep well, my princess," Nightshade whispered.

They drifted off to sleep moments later. This time there were no dreams for Sunstar, just the sound of Nightshade's heartbeat and the warmth from her body.

The next day, the Elves continued the journey back home.

Sunstar felt pleased with herself. Her parents would be thrilled by the treaty. The Goblins had not asked for much. They wanted assistance from the Elves to patrol the borders of their lands. Slavers such as Takhisis and Merton had a lucrative trade and passage across their home, and they wanted to drive them out. In return, they would mine for precious gems for the benefit of both races, but needed safe passage across Elven lands to sell them to the humans.

It was a fair bargain, and Sunstar was happy to seal it with them.

They traveled through the day and night to reach the home city of the Elves, and as they got close, Sunstar could make out two figures waiting at the gates for them.

She hurried down the road with a blindfolded Nightshade in tow. Snakeheart followed close behind, and the rest of the Elven guard broke into a jog.

Darkwood and Morningstar ran toward her and smothered her with hugs and kisses.

"Daughter," Darkwood said. "I thought you were dead. The new bodyguards I assigned you were found dead in the forest."

Sunstar winced.

She looked back at Snakeheart and gave him a sad smile. "My new bodyguard was with me the whole time. Snakeheart, would you consider taking up the post on a more permanent basis?"

Snakeheart, who had been looking gloomy, immediately brightened. "I have nothing left for me as a farmer. I would be honored to be your bodyguard."

"There," she said to her bemused parents. "I have a bodyguard." She tightened her grip on Nightshade's damp hand. "This is Nightshade." She kissed Nightshade's knuckles. "Nightshade, these are my parents, Darkwood and Morningstar."

Darkwood took a step forward and kissed Nightshade's cheeks, followed closely by Morningstar. Both exchanged a contented look.

"Welcome home, Nightshade," Darkwood said.

"Welcome to our family," Morningstar said.

"Thank you," Nightshade said, sounding taken aback. She was quiet for a moment. "Just like that?" she blurted out.

She pushed the blindfold off her eyes. She blinked and smiled in surprise. She seemed to be able to see well enough. She studied Sunstar's parents for a moment.

Darkwood and Morningstar exchanged a glance and laughed softly.

"Just like that," Darkwood said. "It became apparent to us almost as soon as she came back that our daughter loves you very much." He turned and looked at Sunstar. "The Drow queen?"

"Will trouble us no more," Sunstar and Nightshade said together. They exchanged a guilty glance.

"There is no need for guilt, Sunstar," Nightshade murmured. "Believe it or not, we did her a kindness she most certainly did not deserve." She sighed and turned to Darkwood and Morningstar. "The Drow will not be bothering us again."

"Should I ask?" Darkwood watched Nightshade closely.

Nightshade shook her head. "She and the king are ashes."

Darkwood and Morningstar studied her, and she met their gazes unflinchingly.

Nightshade glanced at Sunstar. Sunstar nodded almost imperceptibly.

"We will tell you later," Nightshade said. "The story is a long and troubling one."

"On a brighter note, we now have a trading treaty with the Goblin king," Sunstar said with the ghost of a grin as she handed a slightly tattered scroll to Morningstar.

"What?" Morningstar frowned and unrolled the scroll. She scanned it, and her eyes widened. "Darkwood, we . . . gems . . . and all we have . . ." She looked up at Sunstar. "How did this come about?" She handed the scroll to Darkwood.

"It turns out that the little Goblin boy we rescued was the crown prince," Sunstar said. "His father wants some help to keep slavers out of the forest. I was reasonably certain you would want the same thing, so I said yes."

"I'm not sure we have enough guards for this." Darkwood glanced at Nightshade.

"I'm sure there are more Elves living amongst us that would be happy to defend their new home. There is a lot we could learn from them." Sunstar turned to the nodding Snakeheart. "You could also let us go out on patrol as well." She thought of the forest and solitude with Nightshade.

Darkwood and Morningstar exchanged a glance loaded with parental telepathy.

Darkwood pinned her with a merciless stare. "We'll talk about it."

Nightshade looked back at Windwalker.

The tattered captain of the guard started at her scrutiny.

"Do you mind if Snakeheart and I practice regularly with you?" Nightshade asked. "If we are to go out with the guards our skills must be sharp."

"No," he said. "We would welcome it, actually."

Darkwood turned and gestured down the road toward the city gates. "I want to know what happened. Let's go home."

As they walked toward the city, Sunstar gently squeezed Nightshade's hand. She was rewarded with a gentle caress. She gazed at her beloved Nightshade, feeling the familiar flutter of her heart at the sight of her.

"Home," she murmured. "Home."

"Together," Nightshade replied.

The sun shone down on them both, a benediction and a blessing.

ABOUT THE AUTHOR

Jordan Falconer was born in Sydney, Australia, and from a very young age had an interest in ghoulies, ghosties and long legged beasties and all things that go bump in the night. After surviving Catholic school (twice!) she graduated from Sydney University with an honors degree in Psychology. She currently resides in Canada with her other half and three small, demanding dogs.

Jordan can be reached at jfishmael@hotmail.com

www.ingramcontent.com/pod-product-compliance
Lightning Source LLC
LaVergne TN
LVHW091043080826
845145LV00002B/611

* 9 7 8 1 9 3 9 5 6 2 0 0 5 *